BY JP DELANEY

The Girl Before

Believe Me

The Perfect Wife

Playing Nice

PLAYING NICE

PLAYING NICE

A NOVEL

JP DELANEY

BALLANTINE BOOKS

New York

Copyright © 2020 by Shippen Productions Ltd.

Published in the United States by Ballantine Books, an imprint of Random House, a division of Penguin Random House LLC, New York.

BALLANTINE and the HOUSE colophon are registered trademarks of Penguin Random House LLC.

Hardback ISBN 978-1-9848-2134-8
International edition 978-0-5931-5985-9
Ebook ISBN 978-1-9848-2135-5

Printed in the United States of America on acid-free paper

randomhousebooks.com

2 4 6 8 9 7 5 3 1

First Edition

Book design by Debbie Glasserman

*Then spake the woman whose the living child was unto the
king, for her bowels yearned upon her son, and she said,
O my lord, give her the living child, and in no wise
slay it. But the other said, Let it be neither mine
nor thine, but divide it.*

—1 KINGS 3:26

PLAYING NICE

PETE

IT WAS JUST AN ordinary day.

If this were a color piece or a feature, the kind of thing I used to write on a daily basis, the editor would have rejected it just for that opening sentence. *Openers need to hook people, Pete,* she'd tell me, tossing my pages back at me across my desk. *Paint a picture, set a scene. Be* dramatic. *In travel journalism especially, you need a sense of place. Take me on a* journey.

So: It was just an ordinary day in Willesden Green, north London.

Because the fact is, before that knock on my door, it *was* just an ordinary day. An unusually nice one, admittedly. The sun was shining, the air was crisp and blue. There was still some snow on the ground, hiding in corners, but it had that soft sugary look snow gets when it's all but melted, and none of the kids streaming into the Acol Road Nursery and Preschool could be bothered to get their mittens wet trying to scoop it up for snowballs.

Actually, there was one small thing out of the ordinary. As I took Theo into the nursery, or rather followed him in—we'd given him a scooter for his second birthday, a chunky three-wheeler he was now inseparable from—I noticed three people, a woman and two men, on the other side of the road, watching us. The younger man was roughly my age, thirty or so. The other was in his fifties. Both wore dark suits with dark woolen coats over them, and the woman, a blonde, was wrapped up in a kind of fake-fur parka, the sort of thing you might see on a fashionable ski slope. They looked too smart for our part of London. But then I saw that the older man was holding a document case in his gloved hand. An estate agent, I guessed, showing some prospective buyers the local childcare facilities. The Jubilee Line goes all the way from our Tube station to Canary Wharf, and even the bankers have been priced out of West Hampstead these days.

Something about the younger man seemed familiar. But then I was distracted by Jane Tigman, whose son Zack was already starting to thrash and scream in her arms at the prospect of being left. She hadn't realized that the trick is to make sure they walk into nursery on their own rather than being carried, which simply makes the moment of separation more final. Then there was a note about World Book Day on the nursery door that hadn't been there yesterday—God, yet another costume I'd have to organize—and after that I had to separate Theo from his helmet, gloves, and coat, stuff the gloves deep enough into the coat pockets that they wouldn't fall out—I still hadn't gotten around to putting name tags on them—and help him hang the coat on his peg, deep among all the others, before crouching down to give him a final pep talk.

"Okay, big man. You going to play nicely today?"

He nodded, wide-eyed with sincerity. "Yef, Dad."

"So no grabbing. And take turns. That's very important. Remember we said we'd take turns to choose lunch? So today it's your turn, and tomorrow it'll be mine. What do you want for lunch?"

"Booby smoovy," he announced after a moment's thought.

"Blueberry smoothie," I repeated clearly. "Okay. I'll make some before I pick you up. Have a good morning."

I gave him a kiss and off he went, happy as a clam.

"Mr. Riley?"

I turned. It was Susy, the woman who ran the nursery. It looked as if she'd been waiting for Theo to go. "Can I have a word?" she added.

I snapped my fingers. "The sippy cup. I forgot. I'll get another one today—"

"It isn't about the sippy cup," she interrupted. "Shall we talk in my office?"

"IT'S NOTHING TO WORRY about," she said as we sat down, which of course instantly made me aware that it was definitely something to worry about. "It's just that there was another incident yesterday. Theo hit one of the other children again."

"Ah," I said defensively. That was the third time this month. "Okay. It's something we have been working on at home. According to the internet, it sometimes happens at this age if physical skills get ahead of verbal skills." I smiled ruefully, to show that I wasn't stupid enough to believe every parenting theory I read on the internet, but neither was I one of those entitled middle-class dads who thought that just because my son was now at nursery I wasn't required to put any effort into being his parent anymore; or, even worse, was blind to the possibility of my little darling having any faults in the first place. "And of course, his speech *is* a little delayed. But I'd welcome any suggestions."

Susy visibly relaxed. "Well, as you say, it is typical two-year-old stuff. I'm sure you know this, but it can help if you model the correct behavior. If he sees you getting cross or aggressive, he'll come to believe that aggression is a legitimate response to stress. What about the TV programs he watches? I'm afraid even *Tom and*

Jerry may not be appropriate at this age, at least not until the hitting stage is over. And if you play any violent videogames yourself—"

"I don't play videogames," I said firmly. "Quite apart from anything else, I don't have the time."

"I'm sure. It's just that we don't always think about the consequences of things like that." She smiled, but I could almost see the thought process behind her eyes. *Stay-at-home dad equals aggressive kid*. She wouldn't have asked Jane Tigman if she played *Call of Duty*.

"And we're working on sharing, too," I added. "Taking turns who chooses what to have for lunch, that kind of thing."

"Well, it certainly sounds as if you're on top of it." Susy got to her feet to show the discussion was over. "We'll keep a close watch here, and let's hope he grows out of it."

Understandably, then, I wasn't thinking about the wealthy-looking couple and their estate agent as I left the nursery. I was worrying about Theo, and why he was taking so long to learn to play nicely with the other kids. But I'm pretty sure, looking back, that by the time I reached the street, the three of them were nowhere to be seen.

2

Case no. 12675/PU78B65: AFFIDAVIT UNDER OATH by D. Maguire.

I, Donald Joseph Maguire, make oath and swear as follows:

1. I am the proprietor and chief investigator of Maguire Missing Persons, a London-based investigative agency which traces over two hundred individuals a year on behalf of our clients. We do not advertise. All our work comes by personal referral.

2. Prior to starting this business, I was a senior detective with the Metropolitan Police, a position I held for thirteen years, leaving with the rank of detective inspector.

3. Last August I was approached by Mr. Miles and Mrs. Lucy Lambert, of 17 Haydon Gardens, Highgate, N19 3JZ. They wished me to act for them in the matter of tracing their son.

3

PETE

AT HOME, I TURNED on the coffee machine and opened my laptop. The coffee machine is a Jura, the laptop a top-of-the-line MacBook. They were the only two bits of kit I insisted on when Maddie and I started having the difficult conversations about which of us was going to stay home to look after Theo once her maternity leave was over. The idea was that I'd work from home part-time, at least when Theo got a place at nursery. Having a really good computer and a bean-to-cup coffeemaker made being a stay-at-home dad feel like a step up, a new opportunity, rather than a step down in my career.

Though actually I hate the phrase *stay-at-home dad*. It's a negative, passive construction, the absence of something. No one calls women in my position stay-at-home mums, do they? They're full-time mums, which immediately sounds more positive. Total mums, mums without compromise. *Stay-at-home dad* sounds like you're too lazy or too agoraphobic to leave the house and get a proper job. Which is what many people secretly do think, actually. Or, in the case of Maddie's parents, not-so-secretly. Her father's an Australian businessman with political views slightly to the right of Genghis Khan, and he's made it clear he thinks I'm sponging off her. Though he'd probably phrase it, *The boy's a bloody bludger.*

There was breakfast to clear up, the recycling to sort, and toys to tidy away, but while the Jura whirred and spluttered—grinding beans, frothing milk—I threw in a load of washing and logged onto DadStuff.

> Just seen a poster for World Book Day at my DS's nursery. 7 March. Aargh! Ideas? Really don't want to buy a ready-made costume at Sainos or the motherhood will judge me even more.

Within moments I had a reply. There's a hard core of about a hundred of us who stay online pretty much throughout the day, coming back to the forum in between our parenting duties. Once you got used to the cliquey jargon—*DS* or *DD* means "darling son" or "darling daughter," *OP* means "original poster," while *OH* is "other half" and *AIBU* is "am I being unreasonable?"—it was reassuring to be able to throw questions out there and see what others thought.

> The mouse from The Gruffalo, mate. Brown shirt, white vest, some ears on an Alice band. Sorted.

That was Honker6. I typed back:

> Er, Alice band? Your DDs might go for it but we don't even own one of those.

Greg87 wrote:

What about Peter Rabbit? Little blue jacket, paper ears on baseball hat, face-painted whiskers?

Greg being practical, as usual. *Nice one,* I replied, trying to remember if Peter Rabbit had ever been involved in any age-inappropriate violence that Susy the nursery head might disapprove of. You had to be careful with those Beatrix Potter books.

Then the doorbell rang, so I put my cappuccino down and went to answer it.

ON THE STEP WAS the group I'd seen outside the nursery. My first thought was that they must have made a mistake, because our house wasn't for sale. My second was that it wasn't the group from the nursery, not quite: The woman was no longer with them. So maybe they weren't house buyers, after all—they could be political canvassers, or even journalists. And my third thought, the one that immediately crowded all the others out of my head, was that, now that I saw him up close, the younger of the two men, the one roughly my age, was the spitting image of Theo.

He had dark hair that spilled over his forehead in an unruly comma, a prominent jaw, and deep-set blue eyes—the kind of dark, boyish looks that in Theo are heart-stoppingly cute but in adults always make me think of the word *saturnine,* without really knowing why. Almost six feet, chunky, broad-shouldered. An athlete's physique. There's a picture of the writer Ted Hughes as a young man, glowering at the camera with the same lock of hair falling over his right eye. This guy reminded me of that. A chiseled, granite face, but not unfriendly.

"Hello," he said, without ado. "Can we come in?"

"Why?" I asked stupidly.

"It's about your son," he said patiently. "I really think this would be better done inside."

"All right." And his manner was so brisk and purposeful that I found myself stepping away from the door, even though I was now thinking, *Was it* his *child Theo hit? Am I about to get shouted at?*

"Er—coffee?" I said, leading the way into the lounge—which is to say, taking a few steps back. Like most people in our street, we've ripped out the walls downstairs to create one decent-sized room. The older man shook his head, but I saw the younger man glance at my cappuccino. "I make them fresh," I added, thinking a pause for coffee might defuse the coming row a bit.

"Go on then." There was an awkward wait while I frothed more milk.

"I'm Miles Lambert, by the way," he added when I was done. "And this gentleman is Don Maguire." He took the cup I offered him. "Thanks. Shall we sit down?"

I sat in the only armchair and Miles Lambert took the couch, carefully moving some toys out of the way as he did so. Don Maguire sat in my swivel desk chair. I saw him cast an admiring glance at my MacBook.

"There's no easy way to do this," Miles said when we were all seated. He leaned forward, lacing his fingers together like a rugby player about to take a penalty. "Look, if it was me, I'd want to be told straight, with no bullshit, so that's what I'm going to do. But prepare yourself for a shock." He took a deep breath. "I'm sorry to have to tell you that Theo isn't your son. He's mine."

I gaped at him. Thoughts crowded in on me. *That can't be right,* followed by *So that's why this man looks like Theo.* Disbelief, shell shock, horror, all paralyzed me. I'm not fast in a crisis, unfortunately; Maddie's the one who thinks on her feet.

Maddie. Oh my God. Was this man telling me they had an affair? *Is that what this is? That I'm a—*

The word *cuckold,* with all its medieval ugliness, crashed into my brain like a rock. Maddie and I have had our problems, we're like any couple in that regard, and there have been times over the last year or so when I've sensed her drawing away from me. But I've always put that down to the trauma of Theo's birth—

Theo's birth. Think straight, Pete. Theo was born just over two years ago. So it would have been two and a half years ago when this supposed affair happened. Which was nigh-on impossible. Maddie and I only came back from Australia, where we met, three years back.

I realized both Miles Lambert and Don Maguire were looking at me, waiting for me to react, and I still hadn't said anything. "What are you trying to tell me?" I said numbly.

Miles Lambert simply repeated, "Theo isn't your son. He's mine." His blue eyes held mine, concerned. "I'm sorry. I know it's a shock. Please, take your time."

It was Don Maguire who coughed and added, "You both have sons who were born prematurely, I understand, who were both separated from their mothers briefly when they were transferred to the neonatal intensive care unit at St. Alexander's. It's conceivable that, at some point during that process, the wrong tags were put on the wrong babies. That's our working theory, anyway."

Double negative, the editor shouted at me. *The wrong tags got put on the right babies, you cretin.* Which only goes to show that, at moments of crisis, you think the most bizarre things.

4

PETE

"SO YOU THINK *YOU* have *our* son. Our birth son, that is." In all this chaos, it was the one thing I could grasp.

Miles Lambert nodded. "David. We called him David."

"And what . . ." *What happens now,* I wanted to ask, but my brain just wouldn't go there. "How do you know? That the babies got switched, I mean?"

Miles indicated Don Maguire. "This man's a private investigator. He finds missing people."

"But how do you *know*?" I insisted.

"I took the liberty of removing an item with Theo's DNA on it from his nursery," Don Maguire said apologetically. "I very much regret having to do that, but we didn't want to put you through the strain of this approach if there was any chance we could be wrong." As he spoke he was removing something from a padded envelope. It was Theo's sippy cup, the one the nursery told me had gotten lost.

"The tests came back yesterday," Miles added. "There's absolutely no doubt."

Don Maguire placed the sippy cup on my desk carefully, as if it were fragile bone china. "We'd like to return this to you now, of course."

"Jesus. *Jesus.* You tested my son's DNA without my permission—"

"Well, technically *my* son. But yes, we apologize that was necessary," Miles said.

My son. The words thudded in my head.

"This is a copy of the test results for you," Don Maguire added, taking an envelope from his folder and placing it next to the cup. "As Mr. Lambert says, there really is no doubt. Theo is his biological son."

Theo. I couldn't comprehend what this might mean for him. I put my head in my hands.

"What are you suggesting we do about this?" I managed to ask. "What do you want to happen now?"

Again, it was Maguire who answered. "Please understand, Mr. Riley. Nothing specific is being suggested here. Cases like this are so rare, there's very little precedent—legal precedent, I mean. There's certainly no automatic requirement for the family courts to get involved. It's best for the parents to work out a solution between themselves."

"A *solution?*"

"Whether to swap back, or stay as you are."

The words, so stark and binary, hung in the air.

"Like I said, it's a shock," Miles added apologetically. "It was for me and Lucy, too, but obviously we've had longer to absorb it. You don't need to say anything right now. And of course, you should get your own advice."

I stared at him. The way he said it made it clear he'd already consulted lawyers.

"We're suing the hospital," he added. "Not St. Alexander's— the private one where Lucy gave birth. You may want to join our action, but . . . like I said, that's all TBD. To Be Discussed. There's no rush."

My eye fell on some pieces of red Duplo by his foot. Only that morning, Theo had assembled them into a tommy gun that promptly fell apart under the force of his overenthusiastic shooting-down of my attempts to get him to clean his teeth. A wave of love for him washed over me. And terror, at the abyss that had just opened up beneath us.

"Would you like to see a picture of David?" Miles asked.

Unable to speak, I nodded. Miles took a photograph from an inside pocket and handed it to me. It showed a small boy sitting in a high chair. He had a fine-featured face, fair hair, light-brown eyes. I could see instantly that he looked a lot like Maddie.

"You can keep that, if you like," he added. "And if I could take one of—of Theo . . ."

"Of course," I heard myself say. I looked around, but all my pictures were on my phone. The exception was one that someone had sent us after a birthday party, which I'd stuck to the fridge with a magnet. Theo dressed up as a pirate, complete with an eyepatch, a tricorn hat, and a cardboard cutlass that was raised toward the camera, his eyes alive with mischief. I took it down and handed it to Miles.

"Thanks." He studied it for a moment, his eyes softening. "And this is me," he added briskly, handing me a business card. "Mobile and email. Get in touch when you've had a chance for it all to sink in, yes? And discussed it with Madelyn, of course. Absolutely no pressure, but—I'm here. We both are." He glanced at Don Maguire, then clarified, "Me and Lucy, I mean. Don's part in this is over, I guess."

I looked down at the card. *Miles Lambert, Chief Executive Officer, Burton Investments.* An office address in central London.

Miles reached down and plucked a foam football from the floor, squeezing it in his hand experimentally. "Sportsman, is he?" he asked conversationally. "Can he catch this yet?"

"Most of the time he can. He's quite advanced, physically. A bit *too* advanced, in some ways."

Miles raised his eyebrows, and I explained. "He sometimes gets a bit physical with the other kids at nursery. It's something we're working on."

"Does he, now? Well, I wouldn't worry too much about that if I were you. I was the same at his age. It came in quite handy on the rugby pitch later. Didn't hear anyone complaining then." Something about the way he said it—fond, almost proprietary—made me realize that, despite the surreal calmness of this conversation, I wasn't just making small talk with another dad at a party. I was talking to my son's father. His *real* father. My world had just turned upside down, and nothing was ever going to be the same again.

"We should get you around," Miles was saying. "Make some proper introductions. When you've had a chance to digest it all."

I tried to reply, but the words wouldn't come. There was an awkward moment when I thought I was going to break down. Miles affected not to notice. He raised the picture I'd given him. "Anyway, thanks for this. Lucy will be thrilled. Something to be going on with."

He tucked the photo inside his suit jacket, then held out his hand. His handshake was dry and decisive. "And try not to worry. We're all reasonable people. It's a terrible thing that's happened, but it's how we handle it that matters now. I really believe we'll figure out the best way forward. But for the time being, we'll get out of your hair."

Don Maguire shook my hand, too, and suddenly they were gone. Miles Lambert hadn't touched his coffee. I poured it down the sink. The washing machine beeped and I went to pull it open. Automatically I pulled the wet things out. It was as if I was in a kind of trance. On top of the pile was one of Theo's T-shirts—mustard yellow, with I'M TWO, WHAT'S YOUR EXCUSE? across the front. For a moment I could almost feel Theo's hot little body in my hands, the familiar shrug and wriggle of his tiny ribs as I hoisted him over my shoulder, the kick of his legs. Tears pricked my eyes and my chest heaved, but I knew I couldn't fall apart, not yet. I had to call Maddie.

5

4. Together with my client, Miles Lambert, I visited Mr. Riley at home. There we served notice that the child he believed to be his son was in fact the son of my clients, and that, conversely, the child my clients were bringing up was believed to be Mr. Riley's.

5. Mr. Riley was understandably distressed by this news. At several points during the subsequent discussion he broke down in tears.

6. While he recovered his composure, I took the opportunity to make some observations of my surroundings. This was facilitated by the fact that it was a small space, the sitting room, playroom, kitchen, and dining room all being combined in the area in which we were sitting.

7. There were several indications that Mr. Riley was struggling to cope with his domestic routine. The table bore a number of soiled dishes, plates, and other kitchen utensils. Unwashed laundry was

strewn over the furniture, and there were two empty wine bottles on the floor in the kitchen area. When I glanced at Mr. Riley's computer, I noticed the browser was open at a men-only internet forum on which he appeared to be making an appeal for help with his parenting. (Subsequent investigation confirmed that, under the pseudonym Homedad85, Mr. Riley had made over 1,200 posts of a similar nature.) Another tab was open at a videogame, which was paused. Although Mr. Riley's LinkedIn profile states that he is a freelance journalist, there was no evidence of this, nor of any journalistic work in progress.

8. My client reiterated several times to Mr. Riley that he and his wife wished to try to resolve this situation by means of discussion and reasonable compromise. Mr. Riley did not respond to these assurances. When his manner started to turn hostile, we left.

6

MADDIE

I'M IN A MEETING, going through the casting tapes for a Doritos commercial with the clients, when my phone flashes. We're in the middle of a heated discussion—the director wants edgy, independent, moody teenagers, the client wants wholesome and smiley, a debate I must have chaired at least a hundred times, and we're just starting to get somewhere by focusing on the director's third choice who's also the client's second when the call comes. I glance at the screen. Pete. Or rather, PETER RILEY. The first time we met, four years ago, I put his name and surname into my contacts at the end of the evening, and somehow I've never gotten around to changing it to something less formal.

The phone's on silent, so it goes to voicemail. But he instantly disconnects and rings again. That's our signal something's urgent, so I make an excuse and slip out of the meeting to call him back.

"What's up?"

"It's all right, Theo's fine. He's at nursery. It's—" There's the sound of a couple of deep breaths. "There was a man here just now with a private detective. He claims our babies somehow got mixed up in the NICU. So he thinks the little boy he's got at home is ours and Theo—Theo—"

It takes a moment for what he's saying to sink in. "It could be tested," I say. "A DNA test."

"They've done that. He left us a copy. Mads, this guy looked exactly like Theo." There's a pause. "I think he's telling the truth."

I don't reply. Despite what Pete's just said, I don't really believe it. That sort of thing simply doesn't happen. There must be some other explanation. But Pete's clearly devastated, and he needs me to be there. I make a quick decision. "I'm coming home."

I look through the glass wall into the meeting room. On the TV monitor, an impossibly rosy-cheeked fourteen-year-old is miming awed excitement at the contents of her packet of corn chips. Professional etiquette demands that I go back in and make my excuses, explain to the clients that there's a family crisis; no, nothing life threatening, but I'd really better leave. But I don't. Almost without being aware of it, I prioritize. I send a text to one of my colleagues, asking them to take over, and walk out of the building.

WHEN I WAS PREGNANT, I always assumed it would be me who'd be the primary carer. After all, the fact we were having a baby at all was ultimately down to me—the pregnancy was an accident, the timing bad in all sorts of ways. We even discussed termination, although I could tell Pete was uneasy about the idea, and eventually I admitted I was, too; I'm not always as hard-nosed and practical as my friends like to make out. But the international advertising agency that paid my relocation costs from Sydney to London included a year's private health insurance in the package, and when I checked, it included maternity. Instead of having a baby on a crowded NHS ward, I could have it in the comparatively luxurious surroundings of a private hospital in Harley Street, complete with dedicated midwife, C-section on request, twenty-four-hour consultant care, and postbirth recovery program. Of course, the possibility of a pampered, luxurious birth would be a pretty terrible reason to have a baby—but as a reason to have a baby that already existed, why not?

Looking back, I think I'd already decided to keep it and was just looking for some kind of justification. Telling work was awkward, of course—I'd been in my new job less than four months, and now here I was, announcing I'd be taking a year off—but they were grown up enough to realize that, since they had no choice in the matter, they might as well sound pleased for me and emphasize that the position would still be there when I came back.

In short, it looked like everything was working out ridiculously well. But the gods had other ideas.

I was twenty-seven weeks when Pete and I went to Andy and Keith's wedding. If you can't let your hair down at a gay wedding, when can you? Later, I'd torture myself about that. Was it the glass of champagne I allowed myself with the speeches? The exuberant dancing to Aretha Franklin and Madonna on the packed dance floor afterward? (I still can't hear "Respect" without flinching.) The tumble I took on my way back from the ladies', tripping over that marquee rope in the dark? The consultant told me it probably wasn't any of those, but since he couldn't say what *did* cause it, how could he be sure?

Next morning I had a terrible headache, which I put down to the glass of champagne now I wasn't used to it. But I also realized I hadn't felt the baby move for a while, and when I threw up it somehow felt different from my first-trimester morning sickness. So—since it was a Sunday, and we had a private hospital in Harley Street on tap, staffed by experienced midwives we could go and see anytime we liked—Pete suggested we get the baby checked out, then have brunch on Marylebone High Street.

As it turned out, that brunch plan saved our baby's life.

"I'm just going to do a quick scan" turned into "I'm just going to get the doctor to take a look" and then suddenly a red cord I'd barely noticed in the corner of the room was being pulled and I was surrounded by people. Someone shouted, "Prep for theater." I was bombarded with questions even as they were stripping me of my jewelry—I never did get my Vietnamese bracelet back— and putting in a catheter. Someone else was measuring my legs for stockings, of all things, and Pete was being told to scrub and change into a gown if he wanted to be present at the emergency C-section they were about to perform because of my sudden-onset preeclampsia. I was given an injection to help the baby's lungs and a drip to help with something else, I never caught what. And then a surgeon appeared, took one look at the trace, and said just one word: "Now." After that it was a blur of corridors and faces and gabbled explanations. There was no time for an epidural, another doctor told me. Seconds later, I was unconscious.

I came around in the recovery room to silence. No crying baby, no Pete, just the bleep of a machine. And a doctor looking down at me.

"Your baby's alive," he said. "A baby boy."

Thank God. "Can I see him?" I managed to say.

The doctor—I think he was a doctor; he was just a pair of anonymous eyes over a surgical mask—shook his head. "He's gone straight to the NICU in a specialist ambulance. He's very small and very poorly."

NICU, pronounced *nick-you.* It meant nothing to me at the time, but I was soon to become all too familiar with the different levels of emergency infant care. A neonatal intensive care unit was the very highest.

"Poorly? What with?"

"Babies who are that premature struggle to breathe unaided. He'll probably be put on a ventilator to help his lungs." He paused. "It's possible he might have hypoxia."

"What's that? Is it fatal? Is he going to live?"

All I can remember about this man, who I'd never seen before and would never see again, is his kind brown eyes, even though he politely pulled down his surgical mask before he said gently, "It's when the baby's brain is starved of oxygen. But the NICU at St. Alexander's is the best place for him, and it's very close. If anyone can help him, they can."

I stared at him, horrified. I was just realizing that, far from being a great place to have a baby, this smart hotel-like clinic was actually completely ill equipped to deal with an emergency like mine.

Everything had gone wrong. I had an overwhelming feeling of having failed my baby. I was meant to be keeping him safe inside me for another thirteen weeks, for God's sake. I was his life-support system. And instead, my body had rejected him, spat him out into a world he wasn't ready for.

"Where's Pete?" I croaked.

"Your husband will have gone with the baby. I'm sorry—there was no time for goodbyes."

I don't need to say goodbye to Pete, I wanted to say, *and anyway we're not married.* But then I realized. The doctor meant *goodbye to the baby.* The first time I saw my son, he'd be dead and cold.

I began to weep, tears running down my face even as the doctor checked my womb at the other end; tears of rage and regret and loss for the tiny person who'd been inside me and who was going to die before his own mother had even held him.

7

MADDIE

I COME OUT OF the Underground at Willesden Green with a million questions churning around my head, so I call Pete again as I walk the last quarter mile to our house.

"The thing is, I just don't believe two babies could get mixed up like that in the NICU," I tell him. "Theo was in an incubator the whole time, attached to all those lines. And he had an electronic tag on his leg. It just couldn't have happened."

"Miles said something about it not being St. Alexander's he's suing, it's the private hospital where his wife gave birth. So maybe that could explain it."

That seems more possible. If two very premature babies arrived at St. Alexander's at the same time, perhaps they got mixed up before the tags were even put on. This might be real, after all.

"But weren't you with him the whole time? Hang on, I'm at the front door."

Pete opens the door, lowering his phone as he does so. "Not all the time. There were so many people working on him—getting the tubes in, taking blood . . . And later, they found me a room to sleep in. I didn't even notice when the tag appeared on his leg."

He gnaws his lip, his eyes haunted. I know what he's thinking. "You had to sleep sometimes, Pete. We were there for weeks."

"I keep wondering though—how *come* I didn't notice? How could our baby have been switched with a different one and I didn't spot it?"

"Because the truth is, none of them looked like babies to begin with," I say flatly.

Pete glances at me. He still doesn't like to talk about my reaction to the NICU. "But you sensed it, Mads," he says quietly. "You felt no maternal attachment to Theo. You even wondered out loud if he was really our baby. On some level, you *knew*."

I hesitate, then shake my head. "I didn't have trouble bonding with him because he wasn't ours. It was because he was nothing like the baby I'd always imagined having. They all were. I'd have felt the same about any baby in that place. They—they *disgusted* me, somehow."

At least, that's what I've always told myself. Along with *You're a terrible mother* and *There's something wrong with you.* But now, despite what I've just said to Pete, I can't help wondering— had I known something else was wrong, all along?

MY FIRST IMAGE OF my baby was a grainy shot taken on Pete's phone that he sent while I was still in the recovery room. Blurry, taken over the shoulder of a nurse or doctor, it showed a small pale shape in an incubator, a Christmas tree of tubes and valves attached to a tiny body. There was what looked like bubble wrap encasing his chest, with more tubes coming out of it—I found out later that the doctors had been freezing him, deliberately causing hypothermia to reduce any swelling in his brain. Yet more tubes were taped to his nose. He looked scrawny and sick and barely human.

When I was nine, my parents had a litter from the family Labrador, Maya. Five were born alive and well, but then there was a long gap, so long we'd have thought she was finished if she hadn't so obviously been in distress. Finally, one last puppy popped out—a tiny, hairless fledgling of a thing. It soon became clear it wasn't strong enough to haul itself through the scrum of other puppies for one of Maya's teats, and for her part she never seemed to nudge it into position as she did the others. I kept pulling other puppies off the best teat and putting the runt to it, trying to get it to suck, but it just couldn't get the idea. Two days later, it died.

When I saw that picture on my phone, I was even more convinced that by the time I joined Pete at St. Alexander's, our baby would be dead. The doctor's words kept spinning around my brain. *He's very poorly.*

I was still looking at the picture when Pete called. "I've stepped outside—they don't allow phone conversations in the NICU," he said breathlessly. "I just wanted to check you got the photo."

"I got it."

"Are you okay?"

"He's going to die, isn't he?" I said numbly. It felt surreal to be saying those words out loud. Twenty-four hours before, we'd been helping our friends celebrate their marriage, with three months to go before my due date, and now here I was, the mother of a child on its deathbed.

Pete's voice was calm, but I could tell what an effort it was costing him. "Not necessarily. Mads, there are babies here even smaller than he is. They say the next three days are critical. If he gets through that, there's a good chance." A long silence. "Do you want me to come back?"

"No. Stay with him. One of us should be there."

"Okay. They want me to get some colostrum from you, though. I'll be over in a couple of hours with a breast pump."

"Oh God." I hadn't even begun to think about the mechanics of breastfeeding when me and my dying baby were in two separate hospitals. But Pete was ahead of me.

"They'll freeze your milk for now—he's got a tube in his umbilical stump, with a drip hooked up to it." Another pause. "They're asking what we want to call him."

A name to go on his grave. The thought slipped into my brain, unbidden. Suddenly all the names we'd thought of—quirky, fun names like Jack and Sam and Ed, names that were snappy and bouncy and full of vigor—felt wrong. I couldn't picture them carved on a headstone with his dates underneath. "What about Theo?"

"I thought you didn't like Theo."

"I thought you did."

"Well, I do."

"Let's go with Theo, then." *Because I don't want to give a name I like to a child who's going to die.*

I WAS IN SHOCK, of course. And as it turned out, Theo didn't die. As each day went by, and the syringe pumps were taken off him one by one, we allowed ourselves to hope a little more. And finally, after five days, the doctors did a brain scan and announced they were now cautiously optimistic.

Which isn't to say that from then on it was plain sailing. Pete's updates from the NICU, when he came over to sit with me, were full of references to *desats* and *apneas* and *braddies*—the weird terminology of the baby unit, now becoming all too familiar. Desaturation, low oxygen in the blood, because a premature baby's lungs don't work properly on their own. Apnea, absence of breathing, because sometimes, despite the machine that blew air up his nose, Theo would simply forget to inhale. Bradycardia, a dangerously slow heartbeat, because every so often his heart would just stop for no reason, and then the nurses would gently scratch his foot or rub his shoulders to get him started again. It was like magic, Pete said wide-eyed, seeing them bring him back to life like that.

Prolonging the inevitable, I'd thought at the time.

It was a whole week before I was able to join them. My C-section hadn't healed well and I'd had a virus—even if I'd been able to move, they wouldn't have let me into a ward full of premature babies until it had cleared up. But eventually I was put in a wheelchair and sent by taxi to St. Alexander's, the expensive private hospital off-loading me onto the NHS as casually as if it were scraping a piece of dogshit off its shoe.

I'd thought I was prepared for the NICU. After all, Pete had described it, and I'd seen pictures on my phone. But nothing could have prepared me for the reality. Instead of beds, there were pram-sized electronic pods. It made me think of those science-fiction movies where people are transported through space—but while those movies tried to make their incubators look sleek and futuristic, here each pod was surrounded by a chaotic jumble of wires and equipment. It was warm and humid, too, like a swimming pool changing room. There was no natural light, and some of the pods were bathed in ultraviolet. Those babies were being treated for jaundice, Pete explained later. But it was the noise that hit me the hardest. There was no crying—little lungs couldn't, only mew, and in any case, most of the babies had tubes that went up their noses and down their throats, preventing them from making any sound. Instead, the NICU was a cacophony of electronic bleeps and chimes and bongs. Later I'd come to realize that many weren't even alarms, just machines making their everything-normal-here noises, and that each was different for a reason. Like ewes recognizing the bleat of their particular lamb across a noisy field, the nurses could recognize their patients' sounds and respond to any change.

I had no idea which incubator contained my baby. But then I saw Pete, over in one corner. Most of the pods had see-through covers with holes in the sides, like machines for handling hazardous material, but he was standing next to one that had the top removed. He was attaching a syringe of what looked like breast milk to one end of a tube.

"Over there," I said to the porter who was wheeling me.

Pete looked up and gave me a tender smile, but didn't stop what he was doing. "Mummy's here," he said to the incubator. I got there, peered in, and saw Theo.

It should have been a big moment. The way everyone talks about the maternal bond, that bottomless pit of gushy love people go on about, if for some reason you don't feel an immediate, overwhelming connection to your baby there must be something wrong with you. But I didn't. I simply recoiled. I'd somehow expected from Pete's positive updates that Theo would look like a real baby now. But this stranger's wizened face seemed a hundred years old rather than newborn. Dark, downy hair covered his shoulders, like a little monkey. He was wearing the tiniest nappy I'd ever seen, and he was tucked into a kind of ramshackle nest of comforters and bedding. Electrical pads were stuck to his chest, and a cuff around his left foot glowed red—that was the oxygen sensor, I learned later. His arms and legs were stick-thin, the limbs of a famine victim.

A clear plastic tube went up one tiny nostril—the same tube Pete was gently squeezing breast milk into the other end of. "Shouldn't a nurse be doing that?" I said anxiously.

"They're busy. Besides, I like doing it for him. It makes me feel useful."

"Did you check the pH, Pete?" an Irish voice called. I looked up. A nurse, dark and pretty, was speaking to him from across a nearby incubator.

"Two point five."

"Good man," she said approvingly. Then, to me, "Are you Mum?"

I've always found the way medical staff call every mother Mum and every infant Baby, instead of *the* mum and *the* baby, slightly grating, but I know that's pedantic of me. "Yes. Maddie."

"Welcome to the NICU, Maddie. I know it must seem overwhelming at first, but little Theo's doing really well." With her Irish accent, his name came out as *Teo*. "And Pete's been a total star. If only all husbands were that handy with the NG tube."

"We're not actually married," I said automatically.

"Sorry, my bad—all partners. Don't let him get away, though. He's a catch, that one."

It was just the friendly banter of someone trying to put me at my ease, I knew. But something about it irritated me, perhaps because I still felt a failure for not being able to carry Theo to term. Plus, there was the realization that, while I'd been lying in a cushy private room, Pete had been quietly coping—no, more than coping, *excelling*—here in the brutal environment of the NICU. Generally, I'd have said Pete isn't brilliant in an emergency. But put him in a situation like that, a situation that requires steadfastness and determination, and he comes into his own. It should have made me feel proud and grateful. But actually, it just made me feel even more guilty.

Pete saw me looking at the monitors. "They start to make sense eventually," he said.

It hadn't even occurred to me to try to make sense of them. "What do you mean?"

He indicated the nearest one. "The wavy line is his heartbeat, and the big number is beats per minute. Anything less than a hundred is a braddie—if that happens, try to get his heart going again with a stroke or pat. The one that goes off most often is oxygen desat. If you see that number starting to fall, check the prongs up his nose before you call the nurse—sometimes they work their way loose."

I couldn't imagine doing any of those things. "Have you held him yet?" I asked.

Pete nodded. "Just once, this morning—his temperature was too unstable before. It's an amazing feeling, Mads. You have to be careful because of all the tubes and wires, obviously. But when he stretched out on my bare chest and opened his eyes at me, I choked up."

"I think we all did." That was the Irish nurse again. She looked up, smiling, from the other incubator. "That's one of the best parts of doing this job—seeing a baby get skin-to-skin for the first time."

Once again, I felt a small, unworthy flicker of irritation at the thought of a bare-chested weeping Pete, with this pretty dark-haired nurse kneeling next to him, crying too. I was careful not to let it show, though. Getting on with the staff here was clearly going to be important. So all I said was, "I can't wait."

8

PETE

WHILE MADDIE WAS ON the Tube, I'd done some quick research on my laptop. I briefly considered posting on DadStuff, which was my usual way of researching things, but thought better of it. Instead, still reeling, I googled *Miles Lambert + Burton Investments*. Miles's LinkedIn page came up, although it didn't tell me much except that he was three years older than me, he'd been to Durham University, his office was located in Berkeley Square, and his professional skills had been recommended as "excellent" by sixteen people. But at least it confirmed this wasn't some kind of terrible prank. The DNA test, when I looked at it, seemed authentic, too—rows of numbers and technical language culminating in the words: *Probability of paternity: 98%*.

Next I searched *swapped babies*. It was clearly very rare—or at least, it was very rare for a swap to come to light. The switching of identical twins was discovered most often, presumably because the resemblance between two apparent strangers was more likely to be noticed. In 1992 a Canadian, Brent Tremblay, bumped into his identical twin, now called George Holmes, at university. In 2001 a similar thing happened to identical twins in the Canary Islands, and in 2015 two sets of identical twins were reunited in Bogotá. From these and other cases, combined with the incidence of twins in the general population, someone had calculated that mix-ups of less discoverable infants—that is, non-twins—could be as many as one in a thousand births, about the same as Down syndrome.

Other switches were discovered as a result of paternity testing when parents separated, as happened in Charlottesville, Virginia. The children involved in that case were three years old; the ensuing custody battle went on for years.

In 2006 two newborn girls were accidentally switched in the Czech Republic, with the mix-up discovered a year later. The girls were gradually reintroduced to their original families, by agreement of all four parents.

The son of a UK citizen was switched in a hospital in El Salvador in 2015. He, too, was reunited with his parents after a year.

In countries where switches were discovered there was often a public outcry leading to more stringent precautions, such as double tagging. That wasn't the case in the UK, but there had been some similar problems with attempted baby abductions, and, as a result, security on NHS wards was considered above average.

There was no mention anywhere of what it was like in British private hospitals.

The thing that immediately jumped out at me, though, was that the decision to swap the children back or not was largely a matter of age. If they were over three when the switch was discovered, they usually ended up staying with their existing families. If they were twelve months or less, they were usually returned to their birth parents.

But two? Two years and two weeks, to be precise? That seemed to be a terrifyingly gray area.

Don Maguire's words came back to me. *There's certainly no automatic requirement for the family courts to get involved. It's best for the parents to work out a solution between themselves.*

If we couldn't work something out, did that mean a court would have to decide? Would Theo's fate ultimately rest with some dry legal bureaucrat? The very thought made my blood run cold.

ALL OF THIS I explained, or rather babbled, to Maddie when she was barely through the door.

"But is that what this man was suggesting?" she asked, getting straight to the most important point as usual. "Does he really think we should swap them back?"

"He didn't say. But neither did he say we shouldn't." In fact, now that I thought about it, Miles Lambert had said remarkably little. "He was pretty vague."

"Perhaps he knew it would be a lot to take in and didn't want you to feel he was railroading you," she pointed out. "What was he like?"

"He seemed all right," I admitted. "That is, as all right as it's possible to be when you're breaking news like that. Said he knew what a terrible shock it must be—it affected him the same way, when he found out."

"Well, that's something. But how *did* he find out? I mean, what made him look at his child in the first place and think, *That's not my son?*"

I thought back. "He didn't say that, either."

"And he really didn't give you any clue as to which way they're thinking?"

I shook my head. I wasn't feeling any better as time passed since our encounter. "But he took a picture of Theo, to show his wife. And he left us one of David."

"Can I see?"

I went and got the photograph. I saw Maddie's face change as she looked at it—first with surprise, and then involuntarily softening around the eyes.

"He looks just like you, doesn't he?" I said gently.

"A bit. And he's the spitting image of Robin at that age." I didn't really know Maddie's brothers, who were all in Australia. Robin, the youngest, was the one she missed most. She took a deep breath. "Wow. I guess this is real, isn't it?"

My laptop pinged. Automatically, I turned toward it. It was a notification from LinkedIn, which I still had open. *Miles Lambert wants to join your network.*

I showed Maddie. "Should I accept?"

"Why not? Whatever happens next, we'll need to be in touch."

I clicked ACCEPT. Moments later, a message pinged into my inbox.

Pete,

Thank you for talking to me today, and once again my apologies for crashing into your life with what can only have been disturbing news. I'm sure you'll want to talk things over with Madelyn before you make any decisions, but now you and I have the initial contact out of the way, Lucy and I were wondering if the two of you would like to come and talk it over at our house—and meet David at the same time? It would be entirely up to you whether or not you bring Theo, but of course we would love to meet him too.

This is a difficult and horrible situation, one that none of us chose or ever expected to find ourselves in. But hopefully we can work out what's right and best for all concerned—and, particularly, for our children.

Kind regards,
Miles

"It's a good email," Maddie said, reading over my shoulder. I could hear the relief in her voice. "It really sounds like they don't want to pressurize us into anything."

"Yes," I said uneasily. Despite the email's agreeable tone, I had a sense that events were already starting to move, and that I wasn't in control of them. Once we'd met David, and the Lamberts had met Theo, everything was going to become much more complicated. The train was leaving the station, and I wasn't the one driving it.

9

MADDIE

IT'S ONLY AFTER I see the email from Miles, with the reference to Lucy, that the name Lambert starts to ring a bell. There'd been twenty-one intensive care incubators in the NICU. Twenty-one sets of parents with desperately small or sick babies. Some were only on the ward a few days; some—especially those with preemies—spent months there. Most were just a blur of drawn, haggard faces. I'd gotten to know the ones whose cots were nearest, or who I happened to stand next to when I was washing out my breast pump in the sink area—talking was a way to distract yourself from the tension, to ease the permanent stress lump in the back of your throat—but there were too many, too transient, to remember them all.

Gradually, I got used to being there. I still felt like a failure, but among all those other failures that was less crushing, somehow, than it had been back at the private hospital with the sound of healthy babies' cries wafting into my room. The babies in the

NICU almost never cried, even the older ones without tubes down their throats. Instead, they'd register distress by stretching out a jittery arm or leg, or arching their back, or even just sneezing. You got ridiculously attuned to those signs in your baby, because any of them might herald the onset of an "episode"—the nurses' euphemism for a near-death experience, when the alarms went off and Theo's heart or breathing would have to be restarted.

Watching my baby so obsessively changed how I felt about him. I felt—not *love,* exactly, definitely not that, but an overwhelming, painful feeling of responsibility. I'd already let him down once. I mustn't let him down again.

The skin-to-skin, or "kangaroo care" as the nurses sometimes called it, helped, too. The first time Bronagh—the Irish nurse, who turned out to not be as bad as I'd thought once I got used to her breezy manner—suggested it, I was dubious. It seemed madness to move this tiny, vulnerable being out of his lifesaving incubator and onto the same stomach that had failed him once already. But Bronagh wasn't going to take no for an answer, so while Pete drew the screens, I pulled off my top and Bronagh carefully lowered Theo, complete with all his tangles of lines and wires, onto my chest, like a collapsed puppet.

"You can see if he might latch on to your breast now, if you like," she added when he was settled.

Breastfeed? Really? I was terrified just holding him. He was so tiny—three pounds when he was born, and still under five pounds three weeks later. I knew how babies should feel—plump and squeezy and pinchable. By comparison Theo felt as light as a blown egg. But I obediently pushed up my bra and steered his tiny head toward my nipple. Tiny toothless gums, soft as a little fish's, mouthed at me. Then, abruptly, they fastened on. A pop, a bubble, and suddenly euphoria was flowing out of me into him. He spluttered once, gasped, then went back to sucking.

"He's doing it," Pete breathed. Then: "Mads, look at the stats."

I looked over at the monitor. Theo's heart rate was falling. "Is he all right?" I said anxiously.

"All right? He's just settling down for a nice drink and a sleep," Bronagh said. "Welcome to your new favorite place, Theo."

That was when it first sank in that the doctor at the other hospital might have been wrong. This baby might be destined to live.

I FIRST NOTICED LUCY because she seemed so out of place. She was very well groomed, for one thing, with long blond hair that was either natural or so expertly dyed it must have been done professionally. The cut also looked like it had been done at an expensive salon, a lovely feather-edged fringe that reminded me of a show horse's mane. Her clothes were impeccable—in all the time we were in the NICU, I never saw her turn up in a fleece or tracksuit bottoms, as other mothers did. She wore white linen blouses, little jackets or cashmere cardigans, jeans that showed off her slender legs. She was probably around the same age as me, but somehow seemed older.

One day, we were both in the sink area. She was rinsing breast milk syringes, while I was washing bottles and teats. She glanced across and said, "That looks like a really distant dream." Her voice had that slight drawl posh English people have, so *really* came out like *rarely*. But her smile was friendly, and I could tell she was just breaking the ice, not actually complaining.

"You'll get there," I replied, trying to be encouraging.

Her smile slipped. "I'm not sure we will, actually. The doctors want to talk to us about discontinuing care."

"I'm so sorry," I said immediately. Everyone on the ward knew what *discontinuing care* meant. There'd been an instance just a few days before, a lovely Indian couple who brought in homemade Keralan food for the nurses and whose baby girl had been a micro-preemie—less than eight hundred grams. She'd fought off infection after infection, but each one had left her progressively weaker. She'd already been diagnosed with cerebral palsy, was partially blind, and had never come off a full ventilator. When the doctors did their rounds, they'd confer over her crib in low, quiet voices. Afterward, the mother would be in tears, and sometimes the father, too. And then a day came when the parents simply looked exhausted and defeated, and the whole apparatus— incubator, ventilator, vital signs monitor, and all the connecting tubes—was unplugged and wheeled out of the NICU. They were being taken to a private room, someone said, where they could hold their baby while she died. All of us, even the nurses, were quiet for the rest of that day.

"Well, it's one of those things, I suppose, isn't it," Lucy said. Which might, on the face of it, seem like a completely inadequate response to her child's possible death, but I understood. Everyone in the NICU had to hold themselves together somehow. Some did it by sobbing and wailing, some wept quietly, others did it by bottling up. I was a bottler-upper myself, and so, it seemed, was Lucy.

Talking with Lucy about our babies, we soon realized they'd been admitted on the same day—which meant, of course, that they shared a birthday, although David had been a little further on than Theo, at twenty-nine weeks. But where Theo had progressed, David had been the opposite. Doctors were using the acronym *FTT* about him, Lucy said—failure to thrive.

I felt a mixture of emotions. That was one of the strange things about the NICU—friends were always texting to say *It must be terrible* or *It's incredible how strong you're being,* but in fact, because you were surrounded by so many people who were even worse off than you, most of the time you actually felt quite lucky. So I looked at this sleek, well-bred woman who was desperately trying to be stoic and British about the fact that her child might die, and felt both pity and relief—relief that my baby's health had taken a different path.

After that, Lucy and I smiled and nodded when we saw each other, and once she came over when Theo was having skin-on-skin feeding time. She watched for a while, looking down at him fondly. "He looks so contented, doesn't he?" she commented. "Like a dog curled up in his favorite chair. I'm Lucy, by the way."

"I'm Maddie." We'd told each other our babies' names, but not our own—slipping into the ways of parenthood already. "And that's my partner, Pete," I added, nodding in his direction.

"Oh, I've seen Pete. So good with the baby. All the nurses say so."

"We call him Saint Peter," I said drily. I still wasn't sure how I felt about the way everyone on the NICU now officially adored Pete, or the way he'd so instantly bonded with Theo. I was getting there—or at least, I was slowly becoming more confident about my ability to feed him—but I still didn't worship him unconditionally, the way Pete clearly did. "What about you? Is your partner here?"

Lucy shook her head. "He has one of those ridiculously high-pressure jobs where if he steps away from his emails for ten minutes, he'll get fired. He'll come after work, I expect."

Later, I saw a good-looking young man in a suit standing by David's incubator. He was resting one hand on the clear cover, almost as if he were stroking it in place of the baby. The fingers of his other hand were curled around a BlackBerry.

On another occasion, I happened to go past David's cot on the way to the toilet. The nurses in the NICU gave out little printed cards to mark every milestone: *Today I had cuddles with Daddy, Today I was fed by Mummy, Today I moved to an open cot.* Theo's incubator was by now festooned with these cards. I was struck by how bare David's was by comparison.

Then I saw that the arterial line in David's ankle looked wrong. There was fluid seeping through the bandage, and his toes were white. He must have dislodged it when he moved.

One of the reasons Pete was so effective in the NICU was that he was constantly asking questions—his journalistic training coming into play. So I knew that a dislodged arterial line could cause circulation problems, and was one of the few emergencies that might not trigger an alarm. I went to the nearest nurse, who was doing something for the baby in the next incubator. "Excuse me—I think David Lambert's line might have come loose."

The nurse gave me a brief, uninterested glance. "I'll take a look shortly."

"I think you should look now," I insisted. "His toes have gone a different color."

"I'll be there in a few minutes," she said testily. Her manner was far removed from Bronagh's cheery competence. Her name tag said PAULA.

I went back and took another look. David's toes were now dark purple. "I'm pulling the alarm," I said. I reached for the red cord by David's incubator, and the piercing sound of the crash alarm filled the ward. Paula swore as she stopped what she was doing and hurried over.

As if from nowhere, doctors appeared. "What's going on?" one demanded.

"This woman pulled the cord," Paula said sulkily.

"His line is loose," I pointed out.

The doctor looked down. "So it is. We'll soon have that sorted. And thank you," he added, as they got to work.

10

PETE

I LOOKED AT MY watch. It was already eleven thirty, and I had to collect Theo at noon. Normal life had to continue, if only for his sake. I took a deep breath. "So I'll reply to Miles saying we'll go?"

Maddie nodded. "I guess. But we should get our own position clear beforehand. In our heads, I mean. We need to know what we're trying to achieve."

"Which is what?" I said helplessly.

Maddie looked at me. "Pete . . . The fact is, of the two of us, you're closer to Theo. No—" She stopped my protests with a shake of her head. "Let's be honest. We both love him to bits, but it's you who spends your whole day with him. So tell me what your instincts are saying to you right now."

"If there *is* a decision to be made, it's a joint decision. It's got to be."

"Of course. But you go first. Tell me what you really think."

"Well . . ." I tried to marshal my thoughts. Just like Don Maguire's use of the word *solution* earlier, the word *decision* seemed to open up a great void beneath my feet. "It's a shock, of course, so I may not be thinking very straight. But I suppose—if we're really being honest—my gut instinct is that I don't think paternity and genetics are all that important. Not compared with *love*. If Theo was adopted, would we love him any less? Of course not. Minding whether someone is your flesh and blood—*what* they are, as opposed to *who* they are—it's so Victorian, isn't it? Or even older. Neanderthal. And then there's Theo. What would it do to him to suddenly be told, *Oh, we picked up the wrong kid at the hospital by mistake, out you go*? However nice Miles and Lucy turn out to be, it would *shatter* him." At the thought of telling Theo he wasn't our birth son, let alone that we were abandoning him for another child who was, my throat started to thicken and I had to pause. "I'm not doing it, Mads. I'm not breaking up this family." I stared at her defiantly. "So that's my view, and I'm pretty bloody wedded to it, actually."

In reply, she stepped forward and kissed me.

"And that is why I love you, Pete Riley," she said quietly. "Because of *that*." She prodded the approximate location of my heart.

"So you agree?"

"Of course I agree. That is, I suppose I've got a whole bunch of emotions. When you showed me that photograph of David, just for a moment, I—" She shook her head. "But no, you're right. Absolutely. The overwhelming question here is, what's best for Theo? And the answer is—obviously—for him to go on being brought up by the best dad in the world."

"And the best mum. Do you think the Lamberts will see it that way, though?"

"I don't see why not. After all, they've had longer to think it through, and now that you've said it, it's pretty obvious. Actually, I think that may be what Miles is hinting at in his email—that bit about putting the children's interests first? He says he's not trying to jump us into anything, but he's clear that whatever we do, we should do by agreement, and for the children. That can only lead you to one conclusion really, can't it? That we stay as we are. For their sake."

I nodded. "Maybe we don't have to make it as binary as swap or no swap anyway. We're civilized people in a civilized society, for God's sake. Maybe we can be part of each other's lives some other way." I snapped my fingers as an idea hit me. "We're always saying it's a shame most of Theo's cousins are in Australia. Why can't Theo and David be honorary cousins?"

"That's a great idea. Or what about godchildren? We were saying only the other day we should get Theo baptized now that we're starting church. We could ask Miles and Lucy to be godparents, and we could be David's as well. So there's something formal to recognize the relationship."

"Brilliant." At the realization that there might be a middle way after all, relief flooded through me. "And the two of them could have playdates. After all, they're the same age—"

"Exactly." Maddie nodded. "I'm sure that's the right response to this situation. Dialogue and cooperation and good communication . . . What are you doing?"

I was rummaging in the fridge. "Making us all blueberry smoothies for lunch. I promised Theo I'd do it before I picked him up. It was his turn to choose."

11

MADDIE

IN SOME WAYS, LEAVING the NICU was almost as traumatic as going there had been. The nurses and junior doctors had become my friends. But there was too much pressure on space for Theo to stay a moment longer than he had to, and eventually he met all the criteria for being moved to the special care baby unit, or the fattening-up room as the nurses in the NICU jokingly called it.

"Your baby's a fighter," Bronagh said as she wrote up his notes for the last time. "We've a pretty good track record with preemies, but I've never known one catch up as fast as him."

"How's David Lambert doing?" I hadn't been able to shake off the sense that David and Theo were like A Tale of Two Babies—that despite being admitted on the same day, one had somehow turned left while the other turned right, their fortunes forever diverging from then on.

"Paula told me he's on the mend. They operated on him for a

heart duct that hadn't closed, and that seems to have sorted him out."

"I'm so pleased!" I said. "Will you tell his mother I said hello?"

Bronagh nodded. "And this is for you, Pete." A little shyly, she handed Pete a card. On the front was written *Happy Father's Day*. "We make sure all our babies give cards to their dads on Father's Day—it's a little tradition around here," she explained. "But that's on Sunday and you won't be here, so . . ." I could tell Pete was touched.

We were only in the special care unit for a week. Theo continued to put on weight and sailed through the car-seat test, when the doctors hooked him up to the monitors and strapped him into a car seat for as long as it would take to get home. Pete and I were given training in infant CPR and the loan of an oxygen tank and mask, just in case he ever stopped breathing at home. And then— just like that, eleven weeks after I woke up with a splitting headache and a strange leaden feeling in my womb, and still two weeks before my actual due date—we were out of hospital, discharged, a proper family at last.

"Welcome to the world, little man," Pete said triumphantly as we walked out the hospital doors, lifting the baby seat like a lantern and slowly spinning around so Theo could see. "From now on, things are going to get better."

Except it wasn't that simple. Once, getting Theo home had been the only thing I wanted. Now it was strangely disorienting. When you were used to being able to glance over and check your baby's status on a monitor, not having one there seemed odd. The noise of the machines had become so familiar, its absence was deafening—the bleeps and chimes continued in my head, insistent as the chorus of a song. Instead of relaxing because we were home, I felt increasingly anxious. I worried that we'd scald the inside of Theo's mouth by overheating his bottle, or accidentally push him under the water when we gave him a bath, or drop him when he was wet and slippery afterward. I checked on him every ten minutes while he slept, to make sure he hadn't stopped breathing. And when he sniffed a few times, I was convinced he had an infection and made Pete rush us all straight back to the NICU.

The doctor checked Theo over, then said quietly to me, "And you? How are you coping?"

"I'm fine. Just a bit stressed out."

"Depressed?"

I shook my head. If anything, I was the very opposite of depressed—full of nervous energy.

"Well, if you do get the baby blues, don't ignore them. There are antidepressants your GP can prescribe that won't pass into your breast milk."

I didn't tell him I'd already started supplementing with formula. Breastfeeding reminded me too much of the NICU. I'd hidden the oxygen tank, too. I only had to catch sight of it to feel sick.

Most of all, though, I felt alone. It was so difficult to tell Pete that I still felt no maternal attachment to Theo, only a terrible helplessness. Once I tried to explain to him what it was like, how I felt as if I were only babysitting someone else's child, someone who'd be furious with me if I screwed up, and he looked at me, baffled.

"But of course he's our baby. Who else's could he be?"

"I don't mean I *think* he's someone else's baby. I mean I *feel* as if he is."

Nor did I tell him that the exhaustion, the chapped nipples, the emotional numbness, felt like my punishment for not being a good mother. Pete so clearly adored his son, I'd have felt disloyal even bringing it up.

Sometimes he'd start to say something about the NICU—"Do you remember when those other parents . . ." or "Wasn't it weird when that doctor said . . ."—and I'd cut him off.

"I don't really want to think about all that. Let's put it behind us, shall we?"

"Of course. That's a really healthy attitude, Mads. Let's look to the future."

I'd read that, for some women, the maternal bond came slowly. So I assumed that was what would happen in my case. And it did start kicking in more when Theo was about three months. I'd gotten used to the half smiles and grimaces he made when he was trying to poo—Pete always seized on them as evidence of his affectionate nature, though to me they were simply an indication that Theo found pooing very satisfying. But one time, after I'd given him a bath, I'd wrapped him in a towel and laid him on the floor as usual when he looked up at me and grinned. A part of me knew he was just pleased to be warm and dry again, but that look, the mischief and contentment in his little blue-gray eyes . . . For the first time, I felt a relationship with him. I wasn't just a milk machine. I was the center of his universe, and even if he wasn't yet the center of mine, we were definitely in some kind of planetary orbit, locked into a relationship that would last forever. I thought: *When I am old and gray, you will be my adult son,* and the sudden sense of permanence made me gasp.

Looking back, it wasn't surprising it took so long. I'm not someone who falls in love at the drop of a hat. It took me almost a year to fall for Pete—we used to joke that he didn't so much date me as lay siege to me. Why would I fall in love with a stranger in a plastic box, one who was probably only passing through my life for a few short weeks? If there had been any maternal reflex in me at all, it was the one telling me not to risk getting emotionally involved. I had to wait for him to move on from being in danger, to become a person with a future, before I could allow myself the luxury of loving him.

12

Dear Miles and Lucy,

First, thank you for your email, Miles, and for coming to see me in person before that, which can't have been an easy thing to do. As you say, this is a very difficult situation that none of us chose to be in, but we really appreciate that you're trying to deal with it in a civilized way. We fully intend to do the same.

Having discussed it, we would be very pleased to take up your offer of getting together at your house, and we think it would be good for Theo and David to meet as well. Maddie remembers Lucy from the NICU and says hello.

We're free all day Saturday. Theo tends to be at his best in the mornings, so shall we aim for about 10:30?

Best wishes,
Pete

13

PETE

COME SATURDAY, WE PACKED Theo into the back of our Golf and headed over to Highgate. I'd allowed plenty of time to find somewhere to park, but as it turned out, I needn't have. Where we lived, it was always a scramble to find a space, but the roads in Miles and Lucy's neck of the woods hardly had any cars parked in them at all. It was because the houses were so big and far apart, I realized—fine, wide Victorian villas, with large sash windows and raised ground floors. Very few had been turned into flats, either, which meant even fewer vehicles competing for spaces, while some, like the Lamberts', had off-road parking. We pulled up a few yards from their house and sat waiting for the clock on the dashboard to reach ten thirty, while behind us Theo puffed tunelessly on a plastic kazoo.

"On reflection, that might not have been the best toy to bring," Maddie said after a while.

"I didn't bring it, he found it on the backseat," I pointed

out. "And it's good for his speech to use his fine mouth muscles. But I'm sure David will have lots of other toys to play with."

We were both silent. The truth was, we were wrung out. The days since Miles had knocked on the door with his bombshell had been exhausting. We'd veered between hope and fear—hope that we could somehow make this work, and fear at what might happen if we couldn't. Sometimes, in the depths of the night, I'd jolt awake, gasping with adrenaline. I could almost feel our family, our little unit, being pulled apart, like the segments of an orange. But then I'd tell myself it was going to be all right, that we had a plan. And that, after all, Miles and Lucy must be feeling exactly the same terror as us.

"Why are we doing this?" Maddie said suddenly.

I gave her a sideways look. "Meeting today? Or meeting them at all?"

"Both. Any of it. Perhaps we should just have—I don't know, politely refused to engage. Perhaps that would have been the best thing for everyone, in the long run."

"It's not too late. We could make an excuse—"

She shook her head. "I don't really mean it. And sorry for snapping about the toy. I'm just nervous, I suppose."

"About the meeting? Or seeing Theo's cousin?" We'd agreed not to use the words *our son* in front of Theo. He probably wouldn't understand, but it was best to be careful.

"Both. But mainly David. I just can't help thinking—he's our, our *offspring.* I carried him. And we have absolutely no idea what sort of person he is. That's just *crazy,* isn't it?"

"Big car," Theo said. I looked around. He was pointing at the four-wheel-drive BMW parked in the Lamberts' drive.

"Very big car," I agreed. "But big cars aren't always better. They put lots of dirt into the air, for one thing."

"Come on, let's do this." Maddie reached down and squeezed my hand, then unbuckled her seatbelt.

. . .

WHAT DO YOU TAKE as a gift in that situation? We'd opted for flowers for Lucy, and we'd let Theo choose a small packet of sweets for David. He'd decided on chocolate buttons. I'd mentally run through all the objections Lucy might raise—some mothers were funny about sweets of any kind—but these were only 160 calories, the chocolate was Fairtrade, and, most important, I knew there were exactly ten buttons in every bag, so they were eminently shareable.

We climbed the steps to the front door, which Theo managed by himself; rang the bell—more complicated than it sounds: It turned out the entry intercom was back by the gate into the drive—and then the door opened and there was Miles, casual in a patterned shirt, chinos, and deck shoes without socks. "Come in, come in, good to see you," he said to me and Maddie, before eagerly crouching down to Theo and putting his hand up, palm out, in the universal gesture that means "high five."

"Hey there, Theo," he said gently.

Theo, for reasons of his own, chose to interpret Miles's flat hand as a target to be punched. "Bouff!" he said as he hit him. Miles laughed and stood up.

"Lucy's through here."

He led us to the rear of the house, into a slate-floored kitchen the size of our entire ground floor. The blond woman I'd last seen outside the nursery was standing by a red Aga, making tea. Once again she was stylishly dressed, in tight white jeans and a shawl made of mohair or angora. "Hello!" she said brightly, coming over and kissing us both on the cheek. I sensed she was just as nervous as we were. "Oh, how kind." She took the flowers and reached under the big ceramic sink for a vase.

"And this is David," Miles said behind us. Maddie and I turned as one.

Miles had carried David in from an adjoining room, so he was at our height. He was smaller than Theo—a lot smaller—and in the flesh, you could tell at once there was something fragile about him. His fair hair was very fine, and his features were elfin, almost girlish, which made the resemblance to Maddie even stronger. He looked at us anxiously, a little dull-eyed, as if he'd just woken up.

"Hi," I said, stepping forward and shaking his little hand gently by the wrist. "I'm Pete."

"And I'm Maddie." Maddie reached toward him eagerly with both hands, as if to take him, and David shrank back.

"He's quite a shy little chap, I'm afraid." Miles squatted down, still holding David, so David was in Theo's eyeline. "We weren't allowed to have other children around at all until a couple of months ago—he's still very immunosuppressed. You're just about the first visitors who Lucy hasn't made scrub their arms with alcohol gel."

"Theo," I began, meaning to prompt him to say hello, but Theo had already stepped forward. Being at nursery had made him confident with other children, and now he held up his hand dramatically, thrusting the bag of chocolate buttons at David for inspection like a policeman's badge. "Ho!" he said proudly. David stared at him, uncomprehending.

"He's not allowed chocolate, I'm afraid," Lucy said.

"Oh, I'm sorry," I said apologetically. "I thought, since it was a special occasion . . ."

"It's not that. He can't digest it. He has a reflux condition that's triggered by any kind of fat. When he gets an attack he has to go straight back on oxygen, which he hates."

"I'll take that, Theo," I said quickly, plucking the bag from his hand. He rounded on me, his eyes expressing his outrage, but I'd already pocketed it. I was probably going to make his own snatching problem worse by grabbing it like that, I reflected, but it wasn't the moment to worry about that. "Why don't you ask David to show you some of his toys?" I added.

Miles gently set David down. He was unsteady on his feet, teetering wide-legged like a baby. From the bulkiness of his trousers, it was clear he was still wearing a regular nappy rather than pull-ups or pants.

"Michaela?" Miles called.

"Yes, Mr. Lambert?" A girl of about twenty appeared in the doorway. She, too, was blond, although her hair had black showing at the roots. She sounded Eastern European.

"Could you take David, and show Theo where to find some toys?"

"Of course. Come with me, Theo, they're all in here."

"What toys do you like, David?" Maddie asked gently as Michaela picked him up. He didn't reply, although his head turned toward her curiously. With a stab of horror I realized he hadn't understood the question.

He was brain-damaged. It shouldn't have come as a surprise—the possibility had been drummed into us in the NICU, over and over. But week by week, as Theo had thrived and prematurity slowly lost its grip, we'd started taking normality for granted. Forgetting just how lucky we'd been.

Or rather, how lucky Theo had been. Because—I now realized—the doctor who'd told Maddie how poorly our son was, and how he might not survive that initial episode of oxygen starvation unscathed, had been right. The child he had been talking about was David, and his mind was clearly impaired.

"David's not very chatty," Lucy said nervously. "He's not nearly so advanced as Theo."

I looked at her, aghast. Was it possible she didn't know? Or was she just using a euphemistic understatement for her son's condition? The latter, I decided. It must be. She would have spent the last two years talking to doctors on an almost daily basis.

But then I remembered how, even in the NICU, the doctors had always shrugged and said, *We just can't tell the future. It's impossible to make a long-term prognosis until around the third birthday.*

Either way, I reflected, this was going to make the conversation we'd come here to have a whole lot more difficult.

14

MADDIE

LUCY POURS US ALL tea, and then we stand and watch the children through the doorway of the playroom. They don't play together. David sits on the floor with a baby gym, repetitively spinning the plastic animals around and around the pole, while Theo stomps around, pulling things off shelves and inspecting them. Eventually Michaela finds him a wooden train and he settles down to make it crash into mountains that he constructs from piles of Duplo, while she scurries around picking up the pieces.

I can't stop looking at David. *My son.* When I'd first seen him in Miles's arms and reached for him, it hadn't even been a conscious gesture. And although he'd shrunk back, my hands had briefly made contact with his ribs. The memory of that touch seems to linger in the ends of my fingers, like the sting after an electric shock.

I glance at Miles and Lucy. Miles is watching Theo the same way I've been looking at David—devouring him with his eyes, a half smile playing across his face every time the train smashes into the Duplo. Lucy . . . Lucy is harder to read, her gaze flitting from one child to the other. When she looks at Theo she smiles, amused by his antics, but she seems anxious, too. And when she looks at David, there's something altogether different in her eyes. Sadness, perhaps.

Eventually Miles says, "Shall we . . . ?" and we all turn back to the kitchen. Pete and I sit on high stools on one side of the enormous island, with Miles and Lucy on the other. It feels weirdly like a business meeting at some trendy production company.

"So," Miles begins, "thank you for coming today. And please don't feel there's any pressure from us to make any long-term plans yet. As far as we're concerned, we just wanted the boys to meet, and for us adults to say a proper hello." He pushes the lock of black hair back out of his eyes. "The important thing is, we're talking. In itself, that's a good first step."

Although he seems diffident, even nervous, it strikes me how good at this he is. Charming without coming across as narcissistic, confident without being arrogant. Good-looking, too, but in a boyish, engaging way that stops it being threatening. I can see how he might be worth the enormous salary he's presumably paid, in order to afford such a spectacular house. And he has some of Theo's pent-up energy, too.

The subtext of his words is, *That's enough emotion for one day. Let's leave it there, shall we?* He's thinking of Lucy, I suspect— she still seems very tense; much more so than she ever did two years ago in the NICU. I've noticed he's very protective of her. When they were handing out the tea, for example, I saw how he quietly corrected her when she forgot whether Pete or I was the one who took milk, but under his breath, without making a big deal of it.

For a moment I feel disappointed. When I've geared myself up for a tricky conversation, I find it frustrating not to have it. But Miles is probably right—no point in rushing things.

Pete doesn't read the situation the same way, though, or perhaps he's simply so tense he can't help himself. He glances at me, then back at Miles and Lucy. "You've had longer than us to think about this," he says bluntly. "You must have some idea what you think the right course of action is."

There's a long silence. Miles and Lucy don't look at each other.

"Of course, if you don't want to say . . ." he adds.

"No, it's not—" Miles begins, just as Lucy says, "Well, to us—"

They both stop. "You go," Miles says, turning to her.

"I couldn't bear to lose him," Lucy says in a rush. She looks directly at me, mother-to-mother. "It doesn't really matter which of our wombs they came out of, does it? It's being the one who cares for them day after day that counts. And when they have problems, like David . . . well, some people say it makes you overprotective. Perhaps that's part of it." She glances at her husband. "It certainly makes the bond even more special."

"Actually, darling, it's Pete who's Theo's main carer," Miles says quietly.

"Well, then you *both* must know what I'm talking about." She looks defiantly from me to Pete and back. "Miles and I would love to be part of Theo's life. We would love for the two of them to see each other as family. As for the details, we haven't gotten that far. But we couldn't bear to swap them back. Just couldn't *bear* it."

"We feel *exactly* the same," Pete says. He looks at me, and I nod to show I'm right behind him. "Both of us do."

Lucy puts one hand to her chest. "Oh, thank God. I thought for a moment I might be ruining everything, blurting it out like that—"

Miles puts his hand on her knee. "You did very well."

"We've talked about it, too," Pete says. He lowers his voice so that Theo, in the playroom, won't overhear. "We were trying not to rush the decision, just like you said, but we both feel—instinctively—that it's the right thing for Theo and David not to be ejected from their current families. But we absolutely second what you said about the two of them being part of each other's lives. We wondered if you'd like to be Theo's godparents, for example. And we could be David's."

"That's a *wonderful* idea," Lucy says.

"Although actually, David already has godparents," Miles interjects apologetically. "Billy Cortauld—the Saracens captain—and Lucy's friend Gemma. And I'm pretty sure the Church of England doesn't allow you to add more after the christening. Lifelong commitment and all that. I can check, though . . ." He's tapping his phone screen as he speaks. "No, you can't. Sorry to be the voice of practicality. But we'd be honored to be Theo's, if you haven't chosen any yet."

Pete nods. "And we were thinking about setting up regular playdates, and telling Theo that David's his cousin. We don't have much in the way of family here in London—Maddie's are all in Australia, and mine are up north. So this could actually be a blessing, or at least a silver lining. It's Easter soon—maybe we could all spend the day together. That's just an example, obviously. I mean, it's all got to be worked out properly, hasn't it, but the point is, we *can* sort this."

"That sounds wonderful," Miles says. He looks at Lucy. "Lucy-loo?"

"Absolutely." She clasps her hands. "You know, really we're so lucky. That it's us and you, I mean. Someone else might not have seen it the same way."

"Well," Miles says. He looks at his watch. "I know it's early, but I think this calls for a glass of something special."

THE FEELING OF RELIEF in the room is palpable. As if by mutual agreement, the discussion breaks up not long afterward. Pete makes an admiring comment about the house and Miles offers him a quick tour, while Lucy and I stay to watch the boys.

"Can I hold him?" I hear myself say.

"David? Of course."

I reach down and take David into my arms. He feels so slight after Theo—he must be at least three pounds lighter, like picking up a delicate little girl instead of a chunky, well-built boy. And while Theo, even on one of his quiet days, would wriggle and swing his legs and probably throw himself backward over my arm to see what would happen, David sits quietly, nestled in the crook of my elbow. After a moment he turns his head and examines me solemnly. His eyes are lighter than mine, but even so there's something in them that feels eerily familiar. Involuntarily, I grin at him and bounce him gently on my arm. He doesn't smile back, but he holds my gaze pensively, never looking away.

"They each look so like one parent, don't they?" Lucy comments. "Theo's just like Miles, and David's so like you."

"Yes." I glance at her. "How did you find out, by the way? What made you first think David might not be yours?"

"Oh." Lucy reaches inside the collar of her shawl and frees a row of pearls that she rubs between her fingers a little nervously. "David's problems have always been a bit of a mystery to the doctors. At one point, they wondered if there might be a defective gene involved. So they tested him and, although they didn't find anything directly relevant, they did find an autosomal recessive— a gene inherited from both parents. But it turned out neither of us carried it. That's when it became apparent he couldn't be ours. Miles spoke to an investigator, who immediately homed in on the fact that I'd given birth in a private hospital. That was the weak link, he predicted—the transfer between there and St. Alexander's. Even so, it took months to track you down. The hospitals refused to give out any names to begin with—trying to hide behind data-protection laws. But I remembered your first name and that our boys were born on the same day, so Don had something to work with."

"Pete said you're suing the hospital."

Lucy nods. "It wasn't really about the money, though. It was more about forcing them to give up the names."

"So you'll drop it now?" A little reluctantly, I put David down so he can play with the baby gym again.

"I'm not sure," she says vaguely. "Miles still thinks they should pay for what they've done. To stop them from letting it happen again, I suppose, to somebody else. And even if we don't absolutely need the money, it might come in useful for you."

"What do you mean?"

"Didn't Pete tell you? Miles has invited him to join the action." She gives me a quick smile. "Of course, we probably won't tell them we're all getting on like a house on fire. Because it *is* distressing, isn't it, however reasonable we're all being. At the end of the day, we've both lost our real children. I've shed some tears over that, I can tell you."

"THAT WENT WELL," PETE says when we're in the car. He waves to Miles and Lucy, who've come to the front door to see us off.

"Yes."

He looks at me, alerted by my hesitant tone. "What do you mean?"

I pull my coat around me. "I don't know, exactly. But while you were looking around, Lucy mentioned that David had been tested for a defective gene. That was the word she used—*defective*. I'm not an expert, but I think it means any more children we have could be at risk of being like David as well."

Pete's silent a moment. "I guess we should get ourselves tested, too, then."

"She also talked about us all getting rich from the lawsuit."

"I know. Miles mentioned it when he came to see me. That doesn't feel right, though, does it? Suing a hospital, if we're happy the way we are."

"If it can help Theo's future, maybe we should think about it.

And who knows what problems David will have later on? He may need round-the-clock care. We can't really get in their way."

"I guess not." Pete glances at me as he pulls up for a red light. "You found it hard back there, didn't you?"

"Yes," I admit. "Not *them*, particularly—they seem nice, and as Lucy said, we're lucky that we're all similar people who think the same way about this. But just now, walking out of there and leaving David behind . . . It felt like I was abandoning him. I keep thinking of myself in his position, being left all alone in a stranger's house."

"But they're not strangers. They're his parents."

"*We're* his parents."

"You know what I mean," Pete says gently. "They're the people he loves. It's all good, Mads. We're going to see lots of David as he grows up, and they'll see lots of Theo."

"I know that's the right thing to do. But I can't help how I *feel*." I look out the window. If I'm honest, I'm finding Pete's insistence that not being Theo's biological parent makes absolutely no difference a bit frustrating. Not because I disagree with the principle—love is what matters, and families aren't made in people's tummies but in their hearts, et cetera et cetera. But there *is* a genetic pull as well. It's almost—I think disloyally—as if Pete actually relishes some aspect of this mix-up; or at least, the chance it gives him to prove that there's nothing atavistic or proprietary about his devotion to Theo. He's even shown me a study he found on the internet, proving that, on balance, adoptive parents take better care of their children than natural parents do.

I add, "Back there, when I first saw David and realized there was something wrong with him, just for a moment, I thought . . ."

"Thought what?" Pete's voice is studiedly neutral, which is how I know he'd actually thought exactly the same thing.

"How lucky we are. We've ended up with . . ." Theo's drifting off to sleep in the back, but even so I choose my words carefully. "Everything normal, and they've got something much more challenging, haven't they? You couldn't blame them if, right now, they're thinking that the situation isn't very fair."

Pete snorts. "I doubt they're thinking that. After all, they're the ones with the big house, the brand-new BMW, and the live-in nanny. They're exactly the sort of people who can take a child like David in their stride. And they clearly adore him. We should just thank our lucky stars we all see things the same way."

15

PETE

ON THE WAY HOME I did my best to reassure Maddie, repeating how fortunate we were that this had happened to people with such similar outlooks.

And it was true—we *were* lucky, incredibly so. We could have done so much worse than Miles and Lucy. But even so, I could tell it wasn't going to be plain sailing.

When he showed me around, Miles took me down to the basement—his manshed, as he jokingly called it. It was vast. The previous owners had excavated the original cellar right out under the garden. There was an air-conditioned wine room down there, a gym, even a small swimming pool.

"Wow," I said, which seemed like the only possible reaction.

"It's all right, isn't it?" Miles gazed around. "But it's only material things, Pete. I'd give it all for David to be able to walk and talk properly."

"Is there any chance he'll catch up?"

He shrugged. "The doctors keep saying, *Wait and see.* Their best guess is that he'll be mildly retarded. But he won't be playing for the first eleven, put it that way."

Retarded. The word sounded so harsh. In the NICU they'd tended to use euphemisms like *challenged* or *delayed.*

"We were lucky with Theo," I said. "He seems to be progressing pretty well. In everything but his speech, anyway."

"Yes." Miles hesitated. "Look, I wasn't planning to mention this today, but since we're all getting on so well . . . When Lucy was pregnant and we found out it was a boy, I put down a deposit for my old schools—Radley and the Dragon School. I know it sounds ridiculous, but you need to get their names down at birth to have the faintest chance of getting in these days. Both are out of the question for David now, of course, given how competitive the entrance is. I'd like to put the places into Theo's name. He's clearly bright enough, and you can tell he's going to be sporty. I think he might benefit from the opportunity."

"Oh," I said, taken aback. "That's really kind, but I don't think we'd ever consider sending Theo to a boarding school. We've actually got a really good C of E primary a few streets away. And we've started going to church." Miles looked puzzled, so I added, "You know—*On your knees to save the fees?* The school's massively oversubscribed, but if you're a regular churchgoer, the vicar can allocate you a place."

"Ah." Miles nodded. "Well, you've clearly got it all under control. Boarding and so on can seem a bit antiquated now, can't it? But look, I might as well change the places to Theo's name anyway, and they'll be there if you ever change your mind. You never know, he might turn out to be a Harry Potter fan, and actually quite like the idea of going away."

I didn't tell Maddie any of this in the car. I thought it was best to emphasize the positives. I suppose that's something I've done for her ever since the NICU—being strong for her. People look at her and see someone who's incredibly capable and tough. They don't know about the struggles she had during the first year of Theo's life, particularly after I did that charity ride. If I'm honest, that was one of the reasons I ended up becoming Theo's main carer. Getting back to work was all part of Maddie's recovery, and only I know how fragile she still is.

16

MADDIE

FOR THE FIRST FOUR months after Theo's birth, I held things together. My parents flew over from Australia to see us. The flights had originally been booked around my due dates, of course, and the tickets weren't transferable. Although they'd offered to buy new ones and come when Theo was in the NICU, there hadn't seemed much point. When they did come, of course they wanted to meet Theo—but there's only so long even a doting grandfather can sit with a small baby, let alone a restless grandfather like Jack Wilson, and they wanted to tour the sights of London as well, which kept us all busy. At least they stayed in a hotel, so only Pete could see how sleep-deprived and stressed I was becoming. Time after time I felt myself getting angry with him for no reason, and although I'd been signed off for sex by my GP six weeks after the birth, there was absolutely no chance that was going to happen. I didn't even tell Pete the doctor had said it would be all right. I suspect he googled the timings, though, because one night when

Theo was about three months old he tried to cuddle me. But when I went rigid, he stopped.

"It's all right. There's no rush," he said gently.

"Too right there's no fucking rush," I snapped. Just for an instant, him telling me what was and wasn't all right about my own body seemed like the most presumptuous, patronizing thing ever.

He peered at me by the light of the bedside clock. "Mads? What's up? I only meant, it's not a problem."

But it *was* a problem, I knew—for me, not him. Sex meant childbirth, and people shouting *Now* and slicing my belly open with a scalpel. Sex meant small, monkeylike babies being fed with nasogastric tubes in the NICU. Sex meant exposing my C-section scar, and all the other scars that weren't visible as well. Sex meant adrenaline flooding my veins, and a feeling of nameless dread clenching my insides.

But I didn't tell him any of that, because I didn't want to talk about it.

"I'M THINKING OF DOING a bike ride for the NICU," Pete said, not long after my parents had flown back.

"A *what*?"

"There's a Facebook group—Dads Behind the NICU. The idea is that we'll all raise funds for the appeal."

I didn't even know the NICU was having an appeal. "Why do they need funds? St. Alexander's is part of the NHS."

"Yes, but they have a separate charity for nonessentials—the bits the NHS can't pay for. The main one is, they want to buy a flat near the hospital for parents to stay in while their babies are in the unit. Bronagh and some of the other nurses did a sponsored fun run, but they're still thirty thousand pounds short."

I looked at him, surprised. "Are you still in touch with Bronagh?"

"Well, we're both members of the fundraising group." He saw

my expression. "It's a Facebook page, Mads," he said patiently. "It's not like we're meeting up for coffee."

"I hadn't realized you missed your nursie groupies so much." Even as I said it, I wondered at the venom in my voice. What was happening to me?

"Anyway, the dads are thinking of cycling all the way from Edinburgh to London," Pete went on after a moment. "It's an opportunity to show our appreciation to the hospital for saving our kids, and do something practical for them at the same time."

Put like that, how could I refuse? "What about work? I thought you'd used up all your holiday."

"They've offered to convert the time we spent in the hospital to compassionate leave. They're right behind this. The editor's already pledged two hundred quid, so everyone else should chip in at least twenty. I've been doing some calculations and I reckon I could raise over a grand."

"Well, that sounds like it's sorted, then," I said bitterly. Which was stupid of me, I knew. I could feel myself turning into one of those people who seize any opportunity to make a barbed remark, even when it meant forgoing the chance to tell my partner what I really felt.

So instead of *I don't think I can cope without you,* I just said, "Send me a postcard from Scotland, won't you?"

PETE THREW HIMSELF INTO preparing for the ride. He assembled a bike from parts he hunted down on eBay. He and the other dads met up for several practice rides, all of which seemed to end with them in the pub, slapping one another on the back and telling one another how much their calf muscles ached and how heroic they were.

I was jealous. I didn't have a group like that, or any group for that matter. The prenatal classes I'd booked started three months before my due date, so of course I'd missed those. There was a support group for mothers of preemies, run by people who'd been through it themselves, but I was still burying my head in the sand and the thought of getting together with other NICU veterans and endlessly rehashing the experience repelled me. I wasn't dwelling on the past like them! I was looking forward! Before Theo, my social life had revolved around my job—the hardworking, hard-partying world of advertising. Going on shoots meant long hours on location, often abroad—it wasn't unusual for the call time to be five A.M. or even earlier, but I always had enough energy for drinks in the hotel bar at the end of the day, and the wrap parties after the last day of filming were legendary. I'd made some deep, even intense friendships, but no one in that world really had time for a chat or a coffee with a new mum—they might say they did, and schedule something, but there was always some crisis or other that meant it had to be postponed. And it was an iron rule of advertising that a lunch or coffee rescheduled more than once was never going to happen. After that, it made you look desperate to pursue it. People said it took a village to raise a child, but I didn't even have a cul-de-sac.

Pete set a goal of twelve hundred pounds on JustGiving and started emailing colleagues. Within a week he'd reached two thousand pounds. He read me some of the comments people left with their donations, and every so often he'd have to stop. "Keep going Pete and Maddie and little Theo, we're all thinking of you," "You'll come through this stronger than ever," or even just "Such a great thing you're doing," all reduced him to tears, or at least to manly silence. It had been one of the things I'd first liked about him—that he wasn't afraid to cry in front of me—but since Theo's birth, his emotions seemed to have become a gushing tap, while mine had gone in the other direction.

When I looked through the donations later, I noticed there was a pledge of ten pounds from Bronagh. *Still doing the great work I see Pete!* she'd written. He hadn't read that one out.

Sometimes, feeding Theo in the middle of the night, I'd Skype my parents. It was strange to see them having lunch on the sun terrace while I was shut up in a dark bedroom in London, the streetlights turning the curtains sickly yellow. On one occasion, I put Theo down in his cot before I called them, only for him to start wailing a few minutes later. "Hang on," I said to my mother wearily. "I'll just go and get him."

Then I heard my father's voice, off camera. "She's spoiling that baby. Tell her, Carol. You have to let them cry, or they never learn not to."

I waited for her to say something, to explain that it wasn't like that these days, but she didn't. I stopped Skyping them after that.

I was getting hardly any sleep. "Sleep when the baby sleeps," people said. But what if I couldn't sleep? I felt compelled to be Theo's monitor, to check on him every few minutes. When I lay down, my brain raced; when I got up, the fog descended again and I could barely function.

Pete left for Scotland at the end of July. It was a cool, settled summer—perfect cycling weather. And although cycling from Edinburgh to London sounded arduous, I knew it wasn't, not really. The route followed car-free cycle paths and old railway lines most of the way, and the group had a coach with a trailer that met them every afternoon and took them and the bikes to a hotel. They were planning to cycle about five hours a day, with every fourth day off. I didn't blame them for making it as pleasant as possible, but I did get annoyed by the endless self-congratulatory updates on social media. After all, if you could stop to take a group selfie with a whole gang of other grinning young men in cycle helmets and Lycra every time you came to a nice view, you weren't exactly doing the Tour de France. So pretty soon I stopped attending to what they were up to and retreated into my own private hell.

I felt as though I had to be doing something every moment. Sterilizing bottles. Washing babygrows. Cleaning the house. Checking the baby. Did I turn on the sterilizer? Did I turn off the washing machine? Was Theo breathing? I was shaking and fighting nausea, a captive animal pacing up and down, full of unfocused dread. Without Pete, there was no one to make me eat, no one to interrupt my inner monologue. The stream of thoughts in my head got louder and shoutier. What had begun as my own internal voice became an intrusive, deafening authority figure. I even gave it a name: the doctor. *What if you let the baby get dirty?* the doctor yelled at me. *What if you let the baby suffocate? What if you drop the baby on the floor and smash open his head?* I was too afraid to go for walks in case a car hit Theo's stroller. I became obsessed with watching him, but I stopped touching him in case I did something bad to him. My heart raced constantly and I was short of breath. When the health visitor came, I demanded to know if she thought Theo's eyes were crossed, and if so, whether that meant he had brain damage. She looked at me strangely and I heard her thoughts as clearly as if she'd spoken them out loud. *This woman is a useless mother.* After that, the health visitor joined the doctors in the chorus of voices all shouting at me that I was doing a terrible job.

And that's when the doctors started spying on me.

Later, the psychiatrist spent a lot of time trying to unpick whether I'd been experiencing actual hallucinations, or simply delusions. It mattered for the treatment, apparently. Had I actually seen the doctors on the TV or the screen of my phone, telling me, *Not like that, you're doing it all wrong,* or had I merely believed they were in there? Both, I decided. Why else would I have hurled one of Theo's full nappies at the TV to shut it up? Why else would I have flung my iPhone at the wall? In any case, it was a relief not to have to worry about Pete's increasingly concerned texts—*U still angry with me? Pls call*—but then the bits from the broken phone must have gotten inside the wall because the doctors started using it as a big screen to project their messages on instead. I worked out that if I turned the microwave on to the maximum setting, the radio waves spun out by the revolving turntable would block the messages and give me some relief, and they did.

And then Pete came back.

He'd abandoned the ride in York and boarded a train to London. He found me curled up on the kitchen floor, lying on sheets of tinfoil to protect myself from the doctors' messages. Theo was on his back a few feet away, nappyless. Nearby, I'd lined up twenty full bottles of milk, ready to feed him with. The radio was on to drown the sound of his crying, and I'd hooked up a calculator to the microwave so I could monitor his vital signs.

WHAT HAPPENED AFTER THAT is fuzzy. It didn't take Pete long to realize he had to call an ambulance, and the paramedics arranged an emergency mental health assessment. I was admitted to a psychiatric ward and given antipsychotics and mood stabilizers. There were no spaces in a mother-and-baby unit, so Pete looked after Theo until I was well enough to come home. It took three weeks, and even then they only let me out when I agreed to join the support group I'd spurned before and do a course of cognitive therapy. When I got home, tired but calm again, I found the house full of flowers and a banner over the front door that read WEL-COME HOME MUMMY. Pete had tidied and cleaned—he told me later it had taken two bottles of bleach to get rid of the smell of the soiled nappies I'd been storing under beds and sofas in case the doctors needed to examine them—and even bought Theo a bigger set of babygrows. When I lifted him from Pete's arms into mine, he smelled of fabric conditioner and warm milk and love.

"I'm sorry about the bike ride," Pete said softly.

I shook my head. "Don't be. Besides, how could you have known what was wrong with me? Even the health visitor didn't realize." I looked around. "This place looks great."

"We've been having a good time." Pete stroked Theo's cheek,

now plump and full like a baby's should be. "Though he's missed his mummy, of course," he added quickly.

"You don't have to tiptoe around me now, Pete. I left Horrible Angry Maddie back in the psych ward."

He nodded. "I've arranged to work from home for a while, even so."

"Won't Karen mind?" Karen was his editor, a woman Pete professed to admire but who I always thought sounded petulant and passive-aggressive when Pete described their interactions.

"She's really supportive. It'll mean doing more roundups, but . . ." Pete shrugged. As newspaper budgets were cut, lists—as opposed to actual assignments—were taking up more and more of the travel section. There was even a weekly feature: *Twelve Traveltastic* . . . In the past few months, Pete had compiled "Twelve Traveltastic Beaches," "Twelve Traveltastic Christmas Markets," "Twelve Traveltastic Tapas Bars," and "Twelve Traveltastic Tuscan Villas." There was no actual travel involved, of course—the recommendations were sourced entirely from the internet, reviews from TripAdvisor lightly disguised with the word *expect,* as in "Expect pale-cream rooms and a poolside barbecue," to cover the fact that the journalist hadn't actually been there. It was dispiriting, mechanical work, and the fact that Pete was volunteering to do more of it in order to spend more time with me and our baby filled me with gratitude.

"Saint Peter. Bronagh was right. I'm so lucky to have you."

"I'm the lucky one, Mads. I've got you and Theo." He stroked Theo's head, then glanced at me. "One of the dads who organized the ride—Greg—isn't going back to work. He's planning on being a stay-at-home dad."

"That's brave."

"Funnily enough, he says everyone uses that word. He said to me when we were cycling, 'What's brave about it? No one calls a woman brave when she stops work.'" Pete paused. "He and Kate are in a similar position to us, actually. She earns more than he does."

I frowned. "I'd always assumed we'd both have to work. The mortgage is pretty steep."

"Well . . . I did a few rough calculations, and it's not impossible." He added quickly, "But look, now isn't the time to go into all that. I just thought it was an interesting idea, that's all."

17

Dear Pete and Maddie,

Lucy and I just wanted to say what a pleasure it was meeting you this morning—and of course, Theo too. To be honest, we'd been somewhat apprehensive about what sort of family our birth son would turn out to be living with. I think we can say for sure that both Theo and ourselves have been incredibly fortunate. We really feel we haven't lost a son but gained some new friends.

We were deeply touched by your suggestion that we become Theo's godparents. That's a definite yes from us, if you're sure.

And Pete, I meant to say—let's go out for a beer sometime. Maybe this Wednesday after work? I think Lucy is going to get in touch with Maddie, too.

Very best,
Miles

18

PETE

THE EMAIL FROM MILES was waiting next time I checked my inbox. It had been sent at two P.M., just a couple of hours after we'd left them.

"He's keen," Maddie commented when I showed her.

"Should I? Go for a beer with him, I mean?"

"Why not? You always say you miss going out with your mates after work. And Wednesday evening's a good time—I can be back by six, so you won't need a sitter."

NEXT MORNING, WE HAD a Skype call booked with Maddie's parents. We were both slightly apprehensive—her father is a big character, and the relationship between him and Maddie is definitely a complicated one. They used to clash when she was a teenager—she was impulsive and headstrong, he was authoritarian and domineering—but she talks about him a lot and he's very important to her. I sometimes wonder if part of my own appeal for her is that I'm about as far away from him as she could possibly get, both geographically and personally.

The call started well. Theo was in good form, taking Maddie's iPad and proudly showing his grandparents a tower he'd made from Duplo. Then he used both feet to kick it all apart.

"Pow! Pow! Pick up, Mika!" he told them.

Jack laughed. "Who's Mika?"

"He means Michaela. She's the nanny for some people we visited yesterday." I took a deep breath. "Jack, Carol, there's something we need to tell you. Just hang on a minute while I take the iPad upstairs." Our bedroom was the only place in the house where Theo wouldn't overhear, although unfortunately it meant I was now going to have to break the news to them on my own.

"What's going on?" Jack asked. I didn't reply until I was safely out of Theo's hearing. Then I explained. They didn't say much, just the occasional "Jesus!" and "Bloody hell!" from Jack. When I got to the bit where we'd agreed with the Lamberts that we weren't going to swap back, he was incredulous.

"What? But they've got your bloody son!"

"Yes. Just as we've got theirs."

"Well, if it was one of *my* children, I wouldn't be happy," Jack said with finality. "Carol, what do you think?"

"Of course we're not happy," I said patiently. "We're really shocked and upset. But what other solution is there? Give Theo away?"

"I guess not," Carol began, just as Jack said, "At that age, they'd get over it in no time."

"I don't think that's true," I said coldly.

"Have you spoken to a child psychologist?"

"No," I admitted.

"What about a lawyer?"

"The Lamberts have spoken to a lawyer. But that's because they're talking about suing the hospital—"

"Bloody right they are."

"We just think that the proper way to deal with this is through dialogue and compromise," I said. The words somehow came out sounding wrong—priggish and pompous instead of reasonable and considered. I tried a different tack. "You always say, once lawyers get involved in a deal, everything goes to shit. Why would this be any different?"

"A lawyer's already involved," Jack said darkly. "Just not yours."

Carol started to say something, but he cut her off. "So tell me, Pete. What exactly *have* you done, since being handed this DNA test supposedly confirming that our grandson, our *real* grandson, is living with another family?"

"We've been to meet them. And we've talked. A lot."

"Jesus," Jack muttered under his breath.

"Could we speak to Maddie?" Carol asked.

"Of course," I said, resisting the urge to sigh. I went downstairs and handed the iPad back to Maddie, rolling my eyes to indicate that my part of the conversation hadn't gone well.

"Hi Mum, hi Dad," she said brightly. "Just let me swap places."

She went upstairs and shut the bedroom door—I suspect as much to shield me from whatever her father was about to say as to stop Theo overhearing.

It was fully ten minutes before she came down again. By then Theo had moved on to crashing engines together on his train track. "It wasn't too bad in the end," she said in response to my look. "I think they were just a bit shocked."

"Shocked at how we're dealing with it, you mean."

"I think they just thought we're taking it in our stride a bit *too* much." By which she meant this had simply confirmed her dad's view that I'm a lazy, unambitious loser. "Funnily enough, they came around more when I explained about . . ." She looked at me, not wanting to put her thought into words, and again I wasn't sure if that was because of Theo or me. "When I explained about the other child," she said eventually.

I stared at her, incredulous. "You mean Jack Wilson is now happy because he thinks we got the *better deal*? That in some way we've *won*?"

"He can't help being the way he is," she said quietly.

And I didn't say anything, because part of the unspoken contract between us is that I don't criticize her father, even though she does and he usually deserves it.

"He wants to send us money for a lawyer," she added. "And a psychologist, if we want one."

"I don't want a psychologist. I know what's best for my son."

The word slipped out without my even being aware of it. It was only when Maddie didn't reply that I realized what I'd said. "He *is* our son," I said patiently. "We can't spend the rest of our lives avoiding that word."

She nodded.

"The most I'm prepared to do is consider suing that private hospital," I said. "Assuming it is their fault, of course. I'll talk to Miles about it when I see him on Wednesday."

19

MADDIE

MY DAD'S ANTIPATHY TOWARD Pete started after I got pregnant. Back in Australia, they'd actually gotten on quite well—mainly because Pete, being British, was naturally polite and deferential, which Dad always liked. Even when I followed Pete to London it was simply, in Dad's words, "Madelyn traveling"—like a slightly delayed version of the gap years many Australians still take, working their way around Europe.

When he found out we were buying a house together—something I realized afterward I hadn't told him about until it was actually happening—and that this was it, we were making a life in a distant country, he was baffled as much as hurt. Who was this quiet, reserved pom I'd chosen to spend my life with? What made him so different from all the other young men who'd drifted in and out of my life?

If I'm honest, the fact Pete and I haven't gotten married is a kind of sop to my dad, a balancing of the books. While we're just living together, he can choose to believe there's a chance I'll change my mind. Besides, he's the kind of man who'd like his future son-in-law to ask his permission, and Pete would think that was a ridiculously old-fashioned thing to do.

And perhaps, deep down, it's even more complicated than that. Jack Wilson is also the kind of man who'd love to throw the biggest wedding Adelaide has ever seen, to make the most memorable speech, to walk his daughter down the aisle with a ramrod-straight back and a tear glistening in his eye. So by not getting married, I know I'm telling him that I don't care about any of that, and, by extension, that I'm not his adoring little daddy's girl anymore.

When I phoned home to tell him I was pregnant, he said jokingly, "Better come back and tie the knot quick, girl, before they won't let you on the bloody plane." That was when I told him we wouldn't be doing that, not ever. Pete, overhearing, looked a bit surprised. But neither has he ever gotten down on one knee and proposed.

After the NICU, when I got ill, Dad blamed Pete. It was irrational and wrong—Pete couldn't have been more supportive, and, with the exception of the bike ride, he was there for me and Theo every possible minute. After all, fourteen fathers went on that ride, and only one of them came back to a partner who was having a breakdown. But Dad had gotten it into his head that it was the strain of being a new mother that had pushed me over the edge, and that narrative only worked if Pete was a lazy, unhelpful parent.

Somehow, the narrative managed to survive Pete becoming Theo's full-time carer as well. Pete and I had been talking about it off and on throughout my maternity—doing the sums, wondering how it might work. It took me a couple of months to fully recover from my psychosis, and even then, I stayed on a maintenance dose of antidepressants. Meanwhile, Pete did the bulk of the caring whenever he could—it seemed to come easily to him, while I had to admit that, much as I now loved Theo, I just wasn't as naturally maternal or patient as some other women. I've always been a bit of an adrenaline junkie. As a teenager, my first love was my horse, Peach: We used to go around Australia together, competing at three-day events. It's partly why I'm good at a high-pressure job, I think: At some level, I actually enjoy the constant crises, if only because I've noticed that I'm usually calmer and more clearheaded in those situations than others are. But the flip side is that I found the quiet, placid rhythms of first-year motherhood mind-numbingly dull, and a part of me couldn't wait to get back to my desk. Of course, that was very different from thinking Pete would do it—I'd assumed that, like most couples we knew, we'd use a childminder or nanny share until Theo was old enough to go to nursery. If I'm honest, I was sometimes surprised that Pete enjoyed parenting quite as much as he did. He loved nothing better than to get home from work and start looking after Theo, while for my part, I couldn't wait to hand him over and pour myself a glass of wine.

Perhaps the most serious conversation we had about it was when his newspaper put out a call for voluntary redundancies. He could go freelance, Pete pointed out: With fewer staff, the paper would probably end up using more outside resources anyway, and the kind of stuff he was doing by then—his most recent piece had been "Twelve Traveltastic American Road Trips"—could be done from anywhere. But when we crunched the numbers, there was no getting away from the fact we'd be poor. So, a little reluctantly, we concluded it wasn't the right time.

And then he lost his job anyway.

Hardly anyone had put themselves forward for redundancy, it turned out—a staff job in journalism was now so rare, people tended to cling to the one they had. And the cuts the paper needed to make were far deeper than they'd been letting on. Some of the other journalists, Pete told me later, had seen the call for redundancies as the writing on the wall it was, and had aggressively

lobbied to keep their jobs, writing spurious but eye-catching stories that made them look useful or sucking up to senior management. Pete hadn't done any of that, and now he seemed almost
baffled that those were the journalists management wanted to
keep. The fact was—and this, I ruefully admitted to myself, was
where my dad's assessment of him did contain a tiny grain of
truth—Pete was simply too nice to succeed in an environment like
that, when backs were against the wall and the fighting turned
dirty.

For a couple of months after that, both of us were at home
with Theo while Pete tried to pitch freelance articles. It was a
good time, but scary. The paper wasn't using more freelancers
after all—quite the reverse: The same cost-cutting drive that had
led to the redundancies resulted in a tough no-freelance policy;
they were working the remaining writers twice as hard instead.
With his redundancy payment dwindling fast, I couldn't afford to
take the unpaid part of my maternity leave, so I went back to
work after thirty-nine weeks.

For Theo's first birthday, Pete hatched a plan to go back to the
NICU, taking Theo and a birthday cake. It was something many
of the ex-NICU families did, he said: It boosted the nurses' morale to see the babies they'd saved doing well. Unfortunately, it
clashed with a commercial I was producing with a famous footballer in Barcelona—the agency wasn't given any say over the
schedule; the footballer's agent simply told us we had four hours
on a certain day and expected us to make it work. *Give my love to
your Irish groupie,* I texted Pete from the shoot, but whereas once
I would have felt bitter and angry about the way he and the nurses
got on so well, now I just felt amused.

And that's when I had my first slipup.

After filming we all went out for beers and tapas, then back to
the hotel bar. At some point the attractive-but-wicked camera assistant started flirting with me, which felt exhilarating and fun
after so long being a milk machine and a launderer of babygrows.

One nightcap led to another, and then he leaned in close and whispered his room number in my ear. "If you dare, that is," he added, sitting back again.

And somehow, stupidly, I did.

Afterward, I felt wretched. But strangely, not guilty. It was more as if I was . . . *detached,* the way I'd been in the NICU.

The brutal truth was, the spark just hadn't been there with Pete since Theo's birth. Nice Pete, Saint Pete, the Pete who changed nappies and warmed baby food and raised funds for charity, just wasn't a turn-on. I loved him, I loved my family, but it wasn't *that* sort of love anymore. Walking down the silent, dim-lit hotel corridor toward the camera assistant's door had felt like I was seventeen again, galloping Peach at full speed toward a fence I wasn't sure we could clear.

But it was a one-off, I told myself. A stupid mistake. A reaction to everything that had happened, from the shock of getting pregnant to the NICU and then my illness. It was over and in the past and there was absolutely no reason to confess it to Pete because it would only hurt him.

So I didn't.

20

PETE

I MET UP WITH Miles in a sports bar close to Marylebone Station. It was next to the headquarters of a French merchant bank, and the place was full of loud young men in well-cut suits, talking in French as they watched football on the big screens. Miles paid them no attention, but he was clearly at ease in their company.

"Here," he said, handing me a pint and raising his own. "To parenthood and friendship."

I chinked my glass against his. "Parenthood and friendship."

"And I got you this." He handed me a shopping bag. "Well, not strictly *you,* I suppose."

Inside was a miniature rugby ball—not a toy, a real one. I took it out. The maker's name was Gilbert, which even I knew was the official supplier to the England team, and it was covered with signatures.

"The 2003 England squad," Miles explained. "Best side we ever had."

"That's really kind of you," I said, touched.

Miles waved away my gratitude. "You can't start too early. And maybe . . ."

"What?"

"Maybe I could teach him how to throw it sometime? If that would be all right with you and Maddie, I mean."

"Of course. I spend most of the day with Theo. It'll do him good to see someone else once in a while."

"What about Saturday? We could take him to Gladstone Park."

"Sounds good, but I'd better check with Maddie."

"She handles your diary, does she?" Miles's grin robbed the words of any offense.

"It's just that she doesn't get to spend much time with Theo during the week," I explained.

Miles patted my shoulder. "Don't worry—I know what it's like. Lucy and I are the same. I just turn up where and when I'm told. Speaking of which . . ." He pulled out his phone. "You know we talked about spending Easter together? I thought maybe we could go to Cornwall. There are these fantastic houses right by the beach on Trevose Head—you literally step out onto the dunes and the sea's just there in front of you." He was flicking through photos with his thumb as he spoke. "Sand, rock pools—it'll be cold, but you can get little wet suits, and something tells me Theo's the kind of kid who'd love to build a sandcastle and watch the waves come and knock it down. Here, take a look."

The house he showed me was massive, with vast windows framing a view of picture-perfect Cornish beach. "It looks amazing," I said enviously.

"Great. I'll book it." He scrolled down to a BOOK NOW button.

"But again, I should talk to Maddie," I said quickly. "We may not be able to afford it."

Miles shook his head. "You don't have to, Pete. My shout. And we can always cancel." He tapped the button.

"I can't let you pay for everything."

"Well, you won't need to after the hospitals pay up." He put the phone back into his pocket.

"You really think they will?"

"Of course. The last thing the NHS wants is anxious mothers starting to panic about whether their baby really is their baby. They'll make us sign an NDA to protect their reputation, and then they'll write us a whopping great check."

"The NHS?" I said, frowning. "I thought it was the other hospital you were suing."

Miles shrugged. "Our lawyer thinks it's better to sue both, from a tactical point of view. After all, we can't prove exactly where the mix-up happened. Better to let them fight it out between themselves. And at the end of the day, the NHS has deeper pockets."

"I'm not sure I'd be happy about suing the NHS. As a taxpayer-funded service, I mean," I said uneasily.

Miles looked at me fondly over the top of his pint. "You know what, Pete? I'm coming to realize something about you, which is that you are a really decent bloke. I admire that. But I also know you'd do anything for Theo, am I right? And the way I look at it is, if I can make you and Maddie just a little bit wealthier, or at least more comfortably off, I'll be doing something for Theo, too. As well as removing one of the biggest difficulties about this whole situation."

"Which is?"

"Well." Miles had the grace to look awkward. "That it's currently somewhat . . . asymmetric."

"Asymmetric?" I echoed.

"Yes. To put it bluntly, we've got more money than you have. And obviously, I'd hate to see Theo being held back because of lack of funds. With the payout in your bank account, conversations like the one we had the other day about schools are going to be a whole lot easier, am I right?"

"Not wanting Theo to go to boarding school isn't about money."

"Maybe not at the moment. But when you can afford the best education money can buy, perhaps you'll view things differently. All I'm saying is, it'll give you options, and that can't be a bad thing, can it?"

I felt we were getting into dangerous territory. "Look, I'll talk to Maddie about litigation. But not schools. A boarding school is completely out of the question."

Miles held up his hand, the one that wasn't wrapped around his glass, in a gesture of surrender. "Of course. Your call entirely, Pete. So it's a yes to suing, but a no to Hogwarts. Another pint?"

"Yes. But this time it's my round," I said firmly.

THAT ONE DISAGREEMENT ASIDE, we got on surprisingly well, given the difference in our backgrounds. Three pints in I realized we'd better steer clear of politics, after I mentioned Vladimir Putin and Miles frowned. "Say what you like about the oligarchs, Pete, but at least they've put that country back together." Mostly, though, we talked about our children. Miles never tired of quizzing me about Theo's achievements—"Can he jump with both feet yet? Stand on one foot? What's he like on monkey bars?"— although I noticed he was far more interested in physical milestones than social ones. It would have been awkward not to reciprocate about David, so rather than ask about his progress, which would inevitably have led to negative comparisons with Theo, I asked what he was interested in.

"Oh, you know," Miles said. "Movement. Tops and spinners and things like that. Poor little chap."

"Right," I said. There didn't seem to be anywhere to go with that.

"You know, the worst thing about it is what it's done to Lucy."

Miles's tone was suddenly serious. "She's not like your Maddie. She's . . . fragile. And having a child like David brings out her anxious side. It's made her overprotective, I suppose."

To break the silence, I said, "Actually, Maddie isn't as tough as she looks. She really suffered after the NICU. I won't go into details but . . . it wasn't easy for her. And *all* parents are overprotective, I think. I once lost Theo for twenty minutes in Sainsbury's, and it was one of the most terrifying things that's ever happened to me. It turned out he'd only wandered off to look for cartoons on the back of cereal packets, but . . ." I shook my head. I was a little drunk now, unable to articulate the full horror of that time, the sudden irrational fear that Theo might have been abducted or hit by a car in the car park. "It was *visceral*. That was one of the things that made me realize . . . It's not about genetics, is it? It's about who you love."

"I'll drink to that." Miles clinked his glass against mine. " 'To love.' "

We both drank. "Though a social scientist would probably say this is quite an interesting experiment," he added.

"How so?"

"You know—nature versus nurture, all that stuff. Will our children take after their biological parents, or will they be shaped by their environments? Or, to put it another way, will Theo turn out to be a driven, competitive little bugger like me, or an all-around decent bloke like you?" He nodded. "You should write about that. It'd make an interesting article."

"Maybe they'll get the best of both worlds," I said. "Drive *and* decency."

Miles laughed. "Exactly the answer I would have expected an all-around decent bloke to give. Come on, let's get another."

AND THEN THERE WAS a moment, halfway through the fourth and last pint of the evening, when—our tongues loosened by drink—we were reliving the drama of our first meeting. It seemed almost funny now, looking back.

"You know what I thought, when you first told me Theo was your son?" I demanded.

Miles shook his head. "Elucidate me, Pete. Whadidya think, when I first told you Theo was my son?"

"Just for a moment, I thought you meant you'd shagged Maddie. That you and she . . ." I shook my head in disbelief at how stupid I'd been. "So that's a silver lining, anyway."

"True," Miles said sagely. "Silver lining for *you,* anyway. But I tell you what, Pete old son." He swayed in close and whispered in my ear. "I. Totally. Would. She's gorgeous. And ballsy with it. You are a lucky bastard, Pete. A very lucky bastard." He stuck out his hand for me to shake. "Congratulations. You got the girl. You got the kid. Well done."

21

Case no. 12675/PU78B65, Exhibit 15: Extracts from the internet history of Peter Riley.

Secret Escapes, retrieved 23:12 P.M.:

Tremerrion House, Trevose Head, Cornwall: This stunning property offers up to ten guests luxury self-catering accommodation just a stone's throw from the sea and the South West Coastal Path. From £8,400 pw (low season). Check availability <u>here</u>.

Washington Post, retrieved 23:18 P.M.:

MOTHER OF SWITCHED BABY SUES FOR $31M

The mother of a girl switched at birth with another baby is suing the Virginia hospital she claims is responsible for $31 million, to compensate her for the pain and suffering she says the mix-up inflicted. The other family involved has already accepted a multimillion-dollar settlement from the state.

"STAGGERING" RISE IN NHS PAYOUTS BLAMED
ON NO-FEE LAWYERS

A total of £22.7 billion—nearly one-fifth of the health service's annual budget—is being set aside each year to settle compensation claims, new figures have revealed.

Experts last night said the scale of the NHS's liabilities was "staggering," with English damages now among the highest in the world.

MPs and other commentators have blamed the courts, saying that the UK's broad definitions of medical negligence and malpractice, along with the rise of no-win no-fee legal firms, have made litigation "almost ridiculously easy."

22

MADDIE

I'M IN BED WHEN Pete stumbles in from his drink with Miles. I'm not asleep, but I've finished most of a bottle of wine myself and don't feel like chatting, let alone cuddling, so I don't answer when he whispers, "You awake, babe?"

By half past five, Theo's wriggling into our bed. We both try to ignore him, but there's only so long you can ignore being hit over the head with a woolly rabbit. Eventually I give up and turn over. Luckily, Pete succumbed just before I did. Theo is now straddling his stomach as if riding a horse, impatiently bouncing his bottom whenever Pete stops jiggling.

"How was last night?" I say blearily.

"It was all right." Pete thinks for a moment. "He brought up schools again."

"Bloody hell. What did you say?"

"A very firm no. Ouff! Gently, Theo."

"Did he get the message this time?"

Pete yawns. "Yes, actually. Took it quite well. That's the thing about these City types. They don't go in for nuance. You have to be forceful with them."

"Well, I'm glad you were forceful."

Pete gives me a look, unsure if I'm teasing. "We talked about suing St. Alexander's, too."

"Gee *up*, Daddeee," Theo complains. Reluctantly, Pete resumes bucking.

"And?"

"Maybe it's not such a bad idea. Quite apart from anything else, it'll level the playing field between us and them. Stop it being quite so asymmetric."

I consider. "Well, it'll make Dad happy. And he did say he'd send us money for a lawyer."

"I don't think we'll need it. The solicitors Miles are using are no-win no-fee. If we use someone from the same firm, he thinks they can coordinate to get us both the best payout."

I nod. I've never shared Pete's qualms about suing a hospital anyway. Like many Brits, he seems to have a love-hate relationship with the National Health Service, both incredibly proud of it in principle and totally despairing and frustrated by it in practice. To me, it seems no different from suing any other large organization that's made a mistake. But I am a bit surprised that Miles has managed to get Pete to overcome his scruples so quickly.

23

<u>Case no. 12675/PU78B65, Exhibits 16A–C:</u>
<u>Emails from (A) Miles Lambert to Peter Riley, (B) Peter Riley to Miles</u>
<u>Lambert, and (C) Miles Lambert to Peter Riley.</u>

Hey Pete,

Great to see you last night. Bit of a sore head on the 7:03 this morning (even skipped the run beforehand) . . .

Just did a quick search for sports lessons for two-year-olds and came across these. They look ace!

www.rugbytots.co.uk

www.teddytennis.com

May be worth checking out?

Best, Miles

Hi Miles,

Thanks for the links. To be honest we're pretty snowed under right now, what with Monkey Music, Swim Starz, and SmartyPilates, but I'll add them to the list for when we have time!

Spoke to Maddie about the lawsuit—we're in. What do we do next? Speak to your lawyer?

Best, Pete

Pete,
I'll call you.

M

24

MADDIE

LATER THAT DAY, I get a Facebook request from Lucy. I'm not really into social media—I sometimes dip into it as an alternative to reading before I drift off to sleep, but only for a few minutes; I certainly never manage to get to the bottom of my news feed. But I accept Lucy's request and spend a few minutes glancing through her posts on my phone while I eat a sandwich at my desk.

The first thing I notice is that she has only thirty-eight friends. I might be a low-frequency user, but even so I've managed to collect a couple of hundred—contemporaries from college, girlfriends, colleagues, neighbors, people I've met on shoots, even a few clients. It seems incredible that anyone could have such a small social circle. She hasn't posted much, either—just photographs of David, mostly. Lying on a mat in what looks like a specialist sensory room. In a physiotherapy chair, with the comment, "Trying really hard!" On a breathing ventilator—"Hopefully just a brief trip back to intensive care!" In a ball pool, immobile and a little forlorn, staring at the camera with an anxious expression. With each one, looking at his elfin features, I feel an echo of the same maternal tug I felt when I held his light, slender body in my arms. I think of the last time we took Theo to a ball pool, the exuberance with which he'd flailed his legs, kicking the colored balls into a volcanic blur before deciding to hurl them two at a time at a fair-haired little girl playing in the far corner. We'd had to wade in and forcibly haul him out, his tiny body writhing and kicking so hard in protest that his shirt actually came away in our hands, like podding a broad bean.

I scroll on through the feed, hungry for more images of David. Most of Lucy's posts aren't even real posts, just shares of funny videos that already have millions of views, warnings about scammers, or appeals for children with cancer to be sent a thousand Christmas cards. But finally I reach some pictures of David in his cot at home, posted over a year ago. There's an oxygen tube up his nose—you can just see the cylinder under the cot—and a bundle of wires snaking from under the sheet that suggests the presence of a monitor. He looks so vulnerable and, yes, so like me that something in my heart opens to him. *That's my baby,* I think with a sudden stab of longing. *My firstborn. From inside my womb.* Unexpectedly, I find I'm blinking back tears, right there in our open-plan office. *That's the little boy whose body my body failed.* I feel a pang of anguish that this delicate, fair-haired creature will never burrow under a pile of colored balls then erupt through them like a jack-in-the-box, the way Theo did.

And even sadder that I'll never cuddle him in his sleep and drowsily inhale the scent of his hair, the way I sometimes do with Theo.

I hover my finger over the post and press LIKE.

THAT EVENING I SHOW Pete. "There but for the grace of God."

He studies the picture. "Sweet, isn't he?"

"It made me cry at work."

"Really?" He seems surprised.

"You feel it, too, don't you?" I press. "When you look at that picture, you must feel sorry for him."

Pete frowns. "I see a cute little boy, that's all."

"But do you think they love him? *Really* love him, I mean, the way we love Theo? Or do you think his . . ." I hesitate. "His problems make it different?"

"Mads, of course they love him," Pete says patiently. "After all, if the switch had never happened and David was part of our family, we'd love him, wouldn't we? Why should the Lamberts be any different? Besides, you heard what Lucy said—sometimes the bond is even stronger when they need you more."

"Hmm," I say. I wonder if Pete is being completely honest with me, or if my feelings about David are a can of worms he'd rather not open, in case everything gets feminine and messy.

As I take the iPad back, I see I've got fourteen notifications. Lucy has been through all my posts, liking every photo of Theo and adding comments—"Such a handsome fellow," "Sooooo adorable." I picture her doing the same thing I did earlier, eagerly scrolling through my Timeline, devouring every image of her birth son. I wonder if, like me, the experience made her cry.

25

MADDIE

ON SATURDAY, THEO SWALLOWS salt.

We're having a relaxing morning. Pete and Theo are downstairs making pancakes—butter and lemon for Pete, Nutella for Theo, vanilla and maple syrup with extra-thick batter for me, what back in Australia they call a pikelet. From what I can hear, Pete has his work cut out preventing Theo from dropping eggs on the floor, or mixing Nutella and maple syrup in some crazy new concoction. For my part, I'm lazing in bed, thinking how lucky I am to have a domestic god for a partner, when I hear Pete roar, "No!"

"What's up?" I call.

"Jesus!" Pete says. It takes a lot to make him swear in front of Theo, so I run down.

Pete has the tub of cooking salt in his hand. Theo, who's clambered onto a chair and is now sprawling across the kitchen table, is looking both pleased with himself and slightly apprehensive. In the middle of the table is a big mound of salt and a spoon.

"I turned around and he was just gobbling it up," Pete says. He's gone white.

"I'll call 111," I say, reaching for my phone. I get through to a recording saying that the NHS helpline is currently experiencing high levels of demand. I ring off. "Perhaps we'd better go to the emergency room. Just in case."

"You're meant to make them drink water." While I've been on the phone, Pete's been googling. "Though no one seems a hundred percent sure. Hang on. Someone on DadStuff may know."

"I'm not sure an internet forum is the best way to deal with this." I take Theo over to the sink, trying not to sound as alarmed as I feel. "Okay, Theo. That stuff really isn't good for you, so I need you to drink a very big glass of water."

I find a pint glass in the back of the cupboard and fill it to the brim. He drinks about a third—he's clearly very thirsty.

"I'll put some Ribena in it," Pete says. He only lets Theo have Ribena as an occasional treat, so this is almost guaranteed to make Theo drink more.

I press REDIAL and get the same recorded message.

"It's Saturday morning," Pete points out. "If we're lucky, the wait at the emergency room might only be a few hours."

We look at each other. I know exactly what he's thinking. Two years ago, we made the decision to get my bump checked out, just in case, and it saved our baby's life.

I ring off. "Emergency room it is, then."

"Yuck," Theo says helpfully, licking his lips and making a face. "More 'bena?"

As I drive us to the hospital, I reflect how, not long ago, something like this would have given me flashbacks to the NICU, maybe even a panic attack. But time is a great healer. It helps, of course, that Pete's pretty sure Theo didn't eat more than a few spoonfuls.

"I literally turned my back on him for a minute," he says, turning around to check on him.

"Don't beat yourself up. He's a two-year-old. He probably thought it was sugar."

In the back, Theo's gone very quiet. When I pull up outside the emergency room and Pete lifts him out of the car seat, he throws up.

By the time I've found a parking space and joined them in the hospital, Theo's flopped in Pete's arms, looking very pale, and Pete's talking to a nurse.

"Don't worry," she's saying. "It's hard to do much damage eating salt—it's an emetic, so you did the right thing by giving him plenty of water and letting him get it out of his system. You can stay to see one of the doctors if you want, but he'll probably just go on being sick for an hour or two. Give him plenty of fluids and make him comfortable." Theo chooses that moment to lean out of Pete's arms and throw up again, splattering vomit all over the shiny hospital floor. Pete starts to apologize and the nurse laughs.

"There'll be plenty more of that before the weekend's over. I'll call a cleaner. And find you something for him to be sick in."

She brings us a cardboard bedpan. Theo has by now gone hot and sticky and doesn't want to leave Pete's arms, so I sit beside them, holding it. He vomits three more times before he eventually perks up.

"I think we can probably risk the journey home now," Pete says.

The nearest parking space we can find is a street away from where we live, so it's only when we reach our house on foot, with Pete carrying a tired and floppy Theo, that we see Miles and Lucy outside our front door. Miles is holding a backpack.

"What the hell?" I say to Pete under my breath.

"Don't ask me." He sounds mystified. "Miles did mention something about teaching Theo to throw a rugby ball. But we never made a firm arrangement."

"Bugger." I plaster a smile across my face. "Hi there!"

"Hey, big man!" Miles says to Theo. "Hey Pete, Maddie. Lucy's baked cookies."

"And brought you a bottle of wine," Lucy says anxiously. "I hope you don't mind us randomly turning up like this. We were just around the corner, and David's with the nanny, so . . ."

"No, it's great to see you!" I say brightly. "Though it's lucky you found us in, actually. We've just been to the emergency room."

"Nothing dramatic, I hope?" Miles looks concerned.

"Only a bit of salt Theo swallowed. We're all a bit hot and vomitty, I'm afraid."

"Then it's a bad time," Miles says, picking up on my hint. "We'll come back another day." He reaches into his backpack and pulls out a foam rugby ball. "I'll leave this with you. I bought it on the interweb—apparently they're easier to catch than those little leather ones."

Theo immediately reaches for the ball, perking up as always at the sight of a new toy. Pete says, "Well, maybe we could give it a quick try. The park's only just around the corner."

"Shouldn't Theo be taking it easy for a while?" I ask pointedly.

"We won't be long," he says mildly. "The nurse said to stay quiet for an hour or two, after all, and we're well beyond that. What do you say, Theo? Quiet time or park?"

"Park!" Theo says immediately, as Pete surely knew he would.

"THEY'RE ALL GETTING ON like a house on fire, aren't they?" Lucy says, when they've gone and I'm making the two of us tea.

I nod, though actually I'm wondering about the origins of that phrase. Are houses on fire really a good thing? Or is it one of those innocuous idioms that actually refer to some horrible disaster, like the Great Fire of London or the Black Death?

"Miles really likes Pete," she adds. "This is so good for him. He doesn't have many male friends."

"Really?" I'm surprised. I'd assumed someone as good-looking and charming as Miles would have a huge social circle.

"He used to see a lot of his rugby teammates, the Mayfair Mayflies. But then he damaged his knee and had to stop playing. And he works in a very small office now he's left Hardings and set up on his own—it's just him and three others."

I nod. "It's the same for Pete, working from home. There's a group of dads from the NICU who meet up occasionally, but most of the time they only seem to interact on DadStuff." I glance at her. "Thank you for liking those pictures of Theo, by the way."

"Oh, they're gorgeous. Miles enjoys going through them over a drink when he gets back from work. Most of those likes were his, actually."

"Miles uses your Facebook account?" I say, surprised.

Lucy nods. "He doesn't have one of his own—he always used to say he didn't know why people bothered. But it's different now." She hesitates, then says in a rush, "In fact—if you were able— I mean, I know Pete's the primary carer, but if between you, you could perhaps post, say, one picture every day . . . And we'd do the same for you, of course. It's such a good way of keeping on top of what they're doing, isn't it? And this period when they're small is so precious. They'll grow up so quickly."

"I'll ask Pete. I'm sure he'll be delighted." I'm generally too busy to keep up with the stream of pictures he takes of Theo, so gradually he's stopped sending me all but the most photogenic ones. But it looks as if he's found a receptive audience now.

AT SOME POINT THE door crashes open and they all charge in. Miles has Theo on his back, horsey-style, Theo's feet sticking straight out from under Miles's arms, his little face beaming with excitement over Miles's shoulder. Pete's carrying the foam rugby ball, his jacket and trousers streaked with mud.

"Good time?" I ask.

"Theo just trounced the All Blacks twenty-nine nil on his very first appearance in the England lineup," Miles says proudly. "And he's got a pretty hefty tackle on him already."

"Great," I say. "Though I thought they didn't actually do tackling now, in school rugby. Isn't it all meant to be played by touch?"

"It's good for him to work off some of that energy," Miles says, unperturbed. He lowers Theo to the floor and ruffles his hair. Theo instantly charges into Miles's legs, wrapping his arms around his calves, and Miles obediently sinks to his knees. "Arrgh! Kick on! Anyway, I can't think of anything more fun for a two-year-old than having both his dads' undivided attention in the park."

"I'll make some more tea," I say.

"'BOTH HIS DADS'?" I say quietly to Pete when they've finally gone and Theo is watching CBeebies. "Is that something you agreed to?"

"I could hardly pull him up on it in front of Theo. But we haven't discussed what Miles should call himself, no." He glances at me. "How was Lucy?"

"Anxious." I tell him about the photo request. "I think we're going to need a conversation with them about boundaries."

"Really?" Pete sounds surprised.

"Well . . . When we were making the decision about the park and whether it was too soon for Theo to be playing . . . I felt a bit outnumbered. Like there were suddenly four parents instead of two."

"They didn't take any part in deciding to go to the park, though. That was me."

"Yes, but you knew Miles wanted you to go."

"Okay," Pete says, a word that somehow contains the sentiment *I think you're overreacting but I'm too supportive to call you on it.* "I'll speak to Miles. I'm sure they want clarity just as much as we do. But we did say that we'd try to make sure Theo's a part of their lives." He gets up from the kitchen chair and stretches. "We had a good time today, actually. I'd forgotten how much fun it is just to go and chuck a ball around—it's something I can't really do with Theo on my own."

"Lucy asked me if I'd booked Easter week off yet. I had to stall her—I had no idea what she was talking about."

"Yes, you do. That plan to get together on Easter Day? It's evolved into a few days down in Cornwall. Miles has found this massive house by the sea."

"I'm not sure I want to be stuck with them for a whole long weekend," I say doubtfully. "I mean, yes, they seem like nice people, and it would be lovely to spend more time with David. But we shouldn't rush things—this is way too important to risk getting it wrong and having it blow up in our faces. Besides, the way Lucy was talking it sounded like more than just a couple of days."

Pete shrugs. "I think it could be fun, actually. And I do get a bit stir-crazy sometimes in London, stuck in this tiny house with Theo. But I'm sure they won't mind if we say we can only go for a night. I'll talk to Miles next week."

26

HELP! JUST FOUND TODDLER EATING SALT. WHAT SHOULD WE DO?

Homedad85—Level 5 poster. Member since 2018.
No idea how much. Big pile of cooking salt from one of those plastic tubs. Given him plenty of water. Should we be worried?

Actiondad
NHS Direct

Darren
Yeah, dial 111 for NHS Direct.

Homedad85
Tried 111, still in the queue. Should we go to emergency?

Thedadinator
Give him some water.

Fourlovelydaughters

Surely must be self-limiting as tastes so bitter and horrid? Maybe ask if he wants any more—if he says yes, maybe he likes the taste so could actually be in real danger? I would just give LOTS of water.

Fourlovelydaughters

Mind you I'm not a medical professional so please don't rely on my advice.

Darren

Out of interest, what did you decide to do?

Darren

@Homedad85? Everything ok over there????

Homedad85

Sorry, got back from emergency after three hours (basically, all fine but projectile vomiting—nurse said we'd done exactly the right thing) and found visitors waiting. Had to go and play rugby in the park with DS and DS's new grown-up friend Miles, aka "Moles" as DS calls him. Pretty inspiring story actually— how friendship, positivity, and good communication are making what could have been a really tricky situation into an all-around success.

Darren

Sounds intriguing @Homedad85—do tell?

27

MADDIE

"YOU KNOW, THIS MILES and Lucy thing would make a great feature," Pete says over supper. "I might try to pitch it to a few editors."

I look up, frowning. "Isn't it a bit soon for that?"

"Well, even if someone does go for it, it'll take me a while to write it. And I'll clear it with Miles and Lucy before I send anything out, obviously. But I think it's the kind of thing an editor might really like—unconventional family dynamics, a beacon of cooperation at a time of global division, all that kind of stuff."

"Will you disguise our identities this time?"

"Of course." He sees my expression. "I know that was a mistake, before," he says quietly. "But this is what I do, Mads. I'm a journalist."

· · ·

AFTER HIS REDUNDANCY, PETE struggled. Not with Theo—he loved being a full-time dad—but professionally. It turned out the articles travel editors really wanted now were the ones their over-worked staff writers no longer had time to write, the ones that required actual traveling: fourteen days trekking through Patago-nia, say, or a review of a new hotel in the Arctic made entirely of ice. That was out of the question for Pete, of course, with Theo to look after. So he started pitching more general articles to the family sections: pieces about being a full-time dad, mostly.

He didn't tell me he was writing about my breakdown, not at first. It was about the NICU, he said vaguely, and what we went through when Theo was born. It was only when he showed me a draft that I realized just how frank he'd been. It was all there—how he'd gotten back from the bike ride and found the TV cov-ered in dried shit, bits of broken phone all over the floor, the gibberish I'd babbled about the doctors who were watching me. "My partner is amazing," he'd written. "Because, however good the NHS was at keeping our tiny premature infant alive, when it came to his mother's brain, they were in the Dark Ages. She was left to fight most of that lonely battle by herself."

"What do you think?" he'd asked when I'd finished reading it.

"It's powerful," I said doubtfully. "And very well written. I sup-pose I just wasn't expecting it to be so . . . honest."

"We always say there shouldn't be any stigma around mental health," he pointed out. "How are we going to remove the stigma, if we don't speak out?"

"I'm not sure I want to be the trailblazer, that's all."

"You know how hard it is to find stories that haven't been done to death already," he said quietly. "I really think this one could get picked up, Mads. It could be the break I need to get me noticed as a freelancer. But if you want me to spike it, I will."

Eventually we agreed he wouldn't use my real name. Because he had a different surname, we reasoned, there wouldn't be any direct link to me. And he was right about it being picked up. *The Sunday Times* ran it in the Style section, and it was immediately reposted on various blogs. A well-known yummy mummy with over a hundred thousand Instagram followers posted a link to it, along with a grateful comment about her own struggles after her premature twins spent three weeks in intensive care. I felt good about that—we were doing exactly what Pete had said, starting a conversation around women's experiences of childbirth and mental health. For a week or so there was the exhilaration of checking the blogs and Twitter every few hours, watching the likes and reblogs pouring in, a cascade of affirmation and solidarity. And praise for Pete, of course. Not many men would have had the emotional maturity or the patience to pick their partner up like that, was the consensus, let alone take over the nurturing of our child.

Then I realized people at work had read it, some of whom knew Pete through me and so knew exactly who he was writing about. A few made supportive comments, which was nice. Others said nothing, which made me wonder what they thought. Then I heard I had a new nickname on the creative floor: Maddie Mad Dog. I started to feel furious with Pete for not hiding my identity more thoroughly.

I went to Prague to film a Christmas commercial for a big electrical retailer. This time it was the art director I slipped up with.

Jenny, my CBT therapist, usually shied away from the touchy-feely stuff, but somehow it came out at our next session. She listened patiently as I spilled all my confusion and self-loathing to her.

"Did your father have affairs?" she asked when I'd finished.

I stared at her. Of all the things I'd been expecting her to say, that wasn't one of them. "Yes. At least three that we knew of."

"And your mother accepted them?"

"Well—not happily. But there was always a feeling that it was up to him whether he left us for the other woman or not. That, if he decided to stay, she'd still be there for him."

"Something of a saint, then. Or at any rate, a martyr. And now here you are, the breadwinner of the family, repeating the same behavior. Only this time with the genders reversed." She left a long pause. "I think you need to talk to Pete. Perhaps with the help of a couples therapist. You've clearly got some buried resentment about the way your parenting roles have turned out."

Meanwhile, Pete was trying to follow up the success of his NICU story. He discovered that our local pizza place didn't let men use the baby-changing rooms, which had been designed as part of the female toilets, so he started a campaign to get them to change their corporate policy. It worked, on one level—people were happy to click on the petition when it came up in their Facebook feeds, but they didn't really care enough to post messages of encouragement, the way they had with the mental health piece. The only newspaper he could interest was a local one, and even then, when the article ran, he discovered the editor had cut it to half its original length.

Gradually, he talked less and less about ideas for articles and more and more about being a parent. Theo had pointed at the snow and said, "Bubbles!" Theo had been on the roundabout in the playground. Theo had thrown a tantrum in Sainsbury's. I got used to reaching for a bottle as soon as I got home, letting the red wine take the edge off as I mentally tried to shift gears from the racing-car frenzy that was advertising to the kiddie rides of Pete and Theo's routine. Sometimes it worked. More often, I was still thinking about a knotty production problem with one half of my brain even as I smiled and nodded along to some story of playground peril.

So I completely understand now why Pete wants to write about what we're doing with the Lamberts. It's a chance to be the old Pete again, the journalist, to have people read what he writes. But it's also a chance to be NICU Pete, too, Saint Peter: to bask in the affirmation of an online audience, the invisible crowd of spectators who'll click and like and share and tell him what an inspiration he is.

I don't stop him, of course. How can I? But, disloyally, it does occur to me that, in the olden days, saints all had one thing in common. They didn't have wives or partners to think about.

28

This is a story about two broken families determined to heal.

This is a story about a bolt from the blue that could have led to discord and hatred—but instead has led to friendship, dialogue, and trust.

This is a story about four young professionals, trying to figure out a modern solution to an ancient problem.

In the Bible, King Solomon was famously faced with a nigh-impossible case. Two women both claimed they were the mother of a baby boy. They'd given birth at roughly the same time, but one child had died. Each was now accusing the other of stealing the live infant.

Calling for a sword, Solomon craftily declared there was only one solution: divide the child and give half to each woman. Immediately, one of the women fell to her knees, saying she renounced her claim. She would rather the child was brought up by someone else than see it die as the result of Solomon's brutal justice. Solomon then ordered that the baby be given to her, as she had just proved herself the true mother.

Whatever this tells us about standards of transparency and openness in the family courts circa 900 BC—what would Solomon have done if neither woman had cried out, or both did? Carried out his original judgment, presumably—it speaks to an ancient truth: Our children mean more to us than we do ourselves.

But what if you are suddenly told that the child you are bringing up—the child you have fed, bathed, played with, taught the letters of the alphabet to, *parented* for two whole years—isn't yours? What if you discovered that your child had been mistakenly switched with someone else's at birth?

That is what happened to my partner and me . . .

29

PETE

"OH, PETE. PETEY PETEY Petey."

It was Miles, calling on my mobile. I'd emailed him my article, with a request for a couple of quotes. But I could tell from his tone he wasn't happy.

"It's only a first draft, obviously," I said. "If there's anything you don't want me to use, just say."

There was a short silence. "It's not right. None of it. I'm sorry, Pete."

"In what way?" I said, confused. "I mean—it's true, isn't it? We *are* working things out between us."

"Of course. But eyes on the prize, yes? Think how this is going to read to whoever's given the job of working out how big a check they should be writing us. This looks like *mitigation*, Pete. Instead of mental distress and anguish, everyone's getting along like one big happy family. The way this is written, you'd think *we* should be paying *them*."

"Ah." I hadn't thought of it like that. "So you don't think I should write anything?"

"I'm not saying that. In fact, a newspaper article could provide us with a very good paper trail. But you need to recast it. Basically, ever since I knocked on your door, your life's been a living hell, yes? Every time you look at Theo's sweet little face, you find yourself staring into another man's eyes. Your family's been violated and your relationship with your child upended—"

"Hang on," I said anxiously. "Stuff hangs around online forever these days. I wouldn't want Theo to read it one day and think I found it difficult to love him."

"Fair enough," Miles allowed. "But there might be other ways. You mentioned that Maddie experienced mental health issues after the NICU. Maybe the shock of all this has brought some of her symptoms back."

"I'll have to ask her," I said. "I have a feeling she might not be too keen on that."

"Well, tell her it could be worth an extra half mil. That should be enough to convince her."

30

Case no. 12675/PU78B65, Exhibit 18B, attachment sent by Peter Riley to several newspaper feature editors.

This is a story that will strike fear into the heart of every parent.

This is a story about two broken families, who, just when they were finally recovering from tragedy, heartbreak, and mental illness, were dealt a fresh blow of unimaginable horror.

Because the shocking truth is that, at any moment, a stranger could knock on your door and announce that the child you have fed, bathed, played with, taught the letters of the alphabet to, *parented* for two whole years, isn't yours. And everything you thought you knew about your family could be blown apart in an instant.

I know, because that is what happened to my partner and me . . .

31

PETE

I REWROTE THE PIECE the way Miles had suggested. It wasn't as good—if I'm honest, part of my motivation for doing an article in the first place had been to celebrate the way we were all dealing with this: It was two fingers up to people like Jack Wilson who thought cynicism and distrust were the only correct responses to a problem like ours. But I could see Miles's point, and in any case pitching it as an update to my successful mental health article made it easier to place. The *Daily Mail* picked it up immediately, although they couldn't say when they'd run it. When the sub who was fact-checking it emailed me back with some queries, I saw they'd added a headline: TWO YEARS AGO, A BOTCHED BIRTH LEFT MY WIFE PSYCHOTIC. NOW A DNA TEST REVEALS: IT ISN'T EVEN OUR BABY.

I went to see a solicitor at the medical malpractice firm Miles was using, at their gleaming office with a view over Tower Bridge. I'd had a vague idea that no-win no-fee lawyers were all hustlers, but Justin Watts was bright and personable and charming, clearly a product of the kind of expensive private school Miles would have liked Theo to attend.

He made me go through the whole story again. "Well," he said when I was done, "as actions go, this one seems pretty straightforward—legally speaking, that is. I'll get a letter of claim off and we'll see what they come back with. Presumably you're aware that St. Alexander's has had its NICU downgraded to Level Two?"

I hadn't been. "Why? What happened?"

"Their mortality rate last year was nearly two percent higher than the national average. That might sound small, but it equates to a jump from four deaths a year to nine. Something's not right over there, so Level Three services have been transferred to Guy's while an investigation's carried out. It's good news for you, though. The trust will be hoping they can reopen as a Level Three as quickly as possible, so the last thing they'll want is you kicking up a stink. This has quick settlement written all over it." He tapped my article, lying on his desk. "But hold off getting this published for now, yes? The hospital might well prefer to keep the whole episode quiet, in which case this is only useful leverage until you actually run it."

I nodded. It would annoy the *Mail* to be told they couldn't print the piece yet, but every editor is used to being told that articles are sub judice. "And I really don't have to pay you anything?"

"Well, there'll be some expenses that'll need to be covered as they arise. But once we enter into the Conditional Fee Arrangement, you won't pay for my time unless we win. At that point, we'll charge our fees in full plus a success fee, both of which will get settled by the other side as costs. They'll have to pay back your expenses, too."

"And if we lose?"

"If we lose, in theory the boot's on the other foot and you have to pay their costs. In practice, you'll take out what's called after-the-event insurance to cover that possibility. And you can add the insurance premium to the costs the other side has to pay if you win."

It all sounded too good to be true. I had to remind myself that this was how things worked, that it was someone else's fault we were in this situation in the first place. "And do you know . . ." I hesitated. It seemed poor taste to ask *How much,* but Justin was ahead of me.

"We'll ask for two million. I doubt we'll get quite that much, but it's good to start high. Of course, that's nothing to what the Lamberts will be asking for."

"Why's that?" I'd assumed we'd get roughly the same.

"Because of David's disabilities. Maddie was told by the doctor who performed her cesarean that her baby might have been starved of oxygen—correct?"

I nodded.

"And later, when you sent her that picture from the NICU, it was of Theo being treated for possible oxygen starvation with a cooling blanket. But, assuming the babies had already been swapped by then, it was the wrong baby who was being cooled. The Lamberts can make a good case that David's problems were exacerbated by negligence—and with those like him now living longer and costing more, the payout could potentially be in the very high tens of millions."

MY SECOND MEETING THAT day was with our local vicar, to talk about the christening. The Reverend Sheila Lewis lived in a tiny modern rectory next to the church, a complete contrast with Justin Watts's sleek office. As it was the afternoon, I had Theo with me, but for once he was on his best behavior, happily playing on the floor with an ancient nativity set.

"Will it be a problem that Theo's older than most kids are when they're christened?" I asked.

Reverend Sheila shook her head. She was small and smiley and energetic—I'd heard from other parents that she'd had a successful career as a biochemist before becoming a vicar. "The only requirement is that the godparents have also been baptized. And that they're prepared to take their duties seriously, of course. Can you vouch that's the case here?"

"I'll have to check with them—the baptism bit, that is. I'm sure they'll take their duties seriously." Something made me add, "We haven't actually known them very long."

Reverend Sheila raised her eyebrows. "Choosing a godparent isn't a decision to be made lightly."

"It wasn't. Quite the reverse." I looked around, but Theo was still engrossed in the nativity set, cheerfully impaling the Virgin Mary on the ox's horns. "It's quite an unusual situation, as it happens," I said quietly. "They're actually Theo's real parents."

For the second time that day, I found myself relating the story of the mix-up at St. Alexander's. Reverend Sheila listened with a rather more quizzical expression than Justin Watts had.

"First of all, I think it's wonderful that you're all taking such a positive view of what could clearly be a very difficult situation," she said when I'd finished. "But I have to tell you that this is not a good reason to have a child baptized, or indeed to choose a godparent. Godparents have very specific responsibilities—appointing one isn't simply a gesture of friendship, even if it sometimes seems that way. And I'm very concerned that it will give Theo, not to mention yourselves, no protection if anything goes wrong."

"We're very much hoping nothing *does* go wrong. That's one reason we want to formalize things—to show our commitment. And we'd been intending to have Theo christened anyway."

"Hmm." Reverend Sheila still looked unconvinced. "How about a prayer of blessing for the six of you—Theo, David, and the two sets of parents? That would seem a much more appropriate way of inviting God into this particular relationship."

"We don't actually have many other people we *can* ask to be godparents," I said. "And I'm certain that Miles and Lucy are re-ligious." I had absolutely no idea if that was the case, of course, but I was pretty sure Miles wouldn't mind telling a small white lie.

"Well, given that it's a highly unusual situation, I'll speak to them before I make a decision." Reverend Sheila reached for a pad. "What's their number?"

32

PETE

ON THE WAY HOME Theo demanded a diversion to the park, and then it was time for us to make his tea—arancini balls, baked not fried, made with homemade breadcrumbs—so it was a while before I had a chance to phone Miles and warn him.

"Pete!" he said cheerfully as he picked up. He clearly had my name stored as a contact now. "How's things?"

"Good, thank you. Look, this is just a heads-up. Someone called Reverend Sheila Lewis might call—"

"Too late. She's already done it."

"Really?" That was quick. "How did it go?"

"All sorted. She's actually doing a couple of baptisms during the service this coming Sunday, so I said we'd muck in with those. That all right for you?"

"Er—I think so. I'd probably better—"

"Check with Maddie," he finished for me. "Of course. You've got a great vicar, by the way. Really liked her."

. . .

"IT WAS EXTRAORDINARY," I told Maddie when she got home. "With me, she was almost disapproving. But Miles seems to have had her eating out of his hand."

"Well, he's very charming. And for all we know, he *is* religious."

"Or just very good at lying."

"Persuading people to see things your way isn't necessarily lying. Besides, I thought you really like Miles. The two of you are thick as thieves at the moment."

"I *do* like him," I said. "I like him a lot. I'm just slightly in awe of how effective he is at getting his own way."

"Have you told him yet we're not going to Cornwall for Easter?"

"Not yet. It never seems the right moment."

Maddie raised her eyebrows.

"I know, I know," I said with a sigh. "I suppose I keep putting it off because I feel bad about it. I think I gave him the impression we were definitely up for it."

"Why not say my brother and his family are coming over from Australia? He can hardly object to that. But don't leave it too long. He may need time to find someone else."

33

MADDIE

I FIND THE CHRISTENING awkward. Because it's a joint baptism with three other families, regular members of the congregation who know one another well, it feels like our group are interlopers. It doesn't help, either, that the other children are all babies, only one of whom is even grizzling slightly. Whereas Theo . . . Theo simply doesn't do keeping a low profile.

The church is one of those trendy ones that pride itself on having a box of books to keep kids entertained—there's even a poster advertising something called Messy Church, every third week— but because this is a christening, everything is slightly more formal. Theo is overexcited from the start. As soon as he sees Lucy and Miles he shouts "Moles!" before running at them and trying to rugby-tackle Miles. Miles just laughs and ruffles his hair. Our friends Keith and Andy are with us—Andy has agreed to be the third godparent—so there are muttered introductions and handshakes, and I notice some of the regulars turning around to see who's making all this noise.

Lucy is carrying David. He lies in her arms very quietly, looking around with a slightly fearful expression. I reach out and stroke his fine, soft hair, itching to hold him myself. Like last time, he doesn't react, just looks at me with his big, solemn eyes. But I like to think he's a little less anxious after that.

Theo spots the box of books and makes a beeline for it. But since he can't read, to him it's just a big box of stories that require an adult to read them aloud. "Daddy! Daddy!" he calls eagerly, but Pete only puts his finger to his lips. The vicar has started her introduction now, something about the continued relevance of the Church and how important it is to welcome the next generation of worshippers. Theo takes out some books and starts throwing them at a side chapel like a knife-thrower, using the metal crucifix as his target. When he hits it, it gives an audible *clang!* and the vicar looks over, perturbed.

"Yeah!" Theo shouts happily.

Pete excuses his way out of the pew and goes to deal with him. After a moment, Miles follows. Theo must think it's a game, or perhaps something in Pete's grim expression warns him he's in trouble, because he decides to make himself scarce. Diving beneath the backmost pew, he wriggles between the feet of the people in it and then keeps going, on to the pews in front. Because he's coming from behind, the first anyone knows of it is when a small body pushes its way through their legs. By the time they've realized what's happening, he's gone.

Pete always hates it when Theo doesn't behave well in public—as if it's a reflection on his parenting skills. "Theo!" he says, in a voice that tries to balance sternness with not shouting over the vicar. "Come here! *Now!*" Theo just chortles and commando-crawls his way onward.

"Sorry, chaps. Ball coming through!" Miles contributes cheerfully, keeping pace alongside Theo in the aisle, but not actually able to get to him.

Pete goes to stand at the front, ready to grab Theo when he comes out, but Theo spots him and simply reverses direction. Luckily a woman four rows back has the good sense to clap her legs together, trapping him long enough for Pete, by now red with anger and embarrassment, to make his way along the pew and haul him out.

"Our Lord Jesus Christ has told us that to enter the kingdom of heaven, we must be born again of water and the Spirit," the vicar is saying.

"Naughty step. Now!" Pete hisses, dragging a wriggling Theo toward the door of the church. Then he stops and looks around.

His problem, I realize, is that if he takes Theo outside, he won't know when they're needed for the baptism. So he improvises, putting Theo down on the big stone step that leads from the church door into the nave.

Pete's a big believer in the naughty step. It was invented by some TV supernanny who insists it only works if you follow a set of very precise instructions, which Pete always does, to the letter. First, you take the child to the step in silence and sit them down. Second, you explain to them what they've done wrong. Third, you walk away and set a timer for one minute per year of the child's age. When the timer goes off, you explain a second time why they're on the naughty step. Then they have to apologize before they can get up, at which point you give them hugs and kisses as a reward for apologizing.

Personally, I think Pete believes in the naughty step mainly because it offers some kind of reassurance that he's disciplining Theo the right way, when all the evidence seems to suggest that actually, Theo is almost completely impervious to discipline of any kind. But Pete claims it works, so I never interfere.

Pete bodily pushes Theo down onto the step, then starts to

explain. "This is a church, Theo. In church people are quiet so they can listen to God—"

"*Bababababababab!*" Theo yells, putting his hands over his ears.

"Here we are clothed with Christ, dying to sin that we may live his risen life," the vicar intones.

Theo drums his shoes on the stone floor, making a satisfying echo. "*Babababab!*"

"As children of God, we have a new dignity, and God calls us to fullness of life—"

". . . so we have to sit still, without talking or playing, just like all these other people are . . ."

"Let us now pray, in *silent contemplation*—"

"*Sowwy, Daddy.*"

"It's not time to say sorry yet. You have to wait for the timer. Two minutes."

"*I'm sowwy, Daddy.*"

Miles laughs. "Oh, come on, Pete. Little beggar's said he's sorry." He opens his arms. "C'mon, big man. Give me a hug."

Theo jumps up from the step and runs into Miles's arms. "Huh-hay!" Miles says, swinging him up so their heads are level. "You going to come and sit quietly with me now?"

"*Yesss!*" Theo says, very loud in the contemplative silence.

IT'S A GOOD THING we're still in the middle of the service. Pete's so angry at Miles's intervention, he can't meet my eye as he comes and sits down. Theo sits meekly on Miles's lap, occasionally sneaking glances at Pete over Miles's shoulder. Then—proof that miracles do happen—he starts listening to what the vicar's saying, or perhaps the singsong way she's saying it captures his attention. And soon it's time for the exciting bit, getting all the parents, godparents, and children to come and stand around the font and lighting a long white candle for each child. Theo's eyes go very big when he's given his candle to hold. Since candles are usually for blowing out—he'd been encouraged to blow out the ones on his birthday cake, after all, just a short while back—he takes a big breath and puffs out his cheeks, until the vicar stops him.

"Not yet. You have to wait until I've put water on you."

"*Wow!*" Theo says, amazed, and everyone—not just the people around the front, but in the pews as well—laughs. Somehow he's managed to charm them all. It's only Pete, glowering beside me, who's still furious.

Miles looks at Theo with fatherly pride, and I realize that of course I know exactly where Theo gets his charm from.

"I'M GOING TO HAVE to speak to Miles," Pete says as soon as the service is over.

"Yes," I agree. "You are. But, Pete . . ."

"What?"

I try to choose my words carefully. Pete's a wonderful parent, but sometimes he can take it all a bit seriously. "I think it was a genuine misunderstanding. I don't suppose Miles knows anything about the naughty step and timers and so on. I think he just wanted to help."

"Well, it's time he *did* understand." Pete strides over to where Miles is chatting to Keith and Andy. I hear him say firmly, "Can I have a moment, Miles?" The two of them move off. Andy catches my eye and pulls a face, one of his parody-camp ones—*Ooohh!*—that are only half a parody.

Pete and Miles talk for about a minute. Miles is nodding. Then he claps Pete on the shoulder and puts out his hand, which Pete shakes.

"Everything all right?" I ask Pete when he comes back.

"Fine," he says. He sounds almost surprised. "He completely took my point. Apologized and said it won't happen again."

I look over at Miles. The expression on his face—eager, friendly, alert—is familiar, somehow. Then I recall where I last saw it. It's the same expression Theo had on his face on the naughty step, when he said sorry before it was time.

34

PETE

"MR. RILEY, COULD I have a word?" It was Susy, the woman who ran the nursery, intercepting me as I collected Theo at lunchtime.

"Of course." I followed her into her office. We both sat down, and I waited for her to say it was nothing to worry about.

She didn't.

Instead she said, "I'm afraid we need to have a difficult conversation about Theo."

"In what way, difficult?" I felt the hairs on the back of my neck go up, but I was careful not to let the tension show in my voice. "Is something wrong?"

"This morning he hit another child with a tumbler. On the head, quite hard I'm told. There was bleeding and we had to call the child's mother to take him home."

"Which child was it?"

"I don't think that's relevant. The point is, this was quite deliberate. The other child had a toy Theo wanted to play with. Theo had previously tried to grab it, but been told by the nursery assistant he'd have to wait his turn. She turned her back for a moment, then she heard a cry and found Theo hitting the other child."

"I'm sorry to hear that. The fact is, he's had a rather overstimulating weekend. He was baptized yesterday and all the attention got him quite excited." I smiled. "I'm sure he'll be calmer tomorrow."

"Well, possibly." Susy paused. "The boy's mother has made an official complaint. And because there have been warnings before . . ."

"Hang on. What warnings?"

"We've talked about Theo's behavior on more than one occasion, Mr. Riley."

"Talked, yes. But those weren't formal warnings." I had a horrible feeling that I knew where this conversation was heading.

"There's a pattern of behavior here that we don't seem to be able to change. And the safety of all our learners has to be our number one priority."

"He's two, for Christ's sake. Two-year-olds do this."

"Please, moderate your language. Getting angry won't help anyone."

"I'm not getting angry. Or rather, my anger is justified and appropriate. And before you say that me getting angry might be why Theo is violent, I don't ever lose my temper with him." A thought occurred to me. "No doubt this other parent was angry that her child got hit. I bet you didn't tell *her* it wouldn't help anyone."

Susy blinked. "In the circumstances, we've reluctantly come to the conclusion that Theo needs more structured support than we can offer him at Acol Road."

"You're expelling him. He's two, and you're *expelling* him?"

"We think it would be in Theo's best interests—"

"I'll speak to the other parent. We could put in some supervised playdates, get the two of them to make friends—"

"I did suggest something along those lines. Mrs. Tigman didn't think that would be an effective solution."

"Hang on. So it was *Zack Tigman*? The little boy who cries all the time? You don't think maybe there are bigger issues going on there than whether Theo can share toys?"

"Zack has taken a while to settle at nursery," Susy allowed. "Which is why it's even more important that he doesn't get beaten up while he's here."

"*Beaten up?*" I scoffed. "We're talking about one two-year-old whacking another with a cup. And why was a tumbler full of liquid at hand in the first place, without proper supervision? That's a health and safety violation for a start."

"We don't have the resources to make hitting impossible," Susy said patiently. "And yes, it *is* normal two-year-old behavior—to a certain extent. But if the child doesn't grow out of it, we simply have no choice but to withdraw the offer of a place." She stood up. "I'm sorry things haven't worked out here for Theo. But I really think that, in the long run, this is the best thing for all concerned. We'll refund your fees for the whole of this week."

35

Bloody nursery have expelled Theo for hitting Zack Tigman!!!

WHAT!!!!

Plus given me pompous lecture re him needing "more structured support." TOSSERS.

OMG. What are we going to do?

God knows. I'll do some research.

Want to talk it through? I can step out.

Better not. Still don't trust myself not to rant, and Theo's

here. Haven't told him yet he won't be going in tmrw . . .
ARRGH. He loves it there. Let's talk later XX

Case no. 12675/PU78B65, Exhibit 19B, retrieved from DadStuff.net.

CHILDMINDING A TWO-YEAR-OLD—WHAT DO THE OPTIONS COST?

Homedad85—Level 5 poster. Member since 2018.
My DS has just been excluded from nursery for hitting another child. I'm bloody angry actually as I don't think they've handled it at all well. But at the end of the day, it's their decision.

My question is, what now? Money's pretty tight so we need to look at the cheapest option. Au pair? Nanny share? Childminder? He probably does need a bit more supervision than some other kids his age.

Graham775
In your shoes I would speak to your local nanny/childcare agencies to discuss what you need, and how much you could expect it to cost in your area.

Onefineday
"We need to look at the cheapest option."
This is a child you're talking about, not flat-pack furniture.

ManUman151
"This is a child you're talking about, not flat-pack furniture."
OP is simply asking for some indicative figures to help him reach a decision, Onefineday. :rolleyes:

Zombieparent

Wasn't there a thread recently about au pairs and how legally they can't be given responsibility for under-fives?

Onefineday

Au pairs are NOT qualified childminders. They are young foreigners who get free board and lodging in return for LIGHT domestic duties and OCCASIONAL babysitting.

If your local nursery was run by a group of Romanian teenagers without qualifications or background checks, no first-aid training, no insurance, no experience, no inspection report, and very limited English, would you send your child there?

Tanktop

We pay our nanny £14 ph in southwest London, if that helps. She's self-employed so that includes tax, NI, etc.

Onefineday

"She's self-employed so that includes tax, NI, etc."
Nannies can't be self-employed. She's lying to you—probably because she doesn't have the right paperwork.

Lewishamdad

Registered childminder = £7 ph
Nursery = £8.50 ph
Nanny = £13–£18 ph
Mother's help aged 18–20 = £5.90 (special minimum wage for this age group)

Wouldn't recommend a mother's help though. Ironically the one we had wasn't much help.

Onefineday
"Ironically the one we had wasn't much help."
Perhaps you gave her an easy ride because she was a young girl.

Silverback71
Sounds like your best option is a nanny share. A qualified nanny will understand the relevant child development issues, there'll be at least one other child to interact with, and the cost will be comparable to a nursery.

Lewishamdad
"Perhaps you gave her an easy ride because she was a young girl."
I'm not even going to respond to that, Onefineday.

Onefineday
And yet you did.

Whosthedaddy
Fight, fight, fight . . .

Onefineday
Handbags at dawn.

Homedad85
Thanks to everyone who's answered. Having considered, I reckon our best bet is another nursery. I think I have to come clean though and tell them about the hitting—it may put some off, but at least if they take him it's because they're confident they can deal with it.

36

PETE

I SOON DISCOVERED, THOUGH, honesty wasn't the best policy.

There was another nursery nearby, but when I explained that Theo had been a little rough with another child, they point-blank refused to take him, citing "staff shortages." Strangely, they hadn't mentioned any staff shortages when they were telling me about the fees.

I phoned the only other nursery within walking distance. They had a three-month waiting list. I put Theo on it, just in case.

"It's not even that I mind being with him all day," I told Maddie that evening after a fruitless afternoon of googling and phoning. "It's just clearly not the right thing for him to be isolated from other kids right now. It's them he needs to learn to play with, not me."

She topped up her wine. "There's bound to be a place somewhere."

The doorbell rang. Maddie didn't stir, so I went to answer it before whoever it was rang again. At that time of night, it was probably Deliveroo with a takeaway for next door, which was annoying because Theo had only just gone down and the bell was almost certain to wake him.

It was Miles.

"Surprise," he said. "Hope that's all right. I was passing, so I thought I'd drop by and see my two favorite boys. And girl, of course. Hi, Maddie." As he stepped inside he raised the Hamleys bag he was holding. "This is only for one of you, though."

I took it. Inside was an electronic fire station—I could tell from the box it was going to be all flashing lights, whirring machines, and beeping buttons. Theo would love it, but in a small house like ours it would drive me crazy. "Thanks, Miles. Theo's gone down for the night, actually."

"Already?" Miles looked crestfallen. "I was hoping to give it to him myself. It's only just gone seven."

"He didn't have a nap today." I kept my voice low so it wouldn't float up the stairs. "And it's been a long day for all of us."

"Theo's been kicked out of nursery, and Pete's been scouring north London for a new one," Maddie explained.

"*What!*" Miles was outraged. "Kicked out? Why?"

"He hit Zack over the head with a tumbler."

"He's *two,* for Christ's sake!"

"Exactly what I said." There was a long, drawn-out yell from the baby monitor. Miles's outrage had woken Theo.

"What do you think? Shall we bring him down?" Maddie asked me.

I shook my head. Theo and I had a whole bedtime routine worked out—showing Mummy what we'd made today, bath, milky drink, quiet time, story. Breaking it would mean starting again. Plus he'd only learn that he could get up whenever he liked, if he yelled loud enough.

"Special occasion, though," Miles said winningly. "You could show him his present." He caught the look on my face. "Or maybe not. Best leave them to cry. Your parenting style and all that."

"Actually, we don't just leave him," I began, but then Miles snapped his fingers.

"I'm being dim. Theo doesn't need a nursery. You can share our nanny."

Maddie and I exchanged glances. "Are you sure?" Maddie asked.

Miles nodded. "Of course. It's the perfect solution. Theo and David will get to spend time together, and it'll be good for David to be around another kid—it might even help him catch up a bit."

"We should talk about the cost," I began, but Miles waved the objection away.

"Forget it. We'll settle up when the compensation comes through. It'll be a pleasure to have Theo at ours."

"And we'd need to work out a few ground rules."

"Like what?"

"Well . . . How much time the nanny spends in each house, for example."

"Really?" Miles looked around, clearly puzzled. "I mean, you want to work, don't you? You couldn't really share this room with a nanny and a couple of two-year-olds and expect to get any writing done. But listen, anything you want to change about the setup, just say. That's how this whole thing works, isn't it? Like you said in your article—the original one, I mean. Dialogue and compromise."

"It does sound like a pretty good solution to me," Maddie said. Which was slightly disloyal of her, because she must have realized that, for reasons I couldn't altogether articulate, I was feeling slightly uneasy about this proposal and was trying to think of ways to get out of it, or at least not to commit to it before I'd thought it through.

"And you'll get to see more of David," Miles added. He looked from one to the other of us. "That *is* what you want, isn't it?"

"Of course," I said, surprised.

"It's just that . . ." Miles gestured at his feet. "Here I am. Making an effort to see my birth son. Whereas I can't help noticing that you . . ." His voice trailed off.

"It isn't like that!" Maddie exclaimed, just as I protested, "Of *course* we want to see David."

There was a silence, broken only by a renewed shout from the baby monitor. "I suppose we were waiting for another invitation," I added.

"Well, don't," Miles said. "Just turn up. *Mi casa es su casa.* Anyway, you'll be able to see him when you drop Theo off now, won't you? I'll tell Lucy to expect you tomorrow."

37

PETE

"YOU NEVER HAD THAT conversation, did you?" Maddie whispered.

We were in bed. In the next room Theo was still grizzling, despite the fact he was now exhausted and we'd repeated the whole bedtime routine from milky drink onward. Or rather, I had. Maddie had opened another bottle of red wine and talked to Miles downstairs, while I was upstairs trying to make *Hairy Maclary from Donaldson's Dairy* sound as boring and soporific as possible. When Miles finally left—which took me pointedly putting the empty bottle next to the recycling bin, where it joined the two Maddie had already polished off that week, and saying firmly, "I'm going to bed. Theo'll be awake again by six, and it's been a long day"—we were too tired to do anything except hit the sack.

"Which conversation?" I whispered back.

"The one about boundaries."

"Yes I did. At the church. I said this could only work if we respected each other's parenting styles. And he completely agreed."

"I'm not sure Miles is sensitive enough to realize that means please don't turn up on our doorstep anytime you feel like it."

"You were the one who opened more wine."

"I couldn't really stand there with a glass in my hand and not offer him one."

"Maddie . . ." I said.

"Oh God. Serious voice. What have I done now?"

"You're drinking quite a lot."

"I know. It relaxes me." Her voice had tightened.

"It's not because you're . . . unhappy?"

"Jesus. No. It's because I have a high-stress job and wine helps me switch off."

"Okay. But you will tell me—"

"Don't lecture me, Daddy Pete. Not now. Cuddle me. We haven't made love for ages."

That's because you never want to, I almost said. *Not unless you're drunk.* But of course I didn't say that, because it would be a passion killer, and one of the consequences of not making love for ages is that you take it when it's offered. Even though you know it's only being offered to shut you up, there's a grizzling child next door, and you prefer it when both of you are sober.

I started to kiss her neck, which she likes, then pushed her T-shirt up and moved down her shoulder toward her breasts.

"At least Theo likes Michaela," Maddie added. "I think it'll be fine."

I rubbed her nipple gently with my nose.

"And if it doesn't work out, you've got him on the waiting list for that other nursery. So that'll be good." She yawned. "I think I'll go to sleep, actually. Do you mind? I'm not quite in the zone."

38

PETE

NEXT MORNING I PUT Theo into the car and drove over to High-gate. It was a fiddly, crosstown journey, complicated by having to get through at least half a dozen school drop-off zones. A drive that had taken less than twenty minutes on a Saturday took almost forty in rush hour.

Lucy came to the door in an elegant pair of designer jeans and a knee-length woolen cardigan. "Pete," she said warmly. "How lovely to see you. And hello there, Theo."

"'SMoles here?" Theo asked hopefully.

She laughed. "No, he's at work. That's what daddies do." She stopped. "Sorry, Pete. I didn't mean . . ."

"That's all right. Are you really sure this is okay? I don't want to impose on you."

"No, it's wonderful. Tania's been baking fat-free cakes for them both. Come in and say hello."

"Tania?" I said, puzzled, as I followed her through to the kitchen.

"The nanny. Tania, this is Theo, and Theo's dad, Pete."

A dark-haired young woman turned toward us from the Aga. She was wearing oven gloves and carrying a baking tray, but she immediately put the tray down and took her hand out of the glove to shake mine. "Pleased to meet you," she said politely, in French-accented English. She even gave me a little bob.

I looked at Lucy. "I thought Michaela was the nanny." In the car I'd been keeping Theo's morale up by speculating about what crazy games he and Mika would be playing today.

"We had to let her go. Miles was furious with her, actually."

"Why? What did she do?"

"He doesn't like the nannies being glued to their phone screens when they're being paid to look after David. And he doesn't let them use the coffeemaker whenever they feel like it—they have Nescafé and the internet in their bedroom, for when they're not working. Anyway, last week he saw Michaela on the nannycam, drinking a cappuccino and scrolling through social media. So of course she had to go."

"You have a nannycam?"

Lucy nodded. "You have to, really, don't you? It's not that you even need to look at it very often. Miles says it's just about making sure you can trust them to stick to the rules."

I looked around. I could see a cappuccino maker—a more expensive model than mine—but no camera. Miles must have hidden it, I realized.

"Right, Theo. Better be on your best behavior," I said brightly. "Somebody might be watching you, so think about that."

Slightly self-consciously, I went into the playroom and squatted down next to where David was sitting on the floor. "Hi, David."

His eyes turned toward me curiously. Maddie's eyes, the exact same shape and shade, but without Maddie's energy, her ever-changing, expressive liveliness. He looked away again.

"What are you up to?" I asked gently. Again, nothing.

"I've brought Theo to play with you." I wasn't sure if he recognized Theo's name, or whether it was because Theo just happened to charge in at that moment, but it seemed to me that David shrank back slightly. I patted him on the head. His blond hair was so fine, I could feel the shape of his skull. It was eerily similar to Maddie's, and so different from Theo's heavy black curls.

"Well, I'll see you at twelve thirty," I said to Theo as I got up. "Remember to play nicely."

"There's really no rush," Lucy said. "By the time you've gotten home, you'll be setting off again. Why doesn't Theo stay for lunch? Then he can rest in the car on the way back."

I WENT HOME, BUT it was hard to concentrate. Driving across London had been more tiring than the stroll to the nursery used to be. But it wasn't just that. I kept thinking of David, sitting in that massive playroom, surrounded by shelves of toys he couldn't play with. There'd been something shut-in about him, something passive. It would be so easy to ignore a child like that, particularly with a fireball like Theo around.

Our house is small, so once Theo's grown out of a toy we tend to put it in the attic. I went and found a crate of books he'd enjoyed at eighteen months. Julia Donaldson's *Toddle Waddle,* Eric Hill's Spot stories, Chris Haughton's *Shh! We Have a Plan*. I pulled out some with sliders, flaps, and other gizmos, too.

When I went back that afternoon, I showed Lucy. "Theo doesn't read these anymore, but I thought David might like them."

She looked at them doubtfully. "He's not a big reader, I'm afraid."

"Of course not," I said patiently. "But he might like me to read to him."

I went and sat down next to David in the playroom.

"Look, David," I said gently, holding up *We're Going on a Bear Hunt*. His eyes turned toward it. Theo would have snatched it out of my hands in an instant, as a prelude to either hurling it away, if he wasn't interested, or hitting me with it until I read it, if he was. David did neither. Instead, he reached out and touched it experimentally with his fingers.

Opening it, I started at the first page. " 'We're going on a—' "

"*Mnnneow,*" yelled Theo, charging into the playroom with a Lego rocket in each hand, followed by Tania.

"Hi, Theo. I'm just going to read this with David. You can watch if you want."

"*Neow-neow.*" Theo crashed the rockets into my head, one after the other.

"Tania, could you take Theo into the other room and help him rebuild his rockets? I just want to finish this story with David."

"Of course. Come on, Theo." She led him away.

" 'We're going on a bear hunt,' " I repeated, turning the page.

DAVID SAT RIVETED TO *We're Going on a Bear Hunt,* followed by *Each Peach Pear Plum* and *Where's Spot?* When I brought out *Dear Zoo* he eagerly reached out and turned the flaps to reveal the animals behind them as I read.

" 'The end,' " I said at last, closing *Dear Zoo* and putting it down. I'd done all the noises, though I'd kept the lion's roar to a quiet purr so as not to startle him.

"That was *wonderful,*" Lucy's voice said. "Simply wonderful."

I looked up. She was filming me on her phone. "Pete, you're a marvel," she added.

39

PETE

"PETE, YOU'RE A MARVEL," Maddie said drily.

I laughed into my phone. "Of course. But how did you know?"

"Lucy's put a video of you reading to David on Facebook. You can hear her voice behind the camera."

It was barely four o'clock. "That was quick."

"Well, I guess one has to do something while the nanny's getting tea."

"The nanny looked pretty shell-shocked, actually, after a whole morning of Theo. Speaking of which, Mika's gone. This one's called Tania."

"What's she like?"

"Seems all right," I said guardedly. "Theo's dubbed her Tanner."

"Well, it's only a temporary arrangement. I'd better go, my meeting's about to start." She paused. "It was lovely seeing you read to David, though. It made me want to reach out and put my arms around you both."

AT HALF SIX THE doorbell rang. *Deliveroo or Miles?* I wondered. It was Miles.

"I left work early this time," he said cheerfully, stepping through the door. "Hope that's all right. Ah! There you are, big man. Still up, I see."

"Only just," I said. Theo was on the sofa in his pajamas, watching a cartoon.

"Don't worry, I won't razz him up. We'll just sit quietly for a bit. Here. This is for you." Miles handed me a square package.

"You don't have to bring us gifts," I said automatically.

"You gave us all those books. Small gesture of gratitude."

I opened the box. Inside was an iBaby monitor, one of the expensive ones with a remote-controlled camera.

"It's the dog's knackers," he added. "I have the same model for David. Wi-Fi, 4G, omnidirectional microphone, night vision . . . It claims the humidity sensor can even alert you when there's a wet nappy, though I guess that's not something you need with Theo anymore."

I lifted the camera out of the box. It was satisfyingly heavy, sleek, and rounded, with the lens part mounted in a kind of gyroscope. "It's great, Miles, but . . . Those books were only sitting in the attic."

"That monitor you've got would have been out of date in the Dark Ages. I've set it all up for you—just put in your Wi-Fi password and you're away. It's nothing, really. And Lucy's been raving about how good you were with David today. She sent me a link to the video."

"It was a pleasure," I said, shrugging.

"Mind you, Theo looked quite put out when you sent him

away like that," he added. He sat down next to Theo, ruffling his hair. "Poor little chap."

"Theo gets plenty of attention."

"He's not used to sharing you, though, is he?" Miles took off his tie and put it in his suit pocket. "You could tell he was—what do they call it?—acting out a bit. What are we watching this evening, Theo?"

"*Po'man Pat.*"

"I *love Postman Pat*. Do you know, they had it when I was your age? I bet I already know this one."

MILES WAS STILL THERE, watching TV, when Maddie got back from work. Theo, sleepy now, had collapsed against him, thumb in mouth. Miles beamed at her.

"Hi Maddie," he said in a stage whisper. "Our boy's tired."

"So I see," she said in her normal voice. She went to the fridge and pulled out a bottle.

"Do you want to put him down and read his story?" I asked.

She nodded. "When I've had a glass of wine. Long day."

"I'll do it," Miles said immediately.

"No, really—" I began, but he cut me off.

"You stay here and talk to Maddie. First chance you two have had to talk to each other all day, I bet. I'll just read Theo a story and then I'll be off."

It was the words "I'll be off" that persuaded me. It had been a long day for me, too. "All right. Thank you."

Miles slid his arms under a limp, sleepy Theo, who allowed himself to be carried upstairs.

It was odd, but as they went up the stairs, with Theo draped crosswise over Miles's arms, I couldn't help thinking of a man carrying his bride over a threshold.

. . .

"MI CASA ES SU casa again?" Maddie said when they were upstairs.

"Yup," I agreed.

"And what's this?" She indicated the iBaby.

"It's an internet-enabled baby monitor. A present from Miles."

"Well . . . I suppose you have been complaining about ours for ages."

"Yes. It's very generous of him." I hesitated. "Lucy told me earlier that Miles fired Michaela because he saw her on a nanny-cam, infringing one of his rules."

"Miles has rules? Who knew?"

I nodded. "Surprisingly strict ones. And a one-strike-and-you're-out policy."

Maddie took another swig and topped up her glass. She did that a lot these days, I noticed: drink-and-refill, so her glass was never empty. And she filled it closer to the top than I did. "So?"

"Miles said he's already set it up. All we have to do is enter our Wi-Fi password. Maybe I'm being overcautious, but . . ."

She was silent a moment. "You think he might be technical enough to hack it?"

"I don't think he'd even need to be very technical. Look." I typed some words into my laptop's search engine and showed her. The search *Are baby monitors easy to hack?* gave over ten thousand results, and from what I could see, the answer from all of them was a resounding *yes.* "But if I'm being paranoid, tell me," I added.

"I don't think you *are* being paranoid," she said slowly. "I mean, he may justify it to himself by saying that it's his son, so why can't he watch him sleeping. But there have to be limits, don't there? When he comes down, I'm going to say something. About Easter, too. It's time we got this sorted."

"HE'S ASLEEP." MILES CAME downstairs smiling. "God, he looks peaceful when he closes his eyes, doesn't he? Like a little cherub."

"It's the only time he does," Maddie said drily. "Incidentally, Miles . . ."

"Yes?"

"There are a couple of things we've been meaning to mention. I'm afraid I can't take any time off at Easter—I'm just too busy at work. And one of my brothers and his family are coming over from Australia on the Saturday, so it would be almost impossible to get all the way to Cornwall and back just for one night. I'm really sorry—I think we're going to have to bail."

"No need," Miles said cheerfully. "Bring them, too. The house sleeps ten, so there's plenty of room at the inn."

"I'm sure you'd rather fill it with your own friends."

Miles's smile died. "I said, bring your brother's family, too. Easter was your idea, after all. And the house is booked and paid for. I can't cancel it now."

Maddie looked at me, puzzled. "I thought it could easily be canceled?"

"Well, it can't." Miles sounded peeved.

"Miles—it's my fault. I should have said something earlier," I said. "But Maddie hardly ever gets a chance to see her family—"

"Fine." He gestured at Maddie, a slicing movement of his hand. "Maddie can stay in London and see her brother. You and Theo can come to Cornwall."

"We'll want to spend Easter together," Maddie pointed out. "And my brother will want to see Theo."

"Well, how else are you going to sort this?" Miles demanded. "I want to see Theo, too."

He looked so exactly like Theo when Theo was denied something—mutinous and truculent, his lower lip thrust out—that without thinking I spoke in the same tone I used with my two-year-old. "We can't always have what we want, though, can we?"

I realized as soon as the words were out that it sounded horribly patronizing, but Miles didn't give me time to say so.

"That's so true, Pete. So very true." He sounded strangely distant and unemotional, almost as if he were speaking to himself.

And then he was gone, a blast of cold air from the door he'd left open behind him chilling our little sitting room.

40

<u>Case no. 12675/PU78B65, Exhibit 21, email from Justin Watts, Fox Atkins LLP, to Peter Riley.</u>

Your Matter

Dear Pete,

This is just to confirm that I have submitted our letters of claim and have received a holding response. I will let you know when I have further news.

Kind regards,

Justin Watts

Associate Partner

Fox Atkins LLP

41

PETE

I TOOK THEO TO the Lamberts' next morning feeling slightly apprehensive. The change in Miles's manner had been so abrupt—the cheeriness and bonhomie visibly draining from him—that I was sure he must have been genuinely offended. Not that I regretted what Maddie had said—it was only what I'd been struggling to say myself—but I did regret my own tactless intervention.

On the other hand, I decided, if Miles *had* taken offense, it was a chance to talk it all through and thrash out some details—a weekly timetable of visits, say, or at the very least agreeing to check by text before we turned up at each other's houses. It was becoming increasingly clear that Miles was going to need quite careful handling if we were to keep relations as smooth as they'd been initially.

But in the event, Miles wasn't home, and Lucy seemed her usual friendly, if high-strung, self. "Oh, hello, Pete," she said in her vague way, as if it was a surprise that I'd managed to find my way to Highgate at all, let alone bang on nine A.M. "And Theo. How lovely to see you."

I'd taken an old play mat of Theo's, a quilt with various insects and animals sewn on it—a ladybird, a frog, a caterpillar that squeaked when you squeezed it, a spider hiding under a leaf. I lifted David onto it and read him *The Very Hungry Caterpillar* while he ate some grapes that Tania had washed and cut in half. When I'd finished, I put the book behind me and said gently, "Can you see a hungry caterpillar anywhere on the mat, David?" He looked around, and I pointed toward the caterpillar, then squeezed it, making it squeak. He laughed. I suddenly realized I'd never seen him laugh before. It lit up his whole face, and just for a moment he didn't look brain-damaged. He just looked like any little kid having a good time.

A little kid with Maddie's eyes.

"Squeak squeak!" I said. "I'm still hungry! Give me some grapes!"

I pretended to feed the caterpillar one of the grapes. "Squeak squeak! That means 'thank you' in caterpillar."

"You're so good with him," Lucy said, watching.

"Well, he's sweet."

"Miles thinks he might be musical when he's older. Because he's sensitive, and he listens a lot."

I nodded. I tried to think whether Maddie and I had ever had a conversation about what Theo might do as an adult. But perhaps it was different when your child had a condition like David's.

I patted David's head and got up. "Incidentally, Lucy . . ."

"Yes?"

"Did Miles say anything about last night? Only I think I might have spoken a bit tactlessly."

"Last night?" She looked bemused. "I didn't even know you two were meeting up last night. Did you go for a drink? He didn't say anything when he got home. And I'm afraid I was asleep when he left this morning—he likes to get off to work early, after his run."

"I'm probably overthinking it," I said. "I'll send him a text or something."

AROUND LUNCHTIME I LOOKED at Facebook. Lucy and Tania had taken the children to the zoo. Lucy had already posted half a dozen pictures—Theo at the penguin pool, Theo petting a snake, Theo standing next to a giraffe's leg. David was in a stroller, so there were fewer of him.

The problem with this arrangement, I reflected, was that Theo was never going to learn to share better while he was with a child so much less advanced than him. If anything, he was just going to get used to having the undivided attention of two adults at once. And what was having a nanny with limited English going to do to his speech delay? It really was only a stopgap solution.

But I suspected Miles and Lucy didn't see it that way. I wondered how long it would take to get some kind of payout from the hospital. After that, hopefully, we'd be able to sort out our own childcare again.

THE REST OF THE week passed without incident, and without word from Miles. And on the plus side, now that Theo was no longer at nursery I didn't have to bother with a costume for World Book Day. It gave me quiet pleasure when I bumped into one of the nursery mums by the organic fruit and veg in Sainsbury's and spotted a *Where's Wally?* costume in her trolley. I remembered her name: Sally Russell. She'd been one of the prime movers behind the group I'd dubbed "the motherhood," constantly making snide remarks to the effect that full-time dads made clueless carers.

"How lovely," I said, glancing down. "Harry will look so cute in that."

Sally flushed. "I was going to make one, but he absolutely refused to be a mouse again. And it's only seven pounds fifty."

"So it is," I agreed. "Makes you wonder where they source it, doesn't it? Long-sleeved shirt, trousers, *and* hat. Is it Fairtrade cotton?" I leaned down to look. "Oh. Polyester. Cambodia. Shame."

I shouldn't have been enjoying myself so much, but if the boot had been on the other foot, she'd have shown no mercy. And it didn't take her long to come back swinging.

"And how's poor old Theo?" she said, her voice dripping with concern. "We were all so upset to hear he'd been excluded. Where did you manage to place him, in the end?"

"Theo's fallen on his feet, actually. We've found a really good nanny share with"—I hesitated—"with friends."

"That's great. He probably wasn't quite ready for preschool, was he?"

"Probably not," I agreed. I really wasn't bothered by her barbed comments, which was nice as I was fairly sure she was bothered by mine. "Good to see you, anyway."

As I moved off she said suddenly, "Did you hear about Jane Tigman?"

I turned. "No. What happened?"

"She got knocked off her bike and broke her leg."

"Knocked off how?"

Sally shook her head. "She can't remember anything about it. She thinks it was a car, rather than a van or bus, but she's not absolutely sure. It must have just touched her back wheel, she thinks, and sent her flying. Whoever it was, they didn't stop. Luckily it was just after she'd dropped Zack off, or he'd have been on the bike with her."

"That's terrible," I said. Jane might have been responsible for Theo leaving the nursery, but it was impossible not to feel sorry for her. "Send her my best wishes, will you?"

42

MADDIE

I'M AT WORK, REDOING the budget for a commercial—the client has arbitrarily decided it should cost 20 percent less, but is adamant it shouldn't look 20 percent less good—when Ingi from reception calls.

"Maddie, there are some people here to see you. From the NHS."

"Okay," I say slowly. "Is there anywhere we can talk in private?"

"The Surfer room is free. I'll put them in there, shall I?" All our meeting rooms are named after famous commercials, which tends to confuse the clients.

Obviously, this must be to do with our claim. But I'm surprised they've come to see me without an appointment. Is it some kind of ambush, to catch me off guard? Or is this the way they do things here in the UK? Either way, I decide, there's no point in getting worked up about it before I know what they want.

In the meeting room, a man and a woman are waiting. Both wear suits and open-necked shirts. The man, who's younger, has a laptop in front of him, while the woman, who's short and stocky, is sorting through a bulging folder of paperwork.

"Hello, I'm Maddie Wilson," I say briskly. "I understand you want to speak to me?"

"Yes." It's the woman who answers. "I'm Grace Matthews, and this is Thomas Finlay. We're from NHS Resolution, the part of the health service that deals with litigation."

I sit down. "It's regarding our claim, I assume."

Grace Matthews nods, causing her glasses to slip down her nose. She pushes them up with a finger. "First of all, we wanted to assure you that the NHS takes incidents like this one very seriously. We're working with the private clinics involved to understand what happened."

Now it's my turn to nod. "Good."

"That may take some time, so please don't worry if you don't hear from us for a little while."

"Of course."

"In the meantime, we'll need access to your patient records, to assist our investigation." Grace Matthews takes a form from her folder and slides it toward me. "If you could sign this, to say you give your consent."

I look down at the form. "I should probably get our lawyer to look through it first."

"Well, of course, if you want to." Grace Matthews sounds surprised. "It's the standard form that anyone has to sign when clinical negligence claims are investigated."

I think. "I'll just step outside and call him."

"Could you read me the form?" Justin Watts says when I've explained why I'm calling. I've only gotten through the first few lines when he stops me. "That's all right. It's standard for these cases."

"Does that mean they'll see my psychiatric records, too?"

"Yes, but since we're claiming mental distress, those records will bolster our case, not hinder it."

I feel uneasy. It hadn't really occurred to me that my psychosis might be relevant to our claim, when the truth was, I would have reacted like that irrespective of whether it was Theo or David I went home with. But we're committed to this path now. "Okay. Thanks."

I go back into the meeting room. "He says it's fine."

"Good. I've got a pen here," Grace Matthews says. As I sign, she says casually, "Where's Theo now, by the way? With your partner?"

Still writing, I say, equally casually, "No, with some friends. We have a nanny share. Why?"

Grace Matthews takes her pen back. "Just curious."

43

PETE

"HEY MATE," MILES SAID cheerfully.

"Miles. Hi," I said cautiously into my phone. It was the first time we'd spoken since he left our house so abruptly that night.

"Baby monitor working all right?"

"Fine, thanks." I hadn't actually plugged it in. The thought of Theo being watched—or even more pertinently, listened to with that omnidirectional microphone—spooked me, and our house was so small, you didn't really need a monitor to hear him crying anyway.

"Great. Look, I've got a favor to ask. What was the name of the nurse who looked after Theo in the NICU, the Irish one who looked like she had the hots for you?"

"I think you probably mean Bronagh Walsh? But she didn't have the hots for me."

He laughed. "If you say so."

"Why do you want to know, anyway?"

"It's for the lawyer. He's compiling a list of all the NHS personnel we can remember coming into contact with, for the investigators."

I suddenly felt apprehensive. "Investigators into what?"

"How the mix-up happened, of course. Presumably they have procedures to stop that kind of thing, and in this instance they didn't work. So they'll want to try to find out what went wrong. Which is a good thing, isn't it? Stop this happening to some other poor bastard."

My feeling of anxiety was deepening. "But no one's going to try to pin this on one of the nurses, are they? Because Bronagh was fantastic."

"Well, if you say so, Pete. But someone cocked up, didn't they?"

"I suppose," I said uneasily. "So long as they don't try to scapegoat Bronagh."

"Who definitely didn't have the hots for you, of course. Anyway, better go."

"Miles . . ." I said.

"Yes, mate?"

"We're good, right? There's nothing bothering you?"

"Like what?"

"Just that we haven't seen you for a few days. And last time we spoke I probably didn't express myself very well. I was tired, and somehow—"

He laughed. "There you go again, Pete. Always worrying about what other people think. No, of course we're good. I've just got a big push on at work. Give my love to the big man, would you? Tell him it's a shame about Easter, but I'll see him soon."

"SO WHAT *DO* YOU want to do for Easter, now we're not spending it with the Lamberts?" Maddie asked that evening.

I opened the fridge and took out a beer. "I think an Easter egg hunt is more or less mandatory, isn't it? They're doing one on

Hampstead Heath. And there's a lambing weekend at Forty Hall—it'll be good for Theo to be around some animals. We should probably put in a couple of appearances at church, too, while we're still fresh in Reverend Sheila's memory."

"What about getting some friends over on the Saturday?"

"Good idea. We haven't seen Greg and Kate for ages."

"And they know Sophie from work, don't they? I've been trying to arrange something with her and Richard for a while. Shall we do supper?"

"Blimey. Who's cooking?"

Maddie stretched. "I'll do dessert if you'll do the main."

"Deal."

"God, it'll be nice to have some time off. It's been so full-on recently, hasn't it, what with all the Miles and Lucy stuff? We really need some time to ourselves."

44

MADDIE

IT'S GREAT TO HAVE friends around. Sophie and Richard have booked a babysitter, but Greg and Kate bring Lily and Alfie with them, putting them down in our bed while Pete cooks. Then we all squeeze around the table and drink wine and eat and talk. About our kids, mostly. Kate's like me—she went back to work while Greg stayed at home, so it's nice not to feel judged for once. At one point, when Pete and Greg are getting all competitive about what they cook with their charges—"Well, last week we made arancini balls from panko breadcrumbs and some leftover risotto, and we didn't skimp on the chili flakes, either"—she gives me a sideways glance and rolls her eyes comically, which makes me snort into my wine.

Greg sits back. "I meant to ask you, Pete—you posted something on DadStuff a while back, about some kind of inspiring story you were involved with?"

"Oh yeah." Pete looks at me. "We can talk about this now, right?"

I shrug. "I don't see why not."

So Pete—keeping his voice down, in case Theo is still awake—tells the story of how the babies got swapped, and how we're dealing with the fallout. He's a good storyteller—that's the journalism, I suppose: He knows how to structure facts succinctly and not go off on tangents. But they'd be spellbound in any case. Hearing him relate the whole thing from start to finish, and seeing our friends' stunned reactions, brings it home to me all over again just how extraordinary this whole situation is.

"And what are they *like*?" Kate asks when Pete's finished. "Do you get on?"

"Well," Pete begins, "that's where we've just been incredibly lucky. They're very nice. And really, really committed to making it work."

"They're a bit weird," I say.

Pete shoots me a look. I realize I've spoken a little thickly, but sod it: It isn't as if I'm driving anywhere.

"I mean, Pete's right," I add. "They *are* committed. But it's a relief to have a break from them, actually. They wanted us all to go away together over Easter. I managed to get us out of it, but—put it this way, they're hard work."

"It's a bit like nature versus nurture, this situation of yours, isn't it?" Richard says thoughtfully.

Pete nods. "That's what Miles said, too."

I give him a look. "When was this?"

"When we went out for a drink." Pete looks surprised. "I thought I told you. Miles said, it'll be interesting to see if Theo turns out as successful as him, or whether being with us will make him less competitive. Or words to that effect."

There's a short silence. "That's actually quite insulting, though, isn't it?" Sophie says.

Richard frowns. "He sounds a bit of a prick."

"Well, we have very different ideas of what success looks like," Pete begins, just as the doorbell rings.

For a moment, I think, *It's him.* Then I relax. Of course, it can't be—the Lamberts are 250 miles away in Cornwall, and in any case, Miles comes earlier than this when he wants to see Theo. "I'll go," I say, getting up.

It *is* Miles. And Lucy, both of them smiling expectantly at me as I open the door. Miles is wearing a dark blazer and faded blue jeans. In one hand he has a bottle of expensive-looking wine, in the other a shopping bag.

"Thought we'd come and introduce ourselves," he says cheerfully. I'm so dumbfounded, I let him step past me into the house. He looks around the full room. "Quite a party you've got here."

Pete finds his voice. "Miles. We thought you were in Cornwall."

"Didn't fancy it on our own." Miles waves at the table. "Greetings, one and all."

"Right." Pete nods, a bit too vigorously. "*Miles and Lucy,* everyone."

"I'm guessing you must be Maddie's brother," Miles says to Richard, extending his hand across the table.

"I'm Richard," Richard says, confused. "My wife works with Maddie."

Miles turns to Greg inquiringly. But then a kind of shadow falls across his face.

"We know Pete and Maddie from the NICU," Greg says.

Miles looks at me. "Where are your brother and his family?" he asks quietly. There's a strange, pale light in his eyes, like a big cat's.

"They're not here."

"Why not?"

I barely hesitate. "Their flight was delayed."

"Which airline?" Miles's voice is soft.

"We didn't fancy coming to Cornwall," I say defiantly. "It was a white lie, okay?"

There's a long silence. Miles shakes his head. "No. It is not okay, Madelyn. It is not okay at all." He speaks in the same distant voice I heard last time he was here, eerily calm.

"Mate—" Pete begins. Miles turns.

"I'm not your mate, Pete. Though God knows I've tried to be, for the sake of my son." He looks at the table. "Well, budge up. Two more for dinner, now."

Another silence. There is clearly no way anyone can squeeze up any further.

I take a deep breath. "Miles, Lucy. It's always great to see you, but this isn't a good time. As you can see, we've got guests."

"Guests," Miles repeats. "And they're more important than the mother and father of that little boy upstairs, are they?"

"It's not like that—" Pete protests.

"We're not good enough for you, is that it?" Miles says. "Because we don't work in the media or take drugs or read the fucking *Guardian*?"

"Jesus," Sophie says nervously. "I can't believe I'm hearing this."

"You should go," I say firmly to Miles.

"Yes, Miles." Lucy's voice is little more than a whisper, and when Miles turns toward her, she flinches. It's a tiny movement, barely more than a twitch, but with a sudden flash of intuition I think: *She's scared of him.* "Let's go home."

"Give this to Theo," he says to no one in particular, pulling a box out of the shopping bag. It's an Easter egg, a huge one. He puts it on the table.

I suddenly realize that Pete and I should have gotten something for David. We should have investigated low-protein eggs, or thought of a non-chocolate alternative. But it hadn't even occurred to us.

Miles puts the wine on the table as well. "Come on," he says to his wife. "Let's get out of this shithole."

45

Case no. 12675/PU78B65, Exhibit 23, email from
Peter Riley to Miles Lambert.

Miles,

After a day's reflection, it seems to Maddie and I that none of us handled yesterday evening very well. Certainly, we shouldn't have told that white lie about Maddie's brother coming over from Australia. Please understand that we only did so out of a desire to spare your and Lucy's feelings. We've been seeing quite a lot of you recently, which has been on the whole a great pleasure, and we just wanted a little time to ourselves.

Also on reflection, it was remiss of us not to sit down with you both much sooner and work out some ground rules for how this is going to work. Clearly, the effort we've all been making to keep it friendly and informal is going to have to be supplemented by some agreements about visiting times, responsibilities, how much input we should each have into each other's parenting styles, things like that. And we are all going to have to be very clear about what is and isn't acceptable language to use with each other.

In many ways we think it's a good thing that harsh words have now been spoken and the air has been cleared. That's what happens in families, isn't it—a row, followed by reconciliation. And we definitely are a kind of family, even if it's an unconventional one.

What do you say—shall we agree to put last night behind us, for the sake of our children, and take it from there? There are so many positives to be had from this situation, even if it is going to take effort and commitment on both sides to make it work smoothly.

Best wishes,
Pete and Maddie

46

MADDIE

PERSONALLY, I THINK THE email is way too conciliatory. I'm still furious at the way Miles and Lucy ruined our evening, and it's taken all Pete's powers of persuasion to convince me that the future relationship with them is worth swallowing my anger for.

"Think of David," he said quietly. "Think of our biological son, sitting in that huge house with a father who virtually ignores him because he'll never make the first eleven. Are we really going to walk away from our son just because Miles is turning out to be trickier than we first thought? David needs us to be bigger than that, Mads."

At which, I burst into tears and told him to write whatever he liked. I haven't told Pete this, but sometimes at work I get up that Facebook video of him reading to David on the play mat and watch it over and over. *That's the family I could have had. Should have had, even.* And—much as I adored the family I did have—I didn't find the idea off-putting. Pete just looked so *right* with

David, so natural. So if he's correct, and a mollifying email is what's now required to reset the relationship with the Lamberts, it's a price worth paying.

Our friends, of course, had been stunned by what they'd witnessed. "A nutter as well as a prick" was Richard's assessment, and it did seem apt. As usual, Pete tried to see both sides—"He's just like that. He blows his top, and then it's all forgotten"—but even he had to admit that Miles's behavior had been downright weird.

And besides, Miles hadn't blown his top. That was one of the things that was so strange about it—the eerie calm with which he'd hurled his insults at us.

I made Pete take out a bit in the first draft where he apologized more profusely for not going to Cornwall, though. It might have been our suggestion to spend the day together, I pointed out, but we'd never signed up for a long weekend, let alone a whole week. If we implied we were in the wrong about that, Miles would simply walk all over us.

It was me who insisted on the bit about unacceptable language, too. Because I'm not having some rich entitled pom thinking he can walk into my home and call it a shithole.

WE FINALLY SEND THE email at four P.M. Miles doesn't reply. Not that evening, or on Easter Monday.

"What do I do tomorrow?" Pete says over supper. "Take Theo to the Lamberts' as usual, or keep him here?"

"God, I don't know." I think. "I suppose, if you do take him, at least it'll be a chance to talk to Lucy. Find out where *she* stands."

"Or there might be a massive row. If Miles is there, I mean."

"Maybe a massive row is what's required right now."

"Um," Pete says. "In front of Theo?"

I glance at him. If Pete has a weakness, it's that sometimes he'll try to smooth things over when what's really required is a bit of shouting. But he's right, of course—we shouldn't be teaching Theo that shouting is how adults resolve disagreements, at least not while his own behavior is still so erratic. "Then why not keep him home for a day?" I suggest. "That might give Miles a reason to get back in touch, after all."

47

PETE

SO I KEPT THEO home.

Around eleven, while Theo was drawing what he claimed were dinosaurs on the giant pad we kept especially for rainy days, my phone rang. I glanced at the screen. MILES LAMBERT. Slightly apprehensive, I answered it. "Hello?"

"Pete, mate. What's up?" Miles said cheerfully. "Is Theo all right?"

"Theo's good, thanks. Why?"

"Lucy texted to say you hadn't turned up this morning."

"That's right," I said cautiously. "You hadn't replied to our email, so we weren't sure if you were expecting him."

"Of course we were. That was the deal, right? Daytimes at ours, nights at yours."

I frowned. "I don't think we exactly formalized that into a *deal*, Miles."

Silence.

"Did you read our email?" I added.

"Yes. Well, the first few lines anyway. It was a bit long, to be honest. But I got the gist. Look, apology accepted. Water under the bridge. And let's face it, I probably spoke a little hastily as well."

I took a deep breath. "Miles, we need to sort this out."

"Consider it sorted. Anyway, now we're all good, how soon can you get Theo over to Highgate?"

"I need to think about that," I said firmly. "Definitely not today, and as for tomorrow . . . Look, you should know that we have reservations about how this whole nanny-share thing is going to work. Whether it's really the best thing for Theo. In the long term, I mean."

There was a brief silence. Then, in the calm, distant voice I was getting so familiar with, Miles said, "Well, don't think too fucking long, Pete."

And then the phone went dead.

I RELATED ALL THIS to Maddie when she got home. "It's like a switch inside him suddenly gets thrown. Then, when the switch goes back again, it's as if it never happened."

Maddie nodded. "I think Lucy's scared of him, too."

As if on cue, our doorbell rang. We looked at each other. "Speak of the devil," I said quietly.

I went and pulled the door open, determined that this time I wasn't going to give any ground.

But as the man on the doorstep moved his umbrella, I saw it wasn't Miles. It was Don Maguire, the private investigator. He was holding out a thick white envelope, rapidly spotting with raindrops.

"I need to serve you this," he said. When I took it, he added, "I'm sorry it didn't work out." Then he turned and walked away through the rain.

Mystified and slightly alarmed, I took the envelope indoors and opened it. It contained a thick bundle of documents. At the top were two sheets, slightly damp, both headed *Notice of Proceedings*. I saw Miles's name.

"What is it?" Maddie asked.

"I'm not sure. But whatever it is, it doesn't look good." Quickly, I pulled the papers out and flicked through them. An official-looking document headed *Declaration of Parentage*. A photocopy of a birth certificate—Theo's. Something about mediation. And several blank forms headed *Respondent's Copy*.

"They're legal papers," I said, baffled. "There's a date for some sort of court hearing. But I don't understand. When I spoke to Miles, he didn't say anything about this."

Underneath the Notice of Proceedings was a form headed *C1: Application for an order, Children Act 1989 except care and supervision orders, Section 8 orders and orders related to enforcement of a contact order.* None of the words meant anything to me. I went through it line by line, desperate to understand what was going on. The first section was headed *About you—Person completing this application.* Miles had filled in his own name and address.

Section 2 was headed *The child(ren) and the order(s) applied for. For each child state (1) the full name, and (2) the type of order(s).* Underneath, Miles had written:

1. David Leopold Lambert—Special Guardianship Order

2. Theo Riley—Child Arrangements Order

"Oh my God." I felt the blood drain from my face.

"What?" Maddie said, concerned. "Is it Theo? He's not trying to swap them back after all?"

"It's worse than that," I said slowly. "I think he's trying to get them both."

48

<u>Case no. 12675/PU78B65: CAFCASS "Welcome Pack" letter received by Peter Riley and Madelyn Wilson, signed by Lyn Edwards, Family Court Adviser.</u>

Dear Ms. Wilson and Mr. Riley,

CAFCASS, the Children and Family Court Advisory Service, has been asked by the court to work with you and your child/ren. Our job is to provide the court with advice to help it decide on future arrangements for your child/ren.

I understand that this is a difficult time for you and your family. At CAFCASS our job is to make sure children are safe and that their views and interests are taken into account. This means that I need to ask questions about your situation. In the first instance I will telephone you to discuss any concerns you may have about the safeguarding of your child/ren. I will also telephone other parties in the case to seek their views. Following those calls, I will write a letter to the court setting out whether there are any safeguarding issues that the court should be aware of, and if so, what I think should be done about them.

We recognize that you may not be in agreement with recommendations I may make to the court and this can be challenged during the court proceedings. If, however, you are unhappy with any part of my practice, please tell me or my manager as soon as possible so that we can quickly understand your concerns and try to put things right.

Yours sincerely,
Lyn Edwards
Family Court Adviser

Wherever possible CAFCASS uses recycled paper and black ink to reduce costs and our carbon footprint.

Case no. 12675/PU78B65, Exhibit 24, retrieved from DadStuff.net.

HELP—NEED GOOD CHILD LAW SOLICITOR URGENTLY.

Homedad85—Level 5 poster. Member since 2018.
Need a lawyer who knows about family law. Just been served 2x Notice of Proceedings—first hearing is in THREE WEEKS. Received a bunch of forms (C1, C100, C1A, and a letter from some people called CAFCASS) and SOMEONE APPEARS TO HAVE GOTTEN A COURT TO CHANGE MY SON'S BIRTH CERTIFICATE WITHOUT US BEING TOLD ABOUT IT. The form has our name and address but one letter of our postcode has been changed. That makes it illegal, surely?

Please help asap. Going out of our minds with worry.

Graham775
Your best bet is to find a solicitor using the search engine on the Law Society website.

Onefineday

Birth certificate is for recording child's parents. Someone appears to have convinced a court that your DS isn't actually yours. I wonder how that can have happened?

Tanktop

Went through court and CAFCASS with my ex. Horrible experience, but can't recommend Anita Chowdry highly enough—child lawyer at Burnham Phillips. She's not cheap but she's worth every penny.

Onefineday

"Child lawyer," Tanktop? Wouldn't OP be better off with a grown-up?

49

MADDIE

"IT'S A HIGHLY UNUSUAL situation," Anita Chowdry says, looking up from the bundle. She seems impressed, even fascinated, by just how unusual it is.

"We've been so naïve," Pete says, shaking his head. "I can't believe how stupid we've been."

"Well, you're here now," Anita says briskly. "Would you like me to explain what the applicants have been up to?"

I like Anita. She seems bright and capable and entirely at ease with her hijab and pronounced south London accent. "Yes, please."

"The first thing they did was to apply to the family court for a declaration of parentage order. That involved them getting a court-approved doctor to take DNA samples from Theo—"

"Hang on," Pete says. "They took Theo to a doctor? I thought they used a sippy cup."

Anita glances down at the document. "The doctor came to

their house. The court would need to be sure there was absolutely no chance of misidentification, so they repeated the tests. But the doctor would only have needed cheek swabs, so Theo probably wouldn't have been aware of anything unusual going on. The Lamberts then asked the court to confirm that they're Theo's natural parents, and having done that, to direct that his birth certificate be amended." She holds up her hand to forestall Pete's protests. "Not sending the Notice of Proceedings to the correct address was sneaky, but there's absolutely no chance the court will overturn it on that basis. The Lamberts probably just didn't want to alert you to what they were doing."

"We had no idea," Pete says, shaking his head. "No idea at all."

"In any case, being declared his legal parents means they now have the right to apply for a Child Arrangements Order—what used to be called custody."

Pete puts his head in his hands.

"There was something in the bundle about mediation," I say. "We didn't quite understand it, but it definitely said mediation would take place."

Anita nods. "Actually, it's already happened."

Pete's head shoots up. "*What?*"

"It's a legal requirement that applicants for a Child Arrangements Order attend a mediation meeting. But there's no absolute requirement that they attend with the other party—if they can convince the mediator they've explored all the possibilities and that further discussion wouldn't work, the mediator can simply sign the certificate that allows them to proceed. Besides, you have to remember that mediation is primarily aimed at divorcing couples. Here you've got a situation where a husband and wife both turn up together, singing off the same hymn sheet and probably both saying how accommodating they've tried to be—it's hardly surprising they were waved through."

Pete slumps again. He'd been pinning all his hopes on the mediation, I realize. It's all part of his general belief that reasonableness and dialogue are the answer to everything.

"The court can still order mediation at the initial hearing, if it chooses to," Anita adds. "I wouldn't get your hopes up, though. A judge won't usually do that if the delay could lead to potential harm to the child."

"Harm!" Pete stares at her. "To Theo? What harm? That's ridiculous."

"The definition of harm in the Children Act is pretty broad. The applicants have listed several examples on the C1A which they believe may qualify. One is that you let Theo wander off and get lost on a shopping trip. Another is that you allowed him to eat a tub of salt, resulting in a visit to the emergency room. They also say they have photographic evidence of bruising to his legs—"

"He bruised his legs playing rugby with Miles!" Pete shouts.

"Of course," Anita says calmly. "I'm simply telling you what they've alleged, which is that the bruises were caused by you forcibly holding him down on a church step, in front of witnesses. Oh, and they're asking for an accelerated process because they claim the three of you could be a flight risk." She looks at me. "You're an Australian citizen, I understand? And Theo has an Australian passport?"

I nod. "We visited his grandparents last Christmas. And since Pete and I aren't married, it was easier to get him an Australian one."

"Then I think it's highly likely they'll succeed in getting the process expedited. Which in some ways is unfortunate, because they've already stolen a march on you." Anita turns a page. "They've also asked the court to make a Prohibited Steps Order preventing you from taking Theo abroad, on the basis that the people listed in his passport as his parents no longer have parental responsibility for him."

"What do you mean—'no longer have parental responsibility'?" I say, baffled. "We're still his day-to-day carers, surely? At least until a court decides otherwise?"

Anita considers. "Have you told the council you're private fostering?"

"I don't even know what that is," Pete says despairingly.

"Caring for someone else's child. It might have given you some protection if the council had already looked into the situation and decided you were doing a good job. As it is, notifying them is a legal requirement that you've failed to carry out, which isn't a big deal but probably doesn't help us." The solicitor puts her pen down. "I'm afraid you're in a very unusual situation, legally speaking. Generally, you can only apply for court orders to do with children if you have parental responsibility for them—and while that would automatically include any child who'd lived with you for three years, anything less doesn't count. If the child is two, and you aren't his parents or legal guardians and you're no longer listed as such on his birth certificate, you effectively have no rights over him whatsoever." She pulls another document out of the bundle. "So when, for example, the applicants say they want Theo to continue coming to their house every day to be looked after by their nanny, technically that's their decision to make."

"Over my dead body," Pete says, clenching his fists.

Anita glances at him. "You might want to think through the possible ramifications before you decide not to comply," she says mildly. "As you've probably gathered, there's an organization called CAFCASS that'll be involved—independent social workers who'll make a recommendation to the court based on what they think is best for the child. It's very, very rare for the judge not to go along with their views. If the applicants can argue you're not acting in the child's best interests, and the CAFCASS officer agrees, it may not be helpful to your case."

Pete shakes his head. "This nanny share *isn't* in Theo's best interests. He needs to socialize with children who are the same developmental age as him. Being at the Lamberts' with a nanny who barely speaks English and a child with special needs isn't helping."

"And can you offer him an environment where he *will* be with other children his age?"

After a moment Pete sighs. "Not right now. He was thrown out of nursery for hitting."

"So where is he today?"

"At a neighbor's house. She homeschools, but her kids are older. She's just doing us a favor so we could both come to this meeting."

"Well, I strongly suggest you talk it over with the CAFCASS officer before you go against the biological parents' wishes. But if Theo's been violent with other children, be prepared for them to ask some tough questions about your own parenting style as well."

"Jesus," Pete says. "*Jesus.* I can't believe this is happening."

"That's not to say the Lamberts will succeed in taking Theo away from you," Anita adds. "Usually, the courts work on what's called the no order principle—in other words, when in doubt, leave things as they are. This is clearly a very unusual case, but the bottom line is that the court will have to decide returning Theo to his birth family is in his best interests. Hopefully, they'll conclude that the status quo is actually better for all concerned."

"Well, it *obviously* is," Pete says. "And that's what Miles and Lucy thought, too, before it all went crazy."

"Did they put anything in writing?"

Pete shakes his head. We've been back over every email, looking for something that might prove what the Lamberts agreed to, but there's nothing specific, just vague protestations of friendship and goodwill.

"When did they start all this legal stuff?" I ask.

Anita checks one of the forms. "About eight weeks ago."

"You see?" I say quietly to Pete. "Eight weeks. That would have been just after our first meeting with them."

He doesn't reply. His eyes look haunted.

I turn back to Anita. "And David? What does this mean for him?"

"David's case is completely different from Theo's. The Lamberts are asking the court's permission to apply for a Special Guardianship Order. SGOs are quite a recent invention—they're sometimes called super guardianships, because once you have one, you can overrule the wishes of everyone else connected with the child, even the natural parents—in other words, you. However, it's not clear whether the Lamberts actually qualify as potential guardians under the Children Act—just as you have very few legal rights over Theo, they have very few over David. They're arguing that, as he has such complex needs, they're already his de facto guardians and it's in his best interests for that to be recognized in law. Again, I think the social worker's report will be crucial."

My head is swimming, but I force myself to remain calm. "Will we still be allowed to see him? If they get what they want, I mean?"

Anita consults the bundle. "To a certain extent. One of the things the judge has to consider is whether the natural parents can meet the child's needs. The Lamberts have written a statement to address that point." She reads aloud, " 'The respondents have consistently shown little interest in their birth son, visiting him only when pressed to do so, or when dropping the applicants' birth son off for free childcare. They have displayed little awareness of his medical condition, on one occasion giving him chocolate, which would have necessitated hospital treatment had we not intervened. They have never bought him gifts, apart from some secondhand books the applicants' birth son had grown out of that were stored in their attic. The books were later found to be moldy, causing a chest infection which required hospital treatment. Nevertheless, recognizing the importance which the courts place on parental contact, the applicants will offer the respondents access to David by means of a supervised two-hour session at a registered contact center once a month.'"

"*Unbelievable,*" Pete says furiously. "They've twisted everything. That chocolate was before we even knew David *had* a medical condition. And I swear those books weren't moldy." He snaps his fingers. "Wait a minute. There's proof we care about David. A film of me reading to him on Facebook. And Lucy calling me a marvel."

He gets out his phone and starts scrolling. After a few moments his shoulders sag. "She's deleted it."

"Or rather, Miles has," I say slowly. "He has access to her Facebook account."

"I'm afraid that kind of thing's to be expected," Anita says. "The family courts are, quite literally, a law unto themselves. Everything hinges on the interests of the child—and, since that's a call usually made by a judge sitting on his or her own without a jury, tiny scraps of evidence can become quite significant. But don't despair. They're also pretty good at seeing through all the chaff and focusing on the real issues. And just as with Theo, we'll argue the no order principle with David—that the status quo is best for all concerned. If we can get the social workers on board with that, the court is likely to agree."

Pete nods. "That makes sense. Any social worker worth their salt is bound to see through this nonsense."

I say slowly, "I don't want to do that."

They both turn to me—Pete surprised, Anita concerned.

I add, "We've got to fight for Theo, obviously. But we can't abandon David. Yes, I think Lucy loves him in her own way, but Miles—deep down, I think Miles despises him. I think he only wants to keep him for Lucy's sake, and because he's hoping for a massive payout if his lawsuit's successful. And he's our *son.* I won't leave my child to be brought up by a man like that. I can't. I want to fight for David, too."

50

MADDIE

PETE LOOKS AT ME, aghast. I stare back at him defiantly.

"It'll be harder to argue," Anita says mildly. "Effectively, you'll have to mirror what the Lamberts are doing—a Declaration of Parentage Order, a Child Arrangements Order, *and* a Special Guardianship Order. But you're eight weeks behind them—which means the first hearings in Theo's case will take place before you're even off the starting blocks with David."

"He's my child," I repeat. "I can't leave him to be brought up by that—that *monster*. All along, we've let Miles push us around. Well, it stops now. He's picked the wrong family to bully. If he can fight for both kids, so can we."

"Mads . . ." Pete says. "Are you really sure about this? Bear in mind how complex David's needs are. Could we really cope with that?"

I look at him steadily. "I know what I'm asking is unfair, be- cause as the primary carer you'll be the one who has to do the most for him. Don't forget, we should have access to the money from his hospital settlement, which will help. But even without that, you're a brilliant dad and a really caring person. I think you can do it. But it's got to be a joint decision. If you don't want to, we won't."

After a moment, Pete blows out his cheeks. "All right. Let's beat the bastard at his own game. Christ, I can't believe I'm saying that. But you're right. We need to rescue David, too." He turns back to Anita. "Is there anything else?"

"The final document here is an application for child maintenance for David. Again, you could reciprocate by making a similar claim for Theo, but of course David has significant extra expenses associated with his special needs, including a full-time nanny." Anita looks up from the papers. "Given what you've told me about the Lamberts' situation, I imagine they're just trying to add an element of financial pressure on top of everything else. Speaking of which, you should be aware that fighting for custody of both children is going to be a lot more expensive than arguing for the status quo."

"How much?" Pete asks.

"If the case is straightforward, I'd estimate between fifteen and twenty thousand pounds. But something tells me this one won't be—straightforward, that is. The other side is already throwing everything they've got at it. I think they'll take every opportunity to escalate it further. So really, the sky's the limit."

"I don't suppose you'd act on a no-win no-fee basis," Pete says hopefully.

Anita shakes her head. "My time costs are three hundred pounds an hour plus VAT. And starting from the moment you ask me to act for you, you'll need to pay me weekly. If you get into arrears, I'll have to stop work. I'm sorry if that sounds brutal, but this is a small practice and we're good at what we do. If you need to take out a second mortgage on your home, which is what many of our clients do, I have a colleague who can help with that."

Pete looks at me. "We'd better speak to your dad."

. . .

THAT NIGHT, I SKYPE my parents. I do it in the bedroom, leaving Pete downstairs. He doesn't object. We both know my dad is going to point out that we were bloody fools for not taking his advice sooner.

To be fair, he hears me out. Telling him what's happened, I find myself crying, almost for the first time since the Lamberts' legal bundle arrived. Pete and I are still trying to be positive for each other, reassuring each other that the Lamberts' lies won't be believed. But now, putting everything that's happened into words, I sob like a little girl.

"Okay," Dad says when I finally get to the end. "So what's the plan?"

I smile through the tears. It had been a catchphrase of my childhood—*What's the plan, Madelyn?*—said every time I got into trouble or faced some knotty problem. "We need money. We're going to fight for them both."

There's a long silence before he says, "There is another option."

"Such as?"

"Pack a bag for you and Theo, go to the airport first thing tomorrow, and come home."

I shake my head. "I can't do that. Besides, I think they're going to notify the passport people."

"The judge won't rule on that until the first hearing, though, will he? If you leave tomorrow, you'll be fine. And once you're home, there'll be nothing they can do. We'll tie them up with lawyers if necessary. By the time they get anywhere, Theo will be at school here in Australia and it won't be in his interests to be uprooted again."

"And Pete?" I say gently. "What about him?"

"Well, that's between the two of you. But if he loves you, he'll follow you. It's not like he's leaving behind some high-flying career, is it?"

Just for a moment, I'm tempted. To walk out of this mess, to leave everything behind and flit back to my family on the other side of the world. I'll get another job in advertising, and Pete will be in a foreign country, as a travel journalist should be. Perhaps he can even work for a newspaper again. But I can't do it.

"I can't leave David," I say. "If I came home, I'd be abandoning your grandson."

Dad doesn't reply for a moment. "You were always headstrong, Madelyn."

I start crying again. "Like father, like daughter, then. Will you lend us the money?"

He sighs. "I'm a businessman, girl. A bloody tough one at that. If I'm going to lend you money, I want a return on my investment."

I don't understand. "What do you mean?"

"A time limit on how long you'll stay in the UK."

I stare at his grainy face on the iPad screen.

"I love you," he adds. "And I miss my little girl. I miss you like hell." His own voice cracks. "I can stand another year of this, but then I want you back for good. You can even bring that bludger you've shacked up with—I'll find him a good job in my company if needs be, something to make himself useful. It's not much to ask, is it?"

"I know you love me, Dad," I whisper. "I've always known that."

"Well, then. Let me know how much you need, and I'll wire it to you."

AFTER THE CALL IS over, I cry some more, then wash my eyes with cold water before going downstairs.

"How'd it go?" Pete asks softly.

"It was fine," I say shortly. "We're remortgaging the house."

51

PETE

WE BOTH TOOK THEO to the Lamberts' next morning. We'd talked long into the night about whether to go at all, but, as Maddie pointed out, it would be crazy to pay a lawyer three hundred pounds an hour and then ignore her advice.

I was apprehensive but determined. I'd been awake early, even before Theo came into our bed, running through different versions of the scene in my mind. If Miles was there, I'd decided, I'd be icy but polite. I certainly wasn't going to give him the satisfaction of thinking he'd managed to frighten us.

Maddie and I were both silent in the car, while Theo chuntered quietly in the back. He hadn't been happy about going to our neighbor the day before—when we collected him, she'd told us he'd deliberately kicked her son's prized model of the moon across the room, breaking it. Theo, listening, had only said mutinously, "Want to go to Moles's house." Now, when he recognized the buildings on our route, he started chanting. "Moles's house! Moles's house! *I like Moles's house!*"

"Moles is not as nice as we thought," I said to shut him up. Maddie gave me a warning glance.

"Why?" Theo demanded. "Why, Daddy?"

"Long story."

Theo was silent. He liked stories, but not long ones.

When we climbed the steps to the Lamberts' front door, it felt almost like a rerun of our first visit. But this time, it wasn't Miles who opened the door, but Tania.

"Good morning, good morning, Theo," she said in her heavily accented English. For a moment I thought Lucy must have sent her to the door deliberately, to avoid meeting us, but then Lucy herself appeared in the hallway behind her, elegantly dressed as always in a pair of designer jeans and a black pashmina.

"Hello Pete. Maddie. How nice to see you. And Theo, of course. Are you coming in?"

Maddie said firmly, "Yes. I'd like to see David."

"Of course. He's in the playroom." Lucy indicated the way.

"Lucy . . ." I said, lingering behind.

"Yes?"

I said quietly, "How can you behave as if nothing has happened? You've served Notice of Proceedings on us."

Her vague smile didn't waver. "Well, it's just legal stuff, isn't it? I'm sure you understand. Miles said we have to go through the proper process and it'll all come out in the wash. I'm not really thinking about that side of things, actually," she added nervously as she gestured me toward the playroom. "And as you've always said, we should all try to be nice to each other, whatever's going on."

"That's *not* what I said, Lucy. And I don't think trying to take our son away from us *is* being nice."

Just for a moment, the smile crumbled. She said in a small voice, "If you'd only been a bit more receptive to the school thing.

And then Cornwall. Miles—he's very *fair*. He just doesn't like it when people aren't straight with him."

"'The *school* thing'?" I stared at her. "*That's* what this is about? He's going to all this effort to take Theo away from us, just so he can pack him off to boarding school?" I actually found myself laughing, a short hollow bark at the irony of it all. "Well, it isn't going to happen."

"Miles says . . ." Her voice was barely more than a whisper. "I'm sure you'll love the Dragon School when Theo actually goes there. Miles is usually right about these things. And anyway, the decision's made now, isn't it? We've got parental authority or whatever it's called. So really, there's not much point in getting worked up about it. Would you like some tea?"

I sighed. "No. I really wouldn't like some tea."

Maddie reappeared. She had tears on her cheeks, which she flicked away angrily. "Let's go."

Outside, we lingered on the pavement, delaying the moment when I'd get in the car and she'd head for the Tube station. "Incredible," I said, shaking my head. "Incredible. It's like he's brainwashed her."

"I guess if you're married to Miles Lambert, you have to give him your absolute loyalty," Maddie said drily.

My phone pinged and I checked the screen. "Who's that?" she asked.

"Greg, seeing if we can meet up. I'll tell him no. I want to spend the morning researching CAFCASS."

"Makes sense. I'll see you tonight, then. Love you."

"Love you," I echoed.

She gave me a hug and a kiss on the cheek and was gone. I called after her, "Have a good day," even though I knew that wasn't possible, not with everything that was going on.

Then I lifted my phone and replied to the text from Bronagh.

52

Case no. 12675/PU78B65, Exhibit 26: deleted texts from Peter Riley's iPhone, (a) from Bronagh Walsh to Peter Riley, and (b) from Peter Riley to Bronagh Walsh in reply.

Pete, it's me. You probably don't want to see me right now but I really need to see you. It's all gone to s**te at St A's and I've been suspended pending investigation. Can we meet? x

Just dropped Theo off, so I can do this morning. Say the Pret near Great Portland St station? At ten?

53

Case no. 12675/PU78B65, Incident Report, submitted by Miles Lambert to CAFCASS as part of Applicants' Supporting Documents bundle, pp 32–36.

5. The following day, the respondents brought Theo to our house to use our nanny and facilities as usual. In response to a comment from my wife that we should try to be civil to each other during the legal process, Mr. Riley's response was to shout that she was "trying to take our son away from us," and that our choice of school "wasn't going to happen." (8:47 A.M., captured on tape.) My wife offered them tea, which they forcefully declined.

54

PETE

"THAT JOB'S EVERYTHING TO me. Everything. Ah, shite. There goes my makeup, for the fifteenth time today." Bronagh attempted to slide the tears out of her eyes with her knuckle.

"You're good at it, too. I don't know how we'd have gotten through those first weeks without you. What the hospital's doing to you is just plain wrong."

Bronagh looked at me fondly. "There you go, Pete. Always thinking of someone else. When what you've been through is ten times worse."

I shrugged. "I was made redundant eighteen months ago. So I know what it's like, thinking your bosses appreciate what you do, then discovering that actually they'll kick you out without a second thought if it helps save their own skins."

She nodded ruefully. "It's like one of my friends always says— *Love your job, but don't expect it to love you back.*"

I stirred my cappuccino. "But *why* have they suspended you? I mean, I get that they have to investigate what happened, but how does the finger of blame end up getting pointed at you? There were two babies, after all, and you were only responsible for one of them." I was hoping Bronagh's suspension wasn't anything to do with me giving Miles her name, but since he seemed to have an almost magical ability to make things happen the way he wanted, perhaps it was. Or was I simply becoming paranoid about him?

"Sure, and they've suspended Paula, too." Bronagh looked weary. "The thing is, they could have gone for any of us if they'd wanted. The first thing they did was run a security audit—comparing the number of tag-off incidents recorded by the system with the number each nurse had reported to Security. Well, surprise surprise, we didn't always report them, even though every time a tag comes off you're meant to initiate a lockdown, call Security, and check every single baby on the ward. If we did *that*, we'd never get any nursing done—a tag comes off almost every day, for Pete's sake." She smiled. "Sorry—not Pete's sake, but you know what I mean. Prem babies are small and the tags are designed for regular-sized infants. Never mind that in this case, it wasn't even a tag slipping off that was the problem—that would have meant two tags coming off at the exact same time on the exact same day, then somehow getting from one incubator to another, right across the unit, and why would that happen when it was two separate nurses dealing with those cots? This most likely happened before the tags even got put on."

I remembered Don Maguire saying much the same thing. Mind you, he'd also said there was no reason for all this to end up in the courts. "In which case, it's hardly your fault, is it? It could have been the paramedics, or one of the doctors who dealt with both babies."

Bronagh nodded. "That's what I reckon. Most times, when a preterm baby is delivered in a hospital that isn't equipped to deal with it, they'll call the neonatal ambulance service and request a transfer while they're still doing the C-section. Then, rather than hang around fiddling with tags after they've pulled the wee thing out, they just put it straight in skin wrap to keep it warm—that's like a little plastic bag with a ziplock—"

"Our baby was in one of those," I interrupted. "I remember because it was so unexpected, seeing him inside a bag like that."

"Well, there you go. And then they either pop the tag inside, or—more likely, because they don't want to unzip the bag and let the heat out—just put it inside the mobile incubator, next to the baby. This is a paper tag we're talking about, not the electronic ones we have, because different hospitals have different systems. So when a baby arrives, we transfer it from the mobile incubator to one of ours, and transfer the tag information to our software at the same time."

I thought. "And if there were two loose paper tags like that, they might have gotten mixed up when the mobile cots were next to each other on arrival."

"Exactly."

"Then you're in the clear, surely?"

Bronagh shrugged. "It all depends when the electronic tag got put on, doesn't it? If I put it on as soon as the baby was stable, I followed protocol. If I had a cup of tea and did it at the end of my shift, they'll try to hang this whole thing on me. I'm already looking at a disciplinary for not reporting every tag-off incident, so if they choose to decide I left it too long, I could be out on my ear." She sighed. "And I bet there's plenty of high-ups who'd prefer it to look like a mistake by an individual who didn't follow proper procedures, rather than admit their whole expensive tagging system is shite in a bucket."

"Ah," I said, thinking through the implications. "Because St. Alexander's has been downgraded, you mean? Management wants this done and dusted and swept under the carpet. *Don't worry, we've fired the person who messed up. Lessons have been learned, et cetera. Nothing to see here anymore.*"

She leaned forward, her blue eyes fixed on mine. "The thing is,

Pete, they're obviously going to ask you for your recollections of that day."

"I guess so, yes."

"If you could . . . I mean, I don't want to put words in your mouth, but . . ." She stopped. "Sorry. Bad choice of phrase. And I'm absolutely not saying that you should do it as a favor because of . . . you know. Just that the earlier you saw that tag on Theo's leg, the less this shitestorm is going to fall on me. Or Paula, for that matter."

"I understand," I said slowly. "The fact is, it was all such a muddle that day . . . I don't know exactly what I'll say yet. But I'll work something out. And whatever happens, I'll try to make it clear it couldn't have been down to you." After all, I reasoned, if it *was* me who put Bronagh in the firing line, the least I could do was to get her out of it.

"Thanks Pete. You're massive. Oh Jesus, there I go again." Bronagh blinked back tears. "I could tell you were a good'un as soon as I saw you with Theo. I see a lot of new dads, you know, and I can always tell." She gently touched the top of my finger with hers. "I hope Maddie knows what a lucky woman she is."

55

MADDIE

I GET THE CALL from CAFCASS while I'm at work. There'd been an automated text earlier, saying a family court adviser would call me at three unless I replied to say it's inconvenient. It *is* inconvenient, very, but I feel an obscure urge to comply, to be a model respondent, even though the call is clearly being arranged by a computer and changing the time can't possibly make any difference.

At quarter to three I find an empty office and set out a bottle of water, a pen, a stack of paper, and a list of pertinent facts. At two minutes past, my mobile rings, the ID listed as UNKNOWN NUMBER.

"Hello, Maddie Wilson," I answer formally.

"Maddie, it's Lyn from CAFCASS here. Is now a good time to chat?" The voice is soft, with a slight Welsh lilt to it.

"Of course." I note that word "chat." Somehow I doubt we're going to be having a cozy natter and a gossip.

Lyn has clearly been trained to use a gentle, soothing voice. She explains that this call isn't about the issue the courts are dealing with, only to establish whether the child—"Theo, is it?"—is at any risk of harm. "That could be physical harm arising from abuse or domestic harm, Maddie. Or it could be emotional harm arising from the behavior of the adults. It could even be neglect, do you see?"

"Yes, of course."

"Basically, I have a checklist here I'll go through, and then at the end I'll make sure you've had time to cover the issues *you* want to raise. There are no trick questions, so it's best just to answer honestly, Maddie. Because if you weren't completely honest, and we found out about it later, we would have to tell the court, and then the court would have to take that into account, Maddie, do you see?"

"Right," I say, wondering how many times Lyn is going to say "Maddie" and "do you see."

"So I've run your name through the police database and social services, and I'm pleased to say there's nothing there. But is there anything we might have missed, Maddie? Have you or anyone in the family had any contact with police or social care before now?"

"No."

"Rightio. Has there been any domestic violence at all?" Lyn might have been asking whether I'd prefer to pay by direct debit or card.

"No."

"Have you ever taken any nonprescription or illegal drugs?"

"No, never." Obviously I have, but the last time was three years ago, in Australia, and there's no way they can possibly find out about it.

"Do you drink alcohol?"

"Sometimes, yes."

"How often?"

"I sometimes have a glass of wine in the evenings."

"And how many units would you say you drink a week? If a bottle of wine is, say, ten units?"

"Twenty units?" I know I'm grossly understating, but I suspect that if I tell the truth it might count against me.

"Has any family member been convicted of violence, or had an allegation of child abuse made against them?" Lyn's questions are speeding up now.

"No."

"Is the child exhibiting any concerning behaviors, such as poor performance at school, bedwetting, sexualized behavior, or being clingy?"

"No. Well," I clarify, "there have been a couple of occasions where he's been a bit rough with other kids—grabbed their toys, that kind of thing. But he's two, so it's to be expected to a certain extent. And he's the very opposite of clingy."

"Of course. These are just standard questions, do you see, so I have to ask them all. Has the child ever reported any abuse or harm to you personally?"

"No, never."

"And finally, what do you think the child's wishes are in this situation? Do you think he would rather stay with your partner or yourself?"

"I don't think you understand," I say, baffled. "Pete and I aren't separating."

"Are you not?" Lyn sounds surprised.

"No, it's much more complicated than that." Briefly I explain what's going on.

"Well, that does sound tricky," Lyn says when I've finished. "And yes, I see it does say something about that here, but I must have missed it."

Or didn't bother to read the paperwork properly in the first place, I think cynically.

"But I have to ask the question anyway," Lyn continues. "What do you think Theo's wishes are in this situation?"

"Well, he's two, so we obviously don't want to frighten him by telling him he might be forcibly taken away from the people he thinks of as Mummy and Daddy and handed over to another family," I say patiently. "To that extent, he doesn't even know there *is* a situation. And we've been careful to keep things with the other family as cordial as possible, so as not to upset him."

"That sounds sensible. Let me just check I have everything . . . Oh yes. Do either of you have any mental health issues?"

"No," I say. I take a deep breath. "That is, not recently. I had a brief episode of postpartum psychosis shortly after Theo came home from hospital. But that was two years ago and it resolved with treatment."

I can hear Lyn's keyboard clicking as she writes all this down. "It can't affect this case, can it?" I add.

"Did it involve any harm or neglect to either the child or yourself, Maddie?"

"No. And in any case, it was triggered by my premature baby being in intensive care for five weeks. It's relatively common after childbirth and there's absolutely no possibility of it recurring. I'm not even Theo's primary carer, for Christ's sake—" I stop, conscious of the importance of not getting worked up. "Sorry. I mean 'for goodness' sake.' I just don't see how it can possibly be relevant to what's happening now."

"I don't suppose it is. But I still have to write it all down, do you see? And are you still taking any medication for that condition?"

"No," I say firmly. "I was prescribed antidepressants but I came off them over a year ago. I'm absolutely fine."

"Would you have any objection to me contacting your GP for a copy of your medical notes? Just to confirm what you've told me? I can ask the court to make a formal order for them, but really, it's so much easier if we're all working together, isn't it?"

"Yes, of course," I say. Just for a moment, I feel dizzy. How did an ordinary professional couple come to have so many court cases going on simultaneously? Fighting for Theo, fighting for David, suing the hospitals . . . It feels like each one is a separate series of plates spinning on sticks, a forest of toppling, precarious crockery that has to be kept from smashing to the ground.

You can do this, I tell myself. After all, it's no more complex than a major TV production, and I do a dozen of those every year.

Lyn is saying, "And is there anything you'd like to tell *me,* Maddie, about how you got into this situation, or how it might be resolved?"

I look down at my notes, all the pertinent facts I'd intended to work into the conversation. Suddenly they all seem irrelevant, a catalog of failed attempts at being reasonable in a situation where reason is redundant. "Yes," I say shortly. "A man turned up on our doorstep one day with the intention of taking our son. How would *you* react to that? We didn't want to end up here, but it was probably inevitable. And there's only one way to resolve it. We need to beat him. He needs a court to tell him he's lost and that he can't have Theo, not ever. Otherwise, he'll never stop trying."

56

Case no. 12675/PU78B65, Exhibit 29: statement by Reverend Sheila Lewis, The Vicarage, Willesden Green, NW10 1AQ.

My name is Reverend Sheila Lewis and I am the vicar of All Souls' Church, Willesden Green. I have been asked by Miles Lambert to write a brief note describing an incident that took place at Theo Riley's baptism service.

From the start, Theo seemed agitated and was disruptive, hurling books at a side chapel and cheering when he succeeded in hitting the cross. We are accustomed these days to children being noisy during services and to some extent we tolerate it, but this went far beyond what I would have considered normal. I tried pausing in my liturgy and giving a meaningful glance in Theo's direction, but the parents—that is, Peter Riley and Maddie Wilson—were slow to take the hint. When they did intervene, it became clear why this was: They had almost no control over Theo whatsoever. Theo then burrowed under the pews, a situation from which Mr. Riley seemed powerless to extricate him. When a member of the congregation finally apprehended the child, Mr. Riley was visibly angry and, under the guise of sitting Theo on "the naughty step," pushed him down forcibly by the thighs. I am told by Mr. Lambert that this produced bruising on Theo's legs, which is certainly consistent with what I saw. I understand Mr. Lambert has obtained phone footage of this incident from another member of the congregation.

Theo is a charming little boy who does not seem in the least malevolent or ill tempered, merely boisterous. I suspect he would simply benefit from a more consistent parenting style. This is an opinion I have formed over several visits by him to my church, as Mr. Riley and Ms. Wilson have become regular members of my congregation.

I have also been made aware by Mr. Lambert why this may be. The vicar here at All Souls' is able to make available to long-standing churchgoers a small number of places at the local Church of England primary school, which has been rated Excellent by school inspectors. Mr. Lambert tells me that Mr. Riley used the phrase *On your knees to save the fees* in this context. While I have no way of knowing if this was indeed what Mr. Riley said, and would in any case encourage people to come and worship with us whatever their true purpose, it saddens me to learn that some members of our community may have a cynical motive for doing so.

57

PETE

"IF YOU COULD JUST tell us in your own words what happened that day," Grace Matthews said.

Resisting the urge to ask who else's words I might be tempted to use, I said, "You have to understand, it was all a blur. I'd had to abandon Maddie after an emergency operation. It was clearly touch and go whether our baby would live, and if he did live, whether he'd be brain-damaged. I had no idea what was going on or how I could help." I looked over at Maddie. "To be honest, I was in a complete panic."

We were in an interview room at NHS Resolution, a surprisingly striking modern office building in Buckingham Palace Road. Grace Matthews had asked us in for what she described as an evidence-gathering meeting. We wouldn't be discussing any potential compensation, she emphasized, merely contributing our recollections to the initial investigation.

The lawyer Justin Watts had told us this was normal. "At this stage, they simply want to find out what happened. There's no arguing with the fact that a swap *did* take place, but from their perspective, finding out how it occurred is the most urgent priority."

"Will you be there?" I asked.

"I really shouldn't need to be. And I'm trying to keep our time costs down as much as possible."

Now Grace Matthews nodded in response to my explanation. She looked more like the floor manager of a midlevel department store than a high-flying investigator—dumpy, wearing an ill-fitting suit and matching skirt, with boxy glasses that kept slipping down her nose. "But at some point, you presumably became aware of the tag on Theo's leg. That is, on the leg of the infant you thought was Theo."

"I suppose so. But there were so many things on him by then—intravenous lines, an oxygen sensor, the cooling suit . . . The security tag was the least dramatic of them all."

"Can you say when you *did* first notice it?"

I shrugged helplessly. "Not really. When we got to St. Alexander's, I went with the paramedics who were wheeling the portable incubator. We shared the lift with two more paramedics who also had a mobile cot with them—I suppose that was the one with Theo in, although of course I didn't know that at the time. Then they were both rushed into the NICU, where the doctors were waiting. I got pushed out of the way—"

"Where was Mr. Lambert at this point?" Grace Matthews interjected. "Had he been with you in the lift?"

I shook my head. "I'd have remembered if there was another dad in there. I don't think I saw him at all that day."

Grace Matthews made a note on a lined yellow pad, even though her male colleague was silently transcribing everything I said on his laptop, his fingers flying across the keys without him needing to look at either the keyboard or screen. Grace had a proper pen, I noticed, an old-fashioned one with a nib, which somehow seemed out of kilter with her dowdy appearance. Perhaps it was a present from someone. "Sorry for interrupting," she said as she wrote. "Go on."

"And then they worked on both babies simultaneously. I think the first thing was getting the umbilical lines in. The ambulance staff were doing their handover reports, and people were coming and going—it was pretty chaotic, and the doctors and nurses were turning from cot to cot, doing whatever it was they needed to do. I couldn't get close—I didn't really try to, in case I got in the way. Then there was a bit of a lull, and when the medical team was happy, they took Theo's mobile incubator over to a much bigger one in the corner and transferred him. That's when I met Bronagh—the main nurse responsible for Theo. She looked after the incubators in that area, so she hadn't really been involved before."

Grace Matthews nodded. "And you got a pretty good look at Theo then, presumably? When all the initial interventions were done?"

I thought back. "Yes. I remember thinking I hadn't really been able to see his face before."

"And can you recall seeing a tag on him at that point?"

"I think so," I said cautiously. "I mean, I couldn't absolutely swear to it, but when I try to picture it, it seems to me he had the security tag on his right ankle." I nodded slowly. "In fact, I'm sure that's right—that Theo had a tag on when I saw him in the larger incubator."

A frown touched Grace Matthews's face. "But you didn't actually see the nurse put it on?"

"No. But . . ." I stopped. "This is hard for me to admit. But the moment I found myself in a quiet corner and it felt like the immediate emergency was over, I broke down. I was crying for several minutes. She must have done it then, as soon as she took over. But I literally couldn't see in front of my own nose."

"Of course," Grace Matthews said. "I do understand, Mr. Riley. Seeing your child—or rather, the child you think is yours—being admitted to intensive care is obviously very stressful." She pushed the cap onto her fountain pen and placed it on her yellow pad. "Thank you for speaking to us today."

58

MADDIE

I KEEP QUIET DURING Pete's interview with Grace Matthews. It's him they want to talk to, after all, the person at the scene, and I didn't even get to the NICU until long after the mix-up had happened.

Afterward, we get an Uber home, too exhausted to face the Tube. As we crawl through the traffic, I look across at him. "I didn't realize you saw the tag on Theo's leg so soon."

He goes on looking out the window. "Well, I said I couldn't swear to it."

"Yes. But after that, you said you were certain. You told her you could picture it."

He doesn't reply at first, and for a moment I think he's going to say something else. But all he says is, "Pretty certain, yes."

"So the mix-up must have happened before that, in those first few minutes."

"When the original tags were loose. That's right."

I frown. "Were the tags loose? You didn't mention that."

"They would have come into the NICU separately, when the babies were zipped into the skin-wrap bags," he explains. "Grace Matthews would have known that. Although I didn't actually see them."

Then how do you know . . . I almost say, but he forestalls me. "This is so exhausting, isn't it? All these different legal actions."

"Perhaps that's what Miles is counting on. Perhaps he was always planning it this way, to ramp up the pressure."

Pete only shakes his head. But it's a gesture of despair, not disagreement.

WHEN WE GET HOME, he gets straight in the car to go and pick up Theo. I open my laptop to check my emails—I've told the office I'll work from home for the rest of the day—but something makes me go into my photo stream instead.

I haven't looked at the very first picture of my baby—the picture Pete texted while I was still in the recovery room at the private hospital—since the day it was taken. It's too raw, the memory of my revulsion at it too stark. But it automatically got saved to my iCloud along with all my other pictures, and now here it is. Grainy, a little blurred, taken over the shoulder of a doctor or nurse. No, definitely a nurse: I'd had no way of knowing it at the time, but that's Bronagh's slim back and jet-black hair. And the image might be blurry, but Pete always had the latest gadgets and the camera was a powerful one: As well as the stick-thin limbs and nose prongs that even now make me feel nauseous, you can see the tubes coming out of the cooling suit, the brake-light-red glow around the baby's left ankle from the oxygen sensor.

And no tag. There's no security tag on the other leg. Of that I'm sure.

Or am I? I peer at the photo again. To use Pete's phrase, I

couldn't absolutely swear to it. I can't even say if the wizened little creature in the cooling suit is Theo or David.

And Pete has said what he's said now. There'd be no point whatsoever in sending this picture to Grace Matthews and saying, sorry, he might have been mistaken. We'd effectively be announcing that he's an unreliable witness, someone whose entire testimony might be flawed. And that, in turn, might have repercussions for the payout.

No: Better to leave things as they are. As our lawyer said, finding out how the mix-up happened is an internal matter for the hospital. If Pete made a small mistake over the exact timing, it's hardly a big deal.

59

<u>Case no. 12675/PU78B65, Exhibit 31: deleted texts from</u>
<u>Peter Riley's iPhone, (a) from Peter Riley to Bronagh Walsh,</u>
<u>and (b) from Bronagh Walsh to Peter Riley, in reply.</u>

Saw them today. Said I remembered seeing the tag on Theo's leg a few minutes after he was transferred to your incubator.

You're a star. xxx

60

PETE

I DROVE TO HIGHGATE to collect Theo from the Lamberts' on autopilot. Not because I was worried about the small lie I'd told on Bronagh's behalf—I'd been pretty nonspecific, and in any case, it probably wasn't even a lie—but because I still couldn't get my head around everything that was going on. I even found myself wondering if we shouldn't pull out of suing the hospital—but since that legal action was the only one not costing us anything, and would hopefully raise the funds to pay Anita Chowdry's fees to boot, it seemed crazy to end it now.

I wasn't really thinking about the Lamberts as I walked up the steps to their door. I assumed the buzzer would be answered by Tania, or that possibly Lucy would be there, wittering on about cups of tea and being polite to each other. But the door was opened by Miles. He was wearing a T-shirt and running shorts.

"Pete," he said warmly. "How are you doing?"

I stared at him. I felt something I'd almost never felt in my life—a physical, atavistic hatred, an almost irresistible compulsion to do bloodcurdling violence to another human being. The hairs on the back of my neck rose and my face flushed involuntarily.

"I've come to collect Theo," I said curtly.

"He's just having a wash—finger painting got a bit messy. He'll be along in a minute."

I nodded, unwilling to engage in small talk. Miles put his head on one side and regarded me quizzically.

"You really hate me, don't you, Pete?" he said softly.

"I don't hate you," I said coldly. "I dislike what you're doing and the way you're doing it, that's all."

"Really?" He studied my face. "No, I think you hate me. I never waste time hating people." He stepped forward, pulling the door behind him so we couldn't be overheard. "You know, some pretty dark stuff happens in the scrum. Gouging, punching, a thumb in the shorts, collapsing the front row the moment you've got the ball . . . But after the match is over, you shake hands and buy each other a beer. Because it's the player who hit you hardest who you respect the most."

I stared at him. "This is not some fucking *game*."

"No." Miles shook his head emphatically. "It's a *contest*. A contest I will win. Not because I hate you, but because the prize of this particular contest is my son." He suddenly leaned in very close, so he was almost talking over my shoulder, his lips close to my ear. It was all I could do not to flinch. "But. Just. Remember. This. You have him on loan, nothing more. And if you do anything, anything at all, to undermine my future relationship with him, I will seek you out and I will kill you."

He stood back, smiling, just as Theo pulled the door open and ran out. "Daddeeee!" he cried excitedly, charging into my legs.

"Ready to go, Theo?" Without waiting for an answer, I took his hand and started down the steps.

"Bye, Theo," Miles called cheerily.

"Bye, Moles," Theo called back over his shoulder. "Love youuu!"

61

PETE

"HE DIDN'T MEAN IT," Maddie whispered.

I looked across at Theo, now engrossed in a wildlife documentary in which wolves were tearing a deer to pieces. It probably wasn't very age-appropriate, but for once he was actually looking quite peaceful, sitting cross-legged in front of the TV in his pajamas, sucking his thumb. "I know. Miles almost certainly taught him to say it. Bribed him with sweets or something." I paused. "But I could count on one hand the number of times Theo's spontaneously said that to *me*. And what if the CAFCASS people hear him and assume he does mean it?"

"So we'll tell them. Add it to the list: Miles Lambert has been coaching our son to say, 'I love you.'"

I watched Theo for a few moments. "*Why* doesn't he say it to us?"

"He's a boy. An unusually confident little boy. Which is a credit to your parenting."

"Maybe. Or . . ."

"What?"

The wolves, having brought down the deer, were now defending their meal from a bear three times their size. I said quietly, "Could he be a bit like his father? His biological father, I mean?"

Maddie replied immediately, which is how I knew she'd already thought about this. "In what way?"

"Nasty." There, I'd said it now. "Is Theo going to grow up to be a horrible bastard like Miles?"

Maddie put her hand on mine. "Of course not. Because, unlike Miles, Theo has you for a role model. Which is another reason we can't let the Lamberts get hold of him. If he were raised by them, then sent away to boarding school, he probably *would* turn into a nasty bastard. But here . . . it's like you said to Miles when you went for a drink. Here he'll get the best of both worlds."

"Perhaps." I didn't say that it increasingly felt as if the two worlds couldn't possibly coexist. That at some point they would simply crash into each other and explode. "Miles threatened to kill me today."

"*Seriously?* Was he angry?"

I shook my head. "Deadly calm. Like he always is when he drops the nice-guy act."

Maddie looked horrified. "He wouldn't dare try anything violent. Not in the middle of a court case."

"Let's hope not. But I think we should both be careful. Just in case. There was something about the way he said it . . . It gave me the creeps, put it that way."

I looked over at Theo, engrossed in the standoff between the wolf-pack leader and the bear. The leader, a she-wolf, was trying to wear the bear down, circling so it could never get a decent bite of the dead deer, but at the same time trying to stay out of range of the bear's claws.

As I looked at him, for the second time that day I felt an unfamiliar emotion. I looked at my son's face and felt, just for a moment, some of the visceral, all-consuming hatred I'd felt for his father.

I HAD MY OWN CAFCASS call the next day. At precisely eleven o'clock, my phone rang and Lyn Edwards introduced herself.

Maddie had already run me through the questions she'd been asked, so I knew roughly what to expect. No contact with social workers, no. No allegations of abuse. I tried to remain calm, even when Lyn asked me whether Maddie's mental health issues could affect Theo's safety.

"Maddie doesn't have mental health issues," I said politely. "Any more than someone who had a broken leg two years ago still has a broken leg."

"But someone who broke their leg might still have difficulty walking," Lyn pointed out, still in the same insurance-call-center voice. "Does Maddie, Peter?"

"Have difficulty walking? No."

Lyn didn't respond to my feeble attempt at a joke. "So there are no mental health issues currently, in your opinion."

"None whatsoever," I said firmly.

"And I understand that you're the primary carer?"

"That's correct."

"How would you describe your parenting style, Peter? Are you more of a structured person, do you see, or child-centered?"

"Well," I said carefully, sensing a verbal trap, "I don't really see a distinction between the two. We have boundaries, obviously, and Theo's aware that there are consequences for crossing them. But I also try to listen to his suggestions and opinions."

"I'll put 'both,' shall I? Oh, it won't let me do that. I'm afraid you'll have to choose."

I sighed. "Child-centered."

"Because there have been some concerns, Peter, haven't there? I understand Theo was asked to leave his nursery."

"He's a little late in learning to share toys, take turns, that sort of thing. Sometimes he hits or bites in order to get his own way. It's something we're working on, for example by using the naughty step."

"And what do you think Theo's wishes are in this situation, Peter? What are the outcomes he would like to see?"

"We haven't asked him," I said firmly. "Not because we don't want to take his feelings into account, but because this is much too momentous a decision for a two-year-old to take. It would cause him immense anxiety even to think about it."

"Yes, your partner said the same thing."

"Well, we've obviously discussed it."

"And is there anything you want to tell *me*, Peter?"

"Pete, please. And yes, there is actually. I want to remove Theo from the nanny share with the other party. I think it's holding his development back—he can't really take turns with David, and the nanny has a strong French accent, which isn't good for his delayed speech."

"I think we'd need to see what the court recommends before we make a big change like that, Peter. What would you do with him instead?"

"He's on the waiting list for a different local nursery."

"And have you asked Theo what his wishes are about going to a nursery?"

I hadn't, of course, mainly because I knew what he'd say. At the Lamberts' he was treated like a little prince. He never needed to share a toy. Why would he want to learn to take turns when he could have a well-stocked playroom all to himself, not to mention a nanny to fetch the toys and tidy up after him? I could tell him that nursery would be more fun because there'd be other children there, but the truth was, Theo didn't particularly like other children, not unless they were the meek, pliable kind who could be relied on to hand over their toys whenever he wanted them.

"Theo's wishes are mixed," I said at last. "He loved his last nursery, and it was definitely good for him to learn how to socialize with other children. I also have concerns that he's being overindulged by the current arrangement. For example, they've been coaching him to say 'I love you' to them."

"Have they now?" Lyn said. "And how would you know that?"

"He said it to Miles yesterday, when I collected him."

"But how do you know it was the result of being coached?"

"Well, it stands to reason," I said, exasperated. I was about to add, *Because he hardly ever says it to me,* when I thought better of it.

"I don't think we should make any assumptions when it comes to ascertaining Theo's feelings," Lyn was saying. "I'll write down that you think that, if you like, but also that there's no evidence to back it up."

62

Case no. 12675/PU78B65, Exhibit 32:
Report by Susy Carson, proprietor, Acol Road Nursery and Preschool.

I have been asked to write something about the circumstances that led to Theo Riley leaving Acol Road Nursery. Asking a parent to remove a child is not something we take lightly, we would only do it after a sustained pattern of behavior that has the potential to negatively impact the other children. In line with government guidelines half our staff either hold NVQ or BTech qualifications or are working toward them. We always aim to maintain the recommended staff–child ratios and at the current time are actively recruiting to achieve this. However, in line with many local facilities we do find it hard to retain staff, at the time under discussion we were down from eight persons to six. I was heavily involved in covering the shortfall myself, but providing an individual child with one-to-one shadowing to prevent harm was unfortunately not an option we were able to pursue.

The specific incident that led to Theo's removal was that he hit another two-year-old with a tumbler, leading to a large bruise and bleeding on Zack's forehead. Even had there not been bleeding, we would have written it in the Incident Book and discussed it with both sets of parents. However, this was the fourth hitting/biting incident in five weeks and it was clear previous efforts to teach Theo to play safely with other children were not working. We had previously had several conversations with the father about the situation and the need for consistent strategies including the home. Whether Mr. Riley followed through on these is not known, however Theo's behavior clearly had not improved. When I informed Mr. Riley that Theo would be leaving us he did not take it well and I was forced to ask him to moderate his language.

Although we report incidents to parents anonymously, on this occasion both parents I spoke to were able to identify the other child. I feel it is my duty to mention that soon after Theo left us, Zack Tigman's mother was knocked off her bike by a motorist as she left the nursery, causing her unfortunately to break her leg. Initially she was unable to provide the police with any details, but she has told me recently that she believes the vehicle could have been a Volkswagen, the make of car driven by Mr. Riley.

63

PETE

"NO!" THEO SCREAMED. "NO no no no *no!*"

"It's not a discussion, Theo," I said firmly. "You chose cheesy toast, so you have to eat it all if you want a mini roll for pudding."

"It's *burned*."

Admittedly, the corners of the toast were dark from being left under the grill a minute or so too long. "It's not burned, it's browned. And anyway, you have to eat it."

"*No no no no no no no.*"

"In that case, no mini roll."

In response, Theo slung his cheesy toast on the floor. I retrieved it and put it back on his plate. "There's no point in doing that, because you still have to eat it, and now it won't be as nice." My phone rang. There was no caller ID, which meant it might be one of our lawyers. "Hello?"

"Hello Peter," Lyn's voice said, her Welsh accent emphasized by her slow, careful delivery. "Is it a convenient time? It's just a quick question, really."

"*No! No! No!*" Theo's face was now puce with anger as he banged the table with his fists.

"Yes, I guess so," I said, desperately looking around for somewhere quiet. There wasn't anywhere, not unless I went upstairs, in which case an unsupervised Theo would almost certainly wreak havoc with his tea. "Let me just sort out Theo."

"Of course."

I picked up a mini roll, then hesitated. If I let Theo have it, he'd shut up for a minute or two, granted, but I'd also have committed the cardinal sin of giving in to a tantrum, and I couldn't do that, not even for CAFCASS. I reached into the back of the cupboard for a foil-wrapped biscuit instead, consoling myself with the thought that since it wasn't actually a mini roll, technically I'd carried out my threat. "Here, Theo. Eat some of the cheese on toast, then this." His eyes lit up as he grabbed it. There was no chance he'd eat the toast first, of course, but at least he'd have to unwrap the biscuit, which would be good for his fine motor skills.

"Right," I said into the phone. "Go ahead."

"All it was, was to ask if you would be prepared to attend some parenting classes," Lyn said. "Now, a lot of parents think they wouldn't be useful, or that it's like going back to school, which it isn't at all. Because really, we could all learn something about being better parents, couldn't we? I know I could. And it would help to counter anyone saying that parenting style is a particular issue here, do you see? I'm trying to be helpful, Peter. Because it would show that, if there *were* any behavioral issues, you were just as keen to address them as we are."

For a moment I couldn't speak. I actually felt dizzy with rage. The idea that my parenting was the issue here—when Miles's idea of good parenting was probably teaching Theo how to cheat at rugby—was so ridiculous, so utterly *twisted*, it made me want to throw up.

I heard my voice say, "Well, if you think it could help Theo's turn-taking, of course I'll attend parenting classes."

"Excellent, Peter." Lyn sounded relieved. "I'll put that in my letter, then."

64

MADDIE

AND THEN WE WAIT.

For the next ten days the law takes its slow, winding course. We shouldn't in any case expect too much from the first hearing, Anita's warned us: The judge will simply read the recommendations in the safeguarding letter, encourage the parties to come to an agreement, and set a date for the final hearing, the only one that really matters.

Pete attends his first parenting class. He goes determined to show the instructors he's got nothing to learn, but comes back saying it was actually quite useful.

"There are some children who basically don't learn from punishment, so things like naughty step are wasted on them," he reports. "They respond better to reward. But you have to start off by giving the reward instantly, so they learn you really mean it, before you work up to deferred rewards on a schedule."

He starts by rewarding Theo for quite ordinary things. "Theo, you're playing with that train really nicely. Here's a chocolate button." "Theo, I noticed you've been quiet for five minutes now. Have a raisin." Initially, Theo is somewhat surprised by this sudden shower of treats, but he quickly gets the idea that doing certain things results in a reward. And if a nice drawing, done on paper instead of the wall, leads to a handful of chocolate buttons, what will eating his cheese on toast without complaint provide? Soon the downstairs walls are covered in star charts for bigger prizes—for eating his breakfast quickly, for getting ready for bed, for sleeping through. It seems to work, too. Personally I'm not sure if it's really because of the charts, or if Theo is simply growing out of his terrible twos at last, but the transformation is certainly impressive.

A week before the hearing, CAFCASS's safeguarding letter arrives. The long list of allegations in Miles's application has effectively been ignored, as Anita predicted it would be. Instead, the letter points out that Pete is voluntarily attending parenting lessons and is cooperating fully with the adviser. It recommends no further action on CAFCASS's part.

Anita's positive. "It's as good as you can hope for at this stage. They're laying the foundation for the court to rule that Theo can stay with you."

"And David?" I ask.

"David will be a tougher proposition. Have you heard from the social worker dealing with his case yet?"

We haven't. That's normal, Anita tells us.

The negligence claim against the hospital has also gone quiet, which suits us. With any luck, the custody cases will be done and dusted before we have to concentrate on the hospital one.

Sometimes, when Theo is being particularly trying, I find myself wondering if we've made a mistake fighting for David as well. Can we really cope with two different diets and two completely different levels of need—Theo with his always-on, supercharged brio, and David, with his quiet, vulnerable placidity? But then I think of David sitting in the Lamberts' huge playroom, idly twirl-ing rollers on a baby gym, and my heart overflows. Of course we'll cope. That's what families do when they have a disabled child. And Pete is the man to do it. When I see his infinite patience with Theo, never getting cross or losing his temper, I know we've made the right decision.

When Justin Watts calls Pete late on Friday, therefore, I'm not expecting anything particularly dramatic to have happened. But I can immediately tell by Pete's startled expression, and the way his gaze turns toward me, that it has.

"What is it?" I ask, concerned. "Are they settling?"

He shakes his head. And then—something he never does—he raises his free hand and puts it over his ear to block me out. His face has gone white.

"What is it?" I say again a minute later, as he puts down the phone.

"NHS Resolution are saying it wasn't the fault of any of the hospitals," he says slowly.

"Well, that's ridiculous. They can hardly deny that two fami-lies have ended up with the wrong children—"

"It isn't that," he interrupts. "They're saying the babies must have been swapped deliberately. Mads, I think they're trying to imply that it was us. That you and I somehow stole Theo from the Lamberts."

65

<u>Case no. 12675/PU78B65, Exhibit 33:</u>
<u>NHS Resolution Preliminary Case Investigation Report,</u>
<u>authored by Grace Matthews and Thomas Finlay, extract.</u>

55. SUMMARY AND CONCLUSIONS

55.1 As the evidence from the Consultant Neonatologist and specialist Neonatal Transfer team confirms, there seems little possibility that the paper ID tags were accidentally transferred between the mobile neonatal incubators before admission. Both incubators were closed throughout the transport process, prior to their arrival on the NICU.

55.2 Similarly, the possibility of even one tag being transferred during admission seems remote, given the number of specific procedures that were being carried out on the infants and the correlatingly high number of professionals there to witness them. The chance of both tags simultaneously traveling in opposite directions, therefore, from one incubator to the other and vice versa, seems vanishingly small.

55.3 Even if the paper tags had indeed been transferred in this way, or gotten lost, both neonatal nurses would also have had to attach the security tags without following proper procedures, such as cross-checking with the BadgerNet record system, in order for the electronic tags to have ended up on the wrong babies.

55.4 Mr. Riley asserts that he saw the electronic tag on "his" baby approximately thirty minutes after admission, soon after the baby was transferred to the hospital incubator. This is contradicted by the evidence from the senior registrar, who noticed its absence when checking the cooling suit some two hours later. It is a matter of considerable regret that the senior registrar did not draw this to anyone's attention at the time.

55.5 However, the lack of a security tag at that stage was not directly relevant to the initial misidentification of the two babies. This is evidenced by the fact that Mr. Riley was already standing next to an incubator that he appeared to believe contained "his" baby, rather than beside the other incubator, which actually did. The misidentification had therefore happened, or was in the process of happening, by that stage.

55.6 On the balance of probabilities, therefore, we conclude that the misidentification was caused deliberately—in other words, that during or shortly before the transfer of the two babies from the mobile incubators to the hospital incubators, a person or persons deliberately swapped or removed the two paper tags, and thereafter continued to uphold the deception that each baby was in fact the other.

55.7 This being the case, we are adjourning our investigation and passing our evidence to the Metropolitan Police, for them to investigate the possible wrongful removal of a child without parental consent under the Child Abduction Act 1984.

55.8 Subject to the outcome of any criminal investigation, it may be necessary to further refer our findings to the NHS Counter Fraud Authority.

66

PETE

"CUI BONO," JUSTIN WATTS said. "It means 'who benefits?' And in this case, unfortunately, they've decided it's you."

"But that's crazy," Maddie said desperately. "*Crazy.* Why on earth would we do such a thing?"

It was nine o'clock on Monday morning, and we were sitting in Justin Watts's smart office. We'd tried to get him to see us on Saturday, but no-win no-fee lawyers like their weekends off, apparently. We'd spent the last two days climbing the walls with frustration.

"Well, they're not speculating," he said, glancing through the report again. "But no doubt the police will. And the most likely inference is that you ended up with a healthy, intellectually normal baby and the Lamberts didn't."

"But we couldn't have known that was what would happen," Maddie insisted. "At the time, all they told us was that our baby was very unwell and might have been starved of oxygen." She looked across at me. "That was literally all we knew. Wasn't it?"

"I spoke to the paramedics in the ambulance," I said slowly. "I asked them what hypoxia meant. One of them explained—he was very honest. I didn't tell you at the time, Mads. You were already suffering enough. Besides, he said nothing was certain. So I kept it from you. Everything except the bit about the next few days being crucial."

"Oh Jesus." Maddie stared at me. "So they think you *knew*. They think they can prove motive."

"But not opportunity," Justin Watts said mildly.

I shook my head. "There were times while the doctors were rushing about when I was alone with both incubators. I wish there hadn't been, but if that's all they need to prove . . ." *I'm done for,* I wanted to say, but I knew how melodramatic that would sound and swallowed my words. "It doesn't look good."

"Well, luckily that *isn't* all they have to prove." Justin Watts picked up the report again. "This is ninety percent insinuation and ten percent balance of probability, which is very different from the standard of proof required in the criminal court. You may be asked to go to a police station to be interviewed under caution, but that's as far as I'd expect it to go." He paused. "You'll want to engage a specialist criminal law solicitor to go with you, but if it does come to an interview, my strong advice would be to answer 'no comment' to every question. Currently, they've got nothing, and if you give them nothing else to work on, they'll almost certainly shelve the whole thing."

"'No comment'? Isn't that what guilty people say?" Maddie said disbelievingly.

"It's what people who want to avoid charges say. Believe me, if you can stop this from turning into a criminal trial, you should."

Criminal trial. Jesus, had it come to this? Was I going to stand in a court, in the dock, accused of deliberately snatching Theo? I couldn't get my head around it.

And all because Miles Lambert had walked into our lives. If he hadn't persuaded me to sue the hospital, none of this would have happened.

"Of course," Justin Watts was saying, "a cynic might be tempted to believe that NHS Resolution would prefer this to be a criminal matter, rather than negligence, because it gets them off the hook financially. But nevertheless, the police will have to investigate the allegation on its merits."

"Hang on," I said. "Do you mean that if the NHS succeeds in muddying the waters, they might not have to pay us anything?"

Justin Watts shrugged. "It will certainly put them in a stronger negotiating position. And as they point out in their final paragraph, if either you or the Lamberts were aware of the abduction, it follows that one of you is committing fraud."

Maddie and I exchanged a startled glance.

"I'm afraid it also calls into question the basis of *our* relationship," he added. "You'll recall that the Conditional Fee Arrangement is tied to us having a reasonable likelihood of winning. If circumstances change, we have to get a second opinion. And there's no doubt that this allegation does change things substantially."

"*What?*" I stared at him. "You might leave us in the lurch?"

"Not at all. But we'd have to start invoicing you for our time. And ask you to pay the costs incurred so far, of course."

I put my head in my hands. "We've already remortgaged our house to pay for the family-law solicitor."

"Ah." Justin Watts made a note. Probably reminding himself to get a bill out to us ASAP, I realized, before we ran out of funds.

"What if we pull out?" I said desperately. "What if we just forget about this whole thing?"

"I definitely wouldn't advise that," he said. "If you withdraw now, you'll have to pay all the other side's costs as well as ours. And it might look like you've got something to hide when it comes to the criminal investigation."

"I've had enough of this," Maddie said abruptly. She stood up. "You're our lawyer, for fuck's sake. You're meant to be fighting for us. And instead all you bloody care about is how much money you can make out of us. Well, you won't get a cent unless you come up with a plan for making this go away." Her Australian accent, usually quite muted after almost three years in London, was as strident as I'd ever heard it. "Come on, Pete. Let's leave this gutless limp-dick to it and go home."

67

PETE

"'GUTLESS LIMP-DICK'?" I whispered. "Where did *that* come from?"

We were pressed together in a crowded Jubilee Line carriage, either side of an upright bar.

"I dunno. My dad, I guess."

"This is all shit, isn't it?"

Maddie nodded. Without warning, she started to cry, silent fat tears that ran down her cheeks and dripped onto her collar. Awkwardly I reached around and hugged her, the bar still between us. Like embracing someone from inside a prison cell, I thought, even though of course it wasn't. They don't make prison cells like that anymore, except in movies.

THERE WAS SOMEONE WAITING outside our house—a young man. It was only when he headed rapidly toward us, his phone held out as if he was imploring us to answer it, that I realized who he was. Or rather, what. Journalists don't use notebooks these days. They have recording apps on their phones instead.

"Kieran Keenan, *Daily Mail*. Is it true you stole a baby, Mr. Riley?"

"Go away," I said irritably, pushing past him. At that moment a photographer jumped out from where he'd been hiding between two parked cars. He crouched down to get the classic shot, snap-snap-snap: the guilty party brushing off the journalist who's asking difficult questions.

"Don't you want to put your side of the story, Mr. Riley?" Kieran called after me.

I stopped and turned. "I know your editor," I said disbelievingly. "Well, the travel editor, anyway."

Snap-snap-snap. The photographer was making the most of this.

"I'll give him your regards. What made you do it, Mr. Riley?"

Maddie had gotten the front door open and was already inside, waiting to slam it behind me. But something made me stay where I was, facing the reporter. God, he really was young. He must be an intern. "We didn't do anything. Do your research. We're not the bad guys in this."

"So who is?" he pressed, but I realized I'd already said too much. I stepped in and Maddie slammed the door.

"THAT WAS DOWN TO Miles," Maddie said flatly. "It must have been."

I flopped into a chair. "Of course. His lawyer would have been sent a copy of that report as well. And Miles's first thought would have been to ask himself how he could use it to his advantage. If people think we took Theo deliberately, they'll think we definitely shouldn't be allowed to keep him."

"Can you call your contact at the *Mail*? Ask them not to run the story?"

"I think that might make it even worse."

We sat in silence, too exhausted even to make coffee.

"Why did you lie about the security tag?" Maddie said at last.

I glanced at her uneasily. "What do you mean?"

"When you told Grace Matthews you saw the tag on Theo within minutes of him being moved to the hospital incubator, that wasn't right. You know it wasn't. And now one of the senior doctors has contradicted you."

"I must have been mistaken."

Maddie's eyes searched my face. "Did you do it for Bronagh?"

I didn't answer. I couldn't.

"Why?" Maddie said simply. But nothing was simple in this situation anymore.

"She's been suspended," I said eventually. "I wanted to help her out."

"Oh Jesus." Maddie started to laugh, a hollow laugh that turned into a howl. "We're losing our son, and you wanted to help a nurse. Which in turn has implicated you in a criminal offense. You are . . . You are such a *cretin* sometimes, Pete. Always trying to be the good guy. Always—" She stopped suddenly. "Is that *all* it was?"

"What do you mean?" I said, even though I knew exactly what she meant.

"Is there anything between you and Bronagh that I should know about?" she demanded.

I looked her in the eye. "No. No, absolutely not."

And that was true, if you were thinking like a lawyer and taking her question at its face value. There was nothing she should know about. Very much the reverse, in fact.

68

Case no. 12675/PU78B65, Exhibit 34: Facebook Messenger exchange between Bronagh Walsh and Peter Riley, deleted by Peter Riley the next day and by Bronagh Walsh two years later.

Hey Pete, how's tricks? The bike ride looks amaaaaazing!!! Actually going to be in York next w/e with some friends on a hen so we might look you lot up! We're all qualified nurses so can tend to any walking (cycling?) wounded!!

Thanks Bronagh. Plenty of sore calves, aching groins & pulled muscles over here but we're plowing on. Determined to make the target for the NICU!

Put like that it's almost our duty to come around and patch you up isn't it!!! (Hmm probably can't do much for the pulled muscles or sore calves . . .)

69

MADDIE

THE *DAILY MAIL* ARTICLE appears on page eight, below a picture of a hunted-looking Pete. TIMES JOURNALIST "STOLE BABY"— BUT STILL WANTS OUR NHS TO PAY is the headline. It quotes the most damning bits of NHS Resolution's report, as well as parts of the article Pete himself wrote, the one he'd told them couldn't be printed yet, in which he'd described how traumatic it had been finding out about the mix-up. In this new context, it seems chillingly self-interested—a brazen attempt to paint himself as a victim, in order to prize more money out of the health service. Theo isn't identified by name, "for legal reasons," but instead is described as "Child X, an adorable toddler with a huge grin and an exuberant zest for life."

As for why Pete stole him, the article makes it clear that Pete's a cold-blooded, quick-thinking monster who saw an opportunity to foist his vulnerable, brain-damaged baby on someone else, then tried to profit from his own villainy to boot. Toward the end of the piece is a quote from an "expert," some pop psychologist who's appeared on various morning-TV programs. "I wouldn't be surprised if this turns out to be an example of 'hero syndrome,'" he says helpfully. "We see it sometimes with firefighters and policemen, creating crises and setting fires purely in order to be the one who averts disaster and is admired as a result. But increasingly, we're also seeing it with those who want to be perfect parents or caregivers." The apparent contradiction between Pete as a heartless monster and Pete as someone who wants to be admired for his parenting skills is completely ignored, of course.

Pete himself seems utterly shell-shocked. That it's a newspaper, his old industry, doing this to him only adds insult to injury. He becomes very quiet, his eyes wide, poleaxed and bewildered.

Anita recommends a colleague specializing in criminal law, who arranges for Pete to attend a police interview voluntarily. We should get our initial response in quickly, the new solicitor says, even though his advice relating to the interview itself is identical to Justin Watts's: Answer "no comment" to everything, in the hope the police will decide the allegation is unprovable either way. I can tell Pete hates that strategy, and at the slightest encouragement from me would abandon it. By nature he's someone who likes to cooperate, to be well thought of by authority figures. And we've all seen video footage of child molesters and serial killers monotonously answering "no comment" to the police's questions, the implication being that they're too callous even to admit their own crimes. I make sure I back the lawyer's strategy every inch of the way.

This new solicitor, Mark Cooper, charges £220 an hour plus VAT.

I'd expected the police investigation to be as slow and Byzantine as every other part of the legal processes we're now embroiled in. But while Pete is attending the interview, the doorbell rings. On the doorstep are a uniformed police sergeant, a WPC, and a man in plainclothes who introduces himself as a detective sergeant. He shows me his ID and a warrant to take Pete's laptop and phone.

I don't even have Pete's phone—he has it with him. I watch as they unplug his MacBook and place it in an evidence bag. "Do you want the power supply?" I hear myself saying.

The detective shakes his head. "We've got plenty of those." They're almost the only words we exchange. Five minutes after entering the house, they're gone.

Taking Pete's laptop doesn't fit with Mark Cooper's prediction that the police will only go through the motions, I think. Or is that the point? That now they'll be able to say they looked for evidence and found none?

The more I think about it, the more ridiculous this whole thing is. Even in some mad parallel universe where the allegations were true and Pete did steal Theo, it isn't as if he'd have googled "how to steal a baby" beforehand. And anyone who knows him would realize just how crazy the notion of Pete as a heartless, calculating monster is.

But Pete as a would-be hero? an inner voice whispers disloyally. *That's more feasible.* I remember the way he was so good in the NICU, even syringing my breast milk into Theo's nasogastric tube so that the nurses didn't have to do it. When Theo thrived, Pete, by extension, shared the credit. And yes, he'd undeniably basked in it, just a little. Saint Peter. The best, most caring dad in the NICU . . .

Stop. I dubbed him Saint Peter because he *is* a saint—almost irritatingly so, sometimes, but a saint nonetheless. No one knows better than me that his caring nature isn't an act.

But he might have done it for you, the inner voice says.

And I stop dead, because I know that, at least, could be . . . not *true,* obviously, but not impossible. Pete kept the stark reality about hypoxia from me that day because he wanted to protect me. He would never have stolen a healthy baby for his own sake—but might he, could he, have stolen a healthy baby because he thought *I* couldn't cope with the alternative?

Was it his very sainthood that prompted him to commit the most terrible of acts—not out of heartlessness, but the very opposite, love?

WE RARELY TALK THESE days about the period that brought us together. It was a wild time in my life—I'd moved to Sydney, gotten a job in television production, started working hard and partying even harder. I certainly wasn't looking to fall in love, so when I fell for an older, married TV presenter it came as a shock. For three whirlwind months I convinced myself he was telling the truth when he said he was going to leave his wife and family for me. He didn't, of course. I became depressed; there was a messy cry for help—an overdose I ended up not being able to keep down—followed by a long period of numb recuperation. And a good-looking, well-mannered English boy who didn't seem in the least put off by the fact I was an emotional wreck, or by my frequent reminders that we'd never be anything more than friends. And slowly, friendship became something else—or rather, I suppose, I came to realize that friendship is actually a more important ingredient of a relationship than I'd given it credit for. When I did eventually sleep with him, it was more out of a sense of gratitude than anything else. *There, that's done now.* But somehow, it didn't stay as a one-off. On some level, I liked the comfort that sex with Pete gave me. And once you were sleeping with your best friend, you were effectively in a relationship. He was my rock, the one who cared for me at a time when to be cared for was what I needed more than anything else.

But would he really commit a crime for me? Surely not—the guilty conscience would plague him; his very sense of who he is would be shaken to the core. Yet here we are, with him effectively accused, and me doubting his innocence . . .

This is what happens, I realize. This is how couples get torn apart by circumstances like these. Doubt and mistrust, combined with financial stress and the agony of not knowing whether a judge is going to order our child taken from us, would eat away at the strongest relationship. I mustn't let it happen to me and Pete.

And yet I can't help it, and the suspicion still lingers, deep in the recesses of my mind. That lie Pete told about the tag—was that really just to protect Bronagh, or was there something more to it as well? And what about the other insinuations in the NHS report? If the babies really were swapped deliberately, who else could it have been?

My phone rings. I answer it, thinking it must be Pete, out of his interview at last.

"Hello, Maddie," Lyn the CAFCASS adviser says in her lilting Welsh tones. "Is now a good time? I need to chat with you about Peter, do you see?"

70

MADDIE

"WHAT ABOUT PETE?"

"It's just that I've been alerted to a possible safeguarding issue, Maddie. I understand serious allegations have been made, which the police are now investigating."

"Well," I say slowly, "it's true there have been some allegations— false ones, obviously. It's fairly clear to us that Miles Lambert is somehow responsible—"

"Would you have any evidence regarding that at all, Maddie?" Lyn interrupts.

"Not as such, no."

"Then I think you should be careful not to make statements like that. As it's now a police matter." Lyn's tone, usually so soft and ingratiating, has turned steely.

"Of course. My point was, these are only allegations, with no evidence behind them."

"Even so, my job is to think of Theo in this situation," Lyn

says firmly. "When a man is being investigated for a possible offense against a child, there are procedures, Maddie, do you see?
We have to ask ourselves, is this child safe?"

"But this is the same child he's accused—wrongly—of taking," I say, genuinely baffled. "Of course Theo's safe."

"Nobody wants to be talking about removing Theo into emergency protection at this stage." The steely note in Lyn's voice is
becoming more pronounced.

"*What?* Who said anything—"

"So I think it's best if Pete finds somewhere else to stay, for
now," Lyn continues as if I haven't spoken. "He can still have contact, but it will have to take place when you're in the house. Or it
could be supervised by someone else, do you see—there are specialist centers where that can be arranged. I can give you a list of
addresses."

"I don't understand," I say slowly. "Are you saying you have the
power to *break up* my relationship with Pete?"

"No," Lyn says evenly. "I'm saying I have the power to remove
Theo into safekeeping if I'm not entirely satisfied with the arrangement that currently exists. Which at the present time, I'm
not. However, if you were to give a written undertaking that Pete
won't be staying in the house, won't be alone with Theo, won't
have him in his sole charge, and will otherwise only see him under
supervision in a registered contact center, I could be persuaded
that you're working with us to provide a safer and more acceptable environment. So really, it's your decision, Maddie. Which is it
to be?"

Even though I can barely speak, I know I have no choice. If
Theo is taken away from us now, the chances of keeping him in
the long term will shrink dramatically.

"I'll do whatever it takes to keep Theo and to get David back,"
I hear myself say. "So if you think Pete should go, I'll tell him he
has to move out."

71

MADDIE

I WAIT IN A kind of daze for Pete to get back from the police station. It's as if my brain is refusing to engage with what's happening, unable to process more than one disaster at a time. Perhaps it's a kind of defense mechanism. If I really grasped the enormity of everything that's going on, I'd scream.

It's another hour before I hear his key in the lock. He comes in looking exhausted. He drops his keys onto the desk, next to where his MacBook usually is. He glances at the dangling power lead but says nothing.

"They took it," I say. "The police. They came earlier."

"I know. They've got my phone, too. That's why I couldn't call you when I came out. And then . . ." He blinks, like a boxer who's been hit in the face. "I walked most of the way home. I needed to think."

"Do you know when you'll get them back?"

"Soon, they said." He runs his hand over his head. "They offered me a choice. Give us your PIN and passwords, so we can download everything immediately, or don't give them to us and we'll keep the laptop and phone until our technical people get around to opening them. And since not giving the passwords would look like I had something to hide . . ." He shakes his head.

"Pete, I've got more bad news," I begin, just as he says, "Maddie . . ."

We both stop. "You go first," he says.

"The CAFCASS woman phoned. Lyn. They're claiming that because you're now the subject of a child abduction investigation, Theo isn't safe. I'm so sorry, Pete. She wants you to stay somewhere else until the hearing. And you can't be alone with Theo."

"Jesus. *Jesus.*" He closes his eyes.

"I thought maybe you could go to Greg and Kate's."

"I guess." He looks around our downstairs room, as if for the last time. "*Jesus.*"

"What did *you* want to say?"

He takes a deep breath. When he starts speaking I know immediately this is something he's prepared, that he's been rehearsing it on the long walk home. "There's something I need to tell you. About my laptop. When the police look at it, they're going to know . . ." He stops, then continues. "They'll be able to tell I've been looking at porn."

I stare at him.

"Not illegal porn, obviously," he adds quickly. "But Mark—the solicitor—said if they interview *you*, it's something they might raise. To try to catch you off guard."

"When?" I say.

"When will they interview you? It's not even certain—"

"When do you look at porn?"

He makes a small, defeated gesture. "I don't know. Does it matter? When Theo was at nursery, I guess."

That nursery cost nearly two hundred pounds a week, paid for from my salary. But it was worth it, we'd agreed, if it allowed Pete some time to pitch and write articles. "How long has this been going on?"

He only shrugs. "A while."

I'd had no idea. Perhaps I shouldn't be surprised, given the other problems in our relationship, but it never even occurred to me. It's so contrary to my image of him—to Pete's image of himself, for that matter. Generally, he's so respectful to women, so principled. I think of some of the images I've stumbled across online, and wince. Is *that* who he is, deep down? And, if I'd never known that about him, what else might I not know?

Who is he, really?

He's always said he needed to password-protect his laptop to prevent Theo from playing with it—"No screen time at all until he's two, and no more than thirty minutes a day fully supervised after that. I read an article—in Silicon Valley, the people who really know about this stuff don't even let their five-year-olds play with iPads unsupervised." But had it actually been to protect Theo from coming across his browsing history? Or indeed, to stop me from doing the same?

If he could lie about that so easily, what other lies has he told? Could he even have lied about the most important thing of all?

"I'll go and pack a suitcase," he says when I don't respond. He waits for me to say something. But I can't.

Only as he starts trudging up the stairs do I manage to add, "What else happened at the interview?"

"Oh . . ." He shrugs wearily. "I said 'no comment' to every question. And I could see the detective getting more and more convinced I must have something to hide. So now it's a trade-off— has he gotten so frustrated he'll decide to investigate anyway, or will he think it's a waste of resources when they have so little to go on?"

It seems inevitable to me now that there'll be a full investigation, not least because so far, everything that possibly could go wrong for us has. And because, behind it all, guiding events with a push here and a nod there, I can feel the invisible, irresistible force of Miles Lambert, who'll stop at nothing to get his son.

Perhaps if we'd handled it better, he'd have had less to work with. But now the tiny lie Pete told about seeing the security tag on Theo's leg is the hairline crack that, when more pressure is applied, could shatter our family apart. Theo could be taken away. Pete could go to prison. And what will happen to me in that situation? If they decide I knew all along, my leave to remain in the UK could be revoked as well.

An abyss has opened up, and we're teetering right on the edge.

"I'll call Greg," Pete says. Automatically, his hand reaches into his pocket for his phone. It comes out empty. "Shit," he says, furious at his own stupidity. "*Shit.*" He takes a deep breath, and I know he's trying to hold himself together.

"I'll do it," I say. "You go and pack."

"Tell him . . ." He stops, then continues. "Tell Greg I'll come late. When Theo's asleep. I want to do bedtime. It could be the last one for a while."

72

PETE

AS I UNDRESSED BEFORE lying down on Greg's sofa, something fell out of my pocket. It was a card the police had given me. Headed *Your Release from Custody*, it explained that *Inappropriate contact with anyone linked to your case, either directly or indirectly, through a third party or social media, may constitute a criminal offense. If found guilty, you could face up to life imprisonment.*

Life imprisonment. Could this really get any worse? And what constituted "inappropriate contact," anyway?

When we got to the police station my lawyer, Mark Cooper, had gone to speak to the police on his own. He'd told me to expect that—it was part of the process, apparently, the "disclosure." He came back somber but encouraging.

"Well, they're not obliged to tell me everything, but even so I'd say they've got very little. My advice is, we stick to 'no comment.'"

"Do we have to? It just feels wrong, somehow. When I've got nothing to hide."

"Let me explain something." Mark Cooper was no older than me, but he had the pale, flabby look of someone who'd spent too much time sitting in these grubby rooms with their flickering strip lights and discarded paper cups. "In this country, the criminal law is based on an adversarial system. That means it's the police's goal to get a suspect arrested, charged, and brought to trial, not to worry about whether he's actually guilty—that's someone else's job. On top of that, they face intense pressure to improve their conviction rates. The police are trained in interviewing techniques, and they're often very good at getting suspects to say something that, however innocent, will help to convict them later. Or, even worse, getting them to tell a small lie that will undermine all the rest of their evidence when it comes out in court. Right now, if they had enough evidence to charge you, they'd have done it. So our objective is to leave here today with that situation unchanged, and the surest way to do that is to answer 'no comment.'"

I understood his logic, but it had been agony. When the policeman—a pleasant, cheerful man who introduced himself as Detective Inspector Richards—cautioned me, and got to the words, "If you do not mention now something which you mention later, a court might ask you why you didn't mention it at the first opportunity," I shot Mark an anguished glance. He only shook his head warningly.

When the caution was out of the way, DI Richards asked the first question. "I understand that you transferred to St. Alexander's with your premature baby in an ambulance. That must have been a very difficult time for you."

"On the advice of my solicitor, I am answering, 'No comment.'"

DI Richards looked pained. "We've agreed to speak to you today to hear your side of the story, Pete. I'm neutral in this—I'm just trying to see what's happened."

"On the advice of my solicitor, I am answering, 'No comment.' "

"No one's currently accused you of any crime, Pete. We just want to make sure we've got your version of events as well as NHS Resolution's."

"On the advice of my solicitor, I am answering, 'No comment.' "

DI Richards shrugged and picked up a document. "You told the NHS investigators you were in a state of complete panic when you got to the intensive care unit. Does that sound right to you, that you were panicking?"

I hesitated. Had I really said that? "On the advice of my solicitor, I am answering, 'No comment.' "

"I can understand why you'd be anxious, Pete. You'd had a conversation with the paramedics in the ambulance, hadn't you? They'd told you your little boy was probably going to be brain-damaged. That must have been hard."

"On the advice of my solicitor, I am answering, 'No comment.' "

And so it went on. Even when he asked about Bronagh, and whether I'd been in touch with her since leaving the NICU. I blinked but managed to say, "On the advice of my solicitor, I am answering, 'No comment.' "

And then there'd been the moment, near the end of the interview, when he'd sprung on me that they'd gotten a warrant to examine my computer. I must have looked anxious, because then he asked whether they'd find anything on it that related to the investigation.

I started to shake my head, then remembered. "On the advice of my solicitor, I am answering, 'No comment.' " But inwardly, I was already thinking of what I would now have to tell Maddie.

Finally, he got to the end of his questions. Since I wasn't answering, it hadn't taken long—no more than fifteen minutes. "That's it," he said with a sigh. Then, as I relaxed, "Oh, just one last thing. We've been contacted by a Miles Lambert, who says he has information that may be relevant to our inquiries. Is there anything you'd like to tell me first?"

I tried very hard not to react, but whatever he read in my face—fear, perhaps, or despair, or even loathing—it evidently satisfied him, because he nodded.

"On the advice of my solicitor, I am answering, 'No comment,'" I mumbled, but DI Richards was no longer listening.

GREG AND KATE HAD replaced their downstairs curtains with blinds, which lit up with every car that passed. Sleep was impossible. I lay on their narrow sofa, my mind churning. *Theo*. I'd told him I was going away for a few days. He'd barely reacted, just asked who was going to take him to Moles's house tomorrow. *Maddie*. I couldn't help thinking she didn't seem desperately upset by the social worker's demand that I move out. She'd seemed distant, almost wary of me as I packed my things. Perhaps she needed time to process what I'd told her. Did she despise me now? Did I disgust her? I'd tried so hard to be the person she wanted me to be, but the truth is, I wasn't, and never had been. I was a fraud.

Which was ironic, because if I was convicted of child abduction, I would almost certainly be charged with fraud as well. Everything had gone wrong, and our family was going to pay the price.

And with that thought, finally, I allowed myself to weep; in the darkness, quietly, so as not to wake Greg's sleeping kids upstairs.

73

Case no. 12675/PU78B65, Exhibit 38: Extract from CAFCASS safeguarding letter regarding Theo Riley, addendum to previous recommendations, presented to the family court by Lyn Edwards, Family Court Adviser.

CONCLUSION

In the light of these revised circumstances, the court should direct CAFCASS to complete a Section 7 report to further explore the issues raised, including:

- The possibility of child abduction and any subsequent psychological implications for the child.

- The possibility of alcohol abuse. Madelyn Wilson has stated that she regularly drinks more than double the maximum of ten units per week recommended by NHS guidelines for women.

- Madelyn Wilson's mental health and how it could impact on the child. In addition to a history of psychosis, she has stated that she is no longer taking the medication she was prescribed for her condition, a fact of which her GP was unaware.

- What the child's wishes are. Although Theo is very young, CAF-CASS advisers are trained to use indirect techniques to elicit a young child's feelings in situations such as these.

- Acrimony from Mr. Riley and Ms. Wilson toward the applicants, and how it may alienate or otherwise affect the child.

The report should conclude by making recommendations to the court regarding the child's long-term situation.

Lyn Edwards,

Family Court Adviser

74

MADDIE

THAT NIGHT, I GET drunk—properly, mind-numbingly drunk. With Theo asleep and no Pete to give me disapproving looks every time I top up my glass, I drink myself into a miserable oblivion.

I wake up next morning with a stinking hangover, made worse by having to get Theo dressed, breakfasted, and off to the Lamberts' on my own. Usually, I slink off to the Tube in silence, leaving Pete to do all this. I hadn't really appreciated just how draining Theo can be at this hour.

"Daddy cuts my toast inter *soljers*."

"Daddy isn't here today, Theo."

"Daddy gets my toofbrush *all ready*."

"Like I said, Theo, Daddy isn't here."

I miss him—not just the practical Pete, laying a precise three-millimeter fuse of toddler-safe toothpaste on a brush, but also Pete the warm presence in our bed, making room between our backs for Theo as he clambers between us. Was I too quick to let him go? Should I have fought Lyn's monstrous proposal more fiercely? And should I have been more affectionate before he left? We'd barely spoken as he packed a bag, nor when Theo finally fell asleep, exhausted, in his arms. "Don't forget his snack in the morning," Pete had said as he opened the front door, and I'd simply nodded. The truth was, I didn't know who I was saying goodbye to any longer. It was ridiculous to conflate a commonplace weakness like looking at porn with thinking he could have stolen someone else's child, but I didn't know what to think now. We'd become strangers to each other.

And that was how we parted, with strangers' distant nods.

AT THE LAMBERTS', THEO eagerly runs to push the intercom button, then bounds up the steps without waiting for it to be answered. I'd been expecting Lucy, or possibly Tania, so it's a shock to be met by Miles himself, pulling open the door in a T-shirt and jeans.

"Maddie. How nice to see you."

"Fuck off, Miles."

Miles grins. "Please—I must ask you to moderate your language in front of the children." Theo had briefly rugby-tackled Miles's legs before running into the house, so there was absolutely no chance he could have heard.

He eyes me with amusement. Annoyingly, it makes him even more good-looking. "It's fun, this, isn't it?" he says cheerfully. "Makes life so much more interesting."

"What are you doing here? I thought you'd be at work."

"I might ask *you* the same question. My answer, by the way, is that I'm taking time off to be with my children. It's so important for both parents to be actively involved, don't you think?"

"Again, fuck off." I wonder if he knows Pete has been made to move out. I suspect he does—some weaselly back channel of information, lubricated by money. "And actually, I'm on my way to work now." I hesitate. "I need to ask if you'll have Theo until a bit later for the next few days. Say, four o'clock. I can't really get away any earlier."

"And if I said—how did you put it just now?—'Fuck off, Maddie'?" He waits, but I can tell he's only playing with me. Eventually he sighs happily. "Of course. It will be a pleasure to have my son with us for longer during the day."

As I go down the steps, he adds, "It'll be good preparation for when he moves in permanently. I'm sure the court will see it that way, too. Particularly when they learn that it was your toe-rag of a partner who stole him from us. Who would have thought Perfect Pete had it in him to do a thing like that, Maddie? Perhaps he's not quite the man you thought he was."

Again I don't rise to it, although I'm shaking with fury. As I turn the corner he calls after me, "I'll see you at the hearing. On Tuesday. Make sure you turn up this time, won't you?"

I'D MEANT TO GO straight on to work, but I go home instead. I'm amazed by how focused I am. At the Lamberts' house, listening to Miles's taunts, I'd felt adrenaline coursing through me, the ancient fight-or-flight reflex prickling my skin, blood pounding in my ears.

The CAFCASS letter is waiting on the mat. I open it and read the revised list of recommendations with a mixture of anger and resignation. So now Lyn has me in her sights, as well as Pete. I scrunch the letter up and let it fall to the floor. As if in a dream, I pull two big suitcases out of the understairs cupboard where they're kept. In Theo's room I work quickly, transferring clothes— five T-shirts, five pairs of jeans, ten pairs of socks—into the first case. All so neatly ironed and folded by Pete, still smelling of the eco-friendly fabric conditioner he uses.

For my own suitcase, I just throw in a few things from my wardrobe.

The passports are downstairs, in the desk drawer. I check mine's in date. The photograph shows me with long, unstyled hair down to my chest, an unflattering center parting falling around a fresh, innocent face. So innocent, from a different time. And Theo's—he was less than a year old when his was taken. Incredible to think he'll be eleven when this passport expires.

But of course, he won't be. Miles will get his surname changed to Lambert; a new, British passport issued.

I check Skyscanner. There's a Cathay Pacific flight leaving tonight via Hong Kong. One-way tickets are only six hundred pounds. In a little over forty-eight hours, I could be waking up in my old bedroom at home with Theo beside me. The sun will be shining, my parents will be overjoyed. Dad will be making plans, taking care of things. If I leave it even a few more days it'll be too late: At the hearing, the court will undoubtedly agree to Miles's request and issue an order stopping me and Theo from traveling.

I sit on the bed, the passports in my hands, and sob. Because I know, in my heart, that flight is not an option.

Which only leaves the other thing.

75

MADDIE

I GO TO GREG and Kate's and bang on the door until Greg answers. Behind him I can see Pete at the kitchen table, supervising Play-Doh with Lily and Alfie. The two men, as well as the children, are wearing matching red plastic aprons, and for a moment my heart swells at the sweetness of it all.

"Pete," Greg calls, seeing me. "Maddie's here."

Pete comes to the door. Now that I see him close-up, he looks gaunt. He hasn't shaved and the whites of his eyes are pink. "Yes?" he says blankly.

"We need to fight this," I tell him. "Properly fight it. Not just with lawyers. We need to fight it like Miles is fighting—with every fiber."

"Come in," he says after a moment, holding open the door.

. . .

"THE ONE THING THAT will make all this go away is if we can work out who *did* swap those babies."

Greg has taken the children to Kidzone, to give Pete and me some space. We sit on either side of the kitchen table. Both of us, without thinking, have reached for handfuls of Play-Doh and are kneading it as we talk. Pete's still wearing Kate's apron, which is several sizes too small for him.

"Okay," Pete says cautiously. "But how?"

"The way I see it," I say, pulling a child's pad toward me to make notes, "there are five possibilities. First, that Miles somehow swapped the babies himself."

"But why would he do that?"

"I don't know. But for example, what if he planned to sue the hospital all along? What if it was all some giant moneymaking scheme? After all, he knew he'd be able to use a DNA test to get his own child back whenever he wanted. He just had to make sure he exposed the swap before the children were three years old and we'd acquired parental rights."

Pete stares at me. "But no one, surely . . . He would have to be a—a—"

"A psychopath? But I think that's exactly what Miles Lambert is. I've been reading up about it online. A while back, people used to think psychopaths were all chaotic, disorganized murderers, because those were the ones who ended up in prison and got studied. But there's mounting evidence that many successful CEOs and politicians are actually psychopaths, too; or at least, fall somewhere on the psychopathic spectrum—that is, they score low on tests for remorse, conscience, and moral judgment, and high for fearlessness, quick thinking, and cold-bloodedness. And there are certain psychopathic traits that we *know* Miles has. Something called shallow affect, for example—having a very limited range of emotions. Getting bored easily. Impulsiveness. Charm. Not really caring about other people's feelings, except as a tool to manipulate them by. Having very few long-term friends. Seeing life as a contest where, for you to win, others have to lose. And treating your children as trophies, flattering extensions of yourself."

Pete has been nodding at each point, but now he stops. "The flaw in your theory is that Miles is already stinking rich. Why go to all that trouble, if they don't need the money?"

"I don't know. Because he can? Because he enjoys the game? Or maybe they're not as rich as they look. The mortgage on that house must be millions." I snap my fingers. "Lucy said something about him not having many friends since he left Hardings and set up on his own. Hardings is an investment bank, isn't it? Presumably he earned a fortune there. Maybe now he's losing a fortune instead."

"That theory depends on him having left Hardings by the time he made the swap," Pete points out.

"Which he hadn't," I say, instantly deflated. "I'm pretty sure Lucy also said something back in the NICU, about him getting fired if he spent too long away from his desk."

"But that's interesting in itself, isn't it?" Pete's frowning. "If, back then, he was going through some kind of crisis at work—maybe was right on the verge of getting pushed out—swapping the babies might have seemed like a way out of his problems. He couldn't know he'd end up with a disabled child, of course, and a correspondingly high payout, but he'd know the odds were pretty high."

"Well, that's something we can investigate, then," I say, making a note. "Whether he was in trouble at work."

Pete nods slowly. "Okay. So Miles is suspect number one. Who else?"

"Lucy. Can you remember when she first turned up in the NICU?"

He shakes his head. "I don't think I noticed her at all. Not until she came over to chat to you that day. It was such a blur before then."

"She was definitely around before I was—she told me she'd had a natural birth, rather than a C-section like me. So it seems likely she'd have arrived pretty soon after the babies did."

"But whatever we might think about Miles, Lucy definitely isn't a psychopath," Pete says. "And she of all people had no reason to swap a premature but reasonably healthy baby for one with a high likelihood of disability."

"True. But we can't altogether rule her out."

"All right. And next? You said five possibilities in all."

"Bronagh," I say slowly. "I think it's possible that it was Bronagh who swapped them."

76

MADDIE

"NO." PETE SHAKES HIS head. "No way. *No.*"

"Hear me out," I insist. "It was that article in the *Mail* that got me thinking—that so-called expert saying this might be a case of hero syndrome? I looked it up. It's a bullshit phrase—it's not even officially recognized by psychiatrists. But what *is* true is that, in the caregiving professions, there are a small but significant number of people who deliberately cause crises, either because they enjoy the feeling of power over life and death it gives them, or because they feed on the admiration they get when they sort the crisis out."

"That sounds like some terrible late-night documentary," he scoffs. *"Nurses Who Kill."*

"That's because some nurses *do* kill. Statistically, they're the most prolific serial killers there are. There was one in Germany who killed ninety-nine people, for God's sake. Another in Italy was accused of murdering over eighty. And an unusually high proportion of killer nurses work in pediatrics. There's even a case going through the courts right now—a neonatal nurse who was regarded as brilliant, dedicated, devoted to her job, and who helped organize the fundraising appeal for a new five-million-pound baby unit. Does that sound familiar?"

Pete stares at me.

"Often, they only come under suspicion because someone spots a pattern of abnormally high death rates," I add. "St. Alexander's has been downgraded from a Level Three to a Level Two for exactly that reason, yes?"

"Yes," he says. He sounds stunned. "But not *Bronagh*. She saved Theo's life on a daily basis, Mads. She got his heart going when it stopped—"

"And didn't we all admire her for it?"

He grimaces. "But why *swap* them? It's one thing to say a nurse might do something for attention, but none of the ones you mentioned swapped babies around, did they?"

"True," I admit. "But maybe Bronagh liked having a certain sort of baby in her care. After all, Theo was relatively easy to look after." I hesitate. "And Theo had *you*."

"That is *ridiculous*." He doesn't meet my eye. "For that matter, it could just as easily have been that other nurse—the grumpy one. What was her name? Paula."

"Also true. And in fact, there *was* a strange incident with her, when I pointed out that David's arterial line was loose. Which is why Paula is number four on my list."

"And five? Who's number five?"

"Number five is you, Pete," I say softly. "You're my final suspect."

He sighs despairingly. "Not this—"

"Because I can't rule you out, can I?" I continue. "I don't believe you'd want someone else's baby just because it was healthier than ours. But you knew what I was thinking that day—that our baby was going to die. You knew how badly I was taking it. And you knew I'd had mental health issues in the past. I think you might be capable of doing something like that to protect *me*." I hesitate. "And, for that matter, to protect *us*. Because our lives would have been very different if we'd had David instead of Theo, wouldn't they? We wouldn't have had Miles and Lucy's resources to cushion the blow of his disability. And the brutal truth is, relationships do often break down in circumstances like those. So let's face facts. However unthinkable it is, however unlike you it may seem, you *did* have a motive to take Theo that day."

There's a long silence. Pete closes his eyes, as if in pain.

I add, "And that's why I need to ask you, before we spend a lot of time and money investigating these other possibilities: Did you have anything, anything at all, to do with the swapping of those babies?"

He looks me in the eye. Those kind, gentle brown eyes of his that I've stared into so many times—across the kitchen table as we eat, when we share a knowing glance at parties, when we make love—lock intently onto mine.

"I did not," he says quietly.

But really, what can you tell from someone's eyes? Presumably every one of those nurses I listed had gazes as clear and untroubled as his.

And I still can't shake off the sense that there's something he's not telling me.

"Do you believe me?" he adds.

"Of course," I say, although I don't suppose either of us really thinks I mean it.

77

PETE

I FOUND MURDO MCALLISTER through LinkedIn. I simply set my profile to incognito and browsed Miles's contacts. About a dozen were ex-Hardings. I chose Murdo because his dates showed he'd left the bank around the same time as Miles, and also because under INTERESTS he'd listed "Mayfair Mayflies," the rugby team Lucy said Miles used to play for.

Contacting him was a risk, of course. Murdo might simply forward my email to Miles. But I was betting that Maddie was right, and that what Miles was doing to us was part of a consistent pattern of behavior.

And besides, Maddie was definitely right in saying we had to do something. If nothing else, I had to show her that I was just as committed as she was to clearing my name.

Murdo suggested meeting in a pub in Shepherd Market, off Piccadilly. It wasn't an area I knew—a maze of tiny streets and alleyways where wine merchants and bookshops rubbed shoul-

ders with embassies and pricey antiques dealers. But the tradi-
tional Victorian pub he'd chosen could have been in any market
town in England. As I walked in he stood up and greeted me, a
pleasant, burly man with thinning curly hair and a faint Scottish
accent.

He allowed me to buy him a beer, but only a half. "I don't have
long—I've got a call at one thirty. You said you wanted to talk
about Miles Lambert. You're not about to offer him a job, are
you?"

I shook my head. "It's a bit more complicated than that."

I gave him the short version. When I'd finished, he said flatly,
"What you describe doesn't surprise me in the least."

I pulled out my notebook. "Can you be a bit more specific?"

Just for a moment, Murdo looked anxious. "This is off the record, right?"

"If you like."

He nodded. "I met Miles when he joined Hardings. He was
headed for the top—a golden boy. A few people thought it odd
he'd moved jobs every couple of years before coming to us, but
since he'd always moved to more senior positions or for a bigger
salary, you could read it as smart career planning. This wasn't
long after the crash, and everything was changing—the regulators
were insisting on banks setting up internal compliance depart-
ments, risk assessment experts were getting seats on the board,
that kind of stuff." Murdo took a pull of his beer. "The traders all
hated it, but we could see why it was necessary. Miles's specialty
was spotting gaps in the new regulations and gaming them. Nothing wrong with that, of course—it was what we were paid to do.
And ultimately, if Compliance was happy, fine."

"But Miles went further?"

Murdo nodded. "In that environment, it was all too easy to
start thinking, *How do I package this so Compliance approves it,
even though I know it's actually against the rules?* At the end of
the day, they were just another bunch of muppets you had to out-

smart. And Miles was good at it. He was a bloody professional banker—focused, driven, with an unbelievable work ethic, but he never got stressed or shouted at people. And believe me, that's unusual—trading's a high-pressure environment. He was put in charge of a team, and although he drove them pretty hard, they all seemed to like him."

"So what happened?"

"Rogue trading," Murdo said shortly. "We were both working with complex equity derivatives that most people in the bank couldn't even spell, let alone understand. But essentially, if you made a bet on a particular asset rising, you had to hedge it by making a bet on another asset that could be counted on to move in the opposite direction. That way, you limited the bank's risk, so you were allowed to make a bigger initial bet. It's a bit like taking out an insurance policy against your house burning down—it means you can risk buying a bigger house than you otherwise could. Miles had found a way to make the risky trade without taking out the insurance, by making fictitious hedges. To begin with, he mostly got his bets right, which meant huge profits for his desk. He concealed the source by making more trades, and so on and so on. It was crazy, really—he was bound to get found out eventually. In the event, it was a whistleblower—someone on his team who wasn't quite as brainwashed as the others."

"And Miles got fired?"

"In the end, yes. But before that, there was an investigation. That was the first I knew of it—when the audit people started crawling all over him. The sensible thing to do at that point would have been to clear his position, deny everything, and keep his head down. But he didn't." Murdo shook his head in disbelief. "He came to me after work one day and casually asked if I'd set up a trading account he could use, now the heat was on him. As a fellow Mayfly, he said, he knew he could trust me. I told him I'd have to be mad to do that—I'd end up getting dragged into it, too. He just laughed and said, 'Well, why not? This is the most fun I've had in ages.' He was actually enjoying the whole damn thing. It was as if he thought he was invincible."

"So you refused to help?"

Murdo nodded. "But the bastard told the investigators I'd been part of it anyway. There was absolutely no truth to it, of course. But I knew I was under a shadow after that, so I left."

"When was all this?"

"Just over two years ago."

About the same time David and Theo were in hospital. "And what about the Mayflies? He left the team because of a knee injury, I heard?"

Murdo snorted. "Who told you that? He got thrown out because he took it too damn seriously."

"In what way?"

"Look—we're a pub team. A bunch of guys who all played at a decent level at university and aren't quite ready to hang up our boots. Miles became captain because no one else wanted it. And to be fair, because he was the best player. But he hated losing—just hated it. Pretty soon he was giving us prematch pep talks. We even had to chant stuff out loud—'Desire. Hurt. Dominate. Destroy,' that kind of thing. That one was actually an England dressing room chant from the 2003 World Cup, but we played in a Sunday league, for Christ's sake. And then, in one match, when we were losing sixteen to twelve, there was a scrum in our half near the touchline and Miles gouged out the opposing player's eye with his thumb. The poor guy had to go straight to hospital and have the rest of it removed—he's got a glass eye now. Miles didn't even apologize to him. We took a vote after the game and told Miles he was out. He just shrugged. It was weird, really. He went all quiet and still, almost blank, and said, 'You're losers anyway. I'm bored of the lot of you.' It was as if he'd turned into a robot."

I nodded. "I know that voice."

"So anyway," Murdo said, "my advice to anyone, and the reason I agreed to meet you, is to say: Steer clear of Miles Lambert."

"I wish I could."

Murdo hesitated. "Look, there's something else. It's probably nothing, but . . ."

"What?"

"You know I said it was a whistleblower who first raised concerns about Miles? It's meant to be a confidential process, but the consensus around the office was that it was a guy called Anand, a young analyst who'd only recently transferred onto the team. About a month after Miles left, Anand was out jogging when he was the victim of a hit-and-run. It was raining and visibility was bad—no one saw anything, least of all Anand. He broke his pelvis in five places—he was lucky not to be killed. There was no evidence it was anything to do with Miles. But put it this way, a few of us Mayflies took to running in pairs for a while after that."

I thought of Jane Tigman, knocked off her bike after complaining about Theo.

"I don't think it's nothing," I said slowly. "I think it's what he does."

Murdo nodded, and finished his drink. "And remember, all this is off the record. The last thing I want is Miles waiting outside *my* front door."

78

<u>Case no. 12675/PU78B65, Exhibit 41. Retrieved from</u>
<u>Maddie Wilson's iPad internet history. Peter Riley's laptop</u>
<u>was in police custody at the time.</u>

THE PSYCHOPATH TEST

Do you have psychopathic traits? Take our test to determine whether you share any of the characteristics of a high-functioning psychopath.

People generally take to me straightaway.

○ True   ○ False

I rarely get tongue-tied.

○ True   ○ False

I am easily bored.

○ True   ○ False

I rarely feel guilty.

○ True   ○ False

When I move jobs, I am unlikely to stay in touch with old colleagues.

○ True   ○ False

When I move towns, I am unlikely to stay in touch with old neighbors.

○ True   ○ False

If I fail at something, it is usually because I have been let down by others.

○ True   ○ False

I enjoy taking risks.

○ True   ○ False

Most of my exes are a little bit crazy.

○ True   ○ False

I don't like to stay too long in one situation.

○ True   ○ False

When others panic, I keep a clear head.

○ True   ○ False

I don't get bothered by the suffering of others.

○ True   ○ False

If I accidentally walked out of a restaurant without paying, I wouldn't go back—it's the waiter's fault for not realizing.

○ True   ○ False

Burglars who get shot have only themselves to blame.

○ True   ○ False

I will take responsibility for something, but I will not express remorse.

○ True   ○ False

I would probably be unfaithful if I could be sure there would be no repercussions.

○ True   ○ False

I rarely cry at sad films.

○ True   ○ False

I would make an excuse to avoid going to a colleague's funeral.

○ True   ○ False

Change excites me.

○ True   ○ False

The best decisions are often made quickly.

O True   O False

I don't get mad, I get even.

O True   O False

SCORING: Count all the TRUE boxes you have checked and deduct the number of FALSE boxes. If you have a score of more than +10, you score highly for psychopathic traits.

79

MADDIE

I INSIST ON BEING the one to talk to Bronagh. It makes sense anyway for Pete, as the journalist, to track down Miles's ex-colleagues, but it's more than that. I want to look Bronagh in the eye and ask whether there was ever anything between her and Pete. And while I can tell Pete isn't happy about us meeting, neither can he object without digging himself any deeper into the hole he's in.

Do I really think there's anything to be suspicious of? I'm not sure, any more than I'm sure about the other accusations that have been swirling around him. Of course, if it turns out there *was* something, on one level it would be hypocritical of me to mind, given that I've not been a saint myself. But I would mind, all the same. Pete's loyalty is so much a part of his character that something like that would be a big deal for him. He isn't the sort to have a quick fling and put it out of his head. It would be a sign that our relationship is fundamentally flawed.

What was that line from that old TV show? "The innocent have nothing to fear." And yet here we are, and I *do* fear. Fear losing my family, fear what the courts might order, fear what Miles Lambert might do in his unstoppable drive to get Theo back.

But most of all, fear what I might find out.

I try to push all that from my mind as I enter the Costa on the ground floor of St. Alexander's where Bronagh suggested meeting. She's already there, carrying a smoothie and some kind of cake toward a table, and for a moment I stop and study her. The uniform suits her: The scrubs the neonatal nurses wear, made of thin blue cotton, flatter her lithe frame the way pajamas or a T-shirt would, outlining the shape of her buttocks, the slimness of her shoulders, making her look almost undressed. Today she has her jet-black hair tied in a plait that rests between her shoulder blades. Is she pretty? Yes, I decide, reasonably so. Is she beautiful? Probably not, but then, women don't need to be beautiful to attract men.

I buy myself a coffee, playing for time, then summon up my resolve and go over. "Bronagh. Hi."

"Oh—hi." She raises the cake, which I now see is a chocolate muffin. "Hope you don't mind. This is breakfast *and* lunch." It's almost three P.M.

"You must be really busy. I won't keep you long." I sit down. "You're probably wondering why I wanted to meet."

Bronagh's blue eyes give nothing away. "I guess I was a wee bit surprised when you got in touch."

"And *I* was surprised to find you back at St. Alexander's. Pete told me you'd been suspended."

Bronagh shrugs. "That's routine when they're conducting investigations. It's all cleared up now."

"You mean, the lie he told for you worked," I say quietly.

Something flashes across Bronagh's face. Alarm? Defensiveness? One thing is certain: She definitely knows what I'm talking about. "What lie?"

"When we were interviewed by NHS Resolution, Pete told the investigators he remembered seeing the security tag on Theo's leg within a few minutes of him being transferred into your incubator. But in fact, a registrar noticed it still hadn't been put on hours later."

"Maybe the registrar was wrong, then, and Pete was right."

"He sent me a picture that day—Pete, that is. From his phone, so it's got the time it was taken on it. In that photo, Theo isn't wearing a security tag." I lean forward. "And, partly because of that stupid lie, Pete is now being investigated by the police. They're accusing him of swapping the babies deliberately. He's already been questioned under caution."

"*Jesus.*" Bronagh's hand flies to her mouth. Her look of dismay surely can't be fake.

"As a result of which, he's not allowed to be alone with Theo," I continue, deliberately piling on the pressure. "Which, since we're also facing a custody hearing with the Lamberts, means it's quite possible we'll lose Theo entirely. You can imagine what the prospect of *that* is doing to Pete."

"Shite in a bucket." Bronagh looks appalled. "I had no idea. The fact is, things got pretty crazy around here—there was one lot investigating how Theo and David got mixed up, and another lot crawling over why our mortality rates weren't better. That's when I messaged Pete—when it looked like they were trying to find someone to scapegoat. But as it turned out, once the review was over, they realized they needed every experienced nurse they could get."

I frown. "The mortality review is over?"

Bronagh nods. "And not a moment too soon."

"So what did it find? *Was* there a suspicious pattern of deaths?"

"What?" Bronagh looks pained. "Jesus, no. There's only one thing wrong with our NICU, and that's where it is." When I still look puzzled, she gestures up at the atrium. "Right in the middle of central London. Over half my salary goes to rent, and since I can't afford to live anywhere within fifty minutes of here, half of what's left over goes to travel. Then there's the fact that we do twelve-hour shifts to minimize the number of handovers—it's a pretty grueling schedule even if you're used to it. We're permanently understaffed. I should be looking after one or two babies, tops, but it's a rare week when I don't have three or even four. Plus, our NICU gets all the cases like yours, the babies born in expensive Harley Street clinics that aren't equipped to deal with them, as well as the health tourists and the mothers from deprived areas who maybe don't use the midwifery system as well as they should. Oh, and we just had five years of government thinking we could probably manage just as well on half as much money. It's hardly surprising we had a dip in our outcomes."

"So nothing . . . sinister, then?" I say. "Nothing that could be attributed to an individual?"

"Oh heck. You haven't been watching *Nurses Who Kill,* have you? Look, every single neonatal death here is investigated by postmortem and clinical review. And we're a small team. If we had a Beverley Allitt in our NICU, she or he wouldn't last a month without being spotted."

Is Bronagh telling the truth? There's no reason to think she isn't. But then, if she had somehow been responsible for swapping Theo and David, she'd hardly say so.

"There's something else I have to ask you," I say after a moment.

"What's that?"

"Have you seen Pete at all, since we left the NICU? As opposed to messaging, or speaking to him on the phone?"

Bronagh nods. "He and Theo came back to the NICU around Theo's first birthday. He'd baked a cake. Little Theo looked so sweet, tucked up in that blue papoose Pete wore."

"Any other time? After that? Or before?"

"Let me see." Bronagh looks thoughtful. "I might have bumped into him on that bike ride the lads did. A group of us swung by a bar where they were drinking one night. But I can't recall whether your man was there or not."

And that's how I know she's telling the truth about the mortality review, and there not being anything untoward going on in the NICU. Because, as it now turns out, Bronagh is a very bad liar indeed.

BRONAGH LOOKS ACROSS THE café. "There's Paula." She sounds relieved. "I'd best be getting back upstairs."

I look in the direction of her gaze. Paula, the nurse who'd been so stressy about David that day, is coming toward us. "Do you know Paula well?" I ask.

"Sure, she's a grand girl. Why?"

"There's no chance *she* could have swapped David and Theo, is there?"

Even as I say it, I know how desperate it sounds. Bronagh looks at me askance. "And why in God's name would she do that?"

I can't answer. My suspicions, which had sounded so logical when I was listing them to Pete, now just seem silly and melodramatic. "I don't know," I say helplessly. "Because she could?"

"Look," Bronagh says patiently. "First, she's not a nutter, any more than I am. Second, if a NICU nurse *was* going to go crazy and start playing God, they wouldn't do it by swapping babies around. A simple DNA test, and it would all come out. No— what happened to Theo and David was a tragic mistake in a busy, understaffed ward." She lowers her voice. "I probably shouldn't tell you this, given that you're suing the place. But there were five admissions that day—that's almost double the norm. Every one an emergency. And we were down two nurses, what with the winter vomiting bug that was going around. Everyone knows that's the kind of environment where mistakes get made. And if that isn't mentioned in the case report—well, someone's trying to buff something, because it should be."

Paula's reached our table now. "Coming up?" she asks Bronagh. "Or are you busy?"

"Remember Theo Riley's mum?" Bronagh says, indicating me. "We were just chatting."

Paula looks no more pleased to see me than she did two years ago. "Oh, right. Well, it's almost handover, so . . ."

"Sure." Bronagh stands up.

"Wait," I say quickly. "I've got a question for you, Paula. That first day, when David and Theo got swapped, were either of the Lamberts around?"

Wariness flashes across Paula's face. "I've already told the hospital investigators everything I remember."

"I'm sure. But it might help if you could tell me, too."

Paula shrugs. "Mrs. Lambert got here a couple of hours after the babies were admitted. I'd been given David to look after— I was just setting things up for him when she arrived. That's when I realized no one had thought to put a tag on him." Paula glances at Bronagh. "It didn't occur to me to check with Bron, to see if hers had no tag, too. Why would I? I just typed his details into our software." Her voice catches, and for a moment I think she might be going to cry. "I'm so sorry. It must have caused you so much heartbreak. But I really think it was just a freak accident."

I feel my shoulders sag. If the Lamberts had arrived too late to be responsible for the swap, and it was neither of the nurses, I can see why the finger of suspicion keeps coming back to Pete.

"Besides, I won't forget them in a hurry," Paula says. "The Lamberts, I mean."

My ears prick up. "Why's that?"

"He was a cold fish. Both of them were. You get used to the way people react when they first come onto the NICU—the shock, I mean, and the worry. You could tell *she* was anxious, but with him it was like he was being given a guided tour—as if it was interesting, but nothing personal." She stops. "I remember looking over and seeing your partner, Pete, by Bronagh's station. He was sobbing his eyes out. And why not? A lot of men do that, particularly when they think no one's looking. You've just become a father, maybe a whole couple of months before you thought you would, and suddenly you're on a ward like ours, being told your baby might not live. I remember turning back to my incubator and seeing Mr. Lambert. He was watching your partner, too. *Studying* him, is the only way I can describe it. Like he was fascinated, but also a bit puzzled. And then he looked at his wife and said, 'Well, I'd better get back to my desk.' As if he'd just popped out to get a sandwich. And she only nodded, as if that was totally normal, too."

80

Case no. 12675/PU78B65, Exhibit 43. Texts from Bronagh Walsh to Peter Riley. Peter Riley's iPhone was in police custody at the time.

Just thought you'd want to know—M came to St A's today. Told her the only times we met were when (a) you came to the ward after Theo's birthday and (b) that maybe I'd bumped into you at the bike ride and said hello but couldn't really remember. Didn't mention the other day—she seemed to think it was just messaging. Hope that all tallies?

That OK? X

P? Everything OK? Really hate to cause u any trouble. She told me about the police and Theo etc. Jesus. You poor guys.

P??? You getting these?

81

MADDIE

IT'S NEARLY TIME TO go and pick up Theo. I'd gone to St. Alexander's by car, to give myself more time. Now I sit in a car park on Marylebone Road, looking at Facebook.

Or, more specifically, at Pete's Facebook. So many pictures of Theo, his little limbs gradually shrinking as I scroll backward in time. Theo at eighteen months. Theo crawling. Theo in a babygrow.

And then the bike ride. The pictures I stopped looking at when my psychosis kicked in. The grinning young men in bike helmets taking selfies in Scotland, the Lake District, the Yorkshire Moors . . .

York. A rest day in the city, followed by a whole weekend off. No helmets or Lycra in those photos, just massive breakfasts in cafés and pints of beer in pubs. A night in a club—and yes, there are women around. Nothing untoward, just chatting, drinks in hand.

I do a search for *Bronagh Walsh*. And lo, there's Bronagh's profile. The picture shows her at what looks like a music festival, a sparkler in each hand, pulling a pose. I tap PHOTOS, but she's set them to private. She hasn't done that with her friends, though— all 412 of them. I scroll through until I find Paula, then go to Paula's page. She hasn't made any settings private, so I can look at her pictures and search them by location. Sure enough, some are tagged "York." Facebook even identifies the bar where they were taken—Vudu Lounge, on Swinegate.

With Bronagh Walsh and seven others, it adds helpfully. And there's Bronagh, holding a cocktail, with three other girls, all in short dresses. It's the first time I've seen her with makeup on and her hair down. She's undeniably striking. No sign of Pete, though.

I suddenly feel ashamed. What am I doing, spying on my partner like this? And in any case, what am I hoping to prove? Bronagh's already admitted she was there. It doesn't mean anything happened.

But even so, I'm sure she was being evasive about something. Just as Pete was.

I put the iPad down and start the car. I'm going to be late for Theo. Again.

As I drive to the Lamberts', cutting the traffic lights as fine as I dare, I think about the other things I heard today. Presumably what Bronagh said about the NICU being exonerated by the mortality review could be checked. More interesting, perhaps, was what Paula said about Miles. As I'd told Pete, lack of emotion is typical of a psychopath, as is clearheadedness in a crisis. And studying Pete when he was crying—that, too, is something I'd read about: Without strong feelings of their own, psychopaths learn to study and mimic the emotions of others.

But I can't get away from the fact that Paula said the Lamberts came onto the ward later that day, when the swap must have already happened. And from the sound of it—"I'd better get back to my desk"—Miles hadn't spent much time in the NICU even when he did come.

I'd gone to see Bronagh with such high hopes. But the more I learn, the more I seem to go around in circles. Circles that have at their center just one fixed point, one person with both motive and opportunity.

Pete.

I sigh aloud. At least the traffic is flowing. I reach Haydon Gardens in under thirty minutes. When I buzz the Lamberts' intercom, the front door is opened by someone I haven't seen before, a sandy-haired woman in her thirties.

"Hello," she says pleasantly. "Can I help you?"

"I'm Maddie. Theo's mum?"

"Oh, of course. He's just getting his coat. I'm Jill, by the way."

Now that I look closer, I see she's wearing what could almost be a uniform—dark trousers and a dark-blue pullover, with a lighter-blue polo shirt under it. The pullover has a discreet logo on the chest, a small embroidered N.

"The new nanny," Jill adds smilingly, seeing my incomprehension.

A small fair-haired boy roughly the same age as Theo peers around the edge of the door. "Are you Theo's mummy?" he demands.

"I am, yes. Who are you?"

"I'm Saul."

Lucy appears in the hallway, holding Theo's hand. He's in his coat, carrying a drawing. "Oh, hello Maddie," she says in her usual vague way.

"What's going on?" I say. "Where's Tania?"

"Look, Mummy!" Theo says impatiently, waving the drawing at me. "It's a *exploshun!*"

"You've drawn an explosion. That's a nice drawing, Theo. What's exploding?"

This is a detail Theo clearly hasn't considered. While he's thinking, Lucy says in a rush, "It was Pete's idea, actually."

"Pete's?" I echo.

"Yes—he mentioned it to the CAFCASS woman. About how Theo might benefit from a nanny with better English. And the suggestion there should be another little boy for him to play with. Saul's going to be with us three days a week from now on." As I stand up from looking at Theo's drawing, Lucy adds, "So you see, we *are* listening. When it's something for Theo—something that'll help him—we'll always try to do the right thing. Really, we're very reasonable people. And Jill's terrific. She's a Norland, you know—they're the absolute best. We're already seeing such a difference. I mean, Theo is always adorable, isn't he, but sometimes he can be a bit of a live wire, and not always do what he's asked. He'll do *anything* for Jill."

Theo, looking at his drawing, comes to a decision. " 'S'an exploding *house*, Mummy! Pow! Pow! *Pow!*"

82

PETE

"I ALMOST EXPLODED MYSELF," Maddie said.

"I think I would have." I finished the last mouthful of coffee. "God, I miss this coffee machine. Greg and Kate have one of those pod things."

"What's really annoying is that now Miles and Lucy will take all the credit for the improvement in Theo's behavior. When the truth is, it's down to you." Maddie gestured at my star charts, still Blu-Tacked to the walls. I noticed she hadn't kept up with most of them.

I sighed. "I suppose the chances of getting Theo out of that nanny share and into a nursery are now precisely zilch."

Maddie nodded. "And guess what? I looked up Norland nannies' salaries. Experienced ones earn over sixty grand a year."

"Bloody hell!"

"Which Miles and Lucy will no doubt invoice us for half of, when they claim child maintenance for David." Maddie straightened her back. "But we are not going to let this get us down. We are going to win."

I didn't reply. It increasingly seemed to me that Miles wasn't putting a foot wrong, while we were floundering. "What about St. Alexander's? How did you get on?"

"Oh—they're out of special measures, or whatever it was called. That spike in mortality was due to staff shortages, apparently. And Bronagh and Paula have both been reinstated." Maddie shook her head. "On reflection, that was probably a bit fanciful, to think they might have had anything to do with it. After all, how much of a coincidence would it be if there was a psychopath and a rogue nurse on the same ward at the same time?"

"Which one did you speak to—Bronagh or Paula?" I turned and put my cup under the Jura's spout. "I think I'll have another cup."

"Both. They're friends, actually. Which reminds me—you didn't tell me they came to meet the bike ride in York."

"Didn't I?" I pushed the button, and the noise of the grinding beans meant I had to wait a few moments before replying. "Greg did mention that some of the nurses turned up. But I wasn't there by then. York was where I peeled off and came back here, remember? I got back on the Friday morning."

"Oh." Maddie thought. "Was it Friday? The days were a bit of a blur by then."

I nodded. "So I gathered."

"And when Bronagh told you about her suspension, when exactly was that? She messaged you, presumably?"

"Maddie, what is this?" I protested.

"I'm just trying to get a time line in my head. Unless you don't want to tell me, of course."

I shrugged. "I can't remember the exact date. It was the morning after the Lamberts served the Notice of Proceedings—that day we both took Theo to their house, and Lucy offered to make us tea. And yes, Bronagh messaged." My cappuccino was done now, so I took it out of the machine. "And I messaged back, but she wanted to meet, so we had a coffee at a Starbucks near the hospital."

"I didn't realize you actually met up. She implied it was just a text exchange when I spoke to her."

"Well, it wasn't. Look, I did a stupid thing, okay?" I said, exasperated. "I offered to help her out, and I probably shouldn't have. You would have talked me out of it if you'd known. So yes, my bad. But considering everything else that's going on, is that really the priority?"

"Probably not," Maddie agreed.

We were both silent for a while.

"I think we should try to track down Tania next," Maddie said thoughtfully.

"Why? Presumably she'll have been handsomely paid off by the Lamberts."

"She might be pretty angry, even so. She only had that job a few weeks, which doesn't look good on anyone's CV. And she lived in the house with them. I've a feeling she might be able to tell us something useful."

"All right, then. But let's do it quietly. I'd feel awful if she suffered the same fate as Jane Tigman and that whistleblower." I went and put my coffee cup in the sink. "I'll go and hurry Theo up. I want to read him his story before I head over to Greg and Kate's."

I took the stairs two at a time, relieved that our conversation about Bronagh was now over.

83

MADDIE

THE PRELIMINARY HEARING TAKES place in a bland, 1960s building on Cricklewood Lane—it could be a public library, if it weren't for the royal coat of arms outside. There's a smaller version of the same crest on the wall of the courtroom, which otherwise looks just like any medium-sized meeting room in a slightly run-down office. The judge, a brisk woman in her fifties called Marion Wakefield, wears a gray suit and sits behind a desk on a slightly raised platform.

The Lamberts sit with their barrister and solicitor on one side of a row of chairs facing the judge, and Pete and I sit on the other with Anita. It's all surprisingly informal—none of the lawyers wear a wig or gown, or get to their feet to speak. Lyn the CAF-CASS adviser—who turns out to be a tiny, innocuous-looking woman with sharp eyes—sits on her own, in the second row of chairs.

Judge Wakefield begins by reminding us that this isn't a hearing to consider evidence, only whether the case can be resolved without the court's involvement, and if not, what evidence she'll need at the second hearing to help her make a decision. She looks at the Lamberts, then Pete and me. "So my first question to you, through your legal representatives, is whether there is any possibility you could come to an agreement."

Miles's barrister says, "My clients have tried to explore every avenue for compromise, madam, including becoming Theo's godparents and inviting Theo to share David's nanny. But ultimately, Theo is their son and, like any parent, they want to make the day-to-day decisions regarding his care."

The judge nods. "Ms. Chowdry?"

"My clients have also tried to compromise—the suggestion that the applicants become Theo's godparents actually came from them," Anita says. "They regard Theo as their son, and believe it is in his best interests not to be removed from them at this important stage of his development."

"Thank you," Marion Wakefield says briskly. "This is clearly an unusual and difficult case, and for that reason alone, a fuller hearing seems necessary. I'm going to accept CAFCASS's recommendation that there should be a more detailed report on the safeguarding issues. I'm also going to direct that Theo is assessed by a psychologist to see what impact changing families at his age might have on him." She looks straight at me. "Ms. Wilson, I'm going to direct that you must not travel abroad without the court's permission. And as there has been a question raised about your alcohol intake, I'm going to order that you give blood and hair samples, to be assessed for current and past alcohol intake respectively."

An alcohol test. Anita warned me this might happen, given what Lyn said in her safeguarding letter, and also that there's no way of disguising the amount I've been drinking—although the blood test will only measure what's in my system at the time, the hair sample will show how much I've been drinking over the whole of the last year. I feel my cheeks burn with a mixture of anger and shame.

Anita says calmly, "Madam, we'd like to request that Mr. Riley be allowed back into the family home. While my clients absolutely refute the suggestion that Ms. Wilson could be unfit to care for Theo, it seems illogical to raise that possibility and at the same time bar his primary carer from caring for him."

"I accept that argument," Marion Wakefield says. "Accordingly, I will make no direction about Mr. Riley at this time. But since the present situation is a voluntary one, by arrangement with CAFCASS, it will be up to Ms. Edwards whether she is satisfied with that."

"I am satisfied if the court is satisfied," Lyn says meekly.

"We would also like to ask that the court consolidate all the proceedings in Theo's case," Anita says.

"Mr. Kelly?" The judge turns to the Lamberts' lawyer.

"I was going to suggest the same thing, madam."

"Then we will have one hearing for Theo, in approximately twelve weeks' time, and another at a later date for David." The judge makes a note. "Is there anything else?"

There isn't. The lawyers start shuffling papers together and the judge turns back to her computer. It seems incredible that such a momentous case can be dealt with so quickly, but of course it hasn't been, not really. This is only the opening salvo. And thanks to CAFCASS, Miles has achieved almost everything he wanted. But Pete's allowed to come home. That's something.

Marion Wakefield stays at her desk, making notes, while the rest of us leave. There's a bottleneck at the door, with both sets of parents and lawyers reaching it at the same time. "After you," Miles says politely, just as Pete says firmly, "After you." It's all bizarrely civilized. Eventually Pete waves Lucy through and follows behind, and Miles gestures for me to go ahead of him. I realize he's very close behind me—I can even feel his breath on my neck. No, not just his breath: The bastard is actually blowing on me.

I've worn my hair up, and the sensation on my nape is unmistakable. I stop dead, outraged.

"Such a pity about the hair test," he murmurs. "Some people shave their heads, I gather. But then the doctors use one from down there instead. Do you wax down there, Maddie? I hope not. I picture you with curls."

As he speaks, something insinuates itself between my buttocks. His fingers. I jump forward as if stung, and hear—feel, almost—his chuckle. Furious, I look around. His face is the picture of innocence. All three lawyers, and the judge, are looking at me. I open my mouth to say something. But what? It might look like the act of a desperate woman who didn't get what she wanted at the hearing. A drunk, even. And who would believe that Miles Lambert was reckless enough to grope me in a courtroom?

But I can't do nothing. So I say sharply, "Don't do that."

Miles only grins, the smile of a man who knows he's winning.

84

MADDIE

I DON'T TELL PETE. There's a chance he'll storm off and confront Miles, and I suspect Miles would enjoy that. He might even be hoping he can make Pete look aggressive and hot-tempered, and by implication a bad parent.

After the hearing Pete goes to Greg and Kate's to get his suitcase, while I go back to the house. By the time I get there I'm kicking myself for not making more of a fuss. Shouldn't a strong, confident woman—which is what I know myself to be—have called Miles out? I've always fended off drunken fumbles with a firm stare and a cutting put-down, but promised myself that, if anything more serious happened, I'd stand up for myself; go to the police, if need be. I wouldn't be a victim.

But it had been so quick, so shocking, so hard to take in.

Is that how people like that get away with it, I wonder—sheer effrontery and self-confidence? My anger is growing by the minute, but of course it's too late now. That's another weapon in their armory, I realize—surprise. And the ridiculous British habit of being polite, no matter what the circumstances.

Well, I'm not British. If Miles does it again, I resolve to punch him, courtroom or no courtroom.

Pete arrives, carrying his overnight case. "Welcome home," I say brightly. "I'd open the champagne, but . . ."

He nods and looks around. There's an awkward moment. Probably no one else, looking at the two of us, would even notice it. But we don't hug, or kiss, or fall into each other's arms. We're polite and cheerful and false.

Is it because of what Miles did? Because of not telling Pete? Or is it because of all the other secrets that have started to ooze their way to the surface over the last few weeks, like bubbles squelching out of mud? I want to trust Pete, of course I do, but there's a tiny part of me that knows good people can do bad things, and that loyalty isn't the same as certainty.

Losing Theo isn't the only threat to our relationship, I realize. Even if we get to keep him—which, I have to admit to myself, is looking far from certain—will all the stress and suspicion leave its mark? Can we really survive this as a couple?

I've heard people say there are no winners in legal cases. I'm beginning to understand why.

MY ANGER ABOUT MILES makes me even more determined to speak to Tania, though. What he did to me fits with everything else I know about him, as well as something I read online: "For psychopaths, sex is all about gratification, conquest, risk, and reward."

Where to start? I never took Tania's number. But then I think of Lucy's Facebook, all those pictures of expeditions to the zoo and park. I reach for my iPad.

Sure enough, under the list of people who've liked the pictures is Tania Lefebvre. I message her.

Hi Tania, it's Maddie Wilson here. I know this will seem odd, but could I talk to you about your experience of working for Miles Lambert?

After a little while, a reply comes back.

I think you might be more interested to talk to the nanny before me, Michaela Costea (we share the same agency). Here are her contact details. Bonne chance.

Attached is a phone number.

"MILES LAMBERT FIRED YOU, didn't he? He saw you going through Facebook or whatever, and using his coffee machine when you were meant to be looking after David."

We meet in a café on Finchley Road, a small, bustling place with steamed-up windows where the owners, a family, shout to one another cheerfully in Turkish. Michaela sips her latte and nods.

"Yes. He fired me. But it wasn't how you said."

"What happened?"

Michaela pauses before replying. She's a pretty girl, I decide, although her bleached-white hair does her no favors. "I didn't behave too good myself. Listen, I'm not proud of it. But he was worse."

"Why? What did he do?"

She sighs. "I suppose I was angry with her—with Mrs. Lambert. Who has a coffee machine and stops people using it? 'You're just the nanny. Here, you can drink Nescafé.' I mean, *really*? So when they were out, I made myself a coffee." She shakes her head. "I didn't know it was *his* rule, of course. Everything in that house was him. And yes, while I drank my coffee I looked at my Instagram. Why not? It wasn't like David needed me right then."

"But Miles saw you on his camera."

Michaela nods. "They hadn't told me they were spying on me, either. Not in so many words."

"And then he fired you," I say, not quite sure where this is going. Having a hidden camera is distrustful and controlling, certainly, but I don't think it's illegal.

"Not then, he didn't." Michaela seems to come to a decision. "Okay. He comes to me that night, when she's at her book club. 'I've seen you drinking the coffee,' he says. 'My wife gets very angry about things like that. Personally, I think it's a ridiculous rule. So let's not tell her. Our secret, right?' And then he . . . he . . ." She suddenly looks very young. "Well, you can guess the rest."

"Ah. You slept with him?"

"*Sleeping.* What an English word. We say *a băga regele-n castel* when we want to be polite. Putting the king inside the castle. Yes, we did it. I told myself it was my revenge, to pay his wife back for being so uptight." She shrugs again, an attempt at bravura that doesn't quite work. "I would have done it with him maybe once, then stopped. But he came to my room again a few days later. She was downstairs. I knew it was wrong but he just assumed . . . Somehow it was hard to say no. And then, the next time, we did it in the kitchen when she was right next door, in the playroom. We were behind the big counter in the middle, what she calls the island. He just unzipped himself and put my hand on it. I was wearing a short skirt . . . It was crazy stupid. If she'd come in . . . But you know something? I think he liked it. That we might get caught, I mean."

"Do you think she knew?"

Michaela looks thoughtful. "I don't think so. But she's strange with him, actually. Like she's a little bit scared but she also depends on him for everything. I think she only sees what she wants to see."

"Did you ever see him be violent towards her? Or mistreat David?"

Michaela shakes her head. "No."

That's unfortunate in some ways. Having sex with the nanny behind Lucy's back is gross, but it doesn't help with the case. "And what about you? Did he ever threaten you?"

"Just once." Michaela blinks back tears. "He came to me and said it had to stop. I was . . . you know, relieved, really. I told him he was right and we should never talk about it again. He said I didn't understand. It wasn't stopping because it was wrong. It was because he was bored with me. He threw an envelope on the bed. He said, 'That's five hundred pounds. I'll tell my wife I fired you for drinking the coffee. Now get out of the house.'" Michaela's crying openly now, the tears running down her pale skin. "I didn't want to get fired—the agency will drop you if it happens too often. I said I would stay a bit longer, so it looked okay, then give my notice. And I—I reminded him we had a secret. I wouldn't have told her, but I thought he should consider what he'd done, and maybe behave a bit better. And that's when he changed."

"Changed how?"

"Cold. He went cold. There was nothing—no expression in his face. He said, 'If you ever threaten me again, I will carry you down to the basement and drown you in the swimming pool. The police will think it was an accident.'" Michaela shudders. "I believed him. I was so frightened. I took the money and packed my things right away. I wouldn't go back to that house. Not if you paid me all the money in the world. And I told the next girl to be careful, too."

85

MADDIE

THE WRITTEN DIRECTION FROM the judge says my blood and hair samples have to be taken by a GP. I go to Sharon Randall, a private doctor I used when I first came to London.

"And I need something that'll stop me drinking," I say when the samples have been sealed. "Really stop me, so the judge will know I mean it."

"That would be disulfiram," Sharon says immediately. "Called Antabuse in this country. But I warn you, it's not for the faint-hearted."

"In what way?"

"You know how some Asian people can't tolerate booze, because they can't process acetaldehyde? Antabuse basically makes you very, very Asian. Ten minutes after you've taken it, if you have even the smallest sip of alcohol you'll be vomiting in a way that makes morning sickness look like an attack of the hiccups. And you'll be left with a throbbing headache, diarrhea, lethargy, yellow skin, and acne. In fact, you could get some of those side effects even if you *don't* have a drink."

"It sounds perfect," I say.

"You'll also need to avoid hand sanitizers, perfume, and most types of vinegar, as well as sauces that contain vinegar, such as ketchup. And if you smell someone wearing cologne, run like hell—preferably to the nearest toilet, as you'll probably throw up." Sharon finishes writing the prescription and hands it to me. "Here."

BEFORE I TAKE THE first Antabuse, I collect all the wine bottles in the house and empty them down the sink, then take them outside. As I put them into the recycling, I realize someone is hurrying down the street toward me.

It's that reporter, the one Pete thought was an intern. I can see why: He can't be more than twenty. "Kieran Keenan," he says, waving some press ID. "Could I have a word, Maddie?"

"We've got nothing to say to you."

He says earnestly, "Well, here's the thing, Maddie. Pete said in that article your life had been ruined by finding out your son wasn't really yours. But I've recently discovered that you're in a nanny share with the other family. Why would you do that if it's all so terrible? According to the posts Pete wrote on the Dad-Stuff forum, it's been entirely amicable and friendly from the start."

I almost laugh out loud at the irony of it all. Everything has turned full circle, and the article Pete was made to write by Miles has become reality after all.

I know I should probably keep quiet. But the urge to tell the truth is so strong it's almost impossible to resist.

"It started amicably," I tell him. "Then it wasn't. Which is why we're now having to fight for custody."

Kieran's eyes widen. "You're fighting for custody?" he repeats. He has his phone in his hand, I notice. Recording me.

I've already said too much, I realize. "In the family court. So you're not allowed to report it."

"We can report that a case is happening. So long as we don't identify the child."

"Look," I say desperately, "there's a bigger story here. I don't know exactly what it is yet. But if you help us, you can report it. After the court case is over."

His eyes light up. "You'll do an interview?"

"I need to talk to Pete about it. But in principle, yes."

"YOU DID WHAT?" PETE says, aghast.

He's been to pick up Theo from the Lamberts', his first encounter with Jill. "At least we can be sure Miles won't be trying it on with her. She'd probably floor him," he commented as he took off his coat.

Now he just stares at me, baffled. "Why would you want to do an interview? They're not interested in helping us, Mads. They just want to sell papers."

"It was all I could think of to get him off my back."

"And if you don't go through with it, he'll write the story anyway. Only by then he'll be really pissed off."

"I'm sorry. Oh, this is all shit, isn't it?" I say despairingly. "Everything we do, we're just making things worse. Like we're stuck in quicksand, and fighting it just gets us more stuck."

"Come here," he says gently, opening his arms. "At least we're together again. At least I'm here and you're here and so's Theo. For now."

I let him hug me, feeling the welcome strength of his arms around my shoulders. Perhaps, I think, there might be a way through this after all. I let my cheek fall against his neck. Tonight we might even make love, start to reconnect physically—

"Meeee tooo," Theo yells, wriggling between our legs.

I laugh, pulling Pete closer so Theo's squeezed between the two of us. "Good idea. Family hug."

Theo squeezes back for a few seconds, then wriggles away in search of something more exciting. But when Pete and I finally break apart, Pete's smiling, too.

IT'S STRANGE TO SPEND an evening without enveloping myself in the warm fuzziness of wine. I don't quite know what to do with myself. I give Theo his bath, then read him his story. As I'm tucking him up—I can't resist the temptation to smooth the lock of brown hair off his forehead, even though I know he'll impatiently shake it back as soon as I stop—he says sleepily, "I like my bedroom at Moles's house best."

I feel my blood run cold. "You have a bedroom at Miles and Lucy's house?"

He nods. "'Sgot a rocket. Annit's blue."

"Is it? Well, we could make this bedroom blue if you want. Would you like that?"

He nods again.

"We could all paint it together. Mummy, Daddy, and you. Does that sound good? Because after all, this is the place where you actually sleep."

He yawns. "S'pose. But my other bedroom's bigger."

I go downstairs and grab my iPad. "You won't believe this," I say furiously. "They've given him a bedroom. And painted it blue." I'm finding Lucy's Facebook page as I speak.

Yes, there it is—six photographs, added today. *Theo's new bedroom.* A huge, high-ceilinged room on what looks like the first floor of the Lamberts' house. Blue, just as Theo said, but what he hadn't mentioned is that the ceiling is darker, almost black, and has somehow been printed with a photographic depiction of the night sky, complete with moon, stars, the constellations, and the

Milky Way. The bed is in the shape of a rocket, positioned so the occupant can look up and feel himself drifting through space. And there in the next photo is Theo himself, eyes wide with excitement, clearly seeing it for the first time—you can just make out an adult's hands on either side of his face, slightly blurred: Moments earlier, they must have been covering his eyes.

The final picture shows a pair of pajamas, neatly laid out on the bed. Astronaut pajamas, complete with a NASA badge. Even the pillow is printed with a gold-visored spaceman's helmet.

That last picture has a comment: *Looking forward to our little astronaut moving in for good.*

86

MADDIE

I'M SO ANGRY, I think I'm going to punch something. And there's nothing I can do to take the edge off my fury. Making love is out of the question now, of course. And so, it seems, is sleep. In desperation, at around three in the morning I get up and go in search of something, anything, that might relax me a bit. At the back of a cupboard I find an ancient bottle of some weird elderflower liqueur. Experimentally, I try some. It tastes vile—sugary and slightly musty. But it's alcohol, so I take a longer pull. Within moments I feel my stomach heave, as bad as the time I ate smelly scallops on a beach in Morocco. Something wrings my insides, tighter and tighter. Christ, it's like that scene in *Alien*—it feels as if my colon's going to explode through my cesarean scar. I only just make it to the sink in time, then spend the next hour in the bathroom, throwing up.

Okay, maybe alcohol really isn't an option.

In the morning, after a queasy dawn, I reach for my iPad again.

Pete and I have investigated Miles, Bronagh, and Paula, but the other person on my list is still an enigma.

She's strange with him, actually. Like she's a little bit scared but she also depends on him for everything, Michaela had said.

I need someone who can explain to me why a woman like Lucy would stay married to a man like Miles. Going into my messages, I search for a name I haven't contacted for over a year.

IT WAS MY CBT therapist who originally suggested Pete and I could benefit from some couples counseling. I can't remember now how I found Annette. On the internet, probably. A fiery South African with a huge mane of curly auburn hair, she wasn't anyone's typical idea of a relationship counselor. For one thing, there was nothing gentle or soft about her. Her website said she specialized in PTSD and domestic abuse as well as sex and relationships, using a combination of psychodynamic therapy, energy psychotherapy, and transpersonal techniques. I had no idea what any of that meant, but it sounded as far removed from my CBT sessions as it was possible to get, so I booked an introductory session.

Initially, Pete quite liked the idea of therapy. It fit with his whole outlook on life—that talking and communication were the answer to most problems. And he was quietly desperate for us to start having sex again. What he hadn't anticipated was having to describe in excruciating detail to Annette just what he did, or didn't do, to satisfy me in bed. Annette listened, nodding with what appeared to be an expression of sympathy on her face.

"So what you're basically saying is, you believe it's your duty as a modern man to go down on your partner and give her oral sex until she climaxes," she said when he'd stuttered to a halt. She turned to me. "Maddie, does that sound like a turn-on to you?"

"Not really," I admitted.

"You'd like him to do it because he loves the taste of you and he's caught up in the moment, right?"

"Um," I said. "I guess."

Annette turned back to Pete. "How do you seduce her?" she demanded.

"Seduce her?" Pete echoed blankly.

"When was the last time," Annette said sternly, "that you buried your face in Maddie's hair and inhaled the scent of her?"

"Well . . ." Pete made an attempt to look as if he was counting back the days.

"Tell me how you *flirt* with her," Annette said. "Show me how you *sizzle*."

Pete blinked.

"The reason women don't have sex with men is because men aren't prepared to put the effort into making women *want* to have sex with them," Annette announced firmly. "I want you to woo Maddie, Pete. *Excite* her. Make her fall in lust with you all over again. When you say goodbye to her, don't peck her cheek. Wrap your arms around her and press your body against hers. When you're away from her, send her sexy texts. Make her feel *desired*."

"We do have date nights," Pete said hopefully. "And we cuddle."

"Cuddling," Annette said witheringly, "is the enemy of arousal. When you cuddle, you're leaching all the passion out of your partner's touch."

"Oh," Pete said.

"Which is why I'm going to put the two of you on a sex ban," she added.

Pete looked slightly shocked. After all, ending the sex drought was the main reason he was there in the first place.

"You are going to start touching each other," Annette continued. "Preferably naked. Preferably by candlelight. Massage each other. Arouse each other, if you feel like it. But you are not, repeat not, to have intercourse. Or, God help us, any other kind of sex. I want you to rediscover the pleasure of anticipation." She consulted her pad. "And I'll see you again in three weeks."

To be fair, Pete went along with Annette's instructions. And gradually, I discovered that the combination of relaxing massage and intimate touching without any pressure to have sex *was* arousing, to an extent. Unlike Pete's attempts to woo me with flirtatious texts. It was bad enough to be interrupted in a fraught meeting by a text saying *Can you pick up supper?*, but when it was followed by *What are you wearing, sexy?* it was downright irritating.

You know what I'm wearing. You watched me fish my dirty knickers out of the laundry basket at 7 this morning.

And very erotic it was too, you dirty slut.

Ugh. Pete, not sexy. Takeaway or ready meal?

And when a session of touching finally became too much and I pulled Pete inside me with a moan of pleasure, there was the illicit thrill of knowing we were defying Annette's sex ban. At the next session we sat in front of her like two naughty teenagers and confessed what we'd done.

"Well, of course," Annette said, nodding. "You've learned to excite each other."

She sent us away with more "homework," as she called it— Pete was to surprise me every week with a romantic gift; I was to surprise him with some sexy underwear—and an instruction to come back if things tailed off again. Which they did, but somehow we didn't return. It was just too much of an effort when Theo and work were taking up so much of our time and energy.

The therapy did have one lasting benefit, though. Learning to articulate our problems in front of a stranger had, perversely, made us better at articulating how we felt to each other in private. The problems hadn't gone away, but they felt more like shared problems.

At least, they did back then. But I know it's all too easy to confuse the frankness with which we talked about our sex life with genuine openness. After all, it's not as if I'd shared the not-so-little matter of my own slipups. But on the plus side, neither had I slipped up again. When, on a shoot in Prague, the good-looking director dropped a large hint in my direction—"What happens on location stays on location, right?"—I'd replied firmly that nothing did happen on location. And it didn't.

Has Pete been choosing not to talk about certain matters, too? Are there things he's done that remain as deep-buried as my own secrets are?

I try not to think about that too much, because if I do, everything starts to feel hopeless.

"I WANT TO KNOW why a woman would marry a psychopath," I tell Annette when I'm sitting in her yellow-painted consulting room.

She raises an eyebrow. "Are you not with Pete anymore?"

"Oh—this isn't about me and Pete. Not directly, anyway." Briefly I explain about Miles and Lucy. I include Miles groping me as we left the courtroom.

"And how do you feel about all this?" Annette asks—the classic therapist's opener.

"Right now, angry. But when I don't feel angry . . ." I hesitate. "Sometimes, I just feel the deepest, blackest despair."

Annette nods. "Both are very understandable reactions. And in answer to your question, psychopaths are very easy to fall in love with. For one thing, they know how to charm people. Typically, they throw themselves into the courtship with total commitment—showering their target with gifts, using lines from movies, telling you you're the most beautiful, amazing thing that's ever happened to them. And although it's partly a game to them, it isn't all fake. They're intoxicated by the excitement and the chase, but it's also important to them that they can get *you* to fall in love with *them*—they can't rest until they've sealed the deal and hooked you. It's also typical that they'll propose quickly, while the rush is still there. Again, it's because they crave more and bigger excitement, but they probably know on some level that they can't sustain this sort of intimacy for long. The same applies to getting their partner pregnant. You could meet a psychopath and be married and a mother within a year."

"Because that's the ultimate sealing of the deal?"

"Exactly. And because that's what wives do, so his wife has to do it faster and better than anyone else. She's no longer Emma or Clare or whoever, she's 'my darling wife.' He might even enjoy playing the family guy or doting dad—for a brief scene or two. Then it's on to his next thrill." She hesitates. "I had a psychopath come to therapy once, with his wife. He loved it—it was an hour all about *him*. And he was brilliant at it—at playing it like a game, I mean. I could see him sucking up everything I was doing, using my techniques to become even more charming and deflective and self-justifying. It's the only time I've ever terminated therapy. I told his wife she should get out of the relationship, fast, but the last I heard they were still together."

"But why?" I ask. "If he can't sustain the façade, why would a woman stay with someone like that?"

"Hmm." Annette considers. "Well, based on that couple, I can see how the initial love-bombing and attention could become a kind of drug, particularly if the woman's quite insecure in the first place. Even though the psychopath can't keep it up, he only has to offer her an occasional tiny drop of it to keep the addiction going. And psychopaths are controlling—not least because they think, with some justification, that they're better decision makers than anyone else around them. It's a vicious circle: The more the psychopath makes the decisions, the more the partner believes she's incapable, so the more she lets him make the decisions. Eventually, she just has no confidence left."

That makes sense. I think how different Lucy seemed when we first met in the NICU. Despite the stress of having a premature baby, she'd been engaging and outgoing, a far cry from the vague, anxious creature she is now. I also recall how, the first time we went to the Lamberts', Miles had been so quick to correct her—first when she mixed up who out of Pete and me took milk, and then when she'd failed to pick up that Pete was the primary carer. Tiny, tiny things—at the time I'd taken them for alpha-male protectiveness, but now that I come to think of it, Pete would never have pounced on my mistakes so quickly, or corrected me in quite such a paternalistic way.

"And is there any chance she could become psychopathic herself?" I ask. "That she could, on her own initiative, do something as callous as swapping two babies to get a malpractice payout?"

"You can never completely rule anything out," Annette says cautiously. "Certainly not without talking to the person concerned. But based on what you've told me, I'd say it's unlikely. You're describing someone who's so lacking in confidence she can't even make a cup of tea. The idea that she's capable of making a spur-of-the-moment decision, one with long-lasting consequences, on her husband's behalf, without first securing his permission . . . It just doesn't stack up. Quite apart from anything else, it would force her to confront the reality of her situation— that she's married to a monster. And while there certainly have been psychopathic couples—Bonnie and Clyde, Ian Brady and Myra Hindley—that doesn't sound like the dynamic you're describing. Frankly, I think it's much more likely that the babies got swapped by accident, and you were just unlucky enough to end up with the child of someone you'd normally go a very long way to avoid."

87

Case no. 12675/PU78B65, Exhibit 46. Extract from CAFCASS Section 7 report to the family court's second hearing regarding Theo Riley, compiled by Lyn Edwards, Family Court Adviser.

14. THEO'S WISHES.

I assessed Theo at the home of Mr. and Mrs. Lambert, which Theo visits on a daily basis for his nanny share. Theo is a bright and energetic little boy, if occasionally lacking in self-regulation and awareness of the needs of others. I was able to witness the parenting style of both Mr. and Mrs. Lambert, and noted that they included Theo in making decisions wherever possible.

I then requested to be left alone with Theo so we could have a chat. In the course of our discussion I asked Theo to draw a picture of a place where he would feel safe. In response he drew what looked like a castle. When asked, he identified the castle's location as "Here."

I then asked him to draw some people he thought he might need with him in the castle to keep him safe. After some thought he drew a policeman and what he informed me was a guard dog. I asked if there were any people he knew who he would like in his castle, who could also help to keep him safe. He drew a picture of a stick man with an object. When questioned, he identified this as Mr. Lambert, holding a rugby ball.

I then gently elicited from Theo where Mr. Riley and Ms. Wilson would be in his picture, and also where Mrs. Lambert would be. He indicated that Mrs. Lambert would be next to Mr. Lambert. Mr. Riley and Ms. Wilson would be outside the castle. He drew all three figures, then what he told me was a catapult, firing rugby balls at Mr. Riley.

While Theo is clearly too young to make a reliable direct statement about his wishes, I believe it is clear that in the brief time he has known them he has become very attached to his birth parents, and feels confident and cared for in their company.

In summary, I believe Theo would welcome the opportunity to be returned to his natural family on a permanent basis, and that is my recommendation to the court. Monthly access visits for Mr. Riley and Ms. Wilson should take place in a supervised contact center, to minimize the effects of interfamilial acrimony.

Lyn Edwards
Family Court Adviser

88

PETE

THE COURT-APPROVED PSYCHOLOGIST CAME to see Theo at our house. Perhaps bizarrely, I couldn't help liking the man. His name was Harvey Taylor and he arrived on a touring bike, which led to a discussion about frames and the best width of rim for coping with London potholes.

"Right," Harvey said at last, when I'd made him coffee. He looked around our small living space. "I need to assess Theo without you present, so I guess you'll have to go out for an hour or so."

"Of course. I appreciate you've got a job to do, so I'll let you get on with it. Is there anything you need?"

He indicated his backpack. "It's all here, thanks. Oh, and I have some checklists to go through with you when you get back."

I left the house and paced the streets, too anxious to go and sit in a café. It was strange to think that while I was out walking,

Harvey and Theo were having a conversation that could decide our family's future.

After exactly an hour, I went back. Theo was playing with Duplo on the floor and Harvey was sitting at the kitchen table, writing notes.

"Hi there," he said when he saw me. "Would it be all right if Theo went upstairs for a bit? I'd rather do the checklists on our own."

"Of course. Theo, could you take your Duplo up to your bedroom? I'll come and build something with you later."

When Theo was upstairs, Harvey said, "Before we start, can you tell me about these? I'm curious." He indicated the star charts lining the walls.

"Oh." I explained about the parenting classes, and how I'd learned that some kids react better to reward systems than to punishments. "It's made a massive difference," I added.

He nodded. "That fits with what I'm seeing—that Theo has a very particular learning style."

He pulled out a checklist. "Don't be alarmed if some of these questions sound a bit strange. If another child was upset, would Theo try to help them, for example by giving them a toy?"

I shook my head. "Almost certainly not. In fact, he doesn't really like sharing toys."

Harvey made a note. "Does he like animals?"

"It depends what you mean by 'like,'" I said cautiously. "He enjoys them, certainly. But he tends to do a lot of poking and banging of them to see how they react." There had been an embarrassing occasion when he'd been asked to leave the petting zoo after trying to swing a rabbit around by its ears.

"What about keeping promises and commitments? Is he good at that?"

I pointed at one of the star charts. "As you can see, he's getting better. But it's been a struggle."

There were a dozen more questions—"How responsive is he to

affection? How anxious does he get? How fearful of getting hurt is he? Is he gentle with other children?" At the end Harvey put the checklist down and said, "Again, don't be alarmed by what I'm about to tell you, but Theo almost certainly has what psychologists call CU traits. *CU* stands for 'callous and unemotional.'" He studied my face. "You don't seem very surprised."

"Is it hereditary?"

"Ah." Harvey nodded slowly as the implication of my question sank in. "It can be, yes. Except that, in adults, we would call it psychopathy."

"In that case," I said, "I'm not surprised at all." But then the ramifications of what he'd just said sank in on me. "And if it's hereditary, it can't be cured. Theo will grow up to be just like his father."

"Well, I haven't met his father, so I can't comment on that. But what I can say is that just because something is hereditary, it doesn't mean the future is fixed. We think an underdevelopment of part of the brain called the amygdala may give certain children a disposition toward CU. But personality is malleable, particularly in the very young. A CU diagnosis may simply mean they need a particular kind of parenting to help them learn the human qualities the rest of us pick up without thinking." He indicated the star charts. "You're already doing a lot of it. Punishments mean nothing to kids with CU, but they're very goal-oriented. So rewards are definitely the way to go. Oh, and time-outs don't work—you can forget about the naughty step, for example."

"I'd already worked that out for myself," I said with feeling.

He nodded. "What can definitely help is what we call warm parenting—talking about feelings, displaying lots of emotion yourself, reinforcing any small signs of empathy or emotional literacy that Theo displays. Show him that emotions are good, even enriching, for the person having them. Show him that warmth and positivity and affection are the real measure of success."

"That is *exactly* what I try to do," I said helplessly.

"I'm sure it is." Harvey started packing away his things.

"But can you tell the court that? Can you say I'm a good parent?"

Harvey looked at me sympathetically. "I don't think you understand—that isn't my remit. I'm simply here to assess whether or not Theo would be traumatized by the shock of changing families, if that's what's decided by the judge. And I'm afraid I'm going to have to tell the court that, like any kid with CU traits, he'd hardly bat an eyelid."

89

PETE

"OUR CHILD IS A psychopath," I whispered.

The words had been going around and around my head for so long, it was almost a relief to say them out loud.

"No, he's not," Maddie said. "Children can't be psychopaths. You told me that yourself."

That, at least, was true. Harvey Taylor had told me that a person couldn't be diagnosed as a psychopath until they'd turned eighteen.

"I have a horrible feeling that's a technical distinction. He's a psychopath in embryo form."

"But Theo's got *you*," Maddie persisted. "And you're the very definition of a warm, involved parent."

As if on cue, Theo ran downstairs. "C'mon, Daddeee. Let's *go*," he announced, pulling at my hand. "Swings! Swings! Swings!"

"Okay, Theo," I said, standing up. "But give Mummy a hug first. Because mummies like hugs. It makes them feel happy."

"See?" Maddie said over Theo's head as he hugged her. "You're doing it already."

As Theo went in search of his coat and boots, she added, "I learned something interesting today, too. Annette said psychopaths love-bomb potential partners with attention while they're trying to hook them, then lose interest once they've sealed the deal. It made me think." She gestured in Theo's direction. "What if that's not just true of partners? After all, it's what Miles did to us, in a way—showered us with attention, then switched it off. Maybe, without realizing it, it's what he's doing with Theo as well."

"Oh God." The thought that, after all this, Miles would end up ignoring Theo if he got him just made the situation even more depressing. I could see a future in which Theo would only be able to engage Miles's interest by bringing home an endless succession of sports trophies. And pretty soon that would become Theo's whole attitude to life—that it was all about winning.

"But it is *not* going to happen," Maddie said firmly. "We are going to keep him."

I didn't reply. I knew she only kept saying it to keep my spirits up, but it really wasn't working.

"*Ready*, Daddeee!" Theo announced, jumping up and down by the door.

Maddie's phone rang. I was going out the door as she answered it, so I only just heard her say, "Hang on, I'll get him.

"It's your lawyer," she said as she handed me the phone. "The police want to see you again. Theo, wait," she called after the figure already running down the pavement. "It's me coming with you now, not Daddy. Just let me grab my coat."

90

PETE

"THERE'S GOOD NEWS AND not-so-good news for you, Pete," DI Richards said. He slid a padded envelope across the table. "The good news is, that's your phone. We've finished with it."

He waited for me to ask what the not-so-good news was. I shot my solicitor, Mark Cooper, a look, but he only shook his head slightly.

DI Richards sighed. "The not-so-good news is that your laptop is now evidence in two ongoing investigations." Again he paused, waiting for me to ask what the second investigation was, and again I said nothing.

"On your laptop we found an image or images that appear to be in contravention of the Coroners and Justice Act 2009." He paused again. "We're talking about child pornography, Pete."

Hearing those words said out loud felt like the end of the world. I gaped at him, dumbfounded. My head swam and there was a ringing in my ears.

"Do you have anything to say about that?" DI Richards asked sympathetically.

"On the advice of my solicitor . . ." I couldn't get the words out. The room rocked glassily before my eyes.

DI Richards reached for a file and took out a plastic sleeve with something inside, which he slid across the table. "Specifically, this image," he added.

I stared at it. I couldn't believe what I was looking at. "But it's . . . it's . . ."

Mark touched my arm.

"What you are showing my client is a cartoon drawing in the Japanese style known as manga," he said. "It appears to be a pop-up advertisement with the words CLICK HERE on it."

"What I am showing your client," DI Richards said reasonably, "is a sexualized image of a girl who is clearly under eighteen, since she is wearing a school uniform. This falls under the definition of a Category C nonphotographic indecent image of a minor, and it was found in the internet viewing cache of your client's hard drive. As I'm sure you're aware, the maximum penalty for possession of such images is three years in prison, along with a court order to comply with the notification requirements of the sex offenders' register."

The sex offenders' register. This was like a bad dream.

"This is ridiculous," Mark Cooper said patiently. "No jury is going to convict on the basis of one drawing."

"Possibly not," DI Richards conceded. "Although convictions have been made for possession of cartoons in the past. I'd much rather talk about child abduction and insurance fraud, to be honest."

"Oh—so *that's* it," the solicitor said witheringly. "You're attempting to blackmail my client into giving you a fuller interview on the child abduction charge."

DI Richards looked pained. "We take all offenses against children very seriously."

I put my head in my hands. I couldn't believe this.

"My client isn't going to give you any fuller answers."

"Very well," DI Richards said. "In that case, I will consult with my superiors and the CPS over what action they consider appropriate." He put the image back in the folder and stood up. "Oh, and Pete. We have to liaise quite closely with CAFCASS in investigations like this, as you can imagine. If you change your mind, give me a call."

"What?" My head went up as the implications of what he was saying crashed in on me. "Wait. That's not fair—"

Mark touched my arm. "Not now, Pete."

"I'll do the interview," I said desperately. "I'll do the bloody interview, all right? There is absolutely no reason to involve CAF-CASS—"

"He's trying to wind you up," Mark insisted. "Come on, let's go."

"Well, he's succeeded. There's no way I'm leaving—"

"And there's no way I'm letting you do an interview in this state. Even if I thought it was a good idea, which I don't. We need to go."

DI Richards watched us leave. There was no cheeriness in his eyes at all now, just a look of cold calculation.

91

MADDIE

WHEN MY PHONE RINGS I grab it, thinking it might be Pete, calling from his solicitor's. But it isn't.

"Lyn Edwards here, CAFCASS," Lyn says formally. Her Welsh lilt is more pronounced now. "I'm afraid we have to have a chat about these changed circumstances, Maddie."

"What changed circumstances?"

"There's been child pornography found on Pete's computer."

I can't believe what I'm hearing. "There's been *what*?"

"An indecent image, as I understand it. The CPS will be considering. But my only concern in this is Theo, Maddie, and what it might mean for him. His safety is my responsibility, Maddie, do you see?"

"I don't believe it," I say immediately. "I do not believe that Pete could possibly have been looking at child porn."

"Well, that's as may be. But we have to err on the side of caution, Maddie, do you see?"

"Are you saying you want him to move out again?" I say slowly.

"No, Maddie, that's not what I'm saying. Because, as your own solicitor pointed out, there are also now questions over *your* suitability to act as carer in Pete's absence, aren't there?"

"That wasn't what she—" I begin, but Lyn simply carries on speaking.

"I've looked through the medical reports, Maddie, and frankly they're quite disturbing. Theo found on the floor with—and there's no nice way to say this, Maddie—*feces* all around him."

I feel myself go cold. "I was *ill*."

"That's as may be, Maddie. But who's to say you couldn't become ill again? You're not taking your medication, are you?"

"Are you a doctor?"

There's a brief pause. I can almost picture Lyn's sharp eyes narrowing.

"I'm a qualified social worker, Maddie. We have to use our best judgment in situations like this. Though I have to tell you, I've also been sent a copy of what appears to be a newspaper article written by Peter, saying that the stress of finding out Theo isn't yours has brought back some of your old symptoms. Would that not be correct, then, Maddie?"

That bloody article again. I don't reply.

"We have to take all possible circumstances into account," Lyn continues after a moment. "If that means taking sensible precautions, so be it."

"So if you're not asking Pete to move out, what *are* you suggesting?" I say leadenly.

"I think it's best if Theo stays elsewhere for the time being, Maddie. If you would be so kind as to pack him an overnight bag, he can stay with Mr. and Mrs. Lambert until the hearing."

92

PETE

PACKING THAT SUITCASE WAS the hardest thing I've ever done. Compared with that, our time in the NICU was a doddle. Choosing clothes for Theo to take with him felt like choosing what he'd wear in his grave.

And of course, we had to hide our misery from him. Cheerily, we told him he was going to spend a few nights at David's house, in his new rocket bed, and wouldn't that be fun?

His eyes lit up. "Yeah!" he exclaimed.

We both took him next morning. Just for a moment, as he walked up their steps, he turned and looked at us anxiously. Then he ran back and lifted his arms for a hug.

We squeezed his little body so tight he said, "Ouff! You're *hurting*!" Jill opened the door. We watched him go back up the steps and run inside. We handed her his suitcase.

And just like that, our little boy was gone.

. . .

AT NINE THIRTY I called Mark Cooper and told him I wanted to cooperate fully with the police. He started to say he strongly advised against it. I told him to arrange the interview and hung up.

I saw DI Richards the same day and answered all his questions. At the end of the interview he confirmed that, although the investigation against me for child abduction would remain ongoing while they checked out what I'd told them, everything else would be dropped.

"There, that wasn't so difficult, was it?" he added.

Maddie phoned Lyn and demanded that Theo be allowed to come home now. Lyn said she thought that, on balance, Theo should remain at the Lamberts' "to see how he settles."

"I must say, he does seem very happy there, Maddie. And really, that's everyone's main concern in this situation, isn't it? What's best for Theo, do you see? As his primary carers for the last two years, I'm sure you and Pete must want that for him, too, in the end."

93

PETE

THE DAYS TICKED DOWN toward the hearing. We dug in. That's the only way I can describe it—as if we were underground, enduring, waiting for the bombardment to finish so we could emerge, blinking and shell-shocked, into the real world again.

But all the time, there was a huge, Theo-shaped gap in our hearts. The house seemed very still and quiet. It was like being inside something broken, like a stopped clock.

And I had a horrible feeling that, when all this was over, we wouldn't be emerging into the same world we'd left. If we lost Theo for good, everything would be smashed, including us. Without us even really noticing it, he had become our raison d'être, the point around which our relationship circled.

Not for the first time, I found myself wishing that Maddie hadn't always been so set against marriage. Anything, however intangible, that bound us to each other would have been a help. But now it was hard to see how we could possibly survive as a couple if we lost him. Like parents who split up in the aftermath of a child's death, because the grief would only be survivable with someone who didn't feel the same pain as you, whose agony didn't reflect yours every time you looked into their eyes.

MEANWHILE, THE LEGAL SIDE of things intensified. We had to write statements, go through the evidence—in particular, Lyn Edwards's devastating report. She'd recommended that Theo be returned permanently to the Lamberts. He felt safe there, apparently. But so what? Theo felt safe everywhere. Theo would have felt safe on top of a burning skyscraper.

Even though we'd half expected it, seeing it in black and white like that was another crushing blow. Anita told us encouragingly there were lots of things in the report she could challenge. But I remembered what she'd said about CAFCASS in our very first meeting. *It's very, very rare for the judge not to go along with their views.*

And now that Theo was staying with the Lamberts, they'd become the status quo. There was a reason possession was called nine-tenths of the law. If he was there, and settled, our strongest argument for keeping him—that moving families would cause disruption—now worked in their favor, not ours.

I invented a new word: *CAFCA-esque.* Like Kafkaesque, only with added heartbreak.

I still went to the parenting classes, even though I didn't currently have a child to parent. I didn't want to give CAFCASS any reason, however small, to say we weren't being cooperative.

At the classes I talked to the other parents, and heard tales of unbelievable misery—misery even worse than ours. Parents whose kids had been taken away after anonymous tip-offs by disgruntled neighbors, or because hospitals had concerns about minor injuries, or because a parent had lost their temper with a social worker. Mothers who, having proved they were clean of drugs, relapsed into addiction when the system refused to give their kids back. Or even worse, mothers who stayed clean, only to be told that their kids were now settled and happy with their foster families and it wasn't in their best interests for them to be moved again. Many of the people I spoke to were chaotic, admittedly, or working their way through various rehabilitation programs. But many were just sad and desperate and broken.

And one woman whose story chilled my soul—a woman about Maddie's age, an artist, heavily pregnant, who'd been told that, because she'd been in a psychiatric unit in the past, she was considered "capable of abuse." The psychiatrist who had written those words had never even met her. But unless she could convince a judge his diagnosis was wrong, her baby would be taken from her soon after it was born and given up for adoption. It was all to do with numbers, she told me wearily: Removal of newborns had more than doubled since the government introduced adoption targets. I checked, sure she must have gotten that figure wrong. But she was right.

Once, I would have written about these people, and tried to shine a light on the injustices they were suffering. But even if there'd been a newspaper I could publish in, I wasn't allowed to write anything that related, however tangentially, to our case.

Ironically, as the hearing about Theo neared, the case about David was just getting going. I tried to spend some time researching hypoxia, so I could sound more confident when a social worker asked how we were going to care for him. But the more I read, the more futile it seemed. I looked at our tiny house and wondered how on earth we could accommodate a severely disabled child.

If we even *had* a tiny house. We could barely afford the first mortgage, let alone the second mortgage that was now covering our legal fees. And if we failed to gain custody of David, there was a high likelihood we'd end up having to pay child maintenance for him.

If worse came to worst, and we lost both Theo *and* David, there would be another consequence, too. I would no longer have a child to be a full-time father to. I'd have to get a job—not in journalism, obviously; that ship had sailed, but maybe stacking shelves in the local supermarket. Would that cover our mortgages? I looked to see how much shelf stackers got paid. The answer was no, it wouldn't.

We couldn't sleep. Night after night, we lay side by side, staring at the ceiling and twitching with stress. Even eating was difficult—the tension made it hard to swallow. There was a time when Maddie would have drunk to relax, but now the pills she was taking meant we couldn't even have alcohol in the house.

I started sleeping in Theo's room. There was still a faint, puppyish smell of him lingering in the sheets. I even turned on his nightlight. It helped, somehow.

One night I woke to find Maddie sitting on the side of the bed. I glanced at the clock. It was four A.M.

"Perhaps it's time to let him go," she said softly. "Perhaps we should just stop fighting it. We could go back to Australia, have another child. Start again."

I didn't answer. After a moment she got up and left. In the morning, I wasn't even sure I hadn't dreamed it.

94

MADDIE

PETE IS BRILLIANTLY DOGGED. It's a situation not unlike the NICU—the kind of crisis that requires resilience and determination, not quick thinking or decisiveness. Left to my own devices, I'd probably do something impulsive: shout at Lyn, or try to run away. But Pete just grits his teeth and keeps going. Researching David's condition, writing legal statements, going through the evidence.

We both suspect it's hopeless. But we don't want to get to court and think there was something, anything, more we could have done.

I find myself remembering the period when I first fell in love with him, back in Australia. We were sleeping together, but I still regarded him principally as a friend and I had no expectation that the relationship would ever become anything more. Then I was invited to go and see my grandparents in Tasmania. Pete had never been, so he tagged along, too—we planned to do some hik-

ing after the visit. It was only after we got there that I discovered
the real reason I'd been asked: Grandpa was dying. A series of
small strokes I hadn't been told about had left him barely mobile.
The day after we arrived, a larger one paralyzed his left side and
made him incontinent. Instead of dropping in on an active elderly
couple for a few nights, Pete found himself in the middle of a family drama, with relatives flying in from all over Australia and me
an emotional wreck. He just quietly got on with it—ferrying people from the airport, shopping, cooking, even taking care of soiled
bedsheets. Not once did he mention the missed hiking. When, one
time, I'd started to say *Sorry, I know this isn't what you signed up
for,* he just looked at me as if I was crazy. "Thank you for letting
me take care of you all," he said simply.

Later, after my granddad passed, I was reminiscing with my
grandmother when she patted my knee and said, "I hope you and
Pete will be as happy as me and your granddad were."

"Oh, we're not serious," I began, but then I saw the look on
my grandmother's face. And realized that, of course, we were.
Pete was a keeper, and I'd have been mad to let him go.

I PHONE THE *DAILY MAIL* to say I can't do an interview after all.
But when I get through to the news desk and ask to speak to
Kieran Keenan, there's a pause.

"Are you a relative of his?" the man who picked up asks.

"No. It's in connection with a story he's working on."

"I'm afraid Kieran won't be coming back."

"Won't be back? Why not?"

"He was involved in a traffic accident—quite a bad one. He'll
be in hospital for some time. But if you have a story, tell me and
I'll see if we're still interested."

"What kind of traffic accident?"

"He was hit by a car. Broke his back, poor guy. They say it
could be six months before he's on his feet again."

A terrible notion flits into my brain. "Did they arrest the driver?"

"Usually it's us who ask the questions," the journalist says, amused. "But someone wrote a piece, if you're interested. It's on the website. Now, tell me about this story of yours—"

I've already disconnected.

I FIND THE ARTICLE in between two flickering sidebars of click-bait about the plastic surgery disasters of celebrities I've never heard of. MAIL REPORTER VICTIM OF HIT-AND-RUN. It's only twelve lines long. Kieran was found unconscious by a passerby near his home late one evening. The driver had fled the scene. There were no witnesses.

Did Kieran pick up on my comment about it being a bigger story than it looked, and decide to check out Miles for himself? Coming to the end of his internship, he'd be desperate to make his mark with a big story. And had Miles decided he'd rather not have whatever Kieran found out published?

I have to be wary of reading too much between the lines, I know. But I feel, in my heart, that any one of us could be in danger.

95

MADDIE

THREE DAYS BEFORE THE hearing, we go to a small, anonymous building in Camden to see Theo. The place looks not unlike a nursery or a small school, with rooms full of toys and play mats. But the sign outside says CAMDEN CHILD CONTACT CENTER, and the reception area is plastered with posters saying things like AT CCCC THE MOST IMPORTANT PERSON IS THE CHILD! and PLEASE LEAVE YOUR DISPUTES AT THE DOOR. WE WANT THIS TO BE A POSITIVE PLACE FOR OUR CHILDREN! along with advertisements for women's refuge centers and Childline.

We're led down a long corridor, past room after room of lone dads playing awkwardly with their kids. Despite the drawings on the walls and the jaunty, pastel-colored furniture, it feels like we're walking ever farther into some bureaucrat's version of hell— a surreal cross between a privatized prison and play school. *This is where the detritus of broken families ends up*, I think, looking around. They should send anyone who's contemplating getting divorced here for an afternoon, not to couples therapy. Any marriage, however bad, would surely be more bearable than seeing your child somewhere like this.

Eventually we come to a door marked PENGUIN ROOM. AGE 2–4. Through the glazed panel we can see Theo squatting on the floor, engrossed in a marble run. A middle-aged woman with a notebook sits to one side. That must be Janine, our supervisor. Her job, we've been informed by email, is to write observations on "the quality of our interactions" with Theo for CAFCASS, who may then share them with the court.

I feel strangely nervous as we walk in. Which is ridiculous, I tell myself firmly. This is our son, and we're simply going to play with him. Just like we've done a million times before.

"Hi, Theo," Pete says eagerly. "How are you?"

Theo looks up briefly, then returns his attention to the marble run. "'lo," he mutters.

Undeterred, Pete gets down on the floor next to him. "That looks fun. Can I have a turn?"

Theo shakes his head.

"Come on, Theo. Remember we talked about taking turns?" Pete reaches toward the plastic pot containing the marbles, but Theo snatches it away.

"Mine!" he declares.

I daren't look at Janine to see what she's making of all this. "Theo," I begin, getting down on the floor as well. "Daddy really wants a turn with those marbles—"

For the first time, Theo looks at Pete. "You're not my daddy."

I feel my blood run cold. For a moment Pete's too stunned to react. "Why do you say that, Theo?" he asks at last.

"Daddy Moles is my real daddy." Theo glances at me. "You're not my mummy, too. I was growed in Mummy Lucy's tummy. Daddy Moles told me." He turns back to the marble run and puts a whole fistful of marbles into the top so that they skitter down, one after the other, patter-patter-patter. One bounces out and rolls under Janine's chair.

Pete swivels to Janine. *"Write that down!"* he demands furiously. "Write down that those—the *applicants* have been talking to him about the case. When we all agreed we wouldn't."

But even as he says it, I realize we didn't all agree to that. It was just something Pete and I always assumed. Because telling Theo the truth about his parentage is so irrevocable, so final, that it has literally never occurred to us to do so. We were, I suppose, sticking our heads in the sand and hoping this would somehow go away before it became necessary. And while we'd made it clear to CAFCASS that we weren't telling him, Lyn had never actually confirmed that she agreed with our position.

Janine says calmly, "The applicants asked the CAFCASS officer for permission to undertake some structured life story work with Theo. He has a right to know, after all. The officer thought it was a good idea to do it now, before . . ." She hesitates, and I have the impression she was going to say, *Before he leaves you.* "Before the hearing," she finishes.

"He's *two*," Pete says incredulously. *"Two. Years. Old.* What kind of monstrous *bitch* would allow—"

He manages to stop himself, but the damage is done. "I'm going to terminate this contact now," Janine says sharply, tucking her biro into her notebook to keep her place and standing up. Her hand hovers over a big red button on the wall. "Please go quietly, or I'll have to call Security."

96

MADDIE

OF ALL THE THINGS we've endured—Pete being made to move out, Theo staying at the Lamberts', the police investigations—it's those few brief moments in the contact center that seem to hit Pete hardest. That Miles has managed to weaponize Theo himself in the battle against us seems to rip away the last shreds of hope in his mind.

And that's why Miles has never bothered to kill us, I realize. Not because he wouldn't, but simply because he doesn't need to. The system is on his side, and all he needs to do is let the various processes play out to their conclusion.

THE DAY BEFORE THE hearing, Pete collects his suit from the dry cleaners and I iron a black linen jacket. Funeral clothes, I find myself thinking.

Pete watches me, waiting his turn to iron his shirt. "You know,

I keep thinking about Solomon, and that baby he ordered cut in two," he says glumly. "If CAFCASS had existed back then, they'd probably have taken away *his* children, on the basis he'd threatened violence against a child. As for the women, when the real mother said let the other one have it, they'd have written a report saying she clearly no longer wanted him and was guilty of neglect."

"We shouldn't blame CAFCASS," I say gently. "It's not their fault they've run up against Miles. Think how long it took *us* to see him for what he really is."

"True," he admits.

I go on ironing.

"Wait," he says suddenly. "I've had an idea. Why don't *we* divide the children?"

I look at him. "What do you mean?"

"We have two children between two families, yes? Why don't we simply *share* them? Theo could spend two weeks at ours, say, while David spends two weeks at their house. And then we swap, so David's here and Theo's at theirs. That way, we each have one child at any time. We could *take turns,* the way we're always telling Theo he ought to."

He looks so excited at the idea that some kind of compromise might still be possible that I don't have the heart to tell him Miles will never go for it. Why should he? He's never shown the faintest interest in compromising, not genuinely. And even if he did, who would decide about schools, or holidays, or even little things like haircuts? Perhaps right at the beginning, when things were different, we could have thrashed out an agreement like this. But now, when Miles so nearly has both children within his grasp, it's pointless.

But I don't say any of that. Instead, I say, "Well, it's got to be worth a try."

97

MADDIE

"GOOD MORNING, AND PLEASE take a seat," Marion Wakefield says pleasantly.

I still can't get over how informal the family courts are. It's astonishing to think that every day, in this room, parents are separated from their children.

"First, I'm going to ask you again whether you think any agreement could be reached," the judge continues. "Mr. Kelly?"

"My clients have been open to all suggestions, madam," the Lamberts' barrister says. "It seems a ruling by the court is the only way to resolve this."

The judge nods, clearly expecting that answer. "Ms. Chowdry?"

Anita says, "My clients have a proposal they would like to put forward."

Judge Wakefield looks at her over her glasses. "Would you like to outline it?"

"In brief, to share time with both children fifty–fifty. Theo will spend half his time with the applicants and half with the respondents. David will do the same, but in the opposite rotation. Since the children have very different needs, this will allow each child to get the best care at any one time."

"Very well. We'll take a break for the parties to discuss that."

We all troop out. There are no spare rooms, so we sit in the foyer. Pete and I wait with Anita, while the Lamberts go into a huddle with their barrister and solicitor. After a couple of minutes Miles comes over, smiling.

"Nice try," he says approvingly. "You know you're going to lose, so you thought you'd try to salvage something from the wreckage. But equally, since I know we're going to win, there's absolutely no chance we'll agree. None whatsoever." He wanders back to the others.

"I see what you mean about him," Anita says, watching him go.

"Believe me, that's Miles on a good day," Pete says. He puts his head in his hands.

We return to the court. I make sure I walk in front of Pete rather than Miles.

"Well? How did you get on?" the judge asks.

"My clients don't believe this proposal would be in either child's interests, madam," the Lamberts' barrister says. "The parenting styles of the two families are very different."

"Very well," the judge says briskly. "Let us proceed."

The hearing will begin, Anita has told us, with an opening statement from each side's lawyer, followed by the professional witnesses and CAFCASS. After that, Miles and Lucy will take questions on their written statements. Then it'll be our turn, before each side makes a final summing-up. It's possible the judge will decide to wait and give her judgment at a later date. But Anita thinks it's more likely she'll come to a decision today. This really is the point of no return.

Harvey Taylor, the psychologist, is up first. He comes to the witness box—which is simply a chair and table at the front, sideways on to both the judge and us—and talks through his assessment of Theo in a calm, neutral tone. When he gets to the bit about Theo's callous and unemotional traits, the judge interrupts.

"Are you effectively saying that Theo has special educational needs?"

Harvey nods. "Yes. They may not be comparable to David's in severity, but in their own way they're just as challenging."

"Oh, for God's sake," Miles mutters. The judge looks over at him sharply, but ignores the interruption. She turns back to Harvey Taylor.

"And could you describe what this means for his development?"

"Essentially, he needs a very particular parenting style—what we call warm parenting." The psychologist goes on to explain what that means.

"And can this type of parenting be learned?" the judge asks.

"It can, yes," the psychologist says cautiously. "But, because there can be a hereditary component to CU traits, sometimes the parents of a CU child are the very ones who find it hardest." He hesitates. "I would say, incidentally, that Mr. Riley has grasped it very well."

The Lamberts' barrister says immediately, "Madam, Mr. Harvey was asked by the court to assess whether Theo would be negatively impacted by a permanent move to the applicants' family. His conclusion is that Theo will cope admirably. He wasn't asked to assess either party's parenting capability."

"Mr. Harvey was answering my question," Judge Wakefield says mildly. "And his professional expertise is relevant to the issue of parenting style, which you yourself raised just a short while ago."

Bless you Bless you Bless you, I think.

"The applicants are of course willing to adapt their parenting in whatever way Theo's needs dictate," the barrister says.

"I'm sure they are," the judge says. "Thank you." She nods at Harvey Taylor, and the moment is over.

IT'S ONE SMALL PLUS in a long list of minuses. And, I realize, not even a very significant one. *We* might know that Miles is incapable of warm parenting, but why should the judge be able to tell that? I let my gaze slide toward him. He looks so relaxed, so confident, while beside me, Pete sits slumped in his chair biting his nails, looking like the nervous wreck he is. If I were choosing parents for Theo, which ones would I go for? The well-dressed, good-looking, well-heeled ones, or the ones with a string of criminal investigations, mental health issues, and allegations of alcohol abuse swirling around their heads?

Miles catches me looking at him and smiles.

It really is no contest, I think wearily. Even I would be hard-pressed to decide in our favor. I glance sideways at Pete, wondering if there's anything I can do to prepare him for the worst.

After the psychologist, it's Lyn Edwards's turn. She seems nervous as she comes to the witness box. I'm surprised by that: Court appearances must be a regular part of her job.

"Ms. Edwards," the judge says when Lyn has read out the affirmation, "is there anything you'd like to add to your written report before you take questions?"

Lyn says hesitantly, "There is, actually, madam. But I'm not absolutely sure whether the rules of disclosure allow me to."

The judge raises her eyebrows. "Does it have a direct bearing on the interests of the child?"

Lyn nods. "I believe it does, madam. It concerns some video footage I was sent last night."

"Then I'm going to ask both parties to leave the courtroom, while their representatives discuss whether or not it's admissible." The judge nods at us, then the Lamberts. "If you'd be so kind as to wait outside. The usher will call you back when we're ready."

.   .   .

FOR THE SECOND TIME, we all troop out. This must be some last trick Miles has pulled, I think, some theatrical flourish to round off the proceedings. I look over to where he sits on the other side of the foyer. His face is blank, which seems strange. If this is something he's planned, wouldn't he be savoring the moment? But he just seems impatient to get back inside.

Next to him, Lucy fiddles nervously with her pearls.

"Any idea what it can be?" I ask Pete.

"Beats me," he says, mystified. "But Miles has been leaking stuff to Lyn all along, so it must be him."

Eventually the usher calls us back and we resume our seats. "Thank you for bearing with us," Marion Wakefield says pleasantly. She looks at Lucy. "Mrs. Lambert, I'm going to allow Ms. Edwards to describe the video clip that she referred to earlier. If at any time you want a break to discuss this matter with your legal representatives, or to see the video, feel free to ask. But please bear in mind that if you do request to see it, then the other side, as well as myself, will necessarily be shown it, too." She nods at Lyn. "Please proceed."

"The video appears to be taken with a camera placed on a shelf in Mr. and Mrs. Lambert's playroom," Lyn begins. "It shows Mrs. Lambert sitting with Theo at the table. She's doing a drawing with him—a drawing of what she describes as a safe place. She tells him that really, there's no safer place than their house, because of its thick walls. And she tells him that, if he's ever asked to draw a picture of a place where he feels safe, he should draw the house where she and Miles live, and put the three of them inside it. And finally she says, if he draws a picture like that, his daddy Moles will be proud of him."

There's a short silence. "And what conclusion do you draw from this?" the judge asks.

"I believe she was coaching him in preparation for my visit."

Lyn has the grace to look shamefaced. "It is possible to find old CAFCASS reports online, if you look hard enough—they're meant to be confidential, but parents sometimes ignore that and post them on various forums. And of course, there are only a small number of techniques you can use to elicit very young children's feelings, so it's not hard to work out how we might do it." She looks from the judge to Pete. "Mr. Riley did tell me once that the applicants had been coaching Theo. At the time I assumed he was exaggerating."

"Thank you, Ms. Edwards." The judge looks at Lucy again. "Mrs. Lambert, ordinarily you would give your evidence toward the end of the proceedings, but given what Ms. Edwards has just told us, I'm going to ask you to come to the witness box now."

Lucy's hands are shaking so much, she can barely hold the card with the oath on it, and her voice is little more than a whisper.

"Do you have any comment to make on what Ms. Edwards has described?" Judge Wakefield asks when she's managed to reach the end.

"Well." Lucy touches her pearls. She looks anguished. "I wasn't *coaching* him, not exactly. I just wanted him to do well. I mean, he only gets one chance with CAFCASS, doesn't he, and it would be awful, just awful, if he didn't manage to say the things I know he really wanted to. So I simply tried to give him as much help as possible." She shoots Miles a desperate glance, but his face is impassive. "Because we *do* want his daddy to be proud of him, don't we? Really, it's no different from getting some private tutoring before you take an entrance exam."

This time the silence seems to stretch out forever. Marion Wakefield doesn't say no, it's very different, it's falsifying evidence and contempt of court and probably a whole bunch of other things, too. Neither does she ask a follow-up question. She just leaves Lucy sitting there, stewing, while she writes herself a lengthy note.

Eventually she looks at Anita. "Unless you have questions for Mrs. Lambert about this specific issue, Ms. Chowdry, I suggest we move on."

IT MUST HAVE BEEN one of the nannies, I realize. Tania, most likely. Once Michaela had warned her about the nannycam, Tania must have found a way to access the footage. Perhaps initially it was just to make sure there were no incriminating shots of her drinking coffee or scrolling through Facebook. But when she was abruptly fired to make way for Jill, she must have started looking for something that would allow her to take revenge.

For her own sake, I hope she's safely back in France.

The next part of the hearing is strangely subdued, as if nobody wants to start being bombastic when Lucy still looks as if she might burst into tears. The Lamberts' barrister has clearly decided that the best thing he can do is to carry on as if nothing has happened. And after a while, it almost seems to work. Even I find myself wondering if what Lucy did really makes much difference. After all, trying to work out Theo's wishes from one hastily scribbled drawing was always going to be a nonsense. And all the other factors—my drinking, the accusations against Pete, the fact Theo was thrown out of nursery on our watch—are still there.

But I can't help feeling that, while things looked completely hopeless before, now we have a chance.

98

MADDIE

NEXT, MILES IS CROSS-EXAMINED by Anita. She's good, but she makes little headway. He's unflappable and courteous—the very model of a cooperative witness. And it's hard to argue with the main thrust of his argument—that he and Lucy love Theo, and as his natural parents, believe they're best placed to make decisions about his future. What loving parent wouldn't want the same?

Then it's Pete's turn. The Lamberts' barrister dives straight in. "Can you tell us why you became Theo's full-time carer?"

"Because I enjoy it and I think I'm good at it," Pete replies evenly.

"It wasn't because you lost your job?"

Pete's eyes widen slightly, but his voice stays calm. "No."

"But you *were* made redundant soon after he was born? And then failed to find another position?"

Pete hesitates fractionally. "I went freelance."

"And how many freelance commissions would you say you get each year?"

"Half a dozen?" Pete mutters.

"According to the National Union of Journalists' database, last year it was three." The barrister pauses for that to sink in. "Realistically, could the two of you afford for Ms. Wilson to give up her job?"

"Probably not," Pete admits.

"So becoming Theo's full-time carer was, ultimately, a decision forced on you by economic necessity?"

Pete takes a deep breath. "It was a choice I wanted to make, which also made economic sense. I'm aware I'm very privileged to be doing something I enjoy so much."

"And yet," the barrister says smoothly, "your privilege comes at a cost, doesn't it—it deprives Theo of a full-time mother."

"Your question seems to imply that a full-time father is inherently less competent than a full-time mother," Pete says patiently. "I don't think that's the case. I think it depends on the individual."

Good answer, I think.

The barrister smiles pleasantly. "What is your current ranking on the videogame *Call of Duty*?"

Pete blinks. "I'm not sure."

"Let me refresh your memory. You are currently ranked number twenty-four thousand, two hundred and forty-seven of all players in the UK. Do you play often, to have achieved such a high position?"

Pete sighs. "Not often, no. I achieved that ranking before Theo came along. When I had a full-time job, incidentally."

The barrister still looks skeptical. "Let me read a question you posted on the internet forum DadStuff, about the correct temperature at which to sterilize a baby's bottle." He reads out the post, then pauses. "That's fairly basic information for a full-time parent, surely?"

"It was something I didn't know. So I made sure I found out." Pete grimaces. "Look, no parent gets everything right to begin with. Babies don't come with a manual. But these days, they do come with the internet. And rather than assume I know all the answers, I think it's better to check."

He's winning this exchange, I think. Against a professional inquisitor, Pete's actually holding his own. I can't help feeling proud of him.

The barrister says, "And speaking of the internet, do you look at pornography?"

Pete flinches. But he knows there's no point denying something that's now a matter of record. "I have, yes," he says stiffly.

"And is that something the full-time parent of a small child should do?"

"I'm not proud of it. And I wouldn't ever do it when Theo was in the house."

"But the fact you might be tempted to rather defeats your argument that a mother and a father are interchangeable, doesn't it?"

Pete opens his mouth to answer, but for a moment he can't find the words. "It doesn't make me a bad parent," he says at last.

"What about child pornography? Would that make you a bad parent?" the barrister asks in the same reasonable tone.

Pete says icily, "If I looked at child porn, it would make me a monster. But I don't."

"But you *have* visited websites that feature sexualized images of children. And were interviewed under caution by the police as a result, isn't that right?"

Pete explains that the image was an advertisement on an adult site, that the police were just trying to put pressure on him and no charges were ever brought. But his explanation sounds tortuous and self-justifying even to me. I steal a glance at the judge, trying to gauge her reaction. But she's impossible to read.

"Thank you," the barrister says, and just like that, it's over.

Next it's my turn. I'm ready for a repeat of the same attack on our parenting roles, but the barrister must think he's already made that point, or perhaps he's too clever to have a go at me for being a working mother in front of a female judge.

"How long have you known Mr. Riley?" he asks.

"Four years."

"Would you say yours is a stable relationship?"

For a moment I just stare at him, outraged by the implication. Then I recover. "We own a house together. We had a child together. I left Australia to be with him. Of course it's a stable relationship."

"But you're not actually married, are you?"

"What does that have to do with anything? It's a personal choice."

"Is it a choice you made because you don't want to commit to this relationship for the long term?" the barrister asks mildly.

I look at the judge, furious. Surely he can't be allowed to ask questions like these? But she only looks back, waiting for my answer. I take a breath. "No, it's because I find the idea of marriage outdated and patriarchal." My motives are actually far more complex than that, but I'm certainly not going to start unpacking them here and now.

"Has Pete ever proposed marriage to you?" the barrister asks.

"No, but . . ." I pause. "He knows my views, so he wouldn't."

"Or is it that *he* doesn't want to commit to *you*?"

I blink. Strangely enough, it's a question I've never actually asked myself. I've always taken Pete, and his commitment to me, for granted. "Being married wouldn't make us better parents," I say at last. "Or make our relationship more stable."

"Have you and Pete been to a relationship counselor in the last two years?" the barrister inquires pleasantly.

I gape at him. How the hell does he know about that? Then I realize. Miles must have had his private investigator nosing around, digging up dirt. "We have, yes," I say wearily.

"Why was that?"

"Theo's premature birth was hard on us. We were never in any danger of separating, if that's what you're asking."

"Yet the fact is, if you *did* separate, Pete couldn't afford to go on being Theo's carer, could he?"

"We've never done the sums, because it's not going to happen."

The barrister looks down at his notes. "You travel a lot for work, is that correct?"

"I make television commercials. Mostly they're filmed in this country. Four or five times a year, I have to go abroad. But never for more than a few days."

"Have you had affairs during the time you've been with Pete?"

For a moment there's a ringing in my ears and the room seems to shrink. "No."

"So you've never slept with members of the film crew when you were away?"

I freeze. What should I say? Does he already know the answer? Is he trying to trap me in a lie? My mind's whirring but I can't decide which is the least bad option.

Anita says, "Madam, my client has already denied having affairs, so the question is redundant. And even if she had, it wouldn't be relevant to the issue of whether or not she's a good mother to Theo."

"My point is that the respondents' domestic situation is inherently far less stable than the applicants' is, madam," the Lamberts' barrister says meekly.

"And you have made it," the judge says wryly. "Shall we move on?"

After that, the expected attack on my drinking seems tame by comparison. When I eventually go back to my chair, my cheeks are burning. Pete passes me a note. *That was outrageous. Well done.*

· · ·

THERE'S A LONG BACK-AND-FORTH between the lawyers about the European Human Rights Act and whether the UN Convention on the Rights of the Child—"A child has the right to be cared for by his or her parents"—applies here. It's a vital point, but I'm hardly listening. The barrister's question is still spinning around in my head. *Have you had affairs?* How much do they actually know?

And most important, am I now going to have to tell Pete about my slipups before Miles does?

Eventually all the other evidence is heard, and Pete delivers a final statement on behalf of us both. Normally, Anita would do this, but we've decided that in this case it should be Pete. He's Theo's primary carer. He's the one who needs to impress the judge.

He starts by describing how it felt, that day when Miles knocked on the door and blew our whole world apart with the news Theo wasn't our son. He describes the efforts to compromise, the gradual realization that Miles would stop at nothing to get Theo back. In calm, measured language he describes the pain of having Theo taken away from us, and has to stop because he's in tears. He describes how first the parenting classes, and then Harvey Taylor's visit, have made him a better father to Theo— "So, if you do direct that he should continue to live with us, this whole horrible experience will still have been worthwhile. Because it will have been good for Theo. And in the end, that's all that matters." And finally, he looks directly at Lucy. "That offer still stands, by the way. Despite what you said earlier, despite everything that's happened. We'd be happy to share them both between us. We would always have been happy to do that."

"Thank you," the judge says. "Unless anyone has any further points they wish to raise, I'm going to ask you all to step out while I consider what I've heard."

99

MADDIE

"THANK YOU FOR YOUR patience. I am now ready to give my judgment."

We waited in the crowded foyer for almost two hours—two agonizing hours that seemed to last an eternity. As the end of the day neared, other cases were reaching their conclusion, too—each courtroom spilling out into the foyer in two distinct groups, the elated and the despairing. Parents led away weeping by their lawyers, or punching the air in disinhibited delight.

Eventually the usher called us back and we took our places again. *This is it,* I think disbelievingly. *This is really it.* The moment seems both surreal and oddly mundane at the same time. I realize I've seen so many overwrought TV dramas in which judges bang gavels and lawyers shout "Objection!" that to have this calm, businesslike atmosphere, in which a judge is simply going to announce her decision as if she's the chairperson at an under-attended board meeting, feels all wrong.

Judge Wakefield looks at each of us in turn. "Thank you for coming here today and explaining what it is you want and why. Thank you, too, for allowing your evidence to be tested by the other side's legal representatives. You may have found some of their questioning intrusive, but it has allowed me to form a fuller picture of the options before the court. As you have heard, there is a strong presumption in UK law that children are best brought up within their natural families. However, there is also a duty to place the interests of the child above all else, and that means giving due consideration to such issues as continuity of care and what impact the disruption of existing bonds might have." She goes on to talk about something called the seven-point welfare checklist, and sums up the evidence briefly on each point. It's still impossible to tell which way she's leaning.

Then she pauses. "The right of the child to be brought up by his or her parents is another very important legal principle. We have heard differing views today on how that might apply to this situation. Having considered the matter carefully, I am going to accept Ms. Chowdry's argument that the word *parent,* in this context, should apply not only to the child's biological mother and father, but also to the individuals whom the child regards as his parents, and to whom he is bonded by a million small daily acts of parenting—in short, by the bonds of love. We have heard evidence from Mr. Taylor to the effect that Theo would be better equipped than most two-year-olds are to break those bonds. But we have also heard that he may find it harder than other children to regrow those bonds within a new family. For that reason, I believe both families have a roughly equal potential to provide him with a safe and nurturing home."

Again she pauses. "As you may know, the family courts operate on what is called the no order principle. That is, I have to be certain that whatever new arrangements I direct will be better for the child than those that already exist. Although the present case is a highly unusual one that undoubtedly calls for some clear resolution by the court, the underlying principle remains the same. If Theo were to move families, I have to be absolutely certain that the change will be in his best interests. And since the evidence is in fact finely balanced, I have decided that the previous arrangements should be allowed to stand, and that he should continue to live with the people he considered to be his parents for the first two years of his life."

It takes a moment for her words to sink in, to understand that Theo's coming home. Unbelievably, we've won. Pete reaches for my hand and squeezes it. I squeeze back. But the judge is still talking. "We cannot really have a situation in which Theo is living with the respondents but the applicants still have parental responsibility for him. It follows therefore that the previous order granting the applicants parental responsibility should be revoked, and a new order issued, granting parental responsibility to the respondents . . ."

There's more—the Lamberts are being offered contact visits, access to Theo's future parents' evenings. "I hope in time you may all of you rediscover the original spirit of cooperation with which you first approached this very difficult situation." Miles's face, which I can only see in profile, is a mask, his handsome jaw rigid with barely repressed fury. Clearly, he thought he had this sewn up. He probably did, too, until Lyn received that video. "This hearing has been about Theo, but I would like to remind both parties of the importance of the no order principle, and hope very much that a future hearing about David can be averted." The judge is basically telling us that, having kept Theo, there's little point pursuing our own claim for David, I realize. Everything's going back to the way it was, as if Judge Wakefield is some kind of wizard who can just wave a magic wand and undo the last four months' heartbreak. My gaze moves to Lucy, who's wiping away tears of relief. She loves David, of course she does, and she must quietly have been as terrified of having him taken away from her as Pete and I were of losing Theo. Perhaps it was wrong of us to try to get David, after all. But the pull to rescue my biological offspring from Miles had been so very strong.

And then it's over. The judge clicks something on her computer and nods. The lawyers stand up, followed by the rest of us. *We've won,* I think. *We've won.* I feel Pete's arms reach for me, pulling me into a hug. "We've won," he says. I can feel his body shaking with relief as he weeps into my shoulder. "Oh God. *Theo.* We've won."

"Come on," I say. "Let's go and get our boy."

100

MADDIE

WE BOTH GO TO pick him up from the Lamberts'. When Jill opens the front door he's standing next to her, ready in his coat and shoes, his overnight bag beside him.

"Ouff!" he says when Pete sweeps him into a bear hug, lifting him off the ground and swinging him around and around. "Stop *doing* that!"

He has no idea, of course. No idea why we're both laughing and crying and squeezing him like crazy people.

"Come on, Theo," I say at last, disentangling myself. "I feel an ice cream about to happen."

We walk down the steps. At the bottom Theo looks back, then waves. "Bye Moles! See you tomorrow!"

We look around. Miles is standing at the open door, watching us. There's no expression on his face, none at all. "We'll talk about that in the car, Theo," I say firmly, taking his hand.

Pete says suddenly, "I'm going to say something. After all,

we've got to give them access. Like the judge said, we should try to put things back on a friendly footing."

"Pete, don't," I say, but he's already gone.

Seeing him approach, Miles comes forward. Pete puts out his hand and speaks—I'm too far away to catch all the words, but I think it's, "You've got David and we've got Theo. It's an honorable draw, yes? So let's put this behind us. For their sake." I see Miles take Pete's hand and lean in close, that odd way he has of speaking to someone's ear rather than their face. He keeps a tight hold of Pete's hand and I can tell he's crushing it, squeezing it with all his force. But I'm pretty sure it's what he's saying, not the pressure of his hand, that's causing Pete's face to turn white.

"What did he say?" I ask when Pete returns. He doesn't meet my gaze.

"He said congratulations." Pete gives a quick, tight smile. "He said the best man and woman won."

**Case no. 12675/PU78B65, Exhibit 53: Email from
Harvey Taylor to Peter Riley, retrieved from Peter Riley's iPhone.**

Dear Pete,

Thank you for your email, and the link to the sad news about Judge Wakefield. As it happens, my bike is off the road for repairs, but I will in any case take note of your advice.

Many congratulations on winning your case. If I can be of any help in the future, please don't hesitate to get in touch.

Kind regards,

Harvey Taylor DForenPsy, MBPsS

Registered Psychologist

https://www.lawgazette.com/obituary/tributes-pour-in-for-family-judge-Marion-Wakefield

102

PETE

AS THE DAYS AND weeks went by with no word from Miles, we slowly allowed ourselves to relax. Which isn't to say we weren't vigilant. I didn't use my bike, for one thing. Cycling in London was dangerous enough already, without worrying that someone might drive up behind me and nudge my back wheel with their bumper.

Theo was still on the waiting list for the other nursery, but we managed to get him a temporary place with a childminder a few streets away. It wasn't a long-term solution—the childminder, Rosie, couldn't give him any one-to-one help for his CU—but at least it was away from the Lamberts.

But somehow it all felt like the lull before the storm. What Miles had said to me when we'd collected Theo after the hearing—the things he'd hissed into my ear about Maddie—had been childish and pathetic, but it also suggested he wasn't going to accept the court's judgment and move on. Not that I believed a word of what he'd said, of course. I remembered how, the very first time he'd come to our house, he'd let me think Theo was the result of an affair between him and Maddie. That had been entirely deliberate, I later realized—his first attempt at playing with me, seeing how I'd react. It had been Don Maguire who'd coughed and explained what had really happened. Miles just couldn't resist seeing what made people squirm.

Once, I thought I saw him in his car as I was taking Theo to Rosie's. Since her house was quite close, Theo was on his scooter—although I always made sure he stopped and waited for me before crossing any roads. On this occasion he'd gotten a little bit ahead, but he was safely on the pavement and there were no cars around, so I wasn't too worried. An old lady was pushing a shopping basket on wheels, very slowly. Without stopping, Theo veered around her, wobbling off the pavement and onto the road. Just at that moment, a black BMW four-wheel-drive pulled out from a parking space and sped up the street toward us. *"Theo!"* I screamed. *"Get back on the pavement!"* Theo stopped dead, and instead of doing as I told him, looked over his shoulder, perplexed by the terror in my voice. He was wearing his helmet, but against the bulk of the BMW it would be useless. Then the BMW accelerated past us, and as the driver adjusted her mirror I saw it was a dark-haired woman wearing sunglasses, just another entitled north London mother driving her SUV too fast after dropping off her kids, in a hurry to get to the gym.

My heart pounding, I caught up with Theo. "Don't ever go off the pavement again," I snapped. "Or I'm confiscating your scooter."

Theo only sagged his shoulders comically, as if to say I was overreacting. Which, from his perspective, of course I was.

I'd read how some parents react to traumatic events by catastrophizing—becoming hyper-fearful and protective, seeing imaginary disasters around every corner. Over time, their children soak up those fears, becoming insecure and timid. I couldn't do that to Theo, whose sunny confidence was one of his most endearing characteristics. I mustn't.

I resolved that, whatever terrors still lurked in my own mind, I wasn't going to let Theo be aware of them. We were going to live a normal life.

103

PETE

SO WHEN I LOST him in Sainsbury's, at first I tried not to over-react.

We got most of the big shopping delivered, but once a week Theo and I sat down, planned our meals for the next seven days, then went to the supermarket to buy what we'd need. He loved it, as did I. It was free entertainment that got him out of the house and taught him the rudiments of healthy eating at the same time. I even tried to build in some educational games, such as seeing how quickly he could find, say, a tin of baked beans and bring it back to the trolley, even though I'd probably have to go and swap the tin he'd just grabbed with the correct reduced-sugar-and-salt version while he was doing his next errand.

"Thanks, Theo," I said as he proudly handed me a carton of milk. "Next is melon. We need one of the small yellow ones, okay?"

He nodded and sped off. I used the breathing space to load

some frozen stuff into the trolley. Fish fingers, made with pollack not cod. Peas, no added sugar. Prawns, sustainably sourced. Or were they? That's what it said in big letters on the front of the packet, but that could mean anything. When I checked on the back, there was no MSC certification.

I suddenly realized I'd been able to read the whole of the back of a packet of prawns undisturbed. Theo never took that long finding something. I looked over at the fruit section, concerned but not alarmed. Perhaps he'd gotten distracted. Or started talking to one of the staff.

The store was a sensibly sized one, not one of those vast behemoths that stock everything from saucepans to tracksuits. The fruit section was literally seconds away, in full view of where I was standing with the trolley.

And Theo wasn't there.

I stared at the space where he should be, uncomprehending. That time I'd lost him before on a shopping trip flashed into my mind—the horror of not knowing where your child is, even for a minute.

Beyond the fruit section were the doors to the car park. Automatic doors, that might temptingly open and close if you played grandmother's footsteps with them. But if Theo was doing that, I'd see him.

Wouldn't I? I had a sudden vision of him dropping a melon onto the floor. The melon rolling toward the door. Theo following it . . .

And then what? Going into the car park? Why on earth would he do that? But cars drove around the car park stupidly fast sometimes, and a little boy focusing on a rolling melon might not see one coming—

Stay calm, I told myself. He'd probably just decided to come back to the trolley the long way around, past the checkouts, hoping to grab something interesting from the shelves on the way. It was still less than twenty seconds since I'd realized he was missing, and no more than a minute since I'd last seen him. But I could feel the panic starting to build in my chest. I pushed the trolley rapidly along the row of checkouts, peering down each aisle. Not there, either. But could he now be behind me, given that I'd moved the trolley from where he was expecting it to be? I turned and headed back the other way. Someone blocked me in as they stopped to reach for a packet of cereal. Cursing, I abandoned my trolley so I could move more quickly.

"Theo!" I called at the top of my lungs, all British reserve abandoned. "Theo!"

Still nothing. Frantically I ran to the customer service desk, where they did the PA announcements. But there was no one around.

"Excuse me," I said, butting into the queue for the nearest till and speaking to the youth operating it. "I need to make an announcement. I've lost my son. He's two and a half. Wearing a red hoodie and jeans."

The young man didn't stop scanning his customer's shopping. "I dunno how to use it."

"Oh for God's sake. I'll do it myself."

I ran behind the desk, searching for the microphone, just as the woman whose shopping was being scanned looked up and called, "A red hoodie, did you say?"

"Yes. Have you seen him?"

She pointed. "A little boy in a hoodie just went out with a man in a suit. They looked like they knew each other. I think they were holding hands."

I looked again at the doors. In the magazine racks by the entrance, someone had placed a small yellow melon.

I RAN OUTSIDE, STILL shouting Theo's name. I knew it was probably hopeless, but I pelted down the rows of parked cars anyway, yelling and looking between each one.

Then I caught sight of a black BMW four-wheel-drive pulling out of a space in the far corner. I turned and ran straight toward the exit. Perhaps if I was fast enough, I'd be able to cut them off. Perhaps he'd stop. Perhaps anything.

I was still twenty yards off when the car reached the exit. As he passed, Miles turned and looked at me, his face expressionless. From the back, carefully strapped into a booster seat, Theo waved cheerfully.

104

PETE

I WAS TERRIFIED, OBVIOUSLY. But there was also a part of me that was thinking, *Right, you've done it now.* Because now I could tell the police that Theo had just been abducted in direct defiance of a court order. Now it would be Miles's turn to explain himself to social workers and detectives and lawyers. And in all likelihood, to a judge as well.

Finally, he'd gone too far. I had right on my side, and I was going to make sure the full might of the law came crashing down on him.

I pulled out my phone. Then I hesitated. If I called the police straightaway, they'd tell me to wait where I was until they could get someone out to me. Once they realized it related to an existing custody case, they might even decide it wasn't urgent. And my priority had to be making sure Theo was safe.

I'd call them from outside the Lamberts' house, I decided. That way the police would show up right on Miles's doorstep.

I ran to my car and drove to Highgate, breaking the speed limit all the way.

I got to the Lamberts' house, but the BMW wasn't outside. For a moment I thought I'd simply beaten him to it. But then I realized that was unlikely. Miles must have taken Theo somewhere else.

A shiver ran down my spine. Miles loved his son—adored him. Surely Theo couldn't actually be in danger?

I stabbed the entry buzzer, then impatiently ran up the steps to the front door. It seemed to take an age for anyone to come. When the door finally opened, I saw why: Lucy was on crutches. One foot was bandaged.

It wasn't hard to guess what had happened. Miles must have blamed her for their defeat in court. But right at that moment, I had little sympathy for her.

"Oh, Pete," Lucy began. "How lovely—"

I cut across her. "Where's Miles?"

"Miles?" She stared at me, confused. "He's at work."

"He's got Theo. In the car." I gestured at the empty driveway. "He doesn't usually take the car to work, does he? Think, Lucy. Where could he have taken him?"

She still looked blank. "I don't know."

I must have clenched my hands with impatience, because she flinched and said quickly, "They sometimes go to the Heath. To the boating pond. Theo loves the ponds. And the rugby pitches, of course."

"Thank you." I ran to my car and started it. Just as I was about to drive off, my phone pinged. I looked down at the screen and saw the name. MILES LAMBERT.

And a message.

But the other one said, Let it be neither mine nor thine, but divide it.

105

PETE

I RECOGNIZED IT INSTANTLY, of course. It was from the Old Testament. The woman who said she'd rather go along with Solomon's judgment, and see the disputed child killed, than give up her claim to it.

The police would never understand what it meant, not without knowing the whole background. But I did. It was a death threat. Perhaps not even a threat—this might be Miles's way of telling me what he'd already done.

I felt my bones turn to icy water at the realization that Theo could be dying at that very moment.

I don't know how I drove to the car park beside the Heath. From there you could see how Highgate got its name. Below me, all of London was spread out in one huge, overwhelming vista, from Canary Wharf in the east to Paddington in the west, with St. Paul's and the Shard in the middle. It was a view that had featured in at least a dozen sappy romantic comedies, and I was desperately scouring it for just one thing.

A tiny person in jeans and a red hoodie. Perhaps with a tall man in a well-cut suit by his side.

There was nothing. No one on the rugby pitches. And no one at the boating pond. Just a few dog walkers and joggers, braving a blustery wind.

Then I spotted a black BMW in the car park, right at the end of a row. Empty, but it proved they were here.

Think, Pete. Lucy said, "Theo loves the ponds." Ponds, plural. There were more than half a dozen of them on this side of Hampstead Heath, following the course of some ancient river.

Run, Pete. I set off at a fast pace, but the Heath was vast and I was soon agonizingly short of breath. At the men's swimming pond I drew a blank. The duck pond and the women's pond, ditto. Then came a succession of smaller ponds whose names I didn't know, each one ringed with trees, their surfaces green and shiny with duckweed.

And then, in the smallest pond, right in the middle, so small and still I only just glimpsed it through the trees, I saw a splash of red.

A child's hoodie.

I hurtled through the soggy, squelching mud toward it.

It was Theo. He was floating facedown in the water. The hood was pulled up over his head, his legs sunk under the mat of green duckweed. I ran into the water, almost tripping as the mud gripped my calves, slowing me further even as I desperately tried to reach him. I knew infant CPR—we'd been trained in it at the NICU. If there was a chance, any chance at all, of pummeling the water and weed out of his lungs and breathing life back into him, I could do it. But every second would be vital.

Please don't let him be dead. Anything, anything but that.

But in my heart I knew it was useless. He was motionless, his head bobbing only from the ripples caused by me crashing toward him, making the duckweed undulate and break up. He'd clearly been there for some time.

Under the fluorescent green weed the water was black and noxious, my legs sinking deeper into the silty mud with every yard. I felt breathless, my ears ringing as if I was about to pass out, lactic acid burning in my muscles, my heart thudding in my chest. I was up to my thighs, then my waist, then at last I was close enough to reach out and flip him over—

It was a rugby ball. Inside the red hood, a rugby ball had been placed where Theo's head would be. A stick, jammed in with it, had kept the rest of the hoodie from sinking. The green weed, obscuring where his legs would be, had done the rest.

I stood there, gulping air, a mixture of relief and fear coursing through me. Relief it wasn't Theo. And fear, that Miles still had him.

"I wanted you to know."

I swung around. Miles was standing twenty feet away in the trees, watching me. His face was blank, his tone matter-of-fact.

Of Theo, there was still no sign.

I couldn't speak. Couldn't move, in fact, the mud gripping my burning calves like shackles.

"To know what it feels like to lose your son," Miles continued. "What it's been like for me, these last weeks. What it'll be like for you, too, when he dies."

Theo's alive. I focused on that, managed to pant, "Where is he? What have you done with him?"

"And die he will," Miles went on as if I hadn't spoken. "Next time, it'll be for real, Pete. Gone forever. No third chances. So that's the deal I'm offering you."

"What deal? What are you talking about?"

"Remember how the Bible story goes? Just before the bit I texted you? The real mother says to Solomon, 'Give her the living child, instead of killing it.' She'd rather her son was handed to her deadliest rival, the woman she'd dragged through the courts for justice, than see him die. That's real parenthood, Pete. Putting your own desires second. Sacrificing everything to keep your child safe. Even your own happiness."

He looked at me, considering. "But are you really that person, Pete? I mean, you appear to be. You love playing the part, that's for sure. Doting dad, decent bloke. Unselfish. Principled. Loving. But how genuine is all that, I wonder? Could you really be as self-sacrificing as that mother in the Bible? You should thank me, Pete. I'm giving you a chance to prove you could."

"You're mad," I said disbelievingly. "Completely mad, if you think I'd ever agree to that."

Miles folded his arms. "Give him up voluntarily, or he dies. Don't doubt me, Pete. Don't think I couldn't do it."

"Oh, I know what you're capable of," I said harshly. "I spoke to Murdo McAllister."

For a moment a frown touched Miles's eyes, then cleared again. "Well, then. You know I mean it. After all, look at this from my perspective. What do I have to lose?"

"I'm going straight to the police."

"Yes? To tell them what—that you abandoned your child in a supermarket? It was a good thing I was there, frankly, or anything might have happened. Luckily, Theo saw a familiar adult face and made contact to say he was lost."

I stared at him. He was completely serious, I saw. He really thought this crazy plan of his was going to work. "And David? What about him?"

"David . . ." Miles considered. "The runt dies, too. Not on the same day, obviously, or in exactly the same way. But if you force me to kill my son, I'll kill yours, too, for good measure. Oh, and so you don't delay any longer than necessary, I'll make him suffer in the meantime. Every twenty-four hours until you decide, Pete, I'll make sure David has a little *episode*." He turned, and his voice changed. "Theo, my man. What did you decide, in the end? It's a tough decision, after all. Magnum or Solero?"

Behind him, Theo was approaching, an ice lolly in each hand. "Twisters," he said happily. "I chose Twisters. Green for you and yellow for me." He looked at me curiously. "Why's Daddy in the water?"

"He went to get your rugby ball back," Miles said, taking the lolly Theo offered him. "Silly Pete couldn't catch it, and now he's all covered in slime. That's going to make your car a bit stinky on the way home, isn't it?"

106

PETE

"WHAT ARE WE GOING to do?" Maddie whispered.

We were lying in the darkness. Theo was asleep. We hadn't been able to talk about it before, not properly—I'd had to tell her everything Miles had said piecemeal, in frantic whispered conversations between tea and bath and story, so Theo wouldn't overhear.

"Our only option is the police," I said. "Tell them what he's threatened to do."

"Yes," she agreed. "But do you think they'll take it seriously? Our word against his? In the wake of a custody battle, too?"

"We can get a restraining order."

"We'd have to get the police to prosecute him first. Besides, do we really think Miles Lambert would stick to the terms of a restraining order? By the time the law catches up with him, it could be too late."

"What, then?"

Maddie said slowly, "I suppose the first question is, do we think he's bluffing?"

In my mind I could picture Miles reaching down to take the lolly from Theo, the coldness in his eyes when he spoke to me. I exhaled. "No, I think he really means it. I think he's prepared to kill Theo if he can't have him." At the thought of that tiny breathing body just ten feet away suddenly being extinguished, my throat caught. "*Theo*. Oh God. What are we going to do?"

"Pete . . ." she began, and I knew that what she was about to say was serious. "Perhaps the time for playing by the rules is over. Perhaps we need to fight dirty. The way Miles has always fought."

"If we only had some evidence," I said doggedly. "Something we could show the police that would prove he's killed before."

"We've already looked for that," she said gently. "We talked to everyone we could. And no one had a smoking gun, did they? No one ever realized what Miles was like until it was too late."

"Yes. And for whatever reason, even his wife seems incapable of seeing him for what he really is." I shuddered in the darkness. "When I saw her today, she was on crutches. And when I happened to clench my fists, she flinched."

"That's what happens, though, isn't it? Annette said women like that simply lose the confidence to leave their abuser." Suddenly Maddie gasped. "Oh my God. I've just realized something."

"What is it?"

"I think we need to talk to Lucy," she said slowly. "I think there's something we've been missing in all this."

107

<u>**Case no. 12675/PU78B65, Exhibit 54: Messenger**</u>
<u>**communication (a) from Madelyn Wilson to Tania Lefebvre, and (b)**</u>
<u>**from Tania Lefebvre to Madelyn Wilson.**</u>

Tania, it's Maddie Wilson again. I just want to thank you for sending that video to the CAFCASS adviser—it made a huge difference. Can we talk on the phone?

I'm sorry Maddie, what video? And who is CAFCASS? We can speak if you like but I don't think I can help you.

108

MADDIE

IT'S SURPRISINGLY HARD TO get Lucy on her own. Speaking to her at her house is out of the question, of course—there's one camera that we know of, but I'm fairly sure there'll be others.

Because they're not really for checking on the nanny, I've realized. Or not only that.

They're for checking on *her*.

To make sure she's carrying out his instructions. Coaching Theo, for example—that almost certainly came from Miles. But even when he hasn't given her a specific task to do, just knowing he might be watching—storing up his criticisms for his return each evening—would be enough to undermine anyone's self-confidence.

He's been controlling her from the day they married. I'm sure of it. And now it's time to see if I'm right.

So we wait for Lucy to leave the house, and eventually she does.

She's still on crutches, but she manages to get to the newsagent around the corner, and that's where I tap her on the shoulder.

Despite the crutches, she jumps.

"Oh! Maddie," she says, recovering. "And Pete, too. How nice to see you. Is Theo with you?"

I shake my head. "With a friend. Can we get a coffee?"

"A coffee?" she repeats anxiously. "I'm not sure that's a good idea. Not just at the moment. Miles . . ." Her voice trails off.

"Miles won't know. And we need to talk," I say firmly. "There's a café right next door." I look her in the eye. "You see, we know it was you who sent that footage to the CAFCASS adviser."

SHE DOESN'T ADMIT IT. But she does allow herself to be taken to the café, where we find an empty table among all the young mummies with their buggies and lattes.

"I contacted Tania," I tell her. "At first I thought it must have been her who sent it. So this morning I messaged her. She told me she'd had nothing to do with it. I'd already had my suspicions, but that's when everything fell into place."

"But why would it be *me*?" Lucy's hand has gone to her collar to tug out her pearls. "Of course I wouldn't do a thing like that. That day was horrible for me, absolutely horrible. Miles said I was lucky not to be charged with contempt of court."

"But that was a risk you were prepared to take, wasn't it?" I reach across the table for her free hand, but she flinches away at the movement. "As for why you did it, that's simple. You did it to protect Theo. You did it because you wanted to lose."

THERE'S A LONG SILENCE. Lucy sits absolutely still, her eyes wide. "You can't prove that," she whispers.

"I don't need to," I say gently. "Don't you see—I'm not accusing you of anything except loving your son. And wanting him to grow up in the best place possible. With the best father." I indicate Pete, sitting quietly beside us. "Not Miles. Everyone at this table knows what Miles is, Lucy. You wanted Theo brought up by Pete and me. So he'd be safe."

Her silence tells me I'm right.

"After all," I add, "it's not the first time, is it? You've done it before. You did it two years ago, when you swapped them in the hospital."

109

MADDIE

SHE CRIES THEN. BUT it seems to me they're tears of relief, at least partly. Relief she has someone to share the secret with at last.

"You must think I'm so stupid," she says, drying her eyes on a paper napkin from the jam jar on the table. "Not to have realized before I married him that he has a . . . that he can be quite demanding. But it was all so quick, you see, and I was head-over-heels in love."

She describes those early days to us, and it's almost exactly what Annette predicted. The love-bombing that swept her off her feet—showering her with attention, with compliments, with charm. The proposal of marriage that came within weeks; the wedding that took place within months; the pregnancy that started soon after. The private maternity hospital, because nothing was too good for their child. And then the shock of premature birth—going into labor at twenty-nine weeks, as she did Pilates one morning.

"The obstetrician diagnosed something called cervical incompetence. It was rather unfortunate it was called that, actually. Because it made it clear that even the doctors thought it was my fault. I mean, not deliberately, nobody accused me of that. But it was my body that had been so useless. And there was absolutely nothing that could be done—the baby was on its way, and it couldn't go back in. And Miles . . ." She hesitates, then says quietly, "I'll never forget that moment. He took my hand and bent down so he could whisper in my ear. I expect the nurses thought he was saying something encouraging, to help with the contractions. But his voice—well, he just went still. That's what I call them—Miles's stillnesses. I'm used to them now, of course, as much as anyone can be, but that was the first time. He said . . ." She blinks back tears and swallows hard. "He said, 'If you've killed my son, I swear I'll kill you.'"

She lets me put my hand over hers now. I squeeze reassuringly, but say nothing.

"I suppose I'd started to realize by then anyway. I mean, he'd been so distant all through the pregnancy. Like he didn't need to bother with me anymore. As if everything before had been a massive effort, and now the job was done he could stop pretending. I mean, I'm sure he'd tried to love me, but when I didn't measure up, he started to ignore me instead."

She falls silent, remembering.

"And the baby was sent to the NICU," I say.

"Yes." She glances at Pete. "Where almost the first thing I saw was Pete, crying for *his* baby. I thought—well, that's normal, isn't it? That's what a real father would do. I suppose I envied my child the life that baby was going to have. And then a few minutes later this grumpy nurse—Paula—marched up to the mobile incubators and said, 'Which one's David Lambert? This one?' And I—I nodded, even though she was pointing to the wrong cot. So she wheeled it away, across the ward, and I followed her. It was a moment of madness. I didn't even think it would last, not to begin with—I thought any second the mix-up would be discovered, and my little fantasy would be over. But then, when Paula was off getting something, I looked down and saw a paper tag in the cot as well, lying loose. So I pocketed it."

"And David became Theo," I say softly. "Safely stowed inside another family."

She nods. "How did you guess that's what happened?"

I hold her gaze. It's important she understands this, that she doesn't feel entirely alone. "Because I felt the exact same thing. Not back then, in the NICU. It was when Miles first made his move on Theo and David, and I decided we had to fight for David, too. It was crazy on so many levels, but it wasn't something I thought through rationally. I just *knew*."

I'm so rarely maternal, I hadn't recognized it at first—not until Judge Wakefield was making it clear that, having won Theo, there was little point in pursuing our claim for David. I'd looked across at Lucy, wiping away tears of relief, and thought, *At least he's loved*. And I'd realized that my desire to fight for David had been, at root, pure instinct—the overwhelming, urgent need to protect my son from Miles.

It was only last night, talking to Pete in the darkness, that I'd finally made the connection. If I'd felt that way, what were the chances Theo's mother had, too?

Lucy's saying, "Of course, I didn't know the one I'd taken was brain-damaged, not at first. It was several days before the doctors found that out. When they told us—well, I accepted it as my due. I was pleased for you, actually. I thought, *I* might have done an unforgivable thing, but at least *they* got a baby that's healthy. And I could love David, I knew I could. Perhaps even more than you might have. Because I had no one else, you see. Miles had absolutely no interest in either of us. The child was a failure and I was a failure and that was all there was to it. I mean, he put on a good show of being a caring father when it suited him, but when we were alone . . ." She pauses. "He can be quite cutting," she finishes with vague understatement.

"But you've stayed with him."

"Yes." She grimaces. "You must think I'm so pathetic. I know *you'd* never have stood for it. But somehow we muddled along. And I had David. He needs so much . . . I don't think I could cope with him on my own. And Miles is much better once you've worked out how not to make him angry."

Beside me, Pete twitches. I know he's itching to say that Miles had no right to treat her like that in the first place, and that it certainly shouldn't be her job to placate him, but now isn't the moment. I put my hand on his leg, briefly, then turn back to Lucy.

"Lucy, there are several things about Miles I think you may not know. I suspect you do know that he was having sex with Michaela behind your back." After a moment, Lucy nods reluctantly. "But what you probably don't know is that he's tried to kill people. And in at least one case, we think he's succeeded." I look at Pete. "Tell her."

Pete explains about the hit-and-runs. He lays it out calmly and unemotionally, as if it's an article he's pitching to a newspaper. When he's finished, Lucy takes a deep breath.

"He has a storage unit. I think he may have a second car in it— an old Passat. I found the keys once when I was folding his trousers. He was furious—that's how I knew it was something important. But I don't think it's licensed—I've never seen any paperwork for it."

"Do you know where the storage unit is?"

She shakes her head. "And I don't want to. I don't want anything to do with it."

Pete leans forward and says gently, "I'm afraid you already are something to do with it. And there's more. Lucy, you need to hear what he's threatening to do next. To Theo. And what he's already doing to David."

110

PETE

IT WAS JUST AN ordinary day.

It was just an ordinary day in Willesden Green, north London. Summer had come to the city, but at eight thirty in the morning the streets were still relatively cool as I took Theo on his scooter to the Leyland Avenue Nursery and Preschool. He'd settled in well. Harvey Taylor's report had helped a lot, by setting out exactly what extra support he'd need. It was working, too. Slowly but surely, he was getting there.

Having dropped him off, I went home, turned on my laptop and the coffee machine, then logged onto DadStuff. There was a thread for those whose kids had been diagnosed with CU. Music lessons helped, apparently, and simple body-language games. In any case, it was good to share the problem with others, particularly those whose children were older and had been through this stage already.

Then the doorbell rang, so I put down my cappuccino and went to answer it.

There were five of them. Two in uniform, two in white forensic bodysuits, and one in plainclothes. It was the one in plainclothes who said, "Peter Riley, I am arresting you on suspicion of the murder of Miles Leopold Lambert. You do not have to say anything, but if you do not mention now something which you mention later, a court might ask you why you did not mention it at the first opportunity. I have here a warrant to search these premises and to seize electronic devices or other evidence relating to this investigation."

"I'd better call my solicitor," I said, stepping back to let them in. "Before you take my phone."

111

Case no. 12675/PU78B65: SUMMARY AND CONCLUSION
by Catherine Jackson, Senior Crown Prosecutor.

1. The investigation into the death of Miles Lambert (12675/PU78B65) has now been ongoing for more than ten months, and, in the opinion of the police, is unlikely to yield any further high-quality evidence to assist the Crown Prosecution Service in the decision that must now be made regarding whether or not to bring any charges.

2. The circumstances of Mr. Lambert's death—an apparent hit-and-run while returning home from a morning jog at approximately 6:50 A.M.—undoubtedly indicate a criminal act. However, the vehicle that struck him has not been identified, and none of those questioned by the police have admitted any involvement.

3. Suspicion was initially directed at Peter Riley and Madelyn Wilson, who prior to Mr. Lambert's death had been involved in a court case with him over the custody of his biological son, Theo. There is ample documentation in the bundle showing that, despite initially being

quite amicable, the relationship between the two families had become acrimonious. However, Mr. Riley and Ms. Wilson had been successful in that case, and—the communications with Tania Lefebvre and Harvey Taylor notwithstanding—might therefore be presumed to have little motive to harm Mr. Lambert once the judgment had been handed down.

4. They were also able to give each other consistent alibis for the time at which Mr. Lambert's death occurred. Mr. Riley was engaged in a heated exchange about head lice on the internet forum DadStuff from 7:02 to 7:38, making a total of eleven posts from his home network. Ms. Wilson's assertion that she was making Theo's breakfast is consistent with phone tower data showing that her mobile remained in the house until she left for work as usual at around 8:18.

5. Police also questioned Mr. Lambert's wife, Lucy, but again found nothing that would indicate a motive to harm her husband. Footage from the Lamberts' nannycams places Mrs. Lambert in her house drinking coffee until after the arrival of the emergency services at the scene at 7:14. She told investigating officers that she was unaware her husband lay dying outside their front door until she was alerted by the police at approximately 7:25.

6. Perhaps most important, forensic scrutiny of both the Lamberts' BMW and the Volkswagen Golf owned by Peter Riley yielded no signs that either had been involved in an incident of this nature, and nothing of direct relevance was found in the search histories of any of the electronic devices seized and examined by police.

7. In short, there appears to be no reasonable chance of a conviction in this matter, and I therefore conclude that no further action be taken.
Catherine Jackson
Senior Crown Prosecutor

112

MADDIE

TREVOSE HEAD IS JUST as beautiful as Miles promised—a huge house right on the beach, with only the coast path and the sand dunes between us and the sea. Miles was right, too, in his prediction that Theo would love it. We've bought him a tiny little wet suit to run into the sea in, while Pete, also looking quite cute in his matching shortie, stands sentinel to protect him from the treacherous currents. Even David, it turns out, loves to sit in a rock pool and splash, so most mornings Lucy and I sit with him, our feet in the cool water, chatting.

We rarely talk about Miles. Sometimes Lucy feels the need to say something, and then I simply listen while whatever's on her mind spills out in a rush. Then, just as suddenly, she'll stop, shake her head as if clearing it of the memory, and talk about something else.

But I can see her confidence growing day by day. It'll take years,

I imagine. But already she's a different person than the nervous, jumpy creature we sat opposite in the café almost a year ago.

I suspect she would never have helped us on her own account, though. It took Pete telling her what Miles was threatening to do to the children to do that. She let out a cry, and her hand flew to her mouth. Some of the other mothers in the café glanced at her briefly, then went on with their chatting.

From that moment, her resolve never wavered. It was her who tracked down the address of the storage unit, her who stole the key from Miles's desk. When we went to look, it was just as she'd said—an old Volkswagen station wagon, the tax many years out of date. There were dents on the bonnet, and a crack in the windscreen where it might have been hit by a flying, tumbling skull.

But it was me, not her or Pete, who drove it to Haydon Gardens the next morning. In my mind, there was never any question about that. Pete had been shocked when I first told him what I was planning. Then he said that, if it had to be done, it should be him. But I knew something like that would have eaten away at him afterward. For me, it's different.

It was when I was researching Miles's personality that I began to realize something about myself, something important. Psychopathy is a spectrum, Annette told me: These are traits most people have none of, a few have in abundance, but some have a scattering of—just enough to make them fearless, or lacking in squeamishness, or clearheaded in a crisis. Just enough to make them ruthless, too. When I found the psychopath test online I filled it in out of curiosity, but even before I calculated my score I knew I'd be on a very different part of that spectrum from Pete.

I drove up behind Miles as he got home from his run. The sound, or perhaps some sixth sense, must have alerted him, because he half turned and glimpsed me over his shoulder. For a moment, he kept going—speeded up, in fact, as if he meant to try to outrun me. Then he'd slowed and turned. Facing me. Staring me down, as if his gaze alone might be enough to make me stop.

When I kept on coming, and he saw I meant to hit him, he grinned. There'd been no fear in his eyes, only a kind of alert, exultant excitement.

And a nod. Whether that was a gesture of acceptance, or something else—of recognition; welcome, even—I couldn't have said.

I ALMOST DIDN'T TELL Pete it was done. I felt no guilt, no inner need to confess, and in many ways the less he knew the better. But I had to go home anyway, to get my phone, and I decided that, on balance, he should know our children were now safe.

He sat very quietly, his head bowed. He was torn, I knew— both horrified at the thought I'd actually done it, and relieved our nightmare was over.

"By the way," I added when I'd finished. "I think you should tell me what happened with you and Bronagh now."

He stared at me. "How do you know anything did?"

"Well, for one thing your account didn't quite tally with hers. For another, you told a stupid lie. You said you came back from York on the Friday morning. You were right, of course, that I had no idea what planet I was on by then, let alone what day of the week it was. But it's all there in my medical notes—the date and time I was sectioned and admitted. You got back on the Saturday."

"Oh God." Pete took a deep breath. "It's been eating me up, not telling you. I was *going* to tell you—I spent the whole time on that train working out what I was going to say. And then—well, obviously I couldn't say anything when I found you in the state you were in. Or when you first came back from hospital. So I just kind of left it and then it became harder and harder."

So, hesitantly, he told me. How Bronagh had dropped a heavy

hint or two when they were all drinking at the Vudu Lounge—
"This is my first big night out in six months, Pete. If I don't find a
ride tonight, I think I'll go crazy." A dance. An arm—his—around
a waist—hers, pulling her close. And then she'd looked him in the
eye and said softly, "You do know a blow job wouldn't count, Pete
Riley, don't you? What with you not even being married?"

He stopped, shamefaced.

"And?" I said.

"But that was just the point. Of *course* it would count. And
once she'd said it out loud like that . . . I suddenly realized where
this was heading. How squalid it was. And I—I was just letting it
happen. So I went and packed my bag and got on the first train to
London."

Now it was my turn to stare. "You mean—*nothing* happened?"

He frowned. "*That* happened. It was hardly nothing. I'd realized I'd almost risked everything—you, Theo, everything I care
about—for some stupid, momentary ego boost. And then of
course I came back and found you ill, so I felt even worse. I think
that's why I threw myself into looking after Theo—to try to make
it up to you. And I realized that I loved it. I mean, I loved *him* already, but it was more than that. I loved caring for him. Being his
dad. I'd finally found what I was good at." He looked at me. "Can
you forgive me? It's the only time I've even come close to doing
something like that, I promise."

"Of course I forgive you," I said. "I love you, stupid."

CAN PEOPLE LIKE ME love? *Really* love, the way Pete so clearly
loves me and Theo, from the very bottom of his heart? Opinions
on that are divided, I gather. But then, I'm only marginally on the
spectrum—the way I reacted to the NICU confirms that. And
when I look at Theo, soaking up the emotional literacy Pete's
teaching him, I know that change is possible.

Pete will be my conscience. He's already persuaded me to drop our legal action against the NHS. It's right that David receive a payout to help Lucy look after him, he argued, particularly as Miles left her nothing but debts. But we, and Theo, don't need it. So we settled for getting our costs paid, to get Justin Watts off our backs, and with the police investigation effectively closed, NHS Resolution was only too eager to accept.

As for my own slipups, I don't see any need to confess those to Pete. I guessed that was what Miles was telling him, of course, when we collected Theo after the hearing. I was waiting for Pete to say something to me, or for Miles to follow it up with some evidence—a witness statement through the letterbox, an affidavit pinging into Pete's inbox—but he never did.

He had nothing, I eventually realized. Perhaps it was never much more than a shot in the dark in the first place. Perhaps Don Maguire had picked up some gossip, one of those rumors that float around a busy office like mine. If he'd had more, the Lamberts' barrister would surely have found a way to use it at the hearing. Then I'd have been accused of perjury on top of everything else, and the balance between us and the Lamberts would have tilted yet again—and who knows what the judge's decision would have been then? So gradually, I realized my secret was safe, and with that grew my resolve not to tell Pete. It would only hurt him at a time when our relationship needed rebuilding, not undermining.

Sometimes I find myself wondering what, in the end, the difference is between pretending to be nice, the way people like Miles and, I suppose, I do, and trying to be nice, the way Pete, Lucy, and, it now seems, many other people as well do. Perhaps, I think, it isn't so much about what you actually do, but why. Those like Pete whose hearts are pure—the fundamentally decent, honest, loyal ones, the ones Miles would dismissively sneer at as *the meek*—they're living, somehow, in a bigger, richer way. Psychopaths are like tone-deaf people at a concert, mocking those who cry at the beauty of the music as fools.

So I will try. I will hum along and study the score, and perhaps one day I will hear it—properly hear it, the way my partner does.

And yet, and yet . . . It's struck me there's still a small gap in Lucy's account of how Theo and David got switched. Effectively, she said she'd gone along with Paula's mistake. But how had Paula come to make such a mistake in the first place? She might be brusque, but she's a very competent nurse. Is it possible someone had already changed the mobile incubators around, or positioned them in such a way that a nurse might reasonably take the wrong one?

But then I glance over at Pete, so lean and handsome in his wet suit, and think how ridiculous that is.

He's crouching down now, showing Theo how to smack the surface of David's rock pool gently, making the ripples catch the sunlight so David will laugh. Theo's getting the hang of it; and, what's more, is actually resisting the urge to jump in and make the water explode all over David's face. It looks as if he might even be enjoying making David chortle.

At the end of the day, I decide, you have to let suspicion go, to trust those you love. To do otherwise is to walk in Miles's shoes, and who would want to live that way?

Although it's good to know that, if it ever becomes necessary again, I can wear those shoes for a time. To protect my family.

I look again at Pete. Sometime on this holiday, I think, I'll ask Lucy to mind Theo for a while. Pete and I will go for a walk, up on this beautiful headland. Perhaps it will be just as the sun is setting, a golden yolk bursting into the sea. And there on the cliffs, with the wind twisting our hair into crazy shapes and the spray salty on our lips, we'll start a conversation about marriage.

Acknowledgments

WRITERS ARE OFTEN ASKED WHERE they get their ideas, one of the hardest questions to answer. I don't know what first prompted me to write about swapped babies—although it was, of course, one of the great staples of the Victorian "sensation novel"—but during the writing process I did come to see that the plot was heavily influenced by what was happening in the political world at the time. I wanted, I realized, to write about two ordinary people who try to resolve a near-impossible situation through dialogue and compromise—and when that doesn't work, face the challenge of deciding at what point dialogue and compromise become futile. Hopefully, by the time you're reading this the world has become a more settled place, and that particular aspect of the story has less resonance.

Many people helped with the research for this book. In particular I'd like to thank N, a consultant neonatologist whose hospital trust have asked that she remain anonymous (she has no connection with the hospital in the location the fictional St. Alexander's roughly occupies, or with my fictitious private maternity hospitals), solicitor Monica Rai and His Honour Judge Peter Devlin for their guidance on matters of family law, and consultant psychiatrist Dr. Emma Fergusson for allowing me to pick her brains on everything from postpartum psychosis to high-functioning psychopathy. The errors and liberties that remain in these areas are of course entirely my responsibility.

I'd also like to say a special thank-you to Tobias Jacob Hadi, for allowing me to refresh my memory of what a two-year-old is like, and to his mum, Carolina Walker, for agreeing to what must surely be one of the oddest requests a mother can receive from a total stranger. I should point out, too, that CAFCASS are by no means as difficult as my fictional social worker might imply: For every horror story (and there are a few) there are many stories of empathy and caring by their officers in the most difficult of circumstances.

My thanks to my publishers at Ballantine, and particularly Kara Welsh, Denise Cronin, and Rachel Kind for falling in love with the initial pitch; Stef Bierwerth and all the team at Quercus for believing in it as soon as they heard about it; and Caradoc King, Millie Hoskins, and Kat Aitkin for being such fantastic first readers. Anne Speyer, my editor, made this story so much better, not just once but again and again—thank you.

Finally, it seems appropriate to dedicate a book so focused on family and parenting to my children: Tom, Harry, Ollie, and the memory of Nicholas. In the evocative words of the Old Testament, my bowels yearn upon you all.

About the Author

The *New York Times* bestselling author of *The Girl Before*, *Believe Me*, and *The Perfect Wife*, JP DELANEY has previously written bestselling fiction under other names.

jpdelaney.co.uk
Facebook.com/JPDelaneywriter

About the Type

This book was set in Sabon, a typeface designed by the well-known German typographer Jan Tschichold (1902–74). Sabon's design is based upon the original letter forms of sixteenth-century French type designer Claude Garamond and was created specifically to be used for three sources: foundry type for hand composition, Linotype, and Monotype. Tschichold named his typeface for the famous Frankfurt typefounder Jacques Sabon (c. 1520–80).